Margaret Oliphant (1828–97), née Wilson, was born at Wallyford near Edinburgh. Her father was a businessman and the family moved to Glasgow and then to Liverpool where she spent her girlhood. Her first novel, *Passages in the Life of Mrs Margaret Maitland* (1849), was set in Scotland and proved a considerable success. It was followed by *Caleb Field* and *Merkland* (both 1851) and this led to her becoming a regular contributor to *Blackwoods* magazine in Edinburgh, where over two hundred of her short stories, essays and articles were to appear over the years and where her next novel *Katie Stewart* (1853) and many others were first serialised. She visited Edinburgh on more than one occasion and came to know the Blackwoods and their literary circle. Margaret moved to London in 1852 and married her cousin, the artist Frank Wilson Oliphant in 1857, but he died of tuberculosis only two years later and she was left with three young children to support and debts to pay. She turned to writing with renewed commitment and, starting in 1861, she created a sequence of seven novels, *The Chronicles of Carlingford*, based on a fictional provincial town outside London, rather in the manner of Trollope's Barsetshire novels. The best among these are *A Doctor's Family* (1863) and *Miss Marjoribanks* (1866) later praised by Q.D. Leavis, while the last title, *Phoebe Junior*, appeared in 1876.

By 1865 Oliphant was also supporting her widowed brother, who was an alcoholic, and three of his four children. Over the next thirty-three years she was to achieve an extraordinary output of ninety further titles, many of them three-volume novels, as well as *A Literary History of England* (1882); a study of Francis of Assisi (1868); memoirs of Edward Irving the charismatic preacher (1862); of John Tulloch the Scottish divine (1888); of Thomas Chalmers the Scottish preacher and philosopher (1893); *A Child's History of Scotland* (1895); books on Florence, Edinburgh, Jerusalem and Rome and many, many more. Her most notable novels of Scottish life include *The Minister's Wife* (1869), *Effie Ogilvie* (1886) and especially *Kirsteen* (1890); while *A Beleaguered City* (1880) belongs to the group (including short stories) which she thought of as 'Stories of the Seen and Unseen', haunted by her interest in what happens to the soul after death.

Oliphant's *Autobiography* (published posthumously in 1899) came to reflect on the difficulties of having had to write so much (too much for the good of her critical reputation) and her late memoir, *Annals of a Publishing House: William Blackwood and his Sons, their Magazine and Friends* (1897), is an invaluable record of its time.

Margaret Oliphant

A Beleaguered City
and Other Tales of the Seen and the Unseen

★

CANONGATE

CLASSICS

95

This edition first published as a Canongate Classic in Great Britain in 2000 by Canongate Books Ltd, 14 High Street, Edinburgh EH1 1TE.

10 9 8 7 6 5 4 3 2 1

Introduction, notes and glossary copyright © Jenni Calder 2000

Part of this book is based upon *Selected Short Stories of the Supernatural*, an edition of six of Margaret Oliphant's stories edited and annotated by Margaret K. Gray and published by Scottish Academic Press for the Association for Scottish Literary Studies (1985).

Our grateful thanks go to Margaret K. Gray and to the Association for Scottish Literary Studies for their permission to use these edited texts and notes.

The publishers gratefully acknowledge general subsidy from the Scottish Arts Council towards the publication of the Canongate Classics series and a specific grant towards the publication of this volume.

CANONGATE CLASSICS
Series editor: Roderick Watson
Editorial Board: J.B. Pick, Cairns Craig and Dorothy McMillan

British Library Cataloguing-in-Publication Data
A catalogue record for this book is available on request from the British Library

ISBN 1 84195 060 2

Set in 9.5pt Plantin by Hewer Text Ltd, Edinburgh. Printed and bound by Omnia Books Ltd, Glasgow.

www.canongate.net

Contents

Introduction

Margaret Oliphant has been described as 'one of the greatest writers of ghost stories this country has ever produced'[1] and this collection demonstrates why. Her short novel *A Beleaguered City* and these seven stories have a luminous intensity, a psychological realism and a gripping evocation of place. One of the stories, 'The Library Window', rates among the best in the English language. If some of Oliphant's full-length fiction can, however rewarding, be somewhat daunting, these stories show her at her best, and provide an excellent introduction to her work.

Margaret Oliphant was an extraordinarily prolific writer whose fiction reflects a broad geographical, social and historical perspective. She published over ninety novels in her lifetime, a substantial amount of non-fiction, and many articles, stories and book reviews. She turned her hand to biography, travel writing, history and social comment. Her productivity, unflagging for half a century, told against her reputation. Because she wrote much that was mediocre the fact that she wrote a dozen or so novels and stories that place her in the front rank of Victorian fiction has been largely overlooked.

She wrote with consistent intelligence and an ironic sensibility, with an analytical mind and considerable psychological insight. Henry James said of her that she 'understood life itself in a fine free-handed manner',[2] and this judgment is supported by the confidence of her style and the generous vigour of her examination of human behaviour. Her work challenged many conventional opinions and she engaged in several of the foremost social and intellectual battles of the second half of the nineteenth century – for example, the position of women, double standards of morality, and Darwin's theory of evolution.

Although after her early years she spent most of her life

furth of Scotland, she retained a strong sense of her Scottish
inheritance. Many of her novels and stories are set in Scotland, and many more informed by what Robert Louis Stevenson called 'a strong Scotch accent of the mind'.[3] Her
husband's early death left her as breadwinner of an extended
family at a time when there were limited opportunities for
women to earn. She made no secret of the fact that she had to
write for money, which created a degree of uneasiness in the
literary world. She herself acknowledged that she did not
have the luxury of perfecting her art. She was never in her
lifetime either a popular or a critical success, although she had
her admirers and some of her work sold quite well. The
generous and affectionate response to the predicament of
Walter Scott, also writing his way out of debt and whom
she much admired, was denied her.

In 1880, thirty-one years after the publication of her first
novel, she published *A Beleaguered City*, a tale of the supernatural which drew directly on a lengthy visit she made to
France in 1871. The novel also arose out of Oliphant's
experience of bereavement, especially the loss of three of
her children, two as infants and her beloved daughter
Maggie at the age of ten. She was a believing Christian,
but not an unquestioning one, and her faith did not offer
easy consolation. She responded with interest to the views of
sceptics and agnostics, and was fully aware of the challenge
to the foundations of Christianity that came from Darwin
and others. She was also aware of the more insidious challenge that came from a society that placed its faith in
economic and technological progress and the material
expression of wealth. These themes come together in *A
Beleaguered City*.

It is a short, compact novel, a novella in Victorian terms,
and benefits greatly from this leanness. Many of Oliphant's
longer novels, the product of a contemporary demand for
'three-deckers', novels in three volumes, suffer from obvious
padding. But *A Beleaguered City* has an intensity of focus
which drives the narrative. This is all the more effective as the
story is rooted in the bourgeois preoccupations of provincial
France. It is set in the small town of Semur, which Oliphant
herself had visited, and narrated by the town's mayor, Martin
Dupin, a responsible, reasonable but self-important and
complacent character who finds himself face to face with a

phenomenon he cannot explain. First, a darkness descends over the town. Then:

> There was in the air, in the night, a sensation the most strange I have ever experienced. I have felt the same thing indeed at other times, in face of a great crowd, when thousands of people were moving, rustling, struggling, breathing around me, thronging all the vacant space, filling up every spot. This was the sensation that overwhelmed me here – a crowd: yet nothing to be seen but the darkness, the indistinct line of the road. We could not move for them, so close were they around us. What do I say? There was nobody – nothing.

The townspeople are forced out of the town by a mysterious pressure and the gates close behind them. What is this pressure, who are 'they'? It is the women of the town who first understand what has happened, that Semur has been occupied by the dead. The men look for a rational explanation. The women can 'see' something which they cannot, that the dead have returned to a community who are concerned with material rather than spiritual values, in order to remind them of the power and necessity of faith. When the people recognise what is going on, the dead retreat and they reclaim their homes. Normality is restored. The tale ends with an ironic comment on the fact that life continues pretty much as before, with the men slipping into their traditional roles and no lasting change in attitudes to the women, in spite of the fact that their spirituality and heightened ability to see the 'unseen' have saved the town.

The quality of the narrative owes a great deal to Oliphant's own fervent wish to believe that the dead survive in some way, and have a role and a purpose. When Maggie died she longed for reassurance that she still existed somewhere. 'If I could but have a glimpse of her, a word from her how it would comfort my heart,' she wrote in her autobiography.[4] 'Why should it be a wonder that the dead should come back? The wonder is that they do not,' comments Lecamus, a leading character in *A Beleaguered City*. Lecamus is the only man who shares the women's power of seeing, and he acts as a conduit between the material concerns of the other men and the empathy experienced by the women. He carries an authority from which the women are excluded. But then we get a woman's account of events, and Oliphant's quiet irony comes into play as we see the women dealing with the situation, going about their tasks, sensitive to human need. A striking feature of many of Oliphant's supernatural tales is that women have a heightened perception; and in almost everything she wrote, women have a capability and a pragmatism that is very often lacking in her male characters.

Linked with these different levels of perception are metaphorical patterns of light and dark. They operate strikingly in *A Beleaguered City*. A dark cloud engulfs the town, but the sun shines beyond it. There are gradations of light and dark, a play of shadows, wavering light cast by lanterns and candles. The light, and lack of it, is palpable. In the moonlight 'Semur lay like a blot between the earth and the sky, all dark . . . nothing visible but the line of the ramparts, whitened outside by the moon. One knows what black and strange shadows are cast by the moonlight; and it seemed to all of us that we did not know what might be lurking behind every tree.' But it is in the account of Mme Dupin, M. le Maire's mother, that enlightenment comes. Her interpretation of events is phrased in religious terms, but it is essentially about empathy for the weak. 'This all became clear to me as I sat and pondered, while the morning light grew around me, and the sun rose and shed his first rays . . .' Moments later the towers of Semur's cathedral emerge from darkness.

Behind Oliphant's stories of the supernatural lie two traditions which clearly influenced her. The Gothic tale had by the early nineteenth century established itself firmly, and had many successors. It had given currency to a language of mystery and metaphors for reality beyond the rational. Novelists as different as Charlotte Brontë and Charles Dickens had drawn on this tradition. It had generated not only stories of suspense, but also tales that looked at the darker and less explainable aspects of human feelings and behaviour. Robert Louis Stevenson was a practitioner of the latter: one of the best-known of such stories is his *Strange Case of Dr Jekyll and Mr Hyde* (1886), published some time after Oliphant was well into her own explorations of experience beyond the rational. Indeed, he much admired *A Beleaguered City*, and wrote her an excited letter after reading it.[5]

The second tradition was that of the Scottish ballads, with

their stark confrontations and uncompromising dilemmas. Conflict is at the centre of these ballads, between good and evil, between rivals, between love and duty, between fate and free will. This kind of opposition is also at the root of Calvinism. The link between the older tradition and the later Presbyterian development is strong; indeed Presbyterianism absorbed something of the elemental psychology of the ballads as well as their emotional power. Oliphant was exposed to both currents, the ballads and Calvinism. In addition, stories of the supernatural, ghost stories, were very much a phenomenon of the Victorian period. This was partly in response to the familiarity of death, an intimate experience in most Victorian families. Stories that evoked a spirit world were a way of retaining links with the dead, of circumventing loss. They were also a way of circumventing repression. They allowed the exploration of emotional and psychological phenomena within a context that partly disguised them.

Oliphant did not believe that the scientific or the mechanistic could provide an adequate description of life, and she held out against what she called 'the pretensions of science', that were claiming the possibility of classifying and explaining the whole of life on earth. Science, she believed, was the enemy of the imagination as well as of religion. 'This poor world requires a vast deal of ballast to keep it steady,' she wrote. 'We are not all intellect . . . and there are other kinds of power recognised among us than even the power of genius, or the inferior gifts of cleverness and talent.'[6] She believed that there were aspects of life and nature that could not be explained. These were the province of God, but also of the imagination. 'Poetry, of all things in the world, must be least influenced by steam-engines and electric telegraphs. The external world is but scenery for the true poet.'[7]

The stories collected here were all written in the last twenty years or so of Oliphant's life and they reveal her growing command of the genre, culminating with 'The Library Window' which was one of the last things she wrote and can be read almost as an allegory of her own life. All of them play with notions of perception and enlightenment, with literal and metaphorical darkness and light. In each story the pivotal character can see what others cannot. Sometimes this is actual – a door, a window, a figure. Sometimes it is a sensitivity, a moral and spiritual sensitivity, which leads to an insight into a reality beyond the normal.

More conventional is the story, such as 'The Secret Chamber', which involves the laying of a malignant spirit by a profession of faith. The hero, when he confronts the family ghost, uses the sword he carries as a religious rather than a military weapon, a cross rather than a blade. But most of Oliphant's spirits are tormented rather than destructive, and their relationship with the living is highly personal. 'Old Lady Mary', for example, is an ironic but ultimately anguished tale of a woman coming to the end of an apparently blameless life in complacent comfort, but then after her death having to face the consequences of a thoughtless gesture. From 'the other side' she sees that her self-absorbed action, 'that last frivolity of her old age', has rendered her young ward destitute. She realises how 'she had played with the future of the child she had brought up, and abandoned to the hardest fate – for nothing, for folly, for a jest'. Hell is living with the consequences. 'In the first anguish of that recollection she had to go forth, receiving no word of comfort in respect to it, meeting only with a look of sadness and compassion, which went to her very heart.' Oliphant here is reversing the sense of loss. It is not the living who mourn and suffer, but the dead. Lady Mary begs to be allowed to return to the world of the living to put things right, but there is nothing she can do. In the end she is released from the agony of haunting by the love and forgiveness of the victim of her folly. In other words, the fate of the dead is in the hands of the living.

The idea that haunting is the compulsion of a troubled spirit rather than the persecution of the haunted is an ancient one. Just as common is the haunting that is generated by a state of mind. Often the two phenomena exist side by side, and create a psychological relationship of peculiar intensity. Something of this kind occurs in 'The Open Door', where the disturbance at the heart of the story is of a more radical and more frightening nature.

The powerfully evoked setting of 'The Open Door', not precisely identified but clearly near Midlothian's River Esk, is a contributing factor. A young boy rides home from school every day past a ruined building in the grounds of his parents' home. He hears a tormented cry, which he is convinced is the voice of someone 'in terrible trouble', and pleads with his father to do something to help. The boy becomes ill, not through fear but through anxiety for the tormented soul. The father is sceptical, and the doctor dismisses Roland's distress as 'cerebral excitement'. Neither common sense nor medical science can cope with the chilling experience, and Roland grows weaker. His father turns to the minister for help.

The minister's successful exorcism is based less on faith than on empathy with a spirit, whether ghostly or living, in trouble. He combines moral and spiritual authority with pity and tenderness. It is this, combined with the innocence of the child which allowed him to 'see' – or in this case hear – the unseen that ends the pain. Children often feature significantly in ghost stories, because innocence, a simplicity unadulterated by the sophisticated and the rational, can be the crucial link between the seen and the unseen. There is an undercurrent in much of Oliphant's work which suggests a tension between empiricism and sorrow for lost innocence, and it is certainly present in this story.

'The Open Door' is a story of many layers but at the heart of its success is the way it imposes its own reality. The reality that Oliphant creates is woven out of characters who exemplify the traditional readiness of the Scottish imagination to accommodate the unseen and the unexplainable. She utilises the currents that have contributed to this, the environment, a contentious history brimming with attempts to justify unjustifiable actions, and an uncompromising religion. The contrast with the rationalism of Roland's father and the doctor, and the suggestion of ordered art and industry that is contained in the Georgian house and its surroundings (in which the ruin itself is an anomaly), underlines the strength of these more 'primitive' responses.

Throughout the story are images of light and darkness which reinforce this contrast. When the doctor and the minister, the man of science and the man of God, set out with Roland's father to investigate the 'creature invisible', they are 'fully provided with the means of lighting the place . . . three lights in the midst of darkness'. The doctor carries a flickering taper, the minister an 'old-fashioned lantern' which shines steadily, while Mortimer, Roland's father, also has a lantern which produces 'a stream of light'. He is in the process of transformation from the rational to the spiritual. It is not intellectual enlightenment, the flickering taper of science, that is effective. When it is all over the doctor puts out 'his wild little torch with a quick movement, as if of shame' and offers to carry the minister's lantern. Science was not able to reach what Oliphant called 'the hidden heart of nature'.

There is a moral imperative in the story, as there is in all Oliphant's stories of the supernatural. But the story is also about sensibility and sensitivity. To understand 'the hidden heart of nature' you have to perceive that it is there, and that it is indeed natural. At the heart of this is the need to make connections between different worlds, in this case of the living and the dead. To achieve those connections you need a particular kind of light, a particular ability to see. In Oliphant's view, these abilities have a moral and spiritual, rather than an intellectual, source.

The theme is taken up again in 'The Portrait', in which a young man's kindly impulses open him to female ways of seeing. Here, the vehicle is his mother, who died when he was an infant, and is the subject of the portrait of the title. It is significant that he takes the first steps towards perception independently, before he has seen the painting of his mother. He has shown himself receptive. Again, light and shade ripple through the narrative, and their metaphorical role is consolidated by the final sentence: 'She has passed once more into the secret company of those shadows, who can only become more real in an atmosphere fitted to modify and harmonise all differences, and make all wonders possible – the light of the perfect day.' Harmony, connections, breaking down barriers, eliminating the dividing line between the seen and the unseen – these possibilities provide undercurrents in all the stories in this collection.

Oliphant pushes her antipathy to science and technological progress to an extreme in 'The Land of Darkness'. Here is a brutalised landscape reminiscent of Dickens and Ruskin at their most passionate, 'full of furnaces and clanking machinery and endless work'. The light in this landscape is 'the fury of the fires' with men 'like demons in the flames'. The story, though rather formless, concentrates all Oliphant's fears about the modern world as an environment in which spirituality is dead, and she can only counter this vision of hell by asserting the continued existence of God.

The story is not one of Oliphant's best, but it is interesting

for a number of reasons. The fictional portrayal of indus-
trialisation is rare in nineteenth-century Scottish fiction,
which is curious given the speed and consequences of Scotland's industrial revolution. But more striking is the kinship
with Stevenson's *Jekyll and Hyde*, for 'The Land of Darkness' strips away the surface of civility and 'the pretences of a
world that can still deceive itself' to reveal a jarring reality.
'The only thing that touches you and me is what hurts or
helps ourselves', says the narrative's cynical guide. His argument is that all the good impulses of humanity are the result
of self-interest or hypocrisy. Unwrap men and women from
their decorous clothing and the result is the unbounded
infliction of suffering and pain. Similarly, the brutal Hyde
is unleashed when Jekyll dissolves the barriers of moral
restraint.

Light and dark and shades of perception are at the heart of
the most subtle and most potent of the stories here. 'The
Library Window' is one of the few of Oliphant's stories of the
supernatural in which the central figure and narrator is a
woman, and it takes us back to the female ways of seeing in *A
Beleaguered City*. This is a story about female sensibility – but
the heroine is never named. However vivid her perceptions,
however challenging her grasp of reality, she has an unsub-
stantiality. Like so many women in the nineteenth century,
she is anonymous, hidden. Her physical and mental environ-
ments are limited. She spends her days in her aunt's house,
pinned down by traditional female occupations. Her only
liberation is when she is 'afloat in a dream'.

The pivot of the story is a window in the library across the
street, the High Street of St Rules (St Andrews). Is the
window real, 'a living window' as the heroine puts it, or is
it painted? She becomes increasingly absorbed by the window, until, late on a June evening, she becomes aware of a
'faint greyness as of visible space within'. Gradually a room
beyond the window takes shape and she sees more and more:
'one thing became visible to me after another'. But no one else
shares her perception. 'It did indeed bring tears to my eyes to
think that all those clever people . . . should have the simplest
things shut out from them; and for all their wisdom and their
knowledge be unable to see what a girl like me could see so
easily.'

Finally, she sees a figure in the room, seated at a desk,

absorbed in writing. Gradually this vision takes over from reality, becomes more real than the life going on around her. The moment when she can see through the library window and watch the figure working at his desk becomes the chief object of her day. She longs to make contact. Then comes an invitation to a party in the library: she is shattered to discover that there is no window in the wall opposite her aunt's house. Her 'reality' is turned upside down.

What makes the story so astonishingly powerful is the continual play of light, the quality of perception, the nature of different kinds of reality. It is in the evenings, the long summer evenings, that the narrator sees most.

> . . . in the evening in June in Scotland – then is the time to see. For it is daylight, yet it is not day, and there is a quality in it which I cannot describe, it is so clear, as if every object was a reflection of itself.

When the lamps are lit in the house the light outside becomes dim, artificial light challenges natural light. Trapped inside, the narrator is dependent on what she can see outside. But is she looking out or in? Can her perception take her beyond her own circumscribed world? Can she enter another level of reality? Her own grasp of reality is reversed. The room with its mysterious occupant becomes more real than the 'theatrical illusion' of the people around her. When she discovers that there is no library window, no man at his desk, she is taken home in a state of distress. Her friends think she is hallucinating. But back in her aunt's house she can see him again. Later she sits alone 'in the dark which was not dark, but quite clear light – a light like nothing I ever saw. How clear it was in that room! Not glaring like the gas and the voices, but so quiet, everything so visible, as if it were in another world.'

These changes in the quality of light mark each stage of the story, and are matched by a deepening perception. Finally, the man she watches with such intensity opens the library window and salutes her.

> I watched him with such a melting heart, with such satisfaction as words could not say; for nobody could tell me now that he was not there – nobody could say I was dreaming any more. I watched him as if I could not breathe

– my heart in my throat, my eyes upon him . . . I was in a kind of rapture . . .

The sexual connotations are clear. This is her fulfilment, but she never sees through the library window again. The story does not quite end here, although in a sense the heroine's life does. It is briefly indicated that she marries, has children, is widowed, but nothing recaptures the vivid reality of the library window, and nothing can influence or diminish that reality. In other words, the conventional road to fulfilment for a woman means very little to her.

The story is perhaps the most sustained and luminous piece of prose Oliphant produced, and its intensity has a highly personal flavour. Although the narrator herself has no identity, that in itself encourages us to read this as the author's own narration. There is an underlying irony, in that so fine a story evokes a lost life, the life of the artist and scholar that Oliphant felt had been closed to her through the necessity of supporting and caring for others. Her heroine cannot make the connection with the world of intellectual and creative activity which the man in the library represents. But he has lost a life, too. He is solitary, imprisoned in the library without loving association. This is not a simple story about a woman trapped in a mundane existence, denied the opportunity to develop, but a subtle and complex expression of loneliness and longing.

The moral element in this tense, still drama is present in the heroine's sensibility. She 'sees' the figure in the library not just because she is dreamily dissatisfied with her limited life, but also because she has sympathy and concern. It is a generous emotion that conjures him to life, to which he responds when he finally becomes aware of her. 'At last he had seen me: at last he had found out that somebody, though only a girl, was watching him, looking for him, believing in him.' The relationship between the seen and the unseen is two-way.

As in other stories, the gulf between the natural and the supernatural is bridged by sympathy and a spontaneous unselfishness. The significance of this lies not just in the fact that doors, literally and metaphorically, are opened onto new dimensions of experience and imagination, but that the territory of the unseen allows responses that ordinary realities undervalue. Oliphant herself was too much of a realist to be convinced that 'good' feelings and actions brought much tangible reward. Most of her novels illustrate the opposite; they are full of women, particularly, whose routes to achievement are blocked, whatever their moral sensibility. Oliphant returned again and again to themes that demonstrated, with insight and irony, that most people did not get what they deserved, and those who reached some kind of fulfilment often had to pay for it dearly. But her stories of the supernatural allow her to break free from this, and provide an entry into a time and space where the better impulses of humanity have some effect. The heroine of 'The Library Window' has her moment of intensity and revelation, even if it does not and cannot change her life.

NOTES

1. Richard Dalby (ed.), *The Virago Book of Victorian Ghost Stories*, London, 1988, p. 346.
2. Quoted in Q D Leavis, Introduction, *Autobiography and Letters of Mrs Margaret Oliphant*, ed. Mrs Harry Coghill, Leicester, 1974, p. 10.
3. Robert Louis Stevenson, 'The Foreigner at Home', *Memories and Portraits*, Glasgow, 1990, p. 16 (first published 1887).
4. Elizabeth Jay (ed.), *Autobiography of Mrs Margaret Oliphant*, Oxford, 1990, p. 7.
5. R L Stevenson to Margaret Oliphant, *The Letters of Robert Louis Stevenson*, vol. 2, Bradford A. Booth and Ernest Mehew (eds), New Haven and London, 1994, p. 301.
6. 'Modern Light Literature – Science', *Blackwood's Edinburgh Magazine* 78, p. 319.
7. Ibid., p. 226.

A Beleaguered City

ONE

The Narrative of M. le Maire
The Condition of the City

I, MARTIN DUPIN (de la Clairière), had the honour of holding the office of Maire in the town of Semur, in the Haute Bourgogne, at the time when the following events occurred. It will be perceived therefore, that no one could have more complete knowledge of the facts – at once from my official position, and from the place of eminence in the affairs of the district generally which my family has held for many generations – by what citizen-like virtues and unblemished integrity I will not be vain enough to specify. Nor is it necessary; for no one who knows Semur can be ignorant of the position held by the Dupins, from father to son. The estate La Clairière has been so long in the family that we might very well, were we disposed, add its name to our own, as so many families in France do; and, indeed, I do not prevent my wife (whose prejudices I respect) from making this use of it upon her cards. But, for myself, *bourgeois* I was born and *bourgeois* I mean to die. My residence, like that of my father and grandfather, is at No. 29 in the Grande Rue, opposite the Cathedral, and not far from the Hospital of St Jean. We inhabit the first floor, along with the *rez-de-chaussée*, which has been turned into domestic offices suitable for the needs of the family. My mother, holding a respected place in my household, lives with us in the most perfect family union. My wife (*née* de Champfleurie) is everything that is calculated to render a household happy; but, alas! one only of our two children survives to bless us. I have thought these

details of my private circumstances necessary, to explain the
following narrative; to which I will also add, by way of
introduction, a simple sketch of the town itself and its general
conditions before these remarkable events occurred.

It was on a summer evening about sunset, the middle of the
month of June, that my attention was attracted by an incident
of no importance which occurred in the street, when I was
making my way home, after an inspection of the young vines
in my new vineyard to the left of La Clairière. All were in
perfectly good condition, and none of the many signs which
point to the arrival of the insect were apparent. I had come
back in good spirits, thinking of the prosperity which I was
happy to believe I had merited by a conscientious performance of all my duties. I had little with which to blame
myself: not only my wife and relations, but my dependants
and neighbours, approved my conduct as a man; and even my
fellow-citizens, exacting as they are, had confirmed in my
favour the good opinion which my family had been fortunate
enough to secure from father to son. These thoughts were in
my mind as I turned the corner of the Grande Rue and
approached my own house. At this moment the tinkle of a
little bell warned all the bystanders of the procession which
was about to pass, carrying the rites of the Church to some
dying person. Some of the women, always devout, fell on
their knees. I did not go so far as this, for I do not pretend, in
these days of progress, to have retained the same attitude of
mind as that which it is no doubt becoming to behold in the
more devout sex; but I stood respectfully out of the way, and
took off my hat, as good breeding alone, if nothing else,
demanded of me. Just in front of me, however, was Jacques
Richard, always a troublesome individual, standing doggedly,
with his hat upon his head and his hands in his pockets,
straight in the path of M. le Curé. There is not in all France a
more obstinate fellow. He stood there, notwithstanding the
efforts of a good woman to draw him away, and though I
myself called to him. M. le Curé is not the man to flinch; and
as he passed, walking as usual very quickly and straight, his
soutane brushed against the blouse of Jacques. He gave one
quick glance from beneath his eyebrows at the profane
interruption, but he would not distract himself from his
sacred errand at such a moment. It *is* a sacred errand when
any one, be he priest or layman, carries the best he can give to

the bedside of the dying. I said this to Jacques when M. le Curé had passed and the bell went tinkling on along the street. 'Jacques,' said I, 'I do not call it impious, like this good woman, but I call it inhuman. What! a man goes to carry help to the dying, and you show him no respect!'

This brought the colour to his face; and I think, perhaps, that he might have become ashamed of the part he had played; but the women pushed in again, as they are so fond of doing. 'Oh, M. le Maire, he does not deserve that you should lose your words upon him!' they cried; 'and, besides, is it likely he will pay any attention to you when he tries to stop even the *bon Dieu?*'

'The *bon Dieu!*' cried Jacques. 'Why doesn't He clear the way for himself? Look here. I do not care one farthing for your *bon Dieu*. Here is mine; I carry him about with me.' And he took a piece of a hundred sous out of his pocket (how had it got there?) '*Vive l'argent!*' he said. 'You know it yourself, though you will not say so. There is no *bon Dieu* but money. With money you can do anything. *L'argent c'est le bon Dieu.*'

'Be silent,' I cried, 'thou profane one!' And the women were still more indignant than I. 'We shall see, we shall see; when he is ill and would give his soul for something to wet his lips, his *bon Dieu* will not do much for him,' cried one; and another said, clasping her hands with a shrill cry, 'It is enough to make the dead rise out of their graves!'

'The dead rise out of their graves!' These words, though one has heard them before, took possession of my imagination. I saw the rude fellow go along the street as I went on, tossing the coin in his hand. One time it fell to the ground and rang upon the pavement, and he laughed more loudly as he picked it up. He was walking towards the sunset, and I too, at a distance after. The sky was full of rose-tinted clouds floating across the blue, floating high over the grey pinnacles of the Cathedral, and filling the long open line of the Rue St Etienne down which he was going. As I crossed to my own house I caught him full against the light, in his blue blouse, tossing the big silver piece in the air, and heard him laugh and shout '*Vive l'argent!* This is the only *bon Dieu*.' Though there are many people who live as if this were their sentiment, there are few who give it such brutal expression; but some of the people at the corner of the street laughed too. 'Bravo, Jacques!' they cried; and one said, 'You are right, *mon ami*, the only god to trust in nowadays.' 'It is a short *credo*, M. le Maire,' said another, who caught my eye. He saw I was displeased, this one, and his countenance changed at once.

'Yes, Jean Pierre,' I said, 'it is worse than short – it is brutal. I hope no man who respects himself will ever countenance it. It is against the dignity of human nature, if nothing more.'

'Ah, M. le Maire!' cried a poor woman, one of the good ladies of the market, with entrenchments of baskets all round her, who had been walking my way; 'ah, M. le Maire! did not I say true? it is enough to bring the dead out of their graves.'

'That would be something to see,' said Jean Pierre, with a laugh; 'and I hope, *ma bonne femme*, that if you have any interest with them, you will entreat these gentlemen to appear before I go away.'

'I do not like such jesting,' said I. 'The dead are very dead and will not disturb anybody, but even the prejudices of respectable persons ought to be respected. A ribald like Jacques counts for nothing, but I did not expect this from you.'

'What would you, M. le Maire?' he said, with a shrug of his shoulders. 'We are made like that. I respect prejudices as you say. My wife is a good woman, she prays for two – but me! How can I tell that Jacques is not right after all? A *grosse pièce* of a hundred sous, one sees that, one knows what it can do – but for the other!' He thrust up one shoulder to his ear, and turned up the palms of his hands.

'It is our duty at all times to respect the convictions of others,' I said, severely; and passed on to my own house, having no desire to encourage discussions at the street corner. A man in my position is obliged to be always mindful of the example he ought to set. But I had not yet done with this phrase, which had, as I have said, caught my ear and my imagination. My mother was in the great *salle* of the *rez-de-chaussée*, as I passed, in altercation with a peasant who had just brought us in some loads of wood. There is often, it seems to me, a sort of *refrain* in conversation, which one catches everywhere as one comes and goes. Figure my astonishment when I heard from the lips of my good mother the same words with which that good-for-nothing Jacques Richard had made the profession of his brutal faith. 'Go!' she cried, in anger; 'you are all the same. Money is your god. *De grosses pièces*, that is all you think of in these days.'

'*Eh, bien*, madame,' said the peasant; 'and if so, what then?

Don't you others, gentlemen and ladies, do just the same? What is there in the world but money to think of? If it is a question of marriage, you demand what is the *dot*; if it is a question of office, you ask, Monsieur Untel, is he rich? And it is perfectly just. We know what money can do; but as for *le bon Dieu*, whom our grandmothers used to talk about—'

And lo! our *gros paysan* made exactly the same gesture as Jean Pierre. He put up his shoulders to his ears, and spread out the palms of his hands, as who should say, There is nothing further to be said.

Then there occurred a still more remarkable repetition. My mother, as may be supposed, being a very respectable person, and more or less *dévote*, grew red with indignation and horror.

'Oh, these poor grandmothers!' she cried; 'God give them rest! It is enough to make the dead rise out of their graves.'

'Oh, I will answer for *les morts!* they will give nobody any trouble,' he said with a laugh. I went in and reproved the man severely, finding that, as I supposed, he had attempted to cheat my good mother in the price of the wood. Fortunately she had been quite as clever as he was. She went upstairs shaking her head, while I gave the man to understand that no one should speak to her but with the profoundest respect in my house. 'She has her opinions, like all respectable ladies,' I said, 'but under this roof these opinions shall always be sacred.' And, to do him justice, I will add that when it was put to him in this way Gros-Jean was ashamed of himself.

When I talked over these incidents with my wife, as we gave each other the narrative of our day's experiences, she was greatly distressed, as may be supposed. 'I try to hope they are not so bad as Bonne Maman thinks. But oh, *mon ami!*' she said, 'what will the world come to if this is what they really believe?'

'Take courage,' I said; 'the world will never come to anything much different from what it is. So long as there are *des anges* like thee to pray for us, the scale will not go down to the wrong side.'

I said this, of course, to please my Agnès, who is the best of wives; but on thinking it over after, I could not but be struck with the extreme justice (not to speak of the beauty of the sentiment) of this thought. The *bon Dieu* – if, indeed, that great Being is as represented to us by the Church – must naturally care as much for one-half of His creatures as for the other, though they have not the same weight in the world; and consequently the faith of the women must hold the balance straight, especially if, as is said, they exceed us in point of numbers. This leaves a little margin for those of them who profess the same freedom of thought as is generally accorded to men – a class, I must add, which I abominate from the bottom of my heart.

I need not dwell upon other little scenes which impressed the same idea still more upon my mind. Semur, I need not say, is not the centre of the world, and might, therefore, be supposed likely to escape the full current of worldliness. We amuse ourselves little, and we have not any opportunity of rising to the heights of ambition; for our town is not even the *chef-lieu* of the department, – though this is a subject upon which I cannot trust myself to speak. Figure to yourself that La Rochette – a place of yesterday, without either the beauty or the antiquity of Semur – has been chosen as the centre of affairs, the residence of M. le Préfet! But I will not enter upon this question. What I was saying was, that, notwithstanding the fact that we amuse ourselves but little, that there is no theatre to speak of, little society, few distractions, and none of those inducements to strive for gain and to indulge the senses, which exist, for instance, in Paris – that capital of the world – yet, nevertheless, the thirst for money and for pleasure has increased among us to an extent which I cannot but consider alarming. Gros-Jean, our peasant, toils for money, and hoards; Jacques, who is a cooper and maker of wine casks, gains and drinks; Jean Pierre snatches at every sous that comes in his way, and spends it in yet worse dissipations. He is one who quails when he meets my eye; he sins *en cachette*; but Jacques is bold, and defies opinion; and Gros-Jean is firm in the belief that to hoard money is the highest of mortal occupations. These three are types of what the population is at Semur. The men would all sell their souls for a *grosse pièce* of fifty sous – indeed, they would laugh, and express their delight that any one should believe them to have souls, if they could but have a chance of selling them: and the devil, who was once supposed to deal in that commodity, would be very welcome among us. And as for the *bon Dieu* – *pouff!* that was an affair of the grandmothers – *le bon Dieu c'est l'argent*. This is their creed. I was very near the beginning of my official year as Maire when my attention was called to these matters as I have described above. A man may go on for years keeping quiet himself – keeping out of tumult, religious or political – and make no discovery of the general current of feeling; but when you are forced to serve your country in any official capacity, and when your eyes are opened to the state of affairs around you, then I allow that an inexperienced observer might well cry out, as my wife did, 'What will become of the world?' I am not prejudiced myself – unnecessary to say that the foolish scruples of the women do not move me. But the devotion of the community at large to this pursuit of gain – money without any grandeur, and pleasure without any refinement – that is a thing which cannot fail to wound all who believe in human nature. To be a millionaire – that, I grant, would be pleasant. A man as rich as Monte Christo, able to do whatever he would, with the equipage of an English duke, the palace of an Italian prince, the retinue of a Russian noble – he, indeed, might be excused if his money seemed to him a kind of god. But Gros-Jean, who lays up two sous at a time, and lives on black bread and an onion; and Jacques, whose *grosse pièce* but secures him the headache of a drunkard next morning – what to them could be this miserable deity? As for myself, however, it was my business, as Maire of the commune, to take as little notice as possible of the follies these people might say, and to hold the middle course between the prejudices of the respectable and the levities of the foolish. With this, without more, to think of, I had enough to keep all my faculties employed.

TWO

The Narrative of M. le Maire Continued: Beginning of the Late Remarkable Events

I DO NOT attempt to make out any distinct connection between the simple incidents above recorded, and the extraordinary events that followed. I have related them as they happened; chiefly by way of showing the state of feeling in the city, and the sentiment which pervaded the community – a sentiment, I fear, too common in my country. I need not say that to encourage superstition is far from my wish. I am a man of my century, and proud of being so; very little disposed to yield to the domination of the clerical party, though desirous of showing all just tolerance for conscientious faith, and every respect for the prejudices of the ladies of my family. I am, moreover, all the more inclined to be careful of giving in my adhesion to any prodigy, in consequence of a consciousness that the faculty of imagination has always been one of my characteristics. It usually is so, I am aware, in superior minds, and it has procured me many pleasures unknown to the common herd. Had it been possible for me to believe that I had been misled by this faculty, I should have carefully refrained from putting upon record any account of my individual impressions; but my attitude here is not that of a man recording his personal experiences only, but of one who is the official mouthpiece and representative of the commune, and whose duty it is to render to government and to the human race a true narrative of the very wonderful facts to which every citizen of Semur can bear witness. In this capacity it has become my duty so to arrange and edit the different accounts of the mystery, as to present one coherent and trustworthy chronicle to the world.

To proceed, however, with my narrative. It is not necessary for me to describe what summer is in the Haute Bourgogne. Our generous wines, our glorious fruits, are sufficient proof, without any assertion on my part. The summer with us is as a perpetual *fête* – at least, before the insect appeared it was so, though now anxiety about the condition of our vines may cloud our enjoyment of the glorious sunshine which ripens them hourly before our eyes. Judge, then, of the astonishment of the world when there suddenly came upon us a darkness as in the depth of winter, falling, without warning, into the midst of the brilliant weather to which we are accustomed, and which had never failed us before in the memory of man! It was the month of July, when, in ordinary seasons, a cloud is so rare that it is a joy to see one, merely as a variety upon the brightness. Suddenly, in the midst of our summer delights, this darkness came. Its first appearance took us so entirely by surprise that life seemed to stop short, and the business of the whole town was delayed by an hour or two; nobody being able to believe that at six o'clock in the morning the sun had not risen. I do not assert that the sun did not rise; all I mean to say is that at Semur it was still dark, as in a morning of winter, and when it gradually and slowly became day many hours of the morning were already spent. And never shall I forget the aspect of day when it came. It was like a ghost or pale shadow of the glorious days of July with which we are usually blessed. The barometer did not go down, nor was there any rain, but an unusual greyness wrapped earth and sky. I heard people say in the streets, and I am aware that the same words came to my own lips: 'If it were not full summer, I should say it was going to snow.' We have much snow in the Haute Bourgogne, and we are well acquainted with this aspect of the skies. Of the depressing effect which this greyness exercised upon myself personally, I will not speak. I have always been noted as a man of fine perceptions, and I was aware instinctively that such a state of the atmosphere must mean something more than was apparent on the surface. But, as the danger was of an entirely unprecedented character, it is not to be wondered at that I should be completely at a loss to divine what its meaning was. It was a blight some people said; and many were of the opinion that it was caused by clouds of animalculæ coming, as is described in ancient writings, to destroy the crops, and even to affect the health of the population. The doctors scoffed at this; but they talked about malaria, which, as far as I could understand, was likely to produce exactly the same effect. The night closed in early as the day had dawned late; the lamps were lighted before six o'clock and daylight had only begun about ten! Figure to yourself, a July day! There ought to have been a moon almost at the full; but no moon was visible, no stars – nothing but a grey veil of clouds, growing darker and darker as the moments went on; such I have heard are the days and the nights in England, where the sea-fogs so often blot out the sky. But we are unacquainted with anything of the kind in our *plaisant pays de France*. There was nothing else talked of in Semur all that night, as may well be imagined. My own mind was extremely uneasy. Do what I would, I could not deliver myself from a sense of something dreadful in the air which was neither malaria nor animalculæ. I took a promenade through the streets that evening, accompanied by

M. Barbou, my *adjoint*, to make sure that all was safe; and the darkness was such that we almost lost our way, though we were both born in the town and had known every turning from our boyhood. It cannot be denied that Semur is very badly lighted. We retain still the lanterns slung by cords across the streets which once were general in France, but which, in most places, have been superseded by the modern institution of gas. Gladly would I have distinguished my term of office by bringing gas to Semur. But the expense would have been great, and there were a hundred objections. In summer generally, the lanterns were of little consequence because of the brightness of the sky; but to see them now, twinkling dimly here and there, making us conscious how dark it was, was strange indeed. It was in the interests of order that we took our round, with a fear, in my mind at least, of I knew not what. M. l'Adjoint said nothing, but no doubt he thought as I did.

While we were thus patrolling the city with a special eye to the prevention of all seditious assemblages, such as are too apt to take advantage of any circumstances that may disturb the ordinary life of a city, or throw discredit on its magistrates, we were accosted by Paul Lecamus, a man whom I have always considered as something of a visionary, though his conduct is irreproachable, and his life honourable and industrious. He entertains religious convictions of a curious kind; but, as the man is quite free from revolutionary sentiments, I have never considered it to be my duty to interfere with him, or to investigate his creed. Indeed, he has been treated generally in Semur as a dreamer of dreams – one who holds a great many impracticable and foolish opinions – though the respect which I always exact for those whose lives are respectable and worthy has been a protection to him. He was, I think, aware that he owed something to my good offices, and it was to me accordingly that he addressed himself.

'Good evening, M. le Maire,' he said; 'you are groping about, like myself, in this strange night.'

'Good evening, M. Paul,' I replied. 'It is, indeed, a strange night. It indicates, I fear, that a storm is coming.'

M. Paul shook his head. There is a solemnity about even his ordinary appearance. He has a long face, pale, and adorned with a heavy, drooping moustache, which adds much to the solemn impression made by his countenance. He looked at me with great gravity as he stood in the shadow of the lamp, and slowly shook his head.

'You do not agree with me? Well! the opinion of a man like M. Paul Lecamus is always worthy to be heard.'

'Oh!' he said, 'I am called visionary. I am not supposed to be a trustworthy witness. Nevertheless, if M. Le Maire will come with me, I will show him something that is very strange – something that is almost more wonderful than the darkness – more strange,' he went on with great earnestness, 'than any storm that ever ravaged Burgundy.'

'That is much to say. A tempest now when the vines are in full bearing—'

'Would be nothing, nothing to what I can show you. Only come with me to the Porte St Lambert.'

'If M. le Maire will excuse me,' said M. Barbou, 'I think I will go home. It is a little cold, and you are aware that I am always afraid of the damp.' In fact, our coats were beaded with a cold dew as in November, and I could not but acknowledge that my respectable colleague had reason. Besides, we were close to his house, and he had, no doubt, the sustaining consciousness of having done everything that was really incumbent upon him. 'Our ways lie together as far as my house,' he said, with a slight chattering of his teeth. No doubt it was the cold. After we had walked with him to his door, we proceeded to the Porte St Lambert. By this time almost everybody had re-entered their houses. The streets were very dark, and they were also very still. When we reached the gates, at that hour of the night, we found them shut as a matter of course. The officers of the *octroi* were standing close together at the door of their office, in which the lamp was burning. The very lamp seemed oppressed by the heavy air; it burnt dully, surrounded with a yellow haze. The men had the appearance of suffering greatly from cold. They received me with a satisfaction which was very gratifying to me. 'At length here is M. le Maire himself,' they said.

'My good friends,' said I, 'you have a cold post to-night. The weather has changed in the most extraordinary way. I have no doubt the scientific gentlemen at the Musée will be able to tell us all about it – M. de Clairon—'

'Not to interrupt M. le Maire,' said Riou, of the *octroi*, 'I think there is more in it than any scientific gentleman can explain.'

'Ah! You think so. But they explain everything,' I said, with a smile. 'They tell us how the wind is going to blow.'

As I said this, there seemed to pass us, from the direction of the closed gates, a breath of air so cold that I could not restrain a shiver. They looked at each other. It was not a smile that passed between them – they were too pale, too cold, to smile: but a look of intelligence. 'M. le Maire,' said one of them, 'perceives it too;' but they did not shiver as I did. They were like men turned into ice who could feel no more.

'It is, without doubt, the most extraordinary weather,' I said. My teeth chattered like Barbou's. It was all I could do to keep myself steady. No one made any reply; but Lecamus said, 'Have the gooodness to open the little postern for foot-passengers: M. le Maire wishes to make an inspection out-side.'

Upon these words, Riou, who knew me well, caught me by the arm. 'A thousand pardons,' he said, 'M. le Maire; but I entreat you, do not go. Who can tell what is outside? Since this morning there is something very strange on the other side of the gates. If M. le Maire would listen to me, he would keep them shut night and day till *that* is gone, he would not go out into the midst of it. *Mon Dieu!* a man may be brave. I know the courage of M. le Maire; but to march without necessity into the jaws of hell: *mon Dieu!*' cried the poor man again. He crossed himself, and none of us smiled. Now a man may sign himself at the church door – one does so out of respect; but to use that ceremony for one's own advantage, before other men, is rare – except in the case of members of a very decided party. Riou was not one of these. He signed himself in sight of us all, and not one of us smiled.

The other was less familiar – he knew me only in my public capacity – he was one Gallais of the Quartier St Médon. He said, taking off his hat: 'If I were M. le Maire, saving your respect, I would not go out into an unknown danger with this man here, a man who is known as a pietest, as a clerical, as one who sees visions—'

'He is not a clerical, he is a good citizen,' I said; 'come, lend us your lantern. Shall I shrink from my duty wherever it leads me? Nay, my good friends, the Maire of a French commune fears neither man nor devil in the exercise of his duty. M. Paul, lead on.' When I said the word 'devil' a spasm of alarm passed over Riou's face. He crossed himself again. This time I could not but smile. 'My little Riou,' I said, 'do you know that you are a little imbecile with your piety? There is a time for everything.'

'Except religion, M. le Maire; that is never out of place,' said Gallais.

I could not believe my senses. 'Is it a conversion?' I said. 'Some of our *Carmes déchaussés* must have passed this way.'

'M. le Maire will soon see other teachers more wonderful than the *Carmes déchaussés*,' said Lecamus. He went and took down the lantern from its nail, and opened the little door. When it opened, I was once more penetrated by the same icy breath; once, twice, thrice, I cannot tell how many times this crossed me, as if some one passed. I looked round upon the others – I gave way a step. I could not help it. In spite of me, the hair seemed to rise erect on my head. The two officers stood close together, and Riou, collecting his courage, made an attempt to laugh. 'M. le Maire perceives,' he said, his lips trembling almost too much to form the words, 'that the winds are walking about.' 'Hush, for God's sake!' said the other, grasping him by the arm.

This recalled me to myself; and I followed Lecamus, who stood waiting for me holding the door a little ajar. He went on strangely, like – I can use no other words to express it – a man making his way in the face of a crowd, a thing very surprising to me. I followed him close; but the moment I emerged from the doorway something caught my breath. The same feeling seized me also. I gasped; a sense of suffocation came upon me; I put out my hand to lay hold upon my guide. The solid grasp I got of his arm re-assured me a little, and he did not hesitate, but pushed his way on. We got out clear of the gate and the shadow of the wall, keeping close to the little watch-tower on the west side. Then he made a pause, and so did I. We stood against the tower and looked out before us. There was nothing there. The darkness was great, yet through the gloom of the night I could see the division of the road from the broken ground on either side; there was nothing there. I gasped, and drew myself up close against the wall, as Lecamus had also done. There was in the air, in the night, a sensation the most strange I have ever experienced. I have felt the same thing indeed at other times, in face of a great crowd, when thousands of people were moving, rustling, struggling, breathing around me, thronging all the vacant space, filling up every spot. This was the sensation that overwhelmed me here – a crowd: yet nothing to be seen but the darkness, the indistinct line of the road. We could not move for them, so close were they round us. What do I say? There was nobody – nothing – not a form to be seen, not a face but his and mine. I am obliged to confess that the moment was to me an awful moment. I could not speak. My heart beat wildly as if trying to escape from my breast – every breath I drew was with an effort. I clung to Lecamus with deadly and helpless terror, and forced myself back upon the wall, crouching against it; I did not turn and fly, as would have been natural. What say I? *did* not! I *could* not! they pressed round us so. Ah! you would think I must be mad to use such words, for there was nobody near me – not a shadow even upon the road.

Lecamus would have gone farther on; he would have pressed his way boldly into the midst; but my courage was not equal to this. I clutched and clung to him, dragging myself along against the wall, my whole mind intent upon getting back. I was stronger than he, and he had no power to resist me. I turned back, stumbling blindly, keeping my face to that crowd (there was no one), but struggling back again, tearing the skin off my hands as I groped my way along the wall. Oh, the agony of seeing the door closed! I have buffeted my way through a crowd before now, but I may say that I never before knew what terror was. When I fell upon the door, dragging Lecamus with me, it opened, thank God! I stumbled in, clutching at Riou with my disengaged hand, and fell upon the floor of the *octroi*, where they thought I had fainted. But this was not the case. A man of resolution may give way to the overpowering sensations of the moment. His bodily faculties may fail him; but his mind will not fail. As in every really superior intelligence, my forces collected for the emergency. While the officers ran to bring me water, to search for the eau-de-vie which they had in a cupboard, I astonished them all by rising up, pale, but with full command of myself. 'It is enough,' I said, raising my hand. 'I thank you, Messieurs, but nothing more is necessary;' and I would not take any of their restoratives. They were impressed, as was only natural, by the sight of my perfect self-possession: it helped them to acquire for themselves a demeanour befitting the occasion; and I felt, though still in great physical weakness and agitation, the consoling consciousness of having fulfilled my functions as head of the community.

'M. le Maire has seen a – a – what there is outside?' Riou cried, stammering in his excitement; and the other fixed upon me eyes which were hungering with eagerness – if, indeed, it is permitted to use such words.

'I have seen – nothing, Riou,' I said.

They looked at me with the utmost wonder. 'M. le Maire has seen – nothing?' said Riou. 'Ah, I see! you say so to spare us. We have proved ourselves cowards; but if you will pardon me, M. le Maire, you, too, re-entered precipitately – you too! There are facts which may appal the bravest – but I implore you to tell us what you have seen.'

'I have seen nothing,' I said. As I spoke, my natural calm composure returned, my heart resumed its usual tranquil beating. 'There is nothing to be seen – it is dark, and one can perceive the line of the road for but a little way – that is all. There is nothing to be seen—'

They looked at me, startled and incredulous. They did not know what to think. How could they refuse to believe me, sitting there calmly raising my eyes to them, making my statement with what they felt to be an air of perfect truth? But, then, how account for the precipitate return which they had already noted, the supposed faint, the pallor of my looks? They did not know what to think.

And here, let me remark, as in my conduct throughout these remarkable events, may be seen the benefit, the high advantage, of truth. Had not this been the truth, I could not have borne the searching of their looks. But it was true. There was nothing – nothing to be seen; in one sense, this was the thing of all others which overwhelmed my mind. But why insist upon these matters of detail to unenlightened men? There was nothing, and I had seen nothing. What I said was the truth.

All this time Lecamus had said nothing. As I raised myself from the ground, I had vaguely perceived him hanging up the lantern where it had been before; now he became distinct to me as I recovered the full possession of my faculties. He had seated himself upon a bench by the wall. There was no agitation about him; no sign of the thrill of departing excitement, which I felt going through my veins as through the strings of a harp. He was sitting against the wall, with his head dropping, his eyes cast down, an air of disappointment and despondency about him – nothing more. I got up as soon as I felt that I could go away with perfect propriety; but, before I left the place, called him. He got up when he heard his name, but he did it with reluctance. He came with me because I asked him to do so, not from any wish of his own. Very different were the feelings of Riou and Gallais. They did their utmost to engage me in conversation, to consult me about a hundred trifles, to ask me with the greatest deference what they ought to do in such and such cases, pressing close to me, trying every expedient to delay my departure. When we went away they stood at the door of their little office close together, looking after us with looks which I found it difficult to forget; they would not abandon their post; but their faces were pale and contracted, their eyes wild with anxiety and distress.

It was only as I walked away, hearing my own steps and those of Lecamus ringing upon the pavement, that I began to realise what had happened. The effort of recovering my composure, the relief from the extreme excitement of terror (which, dreadful as the idea is, I am obliged to confess I had actually felt), the sudden influx of life and strength to my brain, had pushed away for the moment the recollection of what lay outside. When I thought of it again, the blood began once more to course in my veins. Lecamus went on by my side with his head down, the eyelids drooping over his eyes, not saying a word. He followed me when I called him: but cast a regretful look at the postern by which we had gone out, through which I had dragged him back in a panic (I confess it) unworthy of me. Only when we had left at some distance behind us that door into the unseen, did my senses come fully back to me, and I ventured to ask myself what it meant. 'Lecamus,' I said – I could scarcely put my question into words – 'what do you think? what is your idea? – how do you explain—' Even then I am glad to think I had sufficient power of control not to betray all that I felt.

'One does not try to explain,' he said slowly; 'one longs to know – that is all. If M. le Maire had not been – in such haste – had he been willing to go farther – to investigate—'

'God forbid!' I said; and the impulse to quicken my steps, to get home and put myself in safety, was almost more than I could restrain. But I forced myself to go quietly, to measure my steps by his, which were slow and reluctant, as if he dragged himself away with difficulty from that which was behind.

What was it? 'Do not ask, do not ask!' Nature seemed to say in my heart. Thoughts came into my mind in such a dizzy crowd, that the multitude of them seemed to take away my senses. I put up my hands to my ears, in which they seemed to be buzzing and rustling like bees, to stop the sound. When I did so, Lecamus turned and looked at me – grave and wondering. This recalled me to a sense of my weakness. But how I got home I can scarcely say. My mother and wife met me with anxiety. They were greatly disturbed about the Hospital of St Jean, in respect to which it had been recently decided that certain changes should be made. The great ward of the hospital, which was the chief establishment for the sick in the town, had hitherto been so placed in communication with the chapel that mass was heard daily by all the patients – a thing which some had complained of as an annoyance disturbing their rest. So many, indeed, had been the complaints received, that we had come to the conclusion either that the opening should be built up, or the office suspended. Against this decision, it is needless to say, the Sisters of St Jean were moving heaven and earth. Equally unnecessary for me to add, that having so decided in my public capacity, as at once the representative of popular opinion and its guide, the covert reproaches which were breathed in my presence, and even the personal appeals made to me, had failed of any result. I respect the Sisters of St Jean. They are good women and excellent nurses, and the commune owes them much. Still, justice must be impartial; and so long as I retain my position at the head of the community, it is my duty to see that all have their due. My opinions as a private individual, were I allowed to return to that humble position, are entirely a different matter; but this is a thing which ladies, however excellent, are slow to allow or to understand.

I will not pretend that this was to me a night of rest. In the darkness, when all is still, any anxiety which may afflict the soul is apt to gain complete possession and mastery, as all who have had true experience of life will understand. The night was very dark and very still, the clocks striking out the hours which went so slowly, and not another sound audible. The streets of Semur are always quiet, but they were more still than usual that night. Now and then, in a pause of my thoughts, I could hear the soft breathing of my Agnès in the adjoining room, which gave me a little comfort. But this was only by intervals, when I was able to escape from the grasp of the recollections that held me fast. Again I seemed to see under my closed eyelids the faint line of the high road which led from the Porte St Lambert, the broken ground with its ragged bushes on either side, and no one – no one there – not a soul, not a shadow: yet a multitude! When I allowed myself to think of this, my heart leaped into my throat again, my blood ran in my veins like a river in flood. I need not say that I resisted this transport of the nerves with all my might. As the night grew slowly into morning my power of resistance increased; I turned my back, so to speak, upon my recollections, and said to myself, with growing firmness, that all sensations of the body must have their origin in the body. Some derangement of the system – easily explainable, no doubt, if one but held the clue – must have produced the impression which otherwise it would be impossible to explain. As I turned this over and over in my mind, carefully avoiding all temptations to excitement – which is the only wise course in the case of a strong impression on the nerves – I gradually became able to believe that this was the cause. It is one of the penalties, I said to myself, which one has to pay for an organisation more finely tempered than that of the crowd.

This long struggle with myself made the night less tedious, though, perhaps, more terrible; and when at length I was overpowered by sleep, the short interval of unconsciousness restored me like a cordial. I woke in the early morning, feeling almost able to smile at the terrors of the night. When one can assure oneself that the day has really begun, even while it is yet dark, there is a change of sensation, an increase of strength and courage. One by one the dark hours went on. I heard them pealing from the Cathedral clock – four, five, six, seven – all dark, dark. I had got up and dressed before the last, but found no one else awake when I went out – no one stirring in the house, – no one moving in the street. The Cathedral doors were shut fast, a thing I have never seen before since I remember. Get up early who will, Père Laserques the sacristan is always up still earlier. He is a good old man, and I have often heard him say God's house should be open first of all houses, in case there might be any miserable ones about who had found no shelter in the dwellings of men. But the darkness had cheated even Père Laserques. To see those great doors closed which stood always open gave me a shiver, I cannot well tell why. Had they been open, there was an inclination in my mind to have gone in, though I cannot tell why; for I am not in the habit of attending mass, save on Sunday to set an example. There were no shops open, not a sound about. I went out upon the ramparts to the Mont St Lambert, where the band plays on Sundays. In all the trees there was not so much as the twitter of a bird. I could hear the river flowing swiftly below the wall, but I could not see it, except as something dark, a ravine of gloom below, and beyond the walls I did not venture to look. Why should I look? There was nothing, nothing, as I knew. But fancy is so uncontrollable, and one's nerves so little to be trusted, that it was a wise precaution to refrain. The gloom itself was oppressive enough; the air seemed to creep with apprehensions, and from time to time my heart fluttered with a sick movement, as if it would escape from my control. But everything was still, still as the dead who had been so often in recent days called out of their graves by one or another. 'Enough to bring the dead out of their graves.' What strange words to make use of! It was rather now as if the world had become a grave in which we, though living, were held fast.

Soon after this the dark world began to lighten faintly, and with the rising of a little white mist, like a veil rolling upwards, I at last saw the river and the fields beyond. To see anything at all lightened my heart a little, and I turned homeward when this faint daylight appeared. When I got back into the street, I found that the people at last were stirring. They had all a look of half panic, half shame upon their faces. Many were yawning and stretching themselves. 'Good morning, M. le Maire,' said one and another; 'you are early astir.' 'Not so early either,' I said; and then they added, almost every individual, with a look of shame, 'We were so late this morning; we overslept ourselves – like yesterday. The weather is extraordinary.' This was repeated to me by all kinds of people. They were half frightened, and they were ashamed. Père Laserques was sitting moaning on the Cathedral steps. Such a thing had never happened before. He had not rung the bell for early mass; he had not opened the Cathedral; he had not called M. le Curé. 'I think I must be going out of my senses,' he said; 'but then, M. le Maire, the weather! Did anyone ever see such weather? I think there must be some evil brewing. It is not for nothing that the seasons change – that winter comes in the midst of summer.'

After this I went home. My mother came running to one door when I entered, and my wife to another. '*O mon fils!*' and '*O mon ami!*' they said, rushing upon me. They wept, these dear women. I could not at first prevail upon them to tell me what was the matter. At last they confessed that they believed something to have happened to me, in punishment for the wrong done to the Sisters at the hospital. 'Make haste, my son, to amend this error,' my mother cried, 'lest a worse thing befall us!' And then I discovered that among the women, and among many of the poor people, it had come to be believed that the darkness was a curse upon us for what we had done in respect to the hospital. This roused me to indignation. 'If they think I am to be driven from my duty by their magic,' I cried; 'it is no better than witchcraft!' not that I believed for a moment that it was they who had done it. My wife wept, and my mother became angry with me; but when a thing is duty, it is neither wife nor mother who will move me out of my way.

It was a miserable day. There was not light enough to see anything – scarcely to see each other's faces; and to add to our alarm, some travellers arriving by the diligence (we are still three leagues from a railway, while that miserable little place, La Rochette, being the *chef-lieu*, has a terminus) informed me that the darkness only existed in Semur and the neighbour-hood, and that within a distance of three miles the sun was shining. The sun was shining! was it possible? it seemed so long since we had seen the sunshine; but this made our calamity more mysterious and more terrible. The people began to gather into little knots in the streets to talk of the strange thing that was happening. In the course of the day M. Barbou came to ask whether I did not think it would be well to appease the popular feeling by conceding what they wished to the Sisters of the hospital. I would not hear of it. 'Shall we own that we are in the wrong? I do not think we are in the wrong,' I said, and I would not yield. 'Do you think the good Sisters have it in their power to darken the sky with their incantations?' M. l'Adjoint shook his head. He went away with a troubled countenance; but then he was not like myself, a man of natural firmness. All the efforts that were employed to influence him were also employed with me; but to yield to the women was not in my thoughts.

We are now approaching, however, the first important incident in this narrative. The darkness increased as the afternoon came on; and it became a kind of thick twilight, no lighter than many a night. It was between five and six o'clock, just the time when our streets are the most crowded, when, sitting at my window, from which I kept a watch upon the Grande Rue, not knowing what might happen – I saw that some fresh incident had taken place. Very dimly through the darkness I perceived a crowd, which increased every moment, in front of the Cathedral. After watching it for a few minutes, I got my hat and went out. The people whom I saw – so many that they covered the whole middle of the *Place*, reaching almost to the pavement on the other side – had their heads all turned towards the Cathedral. 'What are you gazing at, my friend?' I said to one by whom I stood. He looked up at me with a face which looked ghastly in the gloom. 'Look, M. le Maire!' he said; 'cannot you see it on the great door?'

'I see nothing,' said I; but as I uttered these words I did indeed see something which was very startling. Looking towards the great door of the Cathedral, as they all were doing, it suddenly seemed to me that I saw an illuminated placard attached to it, headed with the word 'Sommation' in gigantic letters. '*Tiens!*' I cried; but when I looked again there was nothing. 'What is this? it is some witchcraft!' I said, in spite of myself. 'Do you see anything, Jean Pierre?'

'M. le Maire,' he said, 'one moment one sees something – the next, one sees nothing. Look! it comes again.' I have always considered myself a man of courage, but when I saw this extraordinary appearance the panic which had seized upon me the former night returned, though in another form. Fly I could not, but I will not deny that my knees smote together. I stood for some minutes without being able to articulate a word – which, indeed, seemed the case with most of those before me. Never have I seen a more quiet crowd. They were all gazing, as if it was life or death that was set before them – while I, too, gazed with a shiver going over me. It was as I have seen an illumination of lamps in a stormy night; one moment the whole seems black as the wind sweeps over it, the next it springs into life again; and thus you go on, by turns losing and discovering the device formed by the lights. Thus from moment to moment there appeared before us, in letters that seemed to blaze and flicker, something that looked like a great official placard. 'Sommation!' – this was how it was headed. I read a few words at a time, as it came and went; and who can describe the chill that ran through my veins as I made it out? It was a summons to the people of Semur by name – myself at the head as Maire (and I heard afterwards that every man who saw it saw his own name, though the whole *façade* of the Cathedral would not have held a full list of all the people of Semur) – to yield their places, which they had not filled aright, to those who knew the meaning of life, being dead. NOUS AUTRES MORTS – these were the words which blazed out oftenest of all, so that every one saw them. And 'Go!' this terrible placard said – 'Go! leave this place to us who know the true signification of life.' These words I remember, but not the rest; and even at this moment it struck me that there was no explanation, nothing but this *vraie signification de la vie*. I felt like one in a dream: the light coming and going before me; one word, then another, appearing – sometimes a phrase like that I have quoted, blazing out, then dropping into darkness. For the moment I was struck dumb; but then it came back to my mind that I had an example to give, and that for me, eminently a man of my century, to yield credence to a miracle was something not to be thought of. Also I knew the necessity of doing something to break the impression of awe and terror on the mind of the people. 'This is a trick,' I cried loudly, that all might hear. 'Let some one go and fetch M. de Clairon from the Musée. He will tell us how it has been done.' This, boldly uttered, broke the spell. A number of pale faces gathered round me. 'Here is M. le Maire – he will clear it up,' they cried, making room for me that I might approach nearer. 'M. le Maire is a man of courage – he has judgment. Listen to M. le Maire.' It was a relief to everybody that I had spoken. And soon I found myself by the side of M. le Curé, who was standing among the rest, saying nothing, and with the air of one as much bewildered as any of us. He gave me one quick look from under his eyebrows to see who it was that approached him, as was his way, and made room for me, but said nothing. I was in too much emotion myself to keep silence – indeed, I was in that condition of wonder, alarm, and nervous excitement, that I had to speak or die; and there seemed an escape from something too terrible for flesh and blood to contemplate in the idea that there was trickery here. 'M. le Curé,' I said, 'this is a strange ornament that you have placed on the front of your church. You are standing here to enjoy the effect. Now that you have seen how successful it has been, will not you tell me in confidence how it is done?'

I am conscious that there was a sneer in my voice, but I was too much excited to think of politeness. He gave me another of his rapid, keen looks.

'M. le Maire,' he said, 'you are injurious to a man who is as little fond of tricks as yourself.'

His tone, his glance, gave me a certain sense of shame, but I could not stop myself. 'One knows,' I said, 'that there are many things which an ecclesiastic may do without harm, which are not permitted to an ordinary layman – one who is an honest man, and no more.'

M. le Curé made no reply. He gave me another of his quick glances, with an impatient turn of his head. Why should I have suspected him? for no harm was known of him. He was the Curé, that was all; and perhaps we men of the world have our prejudices too. Afterwards, however, as we waited for M. de Clairon – for the crisis was too exciting for personal resentment – M. le Curé himself let drop something which made it apparent that it was the ladies of the hospital upon whom his suspicions fell. 'It is never well to offend women, M. le Maire,' he said. 'Women do not discriminate the lawful from the unlawful: so long as they produce an effect, it does not matter to them.' This gave me a strange impression, for it seemed to me that M. le Curé was abandoning his own side. However, all other sentiments were, as may be imagined, but as shadows compared with the overwhelming power that held all our eyes and our thoughts to the wonder before us. Every moment seemed an hour till M. de Clairon appeared. He was pushed forward through the crowd as by magic, all making room for him; and many of us thought that when science thus came forward capable of finding out everything, the miracle would disappear. But instead of this it seemed to glow brighter than ever. That great word '*Sommation*' blazed out, so that we saw his figure waver against the light as if giving way before the flames that scorched him. He was so near that his outline was marked out dark against the glare they gave. It was as though his close approach rekindled every light. Then, with a flicker and trembling, word by word and letter by letter went slowly out before our eyes.

M. de Clairon came down very pale, but with a sort of smile on his face. 'No, M. le Maire,' he said, 'I cannot see how it is done. It is clever. I will examine the door further, and try the panels. Yes, I have left some one to watch that nothing is touched in the meantime, with the permission of M. le Curé—'

'You have my full permission,' M. le Curé said; and M. de Clairon laughed, though he was still very pale. 'You saw my name there,' he said. 'I am amused – I who am not one of your worthy citizens, M. le Maire. What can Messieurs les Morts of Semur want with a poor man of science like me? But you shall have my report before the evening is out.'

With this I had to be content. The darkness which succeeded to that strange light seemed more terrible than ever. We all stumbled as we turned to go away, dazzled by it, and stricken dumb, though some kept saying that it was a trick, and some murmured exclamations with voices full of terror. The sound of the crowd breaking up was like a regiment marching – all the world had been there. I was thankful, however, that neither my mother nor my wife had seen anything; and though they were anxious to know why I was so serious, I succeeded fortunately in keeping the secret from them.

M. de Clairon did not appear till late, and then he confessed to me he could make nothing of it. 'If it is a trick (as of course it must be), it has been most cleverly done,' he said; and admitted that he was baffled altogether. For my part, I was not surprised. Had it been the Sisters of the hospital, as M. le Curé thought, would they have let the opportunity pass of preaching a sermon to us, and recommending their doctrines? Not so; here there were no doctrines, nothing but that pregnant phrase, *la vraie signification de la vie*. This made a more deep impression upon me than anything else. The Holy Mother herself (whom I wish to speak of with profound respect), and the saints, and the forgiveness of sins, would have all been there had it been the Sisters, or even M. le Curé. This, though I had myself suggested an imposture, made very unlikely to my quiet thoughts. But if not an imposture, what could it be supposed to be?

THREE

Expulsion of the Inhabitants

I WILL NOT attempt to give any detailed account of the state of
the town during this evening. For myself I was utterly worn
out, and went to rest as soon as M. de Clairon left me, having
satisfied, as well as I could, the questions of the women. Even
in the intensest excitement weary nature will claim her dues. I
slept. I can even remember the grateful sense of being able to
put all anxieties and perplexities aside for the moment, as I
went to sleep. I felt the drowsiness gain upon me, and I was
glad. To forget was of itself a happiness.

I woke up, however, intensely awake, and in perfect possession of all my faculties, while it was yet dark; and at once
got up and began to dress. The moment of hesitation which
generally follows waking – the little interval of thought in
which one turns over perhaps that which is past, perhaps that
which is to come – found no place within me. I got up without
a moment's pause, like one who has been called to go on a
journey; nor did it surprise me at all to see my wife moving
about, taking a cloak from her wardrobe, and putting up linen
in a bag. She was already fully dressed; but she asked no
questions of me any more than I did of her. We were in haste,
though we said nothing. When I had dressed, I looked round
me to see if I had forgotten anything, as one does when one
leaves a place. I saw my watch suspended to its usual hook,
and my pocket-book, which I had taken from my pocket on
the previous night. I took up also the light overcoat which I
had worn when I made my rounds through the city on the
first night of the darkness. 'Now,' I said, 'Agnès, I am ready.'
I did not speak to her of where we were going, nor she to me.
Little Jean and my mother met us at the door. Nor did *she* say
anything, contrary to her custom; and the child was quite
quiet. We went downstairs together without saying a word.
The servants, who were all astir, followed us. I cannot give
any description of the feelings that were in my mind. I had

not any feelings. I was only hurried out, hastened by something which I could not define – a sense that I must go; and
perhaps I was too much astonished to do anything but yield.
It seemed, however, to be no force or fear that was moving
me, but a desire of my own; though I could not tell how it was,
or why I should be so anxious to get away. All the servants,
trooping after me, had the same look in their faces; they were
anxious to be gone – it seemed their business to go – there was
no question, no consultation. And when we came out into the
street, we encountered a stream of processions similar to our
own. The children went quite steadily by the side of their
parents. Little Jean, for example, on an ordinary occasion
would have broken away – would have run to his comrades of
the Bois-Sombre family, and they to him. But no; the little
ones, like ourselves, walked along quite gravely. They asked
no questions, neither did we ask any questions of each other,
as, 'Where are you going?' or, 'What is the meaning of a so-
early promenade?' Nothing of the kind: my mother took my
arm, and my wife, leading little Jean by the hand, came to the
other side. The servants followed. The street was quite full of
people; but there was no noise except the sound of their
footsteps. All of us turned the same way – turned towards the
gates – and though I was not conscious of any feeling except
the wish to go on, there were one or two things which took a
place in my memory. The first was, that my wife suddenly
turned round as we were coming out of the *porte-cochère*, her
face lighting up. I need not say to any one who knows
Madame Dupin de la Clairière, that she is a beautiful woman.
Without any partiality on my part, it would be impossible for
me to ignore this fact: for it is perfectly well known and
acknowledged by all. She was pale this morning – a little paler
than usual; and her blue eyes enlarged, with a serious look,
which they always retain more or less. But suddenly, as we
went out of the door, her face lighted up, her eyes were
suffused with tears – with light – how can I tell what it was? –
they became like the eyes of angels. A little cry came from her
parted lips – she lingered a moment, stooping down as if
talking to some one less tall than herself, then came after us,
with that light still in her face. At the moment I was too much
occupied to enquire what it was; but I noted it, even in the
gravity of the occasion. The next thing I observed was M. le
Curé, who, as I have already indicated, is a man of great

composure of manner and presence of mind, coming out of the door of the Presbytery. There was a strange look on his face of astonishment and reluctance. He walked very slowly, not as we did, but with a visible desire to turn back, folding his arms across his breast, and holding himself as if against the wind, resisting some gale which blew behind him, and forced him on. We felt no gale; but there seemed to be a strange wind blowing along the side of the street on which M. le Curé was. And there was an air of concealed surprise in his face – great astonishment, but a determination not to let any one see that he was astonished, or that the situation was strange to him. And I cannot tell how it was, but I, too, though pre-occupied, was surprised to perceive that M. le Curé was going with the rest of us, though I could not have told why.

Behind M. le Curé there was another whom I remarked. This was Jacques Richard, he of whom I have already spoken. He was like a figure I have seen somewhere in sculpture. No one was near him, nobody touching him, and yet it was only necessary to look at the man to perceive that he was being forced along against his will. Every limb was in resistance; his feet were planted widely yet firmly upon the pavement; one of his arms was stretched out as if to lay hold on anything that should come within reach. M. le Curé resisted passively; but Jacques resisted with passion, laying his back to the wind, and struggling not to be carried away. Notwithstanding his resistance, however, this rough figure was driven along slowly, struggling at every step. He did not make one movement that was not against his will, but still he was driven on. On our side of the street all went, like ourselves, calmly. My mother uttered now and then a low moan, but said nothing. She clung to my arm, and walked on, hurrying a little, sometimes going quicker than I intended to go. As for my wife, she accompanied us with her light step, which scarcely seemed to touch the ground, little Jean pattering by her side. Our neighbours were all round us. We streamed down, as in a long procession, to the Porte St Lambert. It was only when we got there that the strange character of the step we were all taking suddenly occurred to me. It was still a kind of grey twilight, not yet day. The bells of the Cathedral had begun to toll, which was very startling – not ringing in their cheerful way, but tolling as if for a funeral, and no other sound was audible but the noise of footsteps, like an army making a silent march into an enemy's country. We had reached the gate when a sudden wondering came over me. Why were we all going out of our houses in the wintry dusk to which our July days had turned? I stopped, and turning round, was about to say something to the others, when I became suddenly aware that here I was not my own master. My tongue clave to the roof of my mouth; I could not say a word. Then I myself was turned round, and softly, firmly, irresistibly pushed out of the gate. My mother, who clung to me, added a little, no doubt, to the force against me, whatever it was, for she was frightened, and opposed herself to any endeavour on my part to regain freedom of movement; but all that her feeble force could do against mine must have been little. Several other men around me seemed to be moved as I was. M. Barbou, for one, made a still more decided effort to turn back, for, being a bachelor, he had no one to restrain him. Him I saw turned round as you would turn a *roulette*. He was thrown against my wife in his tempestuous course, and but that she was so light and elastic in her tread, gliding out straight and softly like one of the saints, I think he must have thrown her down. And at that moment, silent as we all were, his '*Pardon, Madame, mille pardons, Madame,*' and his tone of horror at his own indiscretion, seemed to come to me like a voice out of another life. Partially roused before by the sudden impulse of resistance I have described, I was yet more roused now. I turned round, disengaging myself from my mother. 'Where are we going? why are we thus cast forth? My friends, help!' I cried. I looked round upon the others, who, as I have said, had also awakened to a possibility of resistance. M. de Bois-Sombre, without a word, came and placed himself by my side; others started from the crowd. We turned to resist this mysterious impulse which had sent us forth. The crowd surged round us in the uncertain light.

Just then there was a dull soft sound, once, twice, thrice repeated. We rushed forward, but too late. The gates were closed upon us. The two folds of the great Porte St Lambert, and the little postern for foot-passengers, all at once, not hurriedly, as from any fear of us, but slowly, softly, rolled on their hinges and shut – in our faces. I rushed forward with all my force and flung myself upon the gate. To what use? it was so closed as no mortal could open it. They told me after, for I was not aware at the moment, that I burst forth with cries and exclamations, bidding them 'Open, open in the name of God!' I was not aware of what I said, but it seemed to me that I heard a voice of which nobody said anything to me, so that it would seem to have been unheard by the others, saying with a faint sound as of a trumpet, 'Closed – in the name of God.' It might be only an echo, faintly brought back to me, of the words I had myself said.

There was another change, however, of which no one could have any doubt. When I turned round from these closed doors, though the moment before the darkness was such that we could not see the gates closing, I found the sun shining gloriously round us, and all my fellow-citizens turning with one impulse, with a sudden cry of joy, to hail the full day.

Le grand jour! Never in my life did I feel the full happiness of it, the full sense of the words before. The sun burst out into shining, the birds into singing. The sky stretched over us – deep and unfathomable and blue, – the grass grew under our feet, a soft air of morning blew upon us, waving the curls of the children, the veils of the women, whose faces were lit up by the beautiful day. After three days of darkness what a resurrection! It seemed to make up to us for the misery of being thus expelled from our homes. It was early, and all the freshness of the morning was upon the road and the fields, where the sun had just dried the dew. The river ran softly, reflecting the blue sky. How black it had been, deep and dark as a stream of ink, when I had looked down upon it from the Mont St Lambert! and now it ran as clear and free as the voice of a little child. We all shared this moment of joy – for to us of the South the sunshine is as the breath of life, and to be deprived of it had been terrible. But when that first pleasure was over, the evidence of our strange position forced itself upon us with overpowering reality and force, made stronger by the very light. In the dimness it had not seemed so certain; now, gazing at each other in the clear light of the natural morning, we saw what had happened to us. No more delusion was possible. We could not flatter ourselves now that it was a trick or a deception. M. de Clairon stood there like the rest of us, staring at the closed gates which science could not open. And there stood M. le Curé, which was more remarkable still. The Church herself had not been able to do anything. We stood, a crowd of houseless exiles, looking at each other, our children clinging to us, our hearts failing us, expelled from our homes. As we looked in each other's faces we saw our own trouble. Many of the women sat down and wept; some upon the stones in the road, some on the grass. The children took fright from them, and began to cry too. What was to become of us? I looked round upon this crowd with despair in my heart. It was I to whom every one would look – for lodging, for direction – everything that human creatures want. It was my business to forget myself, though I also had been driven from my home and my city. Happily there was one thing I had left. In the pocket of my overcoat was my scarf of office. I stepped aside behind a tree, and took it out, and tied it upon me. That was something. There was thus a representative of order and law in the midst of the exiles, whatever might happen. This action, which a great number of the crowd saw, restored confidence. Many of the poor people gathered round me, and placed themselves near me, especially those women who had no natural support. When M. le Curé saw this, it seemed to make a great impression upon him. He changed colour, he who was usually so calm. Hitherto he had appeared bewildered, amazed to find himself as others. This, I must add, though you may perhaps think it superstitious, surprised me very much too. But now he regained his self-possession. He stepped upon a piece of wood that lay in front of the gate. 'My children—' he said. But just then the Cathedral bells, which had gone on tolling, suddenly burst into a wild peal. I do not know what it sounded like. It was a clamour of notes all run together, tone upon tone, without time or measure, as though a multitude had seized upon the bells and pulled all the ropes at once. If it was joy, what strange and terrible joy! It froze the very blood in our veins. M. le Curé became quite pale. He stepped down hurriedly from the piece of wood. We all made a hurried movement farther off from the gate.

It was now that I perceived the necessity of doing something, of getting this crowd disposed of, especially the women and the children. I am not ashamed to own that I trembled like the others; and nothing less than the consciousness that all eyes were upon me, and that my scarf of office marked me out among all who stood around, could have kept me from moving with precipitation as they did. I was enabled, however, to retire at a deliberate pace, and being thus slightly detached from the crowd, I took advantage of the opportunity to address them. Above all things, it was my duty to prevent a tumult in these unprecedented circumstances. 'My friends,' I said, 'the event which has occurred is beyond explanation for the moment. The very nature of it is mysterious; the circumstances are such as require the closest investigation. But take courage. I pledge myself not to leave this place till the gates are open, and you can return to your homes; in the meantime, however, the women and the children cannot remain here. Let those who have friends in the villages near, go and ask for shelter; and let all who will, go to my house of La Clairière. My mother, my wife! recall to yourselves the position you occupy, and show an example. Lead our neighbours, I entreat you, to La Clairière.'

My mother is advanced in years and no longer strong, but she has a great heart. 'I will go,' she said. 'God bless thee, my son! There will no harm happen; for if this be true which we are told, thy father is in Semur.'

There then occurred one of those incidents for which calculation never will prepare us. My mother's words seemed, as it were to open the floodgates; my wife came up to me with the light in her face which I had seen when we left our own door. 'It was our little Marie – our angel,' she said. And then there arose a great cry and clamour of others, both men and women pressing round. 'I saw my mother,' said one, 'who is dead twenty years come the St Jean.' 'And I my little René,' said another. 'And I my Camille, who was killed in Africa.' And lo, what did they do, but rush towards the gate in a crowd – that gate from which they had but this moment fled in terror – beating upon it, and crying out, 'Open to us, open to us, our most dear! Do you think we have forgotten you? We have never forgotten you!' What could we do with them, weeping thus, smiling, holding out their arms to – we knew not what? Even my Agnès was beyond my reach. Marie was our little girl who was dead. Those who were thus transported by a knowledge beyond ours were the weakest among us; most of them were women, the men old or feeble, and some children. I can recollect that I looked for Paul Lecamus among them, with wonder not to see him there. But though they were weak, they were beyond our strength to guide. What could we do with them? How could we force them away while they held to the fancy that those they loved were there? As it happens in times of emotion, it was those who were most impassioned who took the first place. We were at our wits' end.

But while we stood waiting, not knowing what to do, another sound suddenly came from the walls, which made them all silent in a moment. The most of us ran to this point and that (some taking flight altogether; but with the greater part anxious curiosity and anxiety had for the moment extinguished fear), in a wild eagerness to see who or what it was. But there was nothing to be seen, though the sound came from the wall close to the Mont St Lambert, which I have already described. It was to me like the sound of a trumpet, and so I heard others say; and along with the trumpet were sounds as of words, though I could not make them out. But those others seemed to understand – they grew calmer – they ceased to weep. They raised their faces, all with that light upon them – that light I had seen in my Agnès. Some of them fell upon their knees. Imagine to yourself what a sight it was, all of us standing round, pale, stupefied, without a word to say! Then the women suddenly burst forth into replies – '*Oui, ma chérie! Oui, mon ange!*' they cried. And while we looked they rose up; they came back, calling the children around them. My Agnès took that place which I had bidden her take. She had not hearkened to me, to leave me – but she hearkened now; and though I had bidden her to do this, yet to see her do it bewildered me, made my heart stand still. '*Mon ami*,' she said, 'I must leave thee; it is commanded: they will not have the children suffer.' What could we do? We stood pale and looked on, while all the little ones, all the feeble, were gathered in a little army. My mother stood like me – to her nothing had been revealed. She was very pale, and there was a quiver of pain in her lips. She was the one who had been ready to do my bidding: but there was a rebellion in her heart now. When the procession was formed (for it was my care to see that everything was done in order), she followed, but among the last. Thus they went away, many of them weeping, looking back, waving their hands to us. My Agnès covered her face, she could not look at me; but she obeyed. They went some to this side, some to that, leaving us gazing. For a long time we did nothing but watch them, going along the roads. What had their angels said to them? Nay, but God knows. I heard the sound; it was like the sound of the silver trumpets

that travellers talk of; it was like music from heaven. I turned
to M. le Curé, who was standing by. 'What is it?' I cried, 'you
are their director – you are an ecclesiastic – you know what
belongs to the unseen. What is this that has been said to
them?' I have always thought well of M. le Curé. There were
tears running down his cheeks. 'I know not,' he said. 'I am a
miserable like the rest. What they know is between God and
them. Me! I have been of the world, like the rest.'

This is how we were left alone – the men of the city – to take
what means were best to get back to our homes. There were
several left among us who had shared the enlightenment of
the women, but these were not persons of importance who
could put themselves at the head of affairs. And there were
women who remained with us, but these not of the best. To
see our wives go was very strange to us; it was the thing we
wished most to see, the women and children in safety; yet it
was a strange sensation to see them go. For me, who had the
charge of all on my hands, the relief was beyond description –
yet was it strange; I cannot describe it. Then I called upon M.
Barbou, who was trembling like a leaf, and gathered the chief
of the citizens about me, including M. le Curé, that we should
consult together what we should do.

I know no words that can describe our state in the strange
circumstances we were now placed in. The women and the
children were safe; that was much. But we – we were like an
army suddenly formed, but without arms, without any
knowledge of how to fight, without being able to see our
enemy. We Frenchmen have not been without knowledge of
such perils. We have seen the invader enter our doors; we
have been obliged to spread our table for him, and give him
of our best. But to be put forth by forces no man could resist
– to be left outside, with the doors of our own houses closed
upon us – to be confronted by nothing – by a mist, a silence, a
darkness, – this was enough to paralyse the heart of any man.
And it did so, more or less, according to the nature of those
who were exposed to the trial. Some altogether failed us, and
fled, carrying the news into the country, where most people
laughed at them, as we understood afterwards. Some could
do nothing but sit and gaze, huddled together in crowds, at
the cloud over Semur, from which they expected to see fire
burst and consume the city altogether. And a few, I grieve to
say, took possession of the little *cabaret*, which stands at

about half a kilometre from the St Lambert gate, and established themselves there, in hideous riot, which was the worst thing of all for serious men to behold. Those upon whom I could rely I formed into patrols to go round the city, that no opening of a gate, or movement of those who were within, should take place without our knowledge. Such an emergency shows what men are. M. Barbou, though in ordinary times he discharges his duties as *adjoint* satisfactorily enough (though, it need not be added, a good Maire who is acquainted with his duties, makes the office of *adjoint* of but little importance), was now found entirely useless. He could not forget how he had been spun round and tossed forth from the city gates. When I proposed to put him at the head of a patrol, he had an attack of the nerves. Before nightfall he deserted me altogether, going off to his country-house, and taking a number of his neighbours with him. 'How can we tell when we may be permitted to return to the town?' he said, with his teeth chattering. 'M. le Maire, I adjure you to put yourself in a place of safety.'

'Sir,' I said to him, sternly, 'for one who deserts his post there is no place of safety.'

But I do not think he was capable of understanding me. Fortunately, I found in M. le Curé a much more trustworthy coadjutor. He was indefatigable; he had the habit of sitting up to all hours, of being called at all hours, in which our *bourgeoisie*, I cannot but acknowledge, is wanting. The expression I have before described of astonishment – but of astonishment which he wished to conceal – never left his face. He did not understand how such a thing could have been permitted to happen while he had no share in it; and, indeed, I will not deny that this was a matter of great wonder to myself too.

The arrangements I have described gave us occupation; and this had a happy effect upon us in distracting our minds from what had happened; for I think that if we had sat still and gazed at the dark city we should soon have gone mad, as some did. In our ceaseless patrols and attempts to find a way of entrance, we distracted ourselves from the enquiry, Who would dare to go in if the entrance were found? In the meantime not a gate was opened, not a figure was visible. We saw nothing, no more than if Semur had been a picture painted upon a canvas. Strange sights indeed met our eyes –

sights which made even the bravest quail. The strangest of
them was the boats that would go down and up the river,
shooting forth from under the fortified bridge, which is one of
the chief features of our town, sometimes with sails perfectly
well managed, sometimes impelled by oars, but with no one
visible in them – no one conducting them. To see one of these
boats impelled up the stream, with no rower visible, was a
wonderful sight. M. de Clairon, who was by my side, murmured something about a magnetic current; but when I asked
him sternly by what set in motion, his voice died away in his
moustache. M. le Curé said very little: one saw his lips move
as he watched with us the passage of those boats. He smiled
when it was proposed by some one to fire upon them. He read
his Hours as he went round at the head of his patrol. My
fellow townsmen and I conceived a great respect for him; and
he inspired pity in me also. He had been the teacher of the
Unseen among us, till the moment when the Unseen was
thus, as it were, brought within our reach; but with the
revelation he had nothing to do; and it filled him with pain
and wonder. It made him silent; he said little about his
religion, but signed himself, and his lips moved. He thought
(I imagine) that he had displeased Those who are over all.

When night came the bravest of us were afraid. I speak for
myself. It was bright moonlight where we were, and Semur
lay like a blot between the earth and the sky, all dark: even the
Cathedral towers were lost in it; nothing visible but the line of
the ramparts, whitened outside by the moon. One knows what
black and strange shadows are cast by the moonlight; and it
seemed to all of us that we did not know what might be
lurking behind every tree. The shadows of the branches
looked like terrible faces. I sent all my people out on the
patrols, though they were dropping with fatigue. Rather that
than to be mad with terror. For myself, I took up my post as
near the bank of the river as we could approach; for there was
a limit beyond which we might not pass. I made the experiment often; and it seemed to me, and to all that attempted it,
that we did reach the very edge of the stream; but the next
moment perceived that we were at a certain distance, say
twenty metres or thereabout. I placed myself there very often,
wrapping a cloak about me to preserve me from the dew. (I
may say that food had been sent us, and wine from La
Clairière and many other houses in the neighbourhood, where

the women had gone for this among other reasons, that we might be nourished by them.) And I must here relate a personal incident, though I have endeavoured not to be egotistical. While I sat watching, I distinctly saw a boat, a boat which belonged to myself, lying on the very edge of the shadow. The prow, indeed, touched the moonlight where it was cut clean across by the darkness; and this was how I discovered that it was the *Marie*, a pretty pleasure-boat which had been made for my wife. The sight of it made my heart beat; for what could it mean but that some one who was dear to me, some one in whom I took an interest, was there? I sprang up from where I sat to make another effort to get nearer; but my feet were as lead, and would not move; and there came a singing in my ears, and my blood coursed through my veins as in a fever. Ah! was it possible? I, who am a man, who have resolution, who have courage, who can lead the people, *I was afraid!* I sat down again and wept like a child. Perhaps it was my little Marie that was in the boat. God, He knows if I loved thee, my little angel! but I was afraid. O how mean is man! though we are so proud. They came near to me who were my own, and it was borne in upon my spirit that my good father was with the child; but because they had died I was afraid. I covered my face with my hands. Then it seemed to me that I heard a long quiver of a sigh; a long, long breath, such as sometimes relieves a sorrow that is beyond words. Trembling, I uncovered my eyes. There was nothing on the edge of the moonlight; all was dark, and all was still, the white radiance making a clear line across the river, but nothing more.

If my Agnès had been with me she would have seen our child, she would have heard that voice! The great cold drops of moisture were on my forehead. My limbs trembled, my heart fluttered in my bosom. I could neither listen nor yet speak. And those who would have spoken to me, those who loved me, sighing, went away. It is not possible that such wretchedness should be credible to noble minds; and if it had not been for pride and for shame, I should have fled away straight to La Clairière, to put myself under shelter, to have some one near me who was less a coward than I. I, upon whom all the others relied, the Maire of the Commune! I make my confession. I was of no more force than this.

A voice behind me made me spring to my feet – the leap of a mouse would have driven me wild. I was altogether demoralised. 'Monsieur le Maire, it is but I,' said some one quite humble and frightened. '*Tiens!* – it is thou, Jacques!' I said. I could have embraced him, though it is well known how little I approve of him. But he was living, he was a man like myself. I put out my hand, and felt him warm and breathing, and I shall never forget the ease that came to my heart. Its beating calmed, I was restored to myself.

'M. le Maire,' he said, 'I wish to ask you something. Is it true all that is said about these people, I would say, these Messieurs? I do not wish to speak with disrespect, M. le Maire.'

'What is it, Jacques, that is said?' I had called him 'thou' not out of contempt, but because, for the moment, he seemed to me as a brother, as one of my friends.

'M. le Maire, is it indeed *les morts* that are in Semur?'

He trembled, and so did I. 'Jacques,' I said, 'you know all that I know.'

'Yes, M. le Maire, it is so, sure enough. I do not doubt it. If it were the Prussians, a man could fight. But *ces Messieurs là!* What I want to know is: is it because of what you did to those little Sisters, those good little ladies of St Jean?'

'What I did? You were yourself one of the complainants. You were of those who said, when a man is ill, when he is suffering, they torment him with their mass; it is quiet he wants, not their mass. These were thy words, *vaurien*. And now you say it was I!'

'True, M. le Maire,' said Jacques; 'but look you, when a man is better, when he has just got well, when he feels he is safe, then you should not take what he says for gospel. It would be strange if one had a new illness just when one is getting well of the old; and one feels now is the time to enjoy one's self, to kick up one's heels a little, while at least there is not likely to be much of a watch kept *up there* – the saints forgive me,' cried Jacques, trembling and crossing himself, 'if I speak with levity at such a moment! And the little ladies were very kind. It was wrong to close their chapel, M. le Maire. From that comes all our trouble.'

'You good-for-nothing!' I cried, 'it is you and such as you that are the beginning of our trouble. You thought there was no watch kept *up there*; you thought God would not take the trouble to punish you; you went about the streets of Semur tossing a *grosse pièce* of a hundred sous, and calling out, "There is no God – this is my god; *l'argent, c'est le bon Dieu*."'

'M. le Maire, M. le Maire, be silent, I implore you! It is enough to bring down a judgment upon us.'

'It has brought down a judgment upon us. Go thou and try what thy *grosse pièce* will do for thee now – worship thy god. Go, I tell you, and get help from your money.'

'I have no money, M. le Maire, and what could money do here? We would do much better to promise a large candle for the next festival, and that the ladies of St Jean—'

'Get away with thee to the end of the world, thou and thy ladies of St Jean!' I cried; which was wrong, I do not deny it, for they are good women, not like this good-for-nothing fellow. And to think that this man, whom I despise, was more pleasant to me than the dear souls who loved me! Shame came upon me at the thought. I too, then, was like the others, fearing the Unseen – capable of understanding only that which was palpable. When Jacques slunk away, which he did for a few steps, not losing sight of me, I turned my face towards the river and the town. The moonlight fell upon the water, white as silver where that line of darkness lay, shining, as if it tried, and tried in vain, to penetrate Semur; and between that and the blue sky overhead lay the city out of which we had been driven forth – the city of the dead. 'O God,' I cried, 'whom I know not, am not I to Thee as my little Jean is to me, a child and less than a child? Do not abandon me in this darkness. Would I abandon him were he ever so disobedient? And God, if thou art God, Thou art a better father than I.' When I had said this, my heart was a little relieved. It seemed to me that I had spoken to some one who knew all of us, whether we were dead or whether we were living. That is a wonderful thing to think of, when it appears to one not as a thing to believe, but as something that is real. It gave me courage. I got up and went to meet the patrol which was coming in, and found that great good-for-nothing Jacques running close after me, holding my cloak. 'Do not send me away, M. le Maire,' he said, 'I dare not stay by myself with *them* so near.' Instead of his money, in which he had trusted, it was I who had become his god now.

FOUR

Outside the Walls

THERE ARE FEW who have not heard something of the sufferings of a siege. Whether within or without, it is the most
terrible of all the experiences of war. I am old enough to
recollect the trenches before Sebastopol, and all that my
countrymen and the English endured there. Sometimes I
endeavoured to think of this to distract me from what we
ourselves endured. But how different was it! We had neither
shelter nor support. We had no weapons, nor any against
whom to wield them. We were cast out of our homes in the
midst of our lives, in the midst of our occupations, and left
there helpless, to gaze at each other, to blind our eyes trying to
penetrate the darkness before us. Could we have done anything, the oppression might have been less terrible – but what
was there that we could do? Fortunately (though I do not
deny that I felt each desertion) our band grew less and less
every day. Hour by hour some one stole away – first one, then
another, dispersing themselves among the villages near, in
which many had friends. The accounts which these men gave
were, I afterwards learnt, of the most vague description.
Some talked of wonders they had seen, and were laughed
at – and some spread reports of internal division among us.
Not till long after did I know all the reports that went abroad.
It was said that there had been fighting in Semur, and that we
were divided into two factions, one of which had gained the
mastery, and driven the other out. This was the story current
in La Rochette, where they are always glad to hear anything
to the discredit of the people of Semur; but no credence could
have been given to it by those in authority, otherwise M. le
Préfet, however indifferent to our interests, must necessarily
have taken some steps for our relief. Our entire separation
from the world was indeed one of the strangest details of this
terrible period. Generally the diligence, though conveying on
the whole few passengers, returned with two or three, at least,

visitors or commercial persons, daily – and the latter class frequently arrived in carriages of their own; but during this period no stranger came to see our miserable plight. We made shelter for ourselves under the branches of the few trees that grew in the uncultivated ground on either side of the road – and a hasty erection, half tent half shed, was put up for a place to assemble in, or for those who were unable to bear the heat of the day or the occasional chills of the night. But the most of us were too restless to seek repose, and could not bear to be out of sight of the city. At any moment it seemed to us the gates might open, or some loophole be visible by which we might throw ourselves upon the darkness and vanquish it. This was what we said to ourselves, forgetting how we shook and trembled whenever any contact had been possible with those who were within. But one thing was certain, that though we feared, we could not turn our eyes from the place. We slept leaning against a tree, or with our heads on our hands, and our faces toward Semur. We took no count of day or night, but ate the morsel the women brought to us, and slept thus, not sleeping, when want or weariness overwhelmed us. There was scarcely an hour in the day that some of the women did not come to ask what news. They crept along the roads in twos and threes, and lingered for hours sitting by the way weeping, starting at every breath of wind.

Meanwhile all was not silent within Semur. The Cathedral bells rang often, at first filling us with hope, for how familiar was that sound! The first time, we all gathered together and listened, and many wept. It was as if we heard our mother's voice. M. de Bois-Sombre burst into tears. I have never seen him within the doors of the Cathedral since his marriage; but he burst into tears. '*Mon Dieu!* if I were but there!' he said. We stood and listened, our hearts melting, some falling on their knees. M. le Curé stood up in the midst of us and began to intone the psalm: (He has a beautiful voice. It is sympathetic, it goes to the heart.) 'I was glad when they said to me, Let us go up—' And though there were few of us who could have supposed themselves capable of listening to that sentiment a little while before with any sympathy, yet a vague hope rose up within us while we heard him, while we listened to the bells. What man is there to whom the bells of his village, the *carillon* of his city, is not most dear? It rings for him through all his life; it is the first sound of home in the distance when he comes back – the last that follows him like a long farewell when he goes away. While we listened, we forgot our fears. They were as we were, they were also our brethren, who rang those bells. We seemed to see them trooping into our beautiful Cathedral. Ah! only to see it again, to be within its shelter, cool and calm as in our mothers' arms! It seemed to us that we should wish for nothing more.

When the sound ceased we looked into each other's faces, and each man saw that his neighbour was pale. Hope died in us when the sound died away, vibrating sadly through the air. Some men threw themselves on the ground in their despair.

And from this time forward many voices were heard, calls and shouts within the walls, and sometimes a sound like a trumpet, and other instruments of music. We thought, indeed, that noises as of bands patrolling along the ramparts were audible as our patrols worked their way round and round. This was a duty which I never allowed to be neglected, not because I put very much faith in it, but because it gave us a sort of employment. There is a story somewhere which I recollect dimly of an ancient city which its assailants did not touch, but only marched round and round till the walls fell, and they could enter. Whether this was a story of classic times or out of our own remote history, I could not recollect. But I thought of it many times while we made our way like a procession of ghosts, round and round, straining our ears to hear what those voices were which sounded above us, in tones that were familiar, yet so strange. This story got so much into my head (and after a time all our heads seemed to get confused and full of wild and bewildering expedients) that I found myself suggesting – I, a man known for sense and reason – that we should blow trumpets at some time to be fixed, which was a thing the ancients had done in the strange tale which had taken possession of me. M. le Curé looked at me with disapproval. He said, 'I did not expect from M. le Maire anything that was disrespectful to religion.' Heaven forbid that I should be disrespectful to religion at any time of life, but then it was impossible to me. I remembered after that the tale of which I speak, which had so seized upon me, was in the sacred writings; but those who know me will understand that no sneer at these writings or intention of wounding the feelings of M. le Curé was in my mind.

I was seated one day upon a little inequality of the ground, leaning my back against a half-withered hawthorn, and dozing with my head in my hands, when a soothing, which always diffuses itself from her presence, shed itself over me, and opening my eyes, I saw my Agnès sitting by me. She had come with some food and a little linen, fresh and soft like her own touch. My wife was not gaunt and worn like me, but she was pale and as thin as a shadow. I woke with a start, and seeing her there, there suddenly came a dread over me that she would pass away before my eyes, and go over to Those who were within Semur. I cried 'Non, mon Agnès; non, mon Agnès: before you ask, No!' seizing her and holding her fast in this dream, which was not altogether a dream. She looked at me with a smile, that has always been to me as the rising of the sun over the earth.

'Mon ami,' she said surprised, 'I ask nothing, except that you should take a little rest and spare thyself.' Then she added, with haste, what I knew she would say, 'Unless it were this, mon ami. If I were permitted, I would go into the city – I would ask those who are there, what is their meaning: and if no way can be found – no act of penitence. – Oh! do not answer in haste! I have no fear; and it would be to save thee.'

A strong throb of anger came into my throat. Figure to yourself that I looked at my wife with anger, with the same feeling which had moved me when the deserters left us; but far more hot and sharp. I seized her soft hands and crushed them in mine. 'You would leave me!' I said. 'You would desert your husband. You would go over to our enemies!'

'O Martin, say not so,' she cried, with tears. 'Not enemies. There is our little Marie, and my mother, who died when I was born.'

'You love these dead tyrants. Yes,' I said, 'you love them best. You will go to – the majority, to the strongest. Do not speak to me! Because your God is on their side, you will forsake us too.'

Then she threw herself upon me and encircled me with her arms. The touch of them stilled my passion; but yet I held her, clutching her gown, so terrible a fear came over me that she would go and come back no more.

'Forsake thee!' she breathed out over me with a moan. Then, putting her cool cheek to mine, which burned, 'But I would die for thee, Martin.'

'Silence, my wife: that is what you shall not do,' I cried,

beside myself. I rose up; I put her away from me. That is, I
know it, what has been done. Their God does this, they do not
hesitate to say – takes from you what you love best, to make
you better – *you!* and they ask you to love Him when He has
thus despoiled you! 'Go home, Agnès,' I said, hoarse with
terror. 'Let us face them as we may; you shall not go among
them, or put thyself in peril. Die for me! *Mon Dieu!* and what
then, what should I do then? Turn your face from them; turn
from them; go! go! and let me not see thee here again.'

My wife did not understand the terror that seized me. She
obeyed me, as she always does, but, with the tears falling from
her white cheeks, fixed upon me the most piteous look. '*Mon
ami,*' she said, 'you are disturbed, you are not in possession of
yourself; this cannot be what you mean.'

'Let me not see thee here again!' I cried. 'Would you make
me mad in the midst of my trouble? No! I will not have you
look that way. Go home! go home!' Then I took her into my
arms and wept, though I am not a man given to tears. 'Oh! my
Agnès,' I said, 'give me thy counsel. What you tell me I will
do; but rather than risk thee, I would live thus for ever, and
defy them.'

She put her hand upon my lips. 'I will not ask this again,'
she said, bowing her head; 'but defy them – why should you
defy them? Have they come for nothing? Was Semur a city of
the saints? They have come to convert our people, Martin –
thee too, and the rest. If you will submit your hearts, they will
open the gates, they will go back to their sacred homes: and
we to ours. This has been borne in upon me sleeping and
waking; and it seemed to me that if I could but go, and say,
"Oh! my fathers, oh! my brothers, they submit," all would be
well. For I do not fear them, Martin. Would they harm me
that love us? I would but give our Marie one kiss—'

'You are a traitor!' I said. 'You would steal yourself from
me, and do me the worst wrong of all—'

But I recovered my calm. What she said reached my
understanding at last. 'Submit!' I said, 'but to what? To
come and turn us from our homes, to wrap our town in
darkness, to banish our wives and our children, to leave us
here to be scorched by the sun and drenched by the rain, –
this is not to convince us, my Agnès. And to what then do you
bid us submit—?'

'It is to convince you, *mon ami*, of the love of God, who has permitted this great tribulation to be, that we might be saved,' said Agnès. Her face was sublime with faith. It is possible to these dear women; but for me the words she spoke were but words without meaning. I shook my head. Now that my horror and alarm were passed, I could well remember often to have heard words like these before.

'My angel!' I said, 'all this I admire, I adore in thee; but how is it the love of God? – and how shall we be saved by it? Submit! I will do anything that is reasonable; but of what truth have we here the proof—?'

Some one had come up behind as we were talking. When I heard his voice I smiled notwithstanding my despair. It was natural that the Church should come to the woman's aid. But I would not refuse to give ear to M. le Curé, who had proved himself a man, had he been ten times a priest.

'I have not heard what Madame has been saying, M. le Maire, neither would I interpose but for your question. You ask of what truth have we the proof here? It is the Unseen that has revealed itself. Do we see anything, you and I! Nothing, nothing, but a cloud. But that which we cannot see, that which we know not, that which we dread – look! it is there.'

I turned unconsciously as he pointed with his hand. Oh, heaven, what did I see! Above the cloud that wrapped Semur there was a separation, a rent in the darkness, and in mid heaven the Cathedral towers, pointing to the sky. I paid no more attention to M. le Curé. I sent forth a shout that roused all, even the weary line of the patrol that was marching slowly with bowed heads round the walls; and there went up such a cry of joy as shook the earth. 'The towers, the towers!' I cried. These were the towers that could be seen leagues off, the first sign of Semur; our towers, which we had been born to love like our father's name. I have had joys in my life, deep and great. I have loved, I have won honours, I have conquered difficulty; but never had I felt as now. It was as if one had been born again.

When we had gazed upon them, blessing them and thanking God, I gave orders that all our company should be called to the tent, that we might consider whether any new step could now be taken: Agnès with the other women sitting apart on one side and waiting. I recognised even in the excitement of such a time that theirs was no easy part. To sit there silent, to wait till we had spoken, to be bound by what we decided, and to have no voice – yes, that was hard. They thought they knew better than we did: but they were silent, devouring us with their eager eyes. I love one woman more than all the world; I count her the best thing that God has made; yet would I not be as Agnès for all that life could give me. It was her part to be silent, and she was so, like the angel she is, while even Jacques Richard had the right to speak. *Mon Dieu!* but it is hard, I allow it; they have need to be angels. This thought passed through my mind even at the crisis which had now arrived. For at such moments one sees everything, one thinks of everything, though it is only after that one remembers what one has seen and thought. When my fellow-citizens gathered together (we were now less than a hundred in number, so many had gone from us), I took it upon myself to speak. We were a haggard, worn-eyed company, having had neither shelter nor sleep nor even food, save in hasty snatches. I stood at the door of the tent and they below, for the ground sloped a little. Beside me were M. le Curé, M. de Bois-Sombre, and one or two others of the chief citizens. 'My friends,' I said, 'you have seen that a new circumstance has occurred. It is not within our power to tell what its meaning is, yet it must be a symptom of good. For my own part, to see these towers makes the air lighter. Let us think of the Church as we may, no one can deny that the towers of Semur are dear to our hearts.'

'M. le Maire,' said M. de Bois-Sombre, interrupting, 'I speak I am sure the sentiments of my fellow-citizens when I say that there is no longer any question among us concerning the Church; it is an admirable institution, a universal advantage—'

'Yes, yes,' said the crowd, 'yes, certainly!' and some added, 'It is the only safeguard, it is our protection,' and some signed themselves. In the crowd I saw Riou, who had done this at the *octroi*. But the sign did not surprise me now.

M. le Curé stood by my side, but he did not smile. His countenance was dark, almost angry. He stood quite silent, with his eyes on the ground. It gave him no pleasure, this profession of faith.

'It is well, my friends,' said I, 'we are all in accord; and the good God has permitted us again to see these towers. I have called you together to collect your ideas. This change must have a meaning. It has been suggested to me that we might send an ambassador – a messenger, if that is possible, into the city—'

Here I stopped short; and a shiver ran through me – a shiver which went over the whole company. We were all pale as we looked in each other's faces; and for a moment no one ventured to speak. After this pause it was perhaps natural that he who first found his voice should be the last who had any right to give an opinion. Who should it be but Jacques Richard? 'M. le Maire,' cried the fellow, 'speaks at his ease – but who will thus risk himself?' Probably he did not mean that his grumbling should be heard, but in the silence every sound was audible; there was a gasp, a catching of the breath, and all turned their eyes again upon me. I did not pause to think what answer I should give. 'I!' I cried. 'Here stands one who will risk himself, who will perish if need be—'

Something stirred behind me. It was Agnès who had risen to her feet, who stood with her lips parted and quivering, with her hands clasped, as if about to speak. But she did not speak. Well! she had proposed to do it. Then why not I?

'Let me make the observation,' said another of our fellow-citizens, Bordereau the banker, 'that this would not be just. Without M. le Maire we should be a mob without a head. If a messenger is to be sent, let it be some one not so indispensable—'

'Why send a messenger?' said another, Philip Leclerc. 'Do we know that these Messieurs will admit any one? and how can you speak, how can you parley with those –' and he too, was seized with a shiver – 'whom you cannot see?'

Then there came another voice out of the crowd. It was one who would not show himself, who was conscious of the mockery in his tone. 'If there is any one sent, let it be M. le Curé,' it said.

M. le Curé stepped forward. His pale countenance flushed red. 'Here am I,' he said, 'I am ready; but he who spoke speaks to mock me. Is it befitting in this presence?'

There was a struggle among the men. Whoever it was who had spoken (I did not wish to know), I had no need to condemn the mocker; they themselves silenced him; then Jacques Richard (still less worthy of credit) cried out again with a voice that was husky. What are men made of? Notwithstanding everything, it was from the *cabaret*, from the wineshop, that he had come. He said, 'Though M. le Maire will not take my opinion, yet it is this. Let them reopen the chapel in the hospital. The ladies of St Jean—'

'Hold thy peace,' I said, 'miserable!' But a murmur rose. 'Though it is not his part to speak, I agree,' said one. 'And I.' 'And I.' There was well-nigh a tumult of consent; and this made me angry. Words were on my lips which it might have been foolish to utter, when M. de Bois-Sombre, who is a man of judgment, interfered.

'M. le Maire,' he said, 'as there are none of us here who would show disrespect to the Church and holy things – that is understood – it is not necessary to enter into details. Every restriction that would wound the most susceptible is withdrawn; not one more than another, but all. We have been indifferent in the past, but for the future you will agree with me that everything shall be changed. The ambassador – whoever he may be –' he added with a catching of his breath, 'must be empowered to promise – everything – submission to all that may be required.'

Here the women could not restrain themselves; they all rose up with a cry, and many of them began to weep. 'Ah!' said one with a hysterical sound of laughter in her tears. '*Sante Mère!* it will be heaven upon earth.'

M. le Curé said nothing; a keen glance of wonder, yet of subdued triumph, shot from under his eyelids. As for me, I wrung my hands: 'What you say will be superstition; it will be hypocrisy,' I cried.

But at that moment a further incident occurred. Suddenly, while we deliberated, a long loud peal of a trumpet sounded into the air. I have already said that many sounds had been heard before; but this was different; there was not one of us that did not feel that this was addressed to himself. The agitation was extreme; it was a summons, the beginning of some distinct communication. The crowd scattered; but for myself, after a momentary struggle, I went forward resolutely. I did not even look back at my wife. I was no longer Martin Dupin, but the Maire of Semur, the saviour of the community. Even Bois-Sombre quailed: but I felt that it was in me to hold head against death itself; and before I had gone two steps I felt rather than saw that M. le Curé had come to my side. We went on without a word; gradually the others collected behind us, following yet straggling here and there upon the inequalities of the ground.

Before us lay the cloud that was Semur, a darkness defined by the shining of the summer day around, the river escaping from that gloom as from a cavern, the towers piercing through, but the sunshine thrown back on every side from that darkness. I have spoken of the walls as if we saw them, but there were no walls visible, nor any gate, though we all turned like blind men to where the Porte St Lambert was. There was the broad vacant road leading up to it, leading into the gloom. We stood there at a little distance. Whether it was human weakness or an invisible barrier, how can I tell? We stood thus immovable, with the trumpet pealing out over us, out of the cloud. It summoned every man as by his name. To me it was not wonderful that this impression should come, but afterwards it was elicited from all that this was the feeling of each. Though no words were said, it was as the calling of our names. We all waited in such a supreme agitation as I cannot describe for some communication that was to come.

When suddenly, in a moment, the trumpet ceased; there was an interval of dead and terrible silence; then, each with a leap of his heart as if it would burst from his bosom, we saw a single figure slowly detach itself out of the gloom. 'My God!' I cried. My senses went from me; I felt my head go round like a straw tossed on the winds.

To know them so near, those mysterious visitors – to feel them, to hear them, was not that enough? But, to see! who could bear it? Our voices rang like broken chords, like a tearing and rending of sound. Some covered their faces with their hands; for our very eyes seemed to be drawn out of their sockets, fluttering like things with a separate life.

Then there fell upon us a strange and wonderful calm. The figure advanced slowly; there was weakness in it. The step, though solemn, was feeble; and if you can figure to yourself our consternation, the pause, the cry – our hearts dropping back as it might be into their places – the sudden stop of the wild panting in our breasts: when there became visible to us a human face well known, a man as we were. 'Lecamus!' I cried; and all the men round took it up, crowding nearer, trembling yet delivered from their terror; some even laughed in the relief. There was but one who had an air of discontent, and that was M. le Curé. As he said 'Lecamus!' like the rest, there was impatience, disappointment, anger in his tone.

And I, who had wondered where Lecamus had gone;

thinking sometimes that he was one of the deserters who had left us! But when he came nearer his face was as the face of a dead man, and a cold chill came over us. His eyes, which were cast down, flickered under the thin eyelids in which all the veins were visible. His face was grey like that of the dying. 'Is he dead?' I said. But, except M. le Curé, no one knew that I spoke.

'Not even so,' said M. le Curé, with a mortification in his voice, which I have never forgotten. 'Not even so. That might be something. They teach us not by angels – by the fools and offscourings of the earth.'

And he would have turned away. It was a humiliation. Was not he the representative of the Unseen, the vicegerent, with power over heaven and hell? but something was here more strong then he. He stood by my side in spite of himself to listen to the ambassador. I will not deny that such a choice was strange, strange beyond measure, to me also.

'Lecamus,' I said, my voice trembling in my throat, 'have you been among the dead, and do you live?'

'I live,' he said; then looked around with tears upon the crowd. 'Good neighbours, good friends,' he said, and put out his hand and touched them; he was as much agitated as they.

'M. Lecamus,' said I, 'we are here in very strange circumstances, as you know: do not trifle with us. If you have indeed been with those who have taken the control of our city, do not keep us in suspense. You will see by the emblems of my office that it is to me you must address yourself; if you have a mission, speak.'

'It is just,' he said, 'it is just – but bear with me one moment. It is good to behold those who draw breath; if I have not loved you enough, my good neighbours, forgive me now!'

'Rouse yourself, Lecamus,' said I with some anxiety. 'Three days we have been suffering here; we are distracted with the suspense. Tell us your message – if you have anything to tell.'

'Three days!' he said, wondering; 'I should have said years. Time is long when there is neither night nor day.' Then, uncovering himself, he turned towards the city. 'They who have sent me would have you know that they come, not in anger but in friendship: for the love they bear you, and because it has been permitted—'

As he spoke his feebleness disappeared. He held his head high; and we clustered closer and closer round him, not losing a half word, not a tone, not a breath.

'They are not the dead. They are the immortal. They are those who dwell – elsewhere. They have other work, which has been interrupted because of this trial. They ask, "Do you know now – do you know now?" this is what I am bidden to say.'

'What' – I said (I tried to say it, but my lips were dry), 'What would they have us to know?'

But a clamour interrupted me. 'Ah! yes, yes, yes!' the people cried, men and women; some wept aloud, some signed themselves, some held up their hands to the skies. 'Never more will we deny religion,' they cried, 'never more fail in our duties. They shall see how we will follow every office, how the churches shall be full, how we will observe the feasts and the days of the saints! M. Lecamus,' cried two or three together; 'go, tell these Messieurs that we will have masses said for them, that we will obey in everything. We have seen what comes of it when a city is without piety. Never more will we neglect the holy functions; we will vow ourselves to the holy Mother and the saints—'

'And if those ladies wish it,' cried Jacques Richard, 'there shall be as many masses as there are priests to say them in the Hospital of St Jean.'

'Silence, fellow!' I cried; 'is it for you to promise in the name of the Commune?' I was almost beside myself. 'M. Lecamus, is it for this that they have come?'

His head had begun to droop again, and a dimness came over his face. 'Do I know?' he said. 'It was them I longed for, not to know their errand; but I have not yet said all. You are to send two – two whom you esteem the highest – to speak with them face to face.'

Then at once there rose a tumult among the people – an eagerness which nothing could subdue. There was a cry that the ambassadors were already elected, and we were pushed forward, M. le Curé and myself, towards the gate. They would not hear us speak. 'We promise,' they cried, 'we promise everything; let us but get back.' Had it been to sacrifice us they would have done the same; they would have killed us in their passion, in order to return to their city – and afterwards mourned us and honoured us as martyrs. But for the moment they had neither ruth nor fear. Had it been they who were going to reason not with flesh and blood, it would have been different; but it was we, not they; and they hurried us on as not willing that a moment should be lost. I had to struggle, almost to fight, in order to provide them with a leader, which was indispensable, before I myself went away. For who could tell if we should ever come back? For a moment I hesitated, thinking that it might be well to invest M. de Bois-Sombre as my deputy with my scarf of office; but then I reflected that when a man goes to battle, when he goes to risk his life, perhaps to lose it, for his people, it is his right to bear those signs which distinguish him from common men, which show in what office, for what cause, he is ready to die.

Accordingly I paused, struggling against the pressure of the people, and said in a loud voice, 'In the absence of M. Barbou, who has forsaken us, I constitute the excellent M. Félix de Bois-Sombre my representative. In my absence my fellow-citizens will respect and obey him as myself.' There was a cry of assent. They would have given their assent to anything that we might but go on. What was it to them? They took no thought of the heaving of my bosom, the beating of my heart. They left us on the edge of the darkness with our faces towards the gate. There we stood one breathless moment. Then the little postern slowly opened before us, and once more we stood within Semur.

FIVE

The Narrative of Paul Lecamus

M. LE MAIRE having requested me, on his entrance into Semur, to lose no time in drawing up an account of my residence in the town, to be placed with his own narrative, I have promised to do so to the best of my ability, feeling that my condition is a very precarious one, and my time for explanation may be short. Many things, needless to enumerate, press this upon my mind. It was a pleasure to me to see my neighbours when I first came out of the city; but their voices, their touch, their vehemence and eagerness wear me out. From my childhood up I have shrunk from close contact with my fellow-men. My mind has been busy with other thoughts; I have desired to investigate the mysterious and unseen. When I have walked abroad I have heard whispers in the air; I have felt the movement of wings, the gliding of unseen feet. To my comrades these have been a source of alarm and disquiet, but not to me; is not God in the unseen with all His angels? and not only so, but the best and wisest of men. There was a time indeed, when life acquired for me a charm. There was a smile which filled me with blessedness, and made the sunshine more sweet. But when she died my earthly joys died with her. Since then I have thought of little but the depths profound, into which she has disappeared like the rest.

I was in the garden of my house on that night when all the others left Semur. I was restless, my mind was disturbed. It seemed to me that I approached the crisis of my life. Since the time when I led M. le Maire beyond the walls, and we felt both of us the rush and pressure of that crowd, a feeling of expectation had been in my mind. I knew not what I looked for – but something I looked for that should change the world. The 'Sommation' on the Cathedral doors did not surprise me. Why should it be a matter of wonder that the dead should come back? the wonder is that they do not. Ah! that is the wonder. How one can go away who loves you, and never return nor speak, nor send any message – that is the miracle: not that the heavens should bend down and the gates of Paradise roll back and those who have left us return. All my life it has been a marvel to me how they could be kept away. I could not stay in-doors on this strange night. My mind was full of agitation. I came out into the garden though it was dark. I sat down upon the bench under the trellis – she loved it. Often had I spent half the night there thinking of her.

It was very dark that night: the sky all veiled, no light anywhere – a night like November. One would have said there was snow in the air. I think I must have slept toward morning (I have observed throughout that the preliminaries of these occurrences have always been veiled in sleep), and when I woke suddenly it was to find myself, if I may so speak, the subject of a struggle. The struggle was within me, yet it was not I. In my mind there was a desire to rise from where I sat and go away, I could not tell where or why; but something in me said

stay, and my limbs were as heavy as lead. I could not move; I sat
still against my will; against one part of my will – but the other
was obstinate and would not let me go. Thus a combat took
place within me of which I knew not the meaning. While it went
on I began to hear the sound of many feet, the opening of doors,
the people pouring out into the streets. This gave me no
surprise; it seemed to me that I understood why it was; only
in my own case, I knew nothing. I listened to the steps pouring
past, going on and on, faintly dying away in the distance, and
there was a great stillness. I then became convinced, though I
cannot tell how, that I was the only living man left in Semur;
but neither did this trouble me. The struggle within me came to
an end, and I experienced a great calm.

I cannot tell how long it was till I perceived a change in the
air, in the darkness round me. It was like the movement of
some one unseen. I have felt such a sensation in the night,
when all was still, before now. I saw nothing. I heard nothing.
Yet I was aware, I cannot tell how, that there was a great
coming and going, and the sensation as of a multitude in the
air. I then rose and went into my house, where Leocadie, my
old housekeeper, had shut all the doors so carefully when she
went to bed. They were now all open, even the door of my
wife's room of which I kept always the key, and where no one
entered but myself; the windows also were open. I looked out
upon the Grande Rue, and all the other houses were like
mine. Everything was open, doors and windows, and the
streets were full. There was in them a flow and movement of
the unseen, without a sound, sensible only to the soul. I
cannot describe it, for I neither heard nor saw, but felt. I have
often been in crowds; I have lived in Paris, and once passed
into England, and walked about the London streets. But
never, it seemed to me, never was I aware of so many, of
so great a multitude. I stood at my open window, and watched
as in a dream. M. le Maire is aware that his house is visible
from mine. Towards that a stream seemed to be always going,
and at the windows and in the doorways was a sensation of
multitudes like that which I have already described. Gazing
out thus upon the revolution which was happening before my
eyes, I did not think of my own house or what was passing
there, till suddenly, in a moment, I was aware that some one
had come in to me. Not a crowd as elsewhere; one. My heart
leaped up like a bird let loose; it grew faint within me with joy

and fear. I was giddy so that I could not stand. I called out her name, but low, for I was too happy, I had no voice. Besides was it needed, when heart already spoke to heart?

I had no answer, but I needed none. I laid myself down on the floor where her feet would be. Her presence wrapped me round and round. It was beyond speech. Neither did I need to see her face, nor to touch her hand. She was more near to me, more near, than when I held her in my arms. How long it was so, I cannot tell; it was long as love, yet short as the drawing of a breath. I knew nothing, felt nothing but Her, alone; all my wonder and desire to know departed from me. We said to each other everything without words – heart overflowing into heart. It was beyond knowledge or speech.

But this is not of public signification that I should occupy with it the time of M. le Maire.

After a while my happiness came to an end. I can no more tell how, than I can tell how it came. One moment, I was warm in her presence; the next, I was alone. I rose up staggering with blindness and woe – could it be that already, already it was over? I went out blindly following after her. My God, I shall follow, I shall follow, till life is over. She loved me; but she was gone.

Thus, despair came to me at the very moment when the longing of my soul was satisfied and I found myself among the unseen; but I cared for knowledge no longer, I sought only her. I lost a portion of my time so. I regret to have to confess it to M. le Maire. Much that I might have learned will thus remain lost to my fellow-citizens and the world. We are made so. What we desire eludes us at the moment of grasping it – or those affections which are the foundation of our lives pre-occupy us, and blind the soul. Instead of endeavouring to establish my faith and enlighten my judgment as to those mysteries which have been my life-long study, all higher purpose departed from me; and I did nothing but rush through the city, groping among those crowds, seeing nothing, thinking of nothing – save of One.

From this also I awakened as out of a dream. What roused me was the pealing of the Cathedral bells. I was made to pause and stand still, and return to myself. Then I perceived, but dimly, that the thing which had happened to me was that which I had desired all my life. I leave this explanation of my failure[1] in public duty to the charity of M. le Maire.

The bells of the Cathedral brought me back to myself – to that which we call reality in our language; but of all that was around me when I regained consciousness, it now appeared to me that I only was a dream. I was in the midst of a world where all was in movement. What the current was which flowed around me I know not; if it was thought which becomes sensible among spirits, if it was action, I cannot tell. But the energy, the force, the living that was in them, that could no one misunderstand. I stood in the streets, lagging and feeble, scarcely able to wish, much less to think. They pushed against me, put me aside, took no note of me. In the unseen world described by a poet whom M. le Maire has probably heard of, the man who traverses Purgatory (to speak of no other place) is seen by all, and is a wonder to all he meets – his shadow, his breath separate him from those around him. But whether the unseen life has changed, or if it is I who am not worthy their attention, this I know that I stood in our city like a ghost, and no one took any heed of me. When there came back upon me slowly my old desire to inquire, to understand, I was met with this difficulty at the first – that no one heeded me. I went through and through the streets, sometimes I paused to look round, to implore that which swept by me to make itself known. But the stream went along like soft air, like the flowing of a river, setting me aside from time to time, as the air will displace a straw, or the water a stone, but no more. There was neither languor nor lingering. I was the only passive thing, the being without occupation. Would you have paused in your labours to tell an idle traveller the meaning of our lives, before the day when you left Semur? Nor would they: I was driven hither and thither by the current of that life, but no one stepped forth out of the unseen to hear my questions or to answer me how this might be.

You have been made to believe that all was darkness in Semur. M. le Maire, it was not so. The darkness wrapped the walls in a winding sheet; but within, soon after you were gone, there arose a sweet and wonderful light – a light that was neither of the sun nor of the moon; and presently, after the ringing of the bells, the silence departed as the darkness had departed. I began to hear, first a murmur, then the sound of the going which I had felt without hearing it – then a faint tinkle of voices – and at the last, as my mind grew attuned to these wonders, the very words they said. If they spoke in our language or in another, I cannot tell; but I understood. How long it was before the sensation of their presence was aided by the happiness of hearing I know not, nor do I know how the time has passed, or how long it is, whether years or days, that I have been in Semur with those who are now there; for the light did not vary – there was no night or day. All I know is that suddenly, on awakening from a sleep (for the wonder was that I could sleep, sometimes sitting on the Cathedral steps, sometimes in my own house; where sometimes also I lingered and searched about for the crusts that Leocadie had left), I found the whole world full of sound. They sang going in bands about the streets; they talked to each other as they went along every way. From the houses, all open, where everyone could go who would, there came the soft chiming of those voices. And at first every sound was full of gladness and hope. The song they sang first was like this: 'Send us, send us to our father's house. Many are our brethren, many and dear. They have forgotten, forgotten, forgotten! But when we speak, then will they hear.' And the others answered: 'We have come, we have come to the house of our fathers. Sweet are the homes, the homes we were born in. As we remember, so will they remember. When we speak, when we speak, they will hear.' Do not think that these were the words they sang; but it was like this. And as they sang there was joy and expectation everywhere. It was more beautiful than any of our music, for it was full of desire and longing, yet hope and gladness; whereas among us, where there is longing, it is always sad. Later a great singer, I know not who he was, one going past as on a majestic soft wind, sang another song, of which I shall tell you by and by. I do not think he was one of them. They came out to the windows, to the doors, into all the streets and byways to hear him as he went past.

M. le Maire will, however, be good enough to remark that I did not understand all that I heard. In the middle of a phrase, in a word half breathed, a sudden barrier would rise. For a time I laboured after their meaning, trying hard and vainly to understand; but afterwards I perceived that only when they spoke of Semur, of you who were gone forth, and of what was being done, could I make it out. At first this made me only more eager to hear; but when thought came, then I perceived that of all my longing nothing was satisfied. Though I was alone with the unseen, I comprehended it not; only when it touched upon what I knew, then I understood.

At first all went well. Those who were in the streets, and at the doors and windows of the houses, and on the Cathedral steps, where they seemed to throng, listening to the sounding of the bells, spoke only of this that they had come to do. Of you and you only I heard. They said to each other, with great joy, that the women had been instructed, that they had listened, and were safe. There was pleasure in all the city. The singers were called forth, those who were best instructed (so I judged from what I heard), to take the place of the warders on the walls; and all, as they went along sang that song: 'Our brothers have forgotten; but when we speak, they will hear.' How was it, how was it that you did not hear? One time I was by the river *porte* in a boat; and this song came to me from the walls as sweet as Heaven. Never have I heard such a song. The music was beseeching, it moved the very heart. 'We have come out of the unseen,' they sang; 'for love of you; believe us, believe us! Love brings us back to earth; believe us believe us!' How was it that you did not hear? When I heard those singers sing, I wept; they beguiled the heart out of my bosom. They sang, they shouted, the music swept about all the walls: 'Love brings us back to earth, believe us!' M. le Maire, I saw you from the river gate; there was a look of perplexity upon your face; and one put his curved hand to his ear as if to listen to some thin far-off sound, when it was like a storm, like a tempest of music!

After that there was a great change in the city. The choirs came back from the walls marching more slowly, and with a sighing through all the air. A sigh, nay, something like a sob breathed through the streets. 'They cannot hear us, or they will not hear us.' Wherever I turned, this was what I heard: 'They cannot hear us.' The whole town, and all the houses that were teeming with souls, and all the street, where so many were coming and going, was full of wonder and dismay. (If you will take my opinion, they know pain as well as joy, M. le Maire, Those who are in Semur. They are not as gods, perfect and sufficing to themselves, nor are they all-knowing and all-wise, like the good God. They hope like us, and desire, and are mistaken; but do no wrong. This is my opinion. I am no more than other men, that you should accept it without support; but I have lived among them, and this is what I think.) They were taken by surprise; they did not understand it any more than we understand when we have put forth all our strength and fail. They were confounded, if I could judge rightly. Then there arose cries from one to another: 'Do you forget what was said to us?' and, 'We were warned, we were warned.' There went a sighing over all the city: 'They cannot hear us, our voices are not as their voices; they cannot see us. We have taken their homes from them, and they know not the reason.' My heart was wrung for their disappointment. I longed to tell them that neither had I heard at once; but it was only after a time that I ventured upon this. And whether I spoke, and was heard; or if it was read in my heart, I cannot tell. There was a pause made round me as if of wondering and listening, and then, in a moment, in the twinkling of an eye, a face suddenly turned and looked into my face.

M. le Maire, it was the face of your father, Martin Dupin, whom I remember as well as I remember my own father. He was the best man I ever knew. It appeared to me for a moment, that face alone, looking at me with questioning eyes.

There seemed to be agitation and doubt for a time after this; some went out (so I understood) on embassies among you, but could get no hearing; some through the gates, some by the river. And the bells were rung that you might hear and know; but neither could you understand the bells. I wandered from one place to another, listening and watching – till the unseen became to me as the seen, and I thought of the wonder no more. Sometimes there came to me vaguely a desire to question them, to ask whence they came and what was the secret of their living, and why they were here? But if I had asked who would have heard me? and desire had grown faint in my heart; all I wished for was that you should hear, that you should understand; with this wish Semur was full. They thought but of this. They went to the walls in bands, each in their order, and as they came all the others rushed to meet them, to ask, 'What news?' I following, now with one, now with another, breathless and footsore as they glided along. It is terrible when flesh and blood live with those who are spirits. I toiled after them. I sat on the Cathedral steps, and slept and waked, and heard the voices still in my dream. I prayed, but it was hard to pray. Once following a crowd I entered your house, M. le Maire, and went up, though I

scarcely could drag myself along. There many were assembled as in council. Your father was at the head of all.
He was the one, he only, who knew me. Again he looked at me
and I saw him, and in the light of his face an assembly such as
I have seen in pictures. One moment it glimmered before me
and then it was gone. There were the captains of all the bands
waiting to speak, men and women. I heard them repeating
from one to another the same tale. One voice was small and
soft like a child's; it spoke of you. 'We went to him,' it said;
and your father, M. le Maire, he too joined in, and said: 'We
went to him – but he could not hear us.' And some said it was
enough – that they had no commission from on high, that they
were but permitted, – that it was their own will to do it – and
that the time had come to forbear.

Now, while I listened, my heart was grieved that they
should fail. This gave me a wound for myself who had trusted
in them, and also for them. But I, who am I, a poor man
without credit among my neighbours, a dreamer, one whom
many despise, that I should come to their aid? Yet I could not
listen and take no part. I cried out: 'Send me. I will tell them
in words they understand.' The sound of my voice was like a
roar in that atmosphere. It sent a tremble into the air. It
seemed to rend me as it came forth from me, and made me
giddy, so that I would have fallen had not there been a
support afforded me. As the light was going out of my eyes
I saw again the faces looking at each other, questioning,
benign, beautiful heads one over another, eyes that were clear
as the heavens, but sad. I trembled while I gazed: there was
the bliss of heaven in their faces, yet they were sad. Then
everything faded. I was led away, I know not how, and
brought to the door and put forth. I was not worthy to see
the blessed grieve. That is a sight upon which the angels look
with awe, and which bring those tears which are salvation into
the eyes of God.

I went back to my house, weary yet calm. There were many
in my house; but because my heart was full of one who was
not there, I knew not those who were there. I sat me down
where she had been. I was weary, more weary than ever
before, but calm. Then I bethought me that I knew no more
than at the first, that I had lived among the unseen as if they
were my neighbours, neither fearing them, nor hearing those
wonders which they have to tell. As I sat with my head in my

hands, two talked to each other close by: 'Is it true that we have failed?' said one; and the other answered, 'Must not all fail that is not sent of the Father?' I was silent; but I knew them, they were the voices of my father and my mother. I listened as out of a faint, in a dream.

While I sat thus, with these voices in my ears, which a little while before would have seemed to me more worthy of note than anything on earth, but which now lulled me and comforted me, as a child is comforted by the voices of its guardians in the night, there occurred a new thing in the city like nothing I had heard before. It roused me notwithstanding my exhaustion and stupor. It was the sound as of some one passing through the city suddenly and swiftly, whether in some wonderful chariot, whether on some sweeping mighty wind, I cannot tell. The voices stopped that were conversing beside me, and I stood up, and with an impulse I could not resist went out, as if a king were passing that way. Straight, without turning to the right or left, through the city, from one gate to another, this passenger seemed going; and as he went there was the sound as of a proclamation, as if it were a herald denouncing war or ratifying peace. Whosoever he was, the sweep of his going moved my hair like a wind. At first the proclamation was but as a great shout, and I could not understand it; but as he came nearer the words became distinct. 'Neither will they believe – though one rose from the dead.' As it passed a murmur went up from the city, like the voice of a great multitude. Then there came sudden silence.

At this moment, for a time – M. le Maire will take my statement for what it is worth – I became unconscious of what passed further. Whether weariness overpowered me and I slept, as at the most terrible moment nature will demand to do, or if I fainted I cannot tell; but for a time I knew no more. When I came to myself, I was seated on the Cathedral steps with everything silent around me. From thence I rose up, moved by a will which was not mine, and was led softly across the Grande Rue, through the great square, with my face towards the Porte St Lambert; I went steadily on without hesitation, never doubting that the gates would open to me, doubting nothing, though I had never attempted to withdraw from the city before. When I came to the gate I said not a word, nor any one to me; but the door rolled slowly open

before me, and I was put forth into the morning light, into the
shining of the sun. I have now said everything I had to say.
The message I delivered was said through me; I can tell no
more. Let me rest a little; figure to yourselves, I have known
no night of rest, nor eaten a morsel of bread for – did you say it
was but three days?

SIX

M. Le Maire Resumes his Narrative

WE RE-ENTERED BY the door for foot-passengers which is by
the side of the great Porte St Lambert.

I will not deny that my heart was, as one may say, in my
throat. A man does what is his duty, what his fellow-citizens
expect of him; but that is not to say that he renders himself
callous to natural emotion. My veins were swollen, the blood
coursing through them like a high-flowing river; my tongue
was parched and dry. I am not ashamed to admit that from
head to foot my body quivered and trembled. I was afraid –
but I went forward; no man can do more. As for M. le Curé he
said not a word. If he had any fears he concealed them as I
did. But his occupation is with the ghostly and spiritual. To
see men die, to accompany them to the verge of the grave, to
create for them during the time of their suffering after death
(if it is true that they suffer), an interest in heaven, this his
profession must necessarily give him courage. My position is
very different. I have not made up my mind 'upon these
subjects. When one can believe frankly in all the Church
says, many things become simple, which otherwise cause
great difficulty in the mind. The mysterious and wonderful
then find their natural place in the course of affairs; but when
a man thinks for himself, and has to take everything on his
own responsibility, and make all the necessary explanations,
there is often great difficulty. So many things will not fit into
their places, they straggle like weary men on a march. One
cannot put them together, or satisfy one's self.

The sun was shining outside the walls when we re-entered

Semur; but the first step we took was into a gloom as black as night, which did not re-assure us, it is unnecessary to say. A chill was in the air, of night and mist. We shivered, not with the nerves only but with the cold. And as all was dark, so all was still. I had expected to feel the presence of those who were there, as I had felt the crowd of the invisible before they entered the city. But the air was vacant, there was nothing but darkness and cold. We went on for a little way with a strange fervour of expectation. At each moment, at each step, it seemed to me that some great call must be made upon my self-possession and courage, some event happen; but there was nothing. All was calm, the houses on either side of the way were open, all but the office of the *octroi* which was black as night with its closed door. M. le Curé has told me since that he believed Them to be there, though unseen. This idea, however, was not in my mind. I had felt the unseen multitude; but here the air was free, there was no one interposing between us, who breathed as men, and the walls that surrounded us. Just within the gate a lamp was burning, hanging to its rope over our heads; and the lights were in the houses as if some one had left them there; they threw a strange glimmer into the darkness, flickering in the wind. By and by as we went on the gloom lessened, and by the time we had reached the Grande Rue, there was a clear steady pale twilight by which we saw everything, as by the light of day.

We stood at the corner of the square and looked round. Although still I heard the beating of my own pulses loudly working in my ears, yet it was less terrible than at first. A city when asleep is wonderful to look on, but in all the closed doors and windows one feels the safety and repose sheltered there which no man can disturb; and the air has in it a sense of life, subdued, yet warm. But here all was open, and all deserted. The house of the miser Grosgain was exposed from the highest to the lowest, but nobody was there to search for what was hidden. The hotel de Bois-Sombre, with its great *porte-cochère*, always so jealously closed; and my own house, which my mother and wife have always guarded so carefully, that no damp nor breath of night might enter, had every door and window wide open. Desolation seemed seated in all these empty places. I feared to go into my own dwelling. It seemed to me as if the dead must be lying within. *Bon Dieu!* Not a soul, not a shadow; all vacant in this soft twilight; nothing moving, nothing visible. The great doors of the Cathedral were wide open, and every little entry. How spacious the city looked, how silent, how wonderful! There was room for a squadron to wheel in the great square, but not so much as a bird, not a dog; all pale and empty. We stood for a long time (or it seemed a long time) at the corner, looking right and left. We were afraid to make a step farther. We knew not what to do. Nor could I speak; there was much I wished to say, but something stopped my voice.

At last M. le Curé found utterance. His voice so moved the silence, that at first my heart was faint with fear; it was hoarse, and the sound rolled round the great square like muffled thunder. One did not seem to know what strange faces might rise at the open windows, what terrors might appear. But all he said was, 'We are ambassadors in vain.'

What was it that followed? My teeth chattered. I could not hear. It was as if 'in vain! in vain!' came back in echoes, more and more distant from every opening. They breathed all around us, then were still, then returned louder from beyond the river. M. le Curé, though he is a spiritual person, was no more courageous than I. With one impulse, we put out our hands and grasped each other. We retreated back to back, like men hemmed in by foes, and I felt his heart beating wildly, and he mine. Then silence, silence settled all around.

It was now my turn to speak. I would not be behind, come what might, though my lips were parched with mental trouble.

I said, 'Are we indeed too late? Lecamus must have deceived himself.'

To this there came no echo and no reply, which would be a relief, you may suppose; but it was not so. It was well-nigh more appalling, more terrible than the sound; for though we spoke thus, we did not believe the place was empty. Those whom we approached seemed to be wrapping themselves in silence, invisible, waiting to speak with some awful purpose when their time came.

There we stood for some minutes, like two children, holding each other's hands, leaning against each other at the corner of the square – as helpless as children, waiting for what should come next. I say it frankly, my brain and my heart were one throb. They plunged and beat so wildly that I could scarcely have heard any other sound. In this respect I think he was more calm. There was on his face that look of intense listening which strains the very soul. But neither he nor I heard anything, not so much as a whisper. At last, 'Let us go on,' I said. We stumbled as we went, with agitation and fear. We were afraid to turn our backs to those empty houses, which seemed to gaze at us with all their empty windows pale and glaring. Mechanically, scarce knowing what I was doing, I made towards my own house.

There was no one there. The rooms were all open and empty. I went from one to another, with a sense of expectation which made my heart faint; but no one was there, nor anything changed. Yet I do wrong to say that nothing was changed. In my library, where I keep my books, where my father and grandfather conducted their affairs, like me, one little difference struck me suddenly, as if some one had dealt me a blow. The old bureau which my grandfather had used, at which I remember standing by his knee, had been drawn from the corner where I had placed it out of the way (to make room for the furniture I preferred), and replaced, as in old times, in the middle of the room. It was nothing; yet how much was in this! though only myself could have perceived it. Some of the old drawers were open, full of old papers. I glanced over them in my agitation, to see if there might be any writing, any message addressed to me; but there was nothing, nothing but this silent sign of those who had been here. Naturally M. le Curé, who kept watch at the door, was unacquainted with the cause of my emotion. The last room I entered was my wife's. Her veil was lying on the white bed, as if she had gone out that moment, and some of her ornaments were on the table. It seemed to me that the atmosphere of mystery which filled the rest of the house was not here. A ribbon, a little ring, what nothings are these? Yet they make even emptiness sweet. In my Agnès's room there is a little shrine, more sacred to us than any altar. There is the picture of our little Marie. It is covered with a veil, embroidered with needlework which it is a wonder to see. Not always can even Agnès bear to look upon the face of this angel, whom God has taken from her. She has worked the little curtain with lilies, with white and virginal flowers; and no hand, not even mine, ever draws it aside. What did I see? The veil was boldly folded away; the face of the child looked at me across her mother's bed, and upon the frame of the picture was laid a branch of olive, with silvery

leaves. I know no more but that I uttered a great cry, and
flung myself upon my knees before this angel-gift. What
stranger could know what was in my heart? M. le Curé,
my friend, my brother, came hastily to me, with a pale
countenance; but when he looked at me, he drew back and
turned away his face, and a sob came from his breast. Never
child had called him father, were it in heaven, were it on
earth. Well I knew whose tender fingers had placed the
branch of olive there.

I went out of the room and locked the door. It was just that
my wife should find it where it had been laid.

I put my arm into his as we went out once more into the
street. That moment had made us brother and brother. And
this union made us more strong. Besides, the silence and the
emptiness began to grow less terrible to us. We spoke in our
natural voices as we came out, scarcely knowing how great
was the difference between them and the whispers which had
been all we dared at first to employ. Yet the sound of these
louder tones scared us when we heard them for we were still
trembling, not assured of deliverance. It was he who showed
himself a man, not I; for my heart was overwhelmed, the tears
stood in my eyes, I had no strength to resist my impressions.

'Martin Dupin,' he said suddenly, 'it is enough. We are
frightening ourselves with shadows. We are afraid even of our
own voices. This must not be. Enough! Whosoever they were
who have been in Semur, their visitation is over, and they are
gone.'

'I think so,' I said faintly; 'but God knows.' Just then
something passed me as sure as ever man passed me. I started
back out of the way and dropped my friend's arm, and
covered my eyes with my hands. It was nothing that could
be seen; it was an air, a breath. M. le Curé looked at me
wildly; he was as a man beside himself. He struck his foot
upon the pavement and gave a loud and bitter cry.

'Is it delusion?' he said, 'O my God! or shall not even this,
not even so much as this be revealed to me?'

To see a man who had so ruled himself, who had resisted
every disturbance and stood fast when all gave way, moved
thus at the very last to cry out with passion against that which
had been denied to him, brought me back to myself. How
often had I read it in his eyes before! He – the priest – the
servant of the unseen – yet to all of us lay persons had that

been revealed which was hid from him. A great pity was within me, and gave me strength. 'Brother,' I said, 'we are weak. If we saw heaven opened, could we trust to our vision now? Our imaginations are masters of us. So far as mortal eye can see, we are alone in Semur. Have you forgotten your psalm, and how you sustained us at the first? And now, your Cathedral is open to you, my brother. *Lætatus sum*,' I said. It was an inspiration from above, and no thought of mine; for it is well known, that though deeply respectful, I have never professed religion. With one impulse we turned, we went together, as in a procession, across the silent place, and up the great steps. We said not a word to each other of what we meant to do. All was fair and silent in the holy place; a breath of incense still in the air; a murmur of psalms (as one could imagine) far up in the high roof. There I served, while he said his mass. It was for my friend that this impulse came to my mind; but I was rewarded. The days of my childhood seemed to come back to me. All trouble, and care, and mystery, and pain, seemed left behind. All I could see was the glimmer on the altar of the great candlesticks, the sacred pyx in its shrine, the chalice, and the book. I was again an *enfant de chœur* robed in white, like the angels, no doubt, no disquiet in my soul – and my father kneeling behind among the faithful, bowing his head, with a sweetness which I too knew, being a father, because it was his child that tinkled the bell and swung the censer. Never since those days have I served the mass. My heart grew soft within me as the heart of a little child. The voice of M. le Curé was full of tears – it swelled out into the air and filled the vacant place. I knelt behind him on the steps of the altar and wept.

Then there came a sound that made our hearts leap in our bosoms. His voice wavered as if it had been struck by a strong wind; but he was a brave man, and he went on. It was the bells of the Cathedral that pealed out over our heads. In the midst of the office, while we knelt all alone, they began to ring as at Easter or some great festival. At first softly, almost sadly, like choirs of distant singers, that died away and were echoed and died again; then taking up another strain, they rang out into the sky with hurrying notes and clang of joy. The effect upon myself was wonderful. I no longer felt any fear. The illusion was complete. I was a child again, serving the mass in my little surplice – aware that all who loved me were kneeling behind, that the good God was smiling, and the Cathedral bells ringing out their majestic Amen.

M. le Curé came down the altar steps when his mass was ended. Together we put away the vestments and the holy vessels. Our hearts were soft; the weight was taken from them. As we came out the bells were dying away in long and low echoes, now faint, now louder, like mingled voices of gladness and regret. And whereas it had been a pale twilight when we entered, the clearness of the day had rolled sweetly in, and now it was fair morning in all the streets. We did not say a word to each other, but arm and arm took our way to the gates, to open to our neighbours, to call all our fellow-citizens back to Semur.

If I record here an incident of another kind, it is because of the sequel that followed. As we passed by the hospital of St Jean, we heard distinctly, coming from within, the accents of a feeble yet impatient voice. The sound revived for a moment the troubles that were stilled within us – but only for a moment. This was no visionary voice. It brought a smile to the grave face of M. le Curé and tempted me well nigh to laughter, so strangely did this sensation of the actual, break and disperse the visionary atmosphere. We went in without any timidity, with a conscious relaxation of the great strain upon us. In a little nook, curtained off from the great ward, lay a sick man upon his bed. 'Is it M. le Maire?' he said; '*à la bonne heure!* I have a complaint to make of the nurses for the night. They have gone out to amuse themselves; they take no notice of poor sick people. They have known for a week that I could not sleep; but neither have they given me a sleeping drought, nor endeavoured to distract me with cheerful conversation. And today, look you, M. le Maire, not one of the sisters has come near me!'

'Have you suffered, my poor fellow?' I said; but he would not go so far as this.

'I don't want to make complaints, M. le Maire; but the sisters do not come themselves as they used to do. One does not care to have a strange nurse, when one knows that if the sisters did their duty – But if it does not occur any more I do not wish it to be thought that I am the one to complain.'

'Do not fear, *mom ami*,' I said. 'I will say to the Reverend Mother that you have been left too long alone.'

'And listen, M. le Maire,' cried the man; 'those bells, will

they never be done? My head aches with the din they make.
How can one go to sleep with all that riot in one's ears?'

We looked at each other, we could not but smile. So that
which is joy and deliverance to one is vexation to another. As
we went out again into the street the lingering music of the
bells died out, and (for the first time for all these terrible days
and nights) the great clock struck the hour. And as the clock
struck, the last cloud rose like a mist and disappeared in flying
vapours, and the full sunshine of noon burst on Semur.

SEVEN

Supplement by M. de Bois-Sombre

WHEN M. LE Maire disappeared within the mist, we all
remained behind with troubled hearts. For my own part I
was alarmed for my friend. M. Martin Dupin is not noble. He
belongs, indeed, to the *haute bourgeoisie*, and all his antecedents are most respectable; but it is his personal character
and admirable qualities which justify me in calling him my
friend. The manner in which he has performed his duties to
his fellow-citizens during this time of distress has been
sublime. It is not my habit to take any share in public life;
the unhappy circumstances of France have made this impossible for years. Nevertheless, I put aside my scruples when
it became necessary, to leave him free for his mission. I gave
no opinion upon that mission itself, or how far he was right in
obeying the advice of a hare-brained enthusiast like Lecamus.
Nevertheless the moment had come at which our banishment
had become intolerable. Another day, and I should have
proposed an assault upon the place. Our dead forefathers,
though I would speak of them with every respect, should not
presume upon their privilege. I do not pretend to be braver
than other men, nor have I shown myself more equal than
others to cope with the present emergency. But I have the
impatience of my countrymen, and rather than rot here outside the gates, parted from Madame de Bois-Sombre and my
children, who, I am happy to state, are in safety at the country

house of the brave Dupin, I should have dared any hazard. This being the case, a new step of any kind called for my approbation, and I could not refuse under the circumstances – especially as no ceremony of installation was required or profession of loyalty to one government or another – to take upon me the office of coadjutor and act as deputy for my friend Martin outside the walls of Semur.

The moment at which I assumed the authority was one of great discouragement and depression. The men were tired to death. Their minds were worn out as well as their bodies. The excitement and fatigue had been more than they could bear. Some were for giving up the contest and seeking new homes for themselves. These were they, I need not remark, who had but little to lose; some seemed to care for nothing but to lie down and rest. Though it produced a great movement among us when Lecamus suddenly appeared coming out of the city; and the undertaking of Dupin and the excellent Curé was viewed with great interest, yet there could not but be signs apparent that the situation had lasted too long. It was *tendu* in the strongest degree, and when that is the case a reaction must come. It is impossible to say, for one thing, how great was our personal discomfort. We were as soldiers campaigning without a commissariat, or any precautions taken for our welfare; no food save what was sent to us from La Clairière and other places; no means of caring for our personal appearance, in which lies so much of the materials of self-respect. I say nothing of the chief features of all – the occupation of our homes by others – the forcible expulsion of which we had been the objects. No one could have been more deeply impressed than myself at the moment of these extraordinary proceedings; but we cannot go on with one monotonous impression, however serious, we other Frenchmen. Three days is a very long time to dwell in one thought; I myself had become impatient, I do not deny. To go away, which would have been very natural, and which Agatha proposed, was contrary to my instincts and interests both. I trust I can obey the logic of circumstances as well as another; but to yield is not easy, and to leave my hotel at Semur – now the chief residence, alas! of the Bois-Sombres – probably to the licence of a mob – for one can never tell at what moment Republican institutions may break down and sink back into the chaos from which they arose – was impossible. Nor would I forsake the brave Dupin without the strongest motive; but that the situation was extremely *tendu*, and a reaction close at hand, was beyond dispute.

I resisted the movement which my excellent friend made to take off and transfer to me his scarf of office. These things are much thought of among the *bourgeoisie*. '*Mon ami*,' I said, 'you cannot tell what use you may have for it; whereas our townsmen know me, and that I am not one to take up an unwarrantable position.' We then accompanied him to the neighbourhood of the Porte St Lambert. It was at that time invisible; we could but judge approximately. My men were unwilling to approach too near, neither did I myself think it necessary. We parted, after giving the two envoys an honourable escort, leaving a clear space between us and the darkness. To see them disappear gave us all a startling sensation. Up to the last moment I had doubted whether they would obtain admittance. When they disappeared from our eyes, there came upon all of us an impulse of alarm. I myself was so far moved by it, that I called out after them in a sudden panic. For if any catastrophe had happened, how could I ever have forgiven myself, especially as Madame Dupin de la Clairière, a person entirely *comme il faut*, and of the most distinguished character, went after her husband, with a touching devotion, following him to the very edge of the darkness? I do not think, so deeply possessed was he by his mission, that he saw her. Dupin is very determined in his way; but he is imaginative and thoughtful, and it is very possible that, as he required all his powers to brace him for this enterprise, he made it a principle neither to look to the right hand nor the left. When we paused, and following after our two representatives, Madame Dupin stepped forth, a thrill ran through us all. Some would have called to her, for I heard many broken exclamations; but most of us were too much startled to speak. We thought nothing less than that she was about to risk herself by going after them into the city. If that was her intention – and nothing is more probable; for women are very daring, though they are timid – she was stopped, it is most likely, by that curious inability to move a step farther which we have all experienced. We saw her pause, clasp her hands in despair (or it might be in token of farewell to her husband), then, instead of returning, seat herself on the road on the edge of the darkness. It was a relief to all who were looking on to see her there.

In the reaction after that excitement I found myself in face of a great difficulty – what to do with my men, to keep them from demoralisation. They were greatly excited; and yet there was nothing to be done for them, for myself, for any of us, but to wait. To organise the patrol again, under the circumstances, would have been impossible. Dupin, perhaps, might have tried it with the *bourgeois* determination which so often carries its point in spite of all higher intelligence; but to me, who have not this commonplace way of looking at things, it was impossible. The worthy soul did not think in what a difficulty he left us. That intolerable, good-for-nothing Jacques Richard (whom Dupin protects unwisely, I cannot tell why), and who was already half-seas-over, had drawn several of his comrades with him towards the *cabaret*, which was always a danger to us. 'We will drink success to M. le Maire,' he said, '*mes bons amis*! That can do no one any harm; and as we have spoken up, as we have empowered him to offer handsome terms, to *Messieurs les Morts*—'

It was intolerable. Precisely at the moment when our fortune hung in the balance, and when, perhaps, an indiscreet word – 'Arrest that fellow,' I said. 'Riou, you are an official; you understand your duty. Arrest him on the spot, and confine him in the tent out of the way of mischief. Two of you mount guard over him. And let a party be told off, of which you will take the command, Louis Bertin, to go at once to La Clairière and beg the Reverend Mothers of the hospital to favour us with their presence. It will be well to have those excellent ladies in our front whatever happens; and you may communicate to them the unanimous decision about their chapel. You Robert Lemaire, with an escort, will proceed to the *campagne* of M. Barbou, and put him in possession of the circumstances. Those of you who have a natural wish to seek a little repose will consider yourselves as discharged from duty and permitted to do so. Your Maire having confided to me his authority – not without your consent – (this I avow I added with some difficulty, for who cared for their assent? but a Republican Government offers a premium to every insincerity), I wait with confidence to see these dispositions carried out.'

This, I am happy to say, produced the best effect. They obeyed me without hesitation; and, fortunately for me, slumber seized upon the majority. Had it not been for this, I can scarcely tell how I should have got out of it. I felt drowsy myself, having been with the patrol the greater part of the night; but to yield to such weakness was, in my position, of course impossible.

This, then, was our attitude during the last hours of suspense, which were perhaps the most trying of all. In the distance might be seen the little bands marching towards La Clairière, on one side, and M. Barbou's country-house ('La Corbeille des Raisins') on the other. It goes without saying that I did not want M. Barbou, but it was the first errand I could think of. Towards the city, just where the darkness began that enveloped it, sat Madame Dupin. That *sainte-femme* was praying for her husband, who could doubt? And under the trees, wherever they could find a favourable spot, my men lay down on the grass, and most of them fell asleep. My eyes were heavy enough, but responsibility drives away rest. I had but one nap of five minutes' duration, leaning against a tree, when it occurred to me that Jacques Richard, whom I sent under escort half-drunk to the tent, was not the most admirable companion for that poor visionary Lecamus, who had been accommodated there. I roused myself, therefore, though unwillingly, to see whether these two, so discordant, could agree.

I met Lecamus at the tent-door. He was coming out, very feeble and tottering, with that dazed look which (according to me) has always been characteristic of him. He had a bundle of papers in his hand. He had been setting in order his report of what had happened to him, to be submitted to the Maire. 'Monsieur,' he said, with some irritation (which I forgave him), 'you have always been unfavourable to me. I owe it to you that this unhappy drunkard has been sent to disturb me in my feebleness and the discharge of a public duty.'

'My good Monsieur Lecamus,' said I, 'you do my recollection too much honour. The fact is, I had forgotten all about you and your public duty. Accept my excuses. Though indeed your supposition that I should have taken the trouble to annoy you, and your description of that good-for-nothing as an unhappy drunkard, are signs of intolerance which I should not have expected in a man so favoured.'

This speech, though too long, pleased me, for a man of this species, a revolutionary (are not all visionaries revolutionaries?) is always, when occasion offers, to be put down. He disarmed me, however, by his humility. He gave a look round. 'Where can I go?' he said, and there was pathos in his voice. At length he perceived Madame Dupin sitting almost motionless on the road. 'Ah!' he said, 'there is my place.' The man, I could not but perceive, was very weak. His eyes were twice their natural size, his face was the colour of ashes; through his whole frame there was a trembling; the papers shook in his hand. A compunction seized my mind: I regretted to have sent that piece of noise and folly to disturb a poor man so suffering and weak. 'Monsieur Lecamus,' I said, 'forgive me. I acknowledge that it was inconsiderate. Remain here in comfort, and I will find for this unruly fellow another place of confinement.'

'Nay,' he said, 'there is my place,' pointing to where Madame Dupin sat. I felt disposed for a moment to indulge in a pleasantry, to say that I approved his taste; but on second thoughts I forebore. He went tottering slowly across the broken ground, hardly able to drag himself along. 'Has he had any refreshment?' I asked of one of the women who were about. They told me yes, and this restored my composure; for after all I had not meant to annoy him, I had forgotten he was there – a trivial fault in circumstances so exciting. I was more easy in my mind, however, I confess it, when I saw that he had reached his chosen position safely. The man looked so weak. It seemed to me that he might have died on the road.

I thought I could almost perceive the gate, with Madame Dupin seated under the battlements, her charming figure relieved against the gloom, and that poor Lecamus lying, with his papers fluttering at her feet. This was the last thing I was conscious of.

EIGHT

Extract from the Narrative of Madame Dupin de la Clairière (née de Champfleurie)

I WENT WITH my husband to the city gate. I did not wish to distract his mind from what he had undertaken, therefore I took care he should not see me; but to follow close, giving the sympathy of your whole heart, must not that be a support? If I am asked whether I was content to let him go, I cannot answer yes; but had another than Martin been chosen, I could not have borne it. What I desired, was to go myself. I was not afraid: and if it had proved dangerous, if I had been broken and crushed to pieces between the seen and the unseen, one could not have had a more beautiful fate. It would have made me happy to go. But perhaps it was better that the messenger should not be a woman; they might have said it was delusion, an attack of the nerves. We are not trusted in these respects, though I find it hard to tell why.

But I went with Martin to the gate. To go as far as was possible, to be as near as possible, that was something. If there had been room for me to pass, I should have gone, and with such gladness! for God He knows that to help to thrust my husband into danger, and not to share it, was terrible to me. But no; the invisible line was still drawn, beyond which I could not stir. The door opened before him, and closed upon me. But though to see him disappear into the gloom was anguish, yet to know that he was the man by whom the city should be saved was sweet. I sat down on the spot where my steps were stayed. It was close to the wall, where there is a ledge of stonework round the basement of the tower. There I sat down to wait till he should come again.

If any one thinks, however, that we, who were under the shelter of the roof of La Clairière were less tried than our husbands, it is a mistake; our chief grief was that we were parted from them, not knowing what suffering, what exposure they might have to bear, and knowing that they would not accept, as most of us were willing to accept, the interpretation of the mystery; but there was a certain comfort in the fact that we had to be very busy, preparing a little food to take to them, and feeding the others. La Clairière is a little country house, not a great château, and it was taxed to the utmost to afford some covert to the people. The children were all sheltered and cared for; but as for the rest of us we did as we could. And how gay they were, all the little ones! What was it to them all that had happened? It was a fête for them to be in the country, to be so many together, to run in the fields and the gardens. Sometimes their laughter and their happiness were more than we could bear. Agathe de Bois-Sombre, who takes life hardly, who is more easily deranged than I, was one who was much disturbed by this. But was it not to preserve the children that we were commanded to go to La Clairière? Some of the women also were not easy to bear with. When they were put into our rooms they too found it a fête, and sat down among the children, and ate and drank, and forgot what it was; what awful reason had driven us out of our homes. These were not, oh let no one think so! the majority; but there were some, it cannot be denied; and it was difficult for me to calm down Bonne Maman, and keep her from sending them away with their babes. 'But they are *misérables*,' she said. 'If they were to wander and be lost, if they were to suffer as thou sayest, where would be the harm? I have no patience with the idle, with those who impose upon thee.' It is possible that Bonne Maman was right – but what then? 'Preserve the children and the sick,' was the mission that had been given to me. My own room was made the hospital. Nor did this please Bonne Maman. She bid me if I did not stay in it myself to give it to the Bois-Sombres, to some who deserved it. But is it not they who need most who deserve most? Bonne Maman cannot bear that the poor and wretched should live in her Martin's chamber. He is my Martin no less. But to give it up to our Lord is not that to sanctify it? There are who have put Him into their own bed when they imagined they were but sheltering a sick beggar there; that He should have the best was sweet to me: and could not I pray all the better that our Martin should be enlightened, should come to the true sanctuary? When I said this Bonne Maman wept. It was the grief of her heart that Martin thought otherwise than as we do. Nevertheless she said, 'He is so good; the *bon Dieu* knows how good he is;' as if even his mother could know that so well as I!

But with the women and the children crowding everywhere, the sick in my chamber, the helpless in every corner, it will be seen that we, too, had much to do. And our hearts were elsewhere, with those who were watching the city, who were face to face with those in whom they had not believed. We were going and coming all day long with food for them, and there never was a time of the night or day that there were not many of us watching on the brow of the hill to see if any change came in Semur. Agathe and I, and our children, were all together in one little room. She believed in God, but it was not any comfort to her; sometimes she would weep and pray all day long; sometimes entreat her husband to abandon the city, to go elsewhere and live, and fly from this strange fate. She is one who cannot endure to be unhappy – not to have what she wishes. As for me, I was brought up in poverty, and it is no wonder if I can more easily submit. She was not willing that I should come this morning to Semur. In the night the Mère Julie had roused us, saying she had seen a procession of angels coming to restore us to the city. Ah! to those who have no knowledge it is easy to speak of processions of angels. But to those who have seen what an angel is – how they flock upon us unawares in the darkness, so that one is confused, and scarce can tell if it is reality or a dream; to those who have heard a little voice soft as the dew coming out of heaven! I said to them – for all were in a great tumult – that the angels do not come in processions, they steal upon us unaware, they reveal themselves in the soul. But they did not listen to me; even Agathe took pleasure in hearing of the revelation. As for me, I had denied myself, I had not seen Martin for a night and a day. I took one of the great baskets, and I went with the women who were the messengers for the day. A purpose formed itself in my heart, it was to make my way into the city, I know not how, and implore them to have pity upon us before the people were distraught. Perhaps, had I been able to refrain from speaking to Martin, I might have found the occasion I wished; but how could I conceal my desire from my husband? And now all is changed, I am rejected and he is gone. He was more worthy. Bonne Maman is right. Our good God, who is our father, does He require that one should make profession of faith, that all should be alike? He sees the heart; and to choose my Martin, does not that prove that He loves best that which is best, not I, or a priest, or one who makes professions? Thus, I sat down at the gate with a great confidence, though also a trembling in my heart. He who had known how to choose him among all the others, would not He guard him? It was a proof to me once again that heaven is true, that the good God loves and comprehends us all, to see how His wisdom, which is un-erring, had chosen the best man in Semur.

And M. le Curé, that goes without saying, he is a priest of priests, a true servant of God.

I saw my husband go: perhaps, God knows, into danger, perhaps to some encounter such as might fill the world with awe – to meet those who read the thought in your mind before it comes to your lips. Well! there is no thought in Martin that is not noble and true. Me, I have follies in my heart, every kind of folly; but he! – the tears came in a flood to my eyes, but I would not shed them, as if I were weeping for fear and sorrow – no – but for happiness to know that falsehood was not in him. My little Marie, a holy virgin, may look into her father's heart – I do not fear the test.

The sun came warm to my feet as I sat on the foundation of our city, but the projection of the tower gave me a little shade. All about was a great peace. I thought of the psalm which says, 'He will give it to His beloved sleeping' – that is true; but always there are some who are used as instruments, who are not permitted to sleep. The sounds that came from the people gradually ceased; they were all very quiet. M. de Bois-Sombre I saw at a distance making his dispositions. Then M. Paul Lecamus, whom I had long known, came up across the field, and seated himself close to me upon the road. I have always had a great sympathy with him since the death of his wife; ever since there has been an abstraction in his eyes, a look of desolation. He has no children or any one to bring him back to life. Now, it seemed to me that he had the air of a man who was dying. He had been in the city while all of us had been outside.

'Monsieur Lecamus,' I said, 'you look very ill, and this is not a place for you. Could not I take you somewhere, where you might be more at your ease?'

'It is true, Madame,' he said, 'the road is hard, but the sunshine is sweet; and when I have finished what I am writing for M. le Maire, it will be over. There will be no more need—'

I did not understand what he meant. I asked him to let me help him, but he shook his head. His eyes were very hollow, in great caves, and his face was the colour of ashes. Still he smiled. 'I thank you, Madame,' he said, 'infinitely; everyone knows that Madame Dupin is kind; but when it is done, I shall be free.'

'I am sure, M. Lecamus, that my husband – that M. le Maire – would not wish you to trouble yourself, to be hurried—'

'No,' he said, 'not he, but I. Who else could write what I have to write? It must be done while it is day.'

'Then there is plenty of time, M. Lecamus. All the best of

the day is yet to come; it is still morning. If you could but get as far as La Clairière. There we would nurse you – restore you.'

He shook his head. 'You have enough on your hands at La Clairière,' he said; and then, leaning upon the stones, he began to write again with his pencil. After a time, when he stopped, I ventured to ask – 'Monsieur Lecamus, is it, indeed, those – whom we have known, who are in Semur?'

He turned his dim eyes upon me. 'Does Madame Dupin,' he said, 'require to ask?'

'No, no. It is true. I have seen and heard. But yet, when a little time passes, you know? one wonders; one asks one's self, was it a dream?'

'That is what I fear,' he said. 'I, too, if life went on, might ask, notwithstanding all that has occurred to me, Was it a dream?'

'M. Lecamus, you will forgive me if I hurt you. You saw – *her?*'

'No. Seeing – what is seeing? It is but a vulgar sense, it is not all; but I sat at her feet. She was with me. We were one, as of old—.' A gleam of strange light came into his dim eyes. 'Seeing is not everything, Madame.'

'No, M. Lecamus. I heard the dear voice of my little Marie.'

'Nor is hearing everything,' he said hastily. 'Neither did she speak; but she was there. We were one; we had no need to speak. What is speaking or hearing when heart wells into heart? For a very little moment, only for a moment, Madame Dupin.'

I put out my hand to him; I could not say a word. How was it possible that she could go away again, and leave him so feeble, so worn, alone?

'Only a very little moment,' he said, slowly. 'There were other voices – but not hers. I think I am glad it was in the spirit we met, she and I – I prefer not to see her till – after—'

'Oh, M. Lecamus, I am too much of the world! To see them, to hear them – it is for this I long.'

'No, dear Madame. I would not have it till – after—. But I must make haste, I must write, I hear the hum approaching—'

I could not tell what he meant; but I asked no more. How still everything was! The people lay asleep on the grass, and I, too, was overwhelmed by the great quiet. I do not know if I slept, but I dreamed. I saw a child very fair and tall always near me, but hiding her face. It appeared to me in my dream that all I wished for was to see this hidden countenance, to know her name; and that I followed and watched her, but for a long time in vain. All at once she turned full upon me, held out her arms to me. Do I need to say who it was? I cried out in my dream to the good God, that He had done well to take her from me – that this was worth it all. Was it a dream? I would not give that dream for years of waking life. Then I started and came back, in a moment, to the still morning sunshine, the sight of the men asleep, the roughness of the wall against which I leant. Some one laid a hand on mine. I opened my eyes, not knowing what it was – if it might be my husband coming back, or her whom I had seen in my dream. It was M. Lecamus. He had risen up upon his knees – his papers were all laid aside. His eyes in those hollow caves were opened wide, and quivering with a strange light. He had caught my wrist with his worn hand. 'Listen!' he said; his voice fell to a whisper; a light broke over his face, 'Listen!' he cried; 'they are coming.' While he thus grasped my wrist, holding up his weak and wavering body in that strained attitude, the moments passed very slowly. I was afraid of him, of his worn face and thin hands, and the wild eagerness about him. I am ashamed to say it, but so it was. And for this reason it seemed long to me, though I think not more than a minute, till suddenly the bells rang out, sweet and glad as they ring at Easter for the resurrection. There had been ringing of bells before, but not like this. With a start and universal movement the sleeping men got up from where they lay – not one but every one, coming out of the little hollows and from under the trees as if from graves. They all sprang up to listen, with one impulse; and as for me, knowing that Martin was in the city, can it be wondered at if my heart beat so loud that I was incapable of thought of others! What brought me to myself was the strange weight of M. Lecamus on my arm. He put his other hand upon me, all cold in the brightness, all trembling. He raised himself thus slowly to his feet. When I looked at him I shrieked aloud. I forgot all else. His face was transformed – a smile came upon it that was ineffable – the light blazed up, and then quivered and flickered in his eyes like a dying flame. All this time he was leaning his weight upon my arm. Then suddenly he loosed his hold of me, stretched out his hands, stood up, and – died. My God! shall I ever forget him as he stood – his head raised, his hands held out, his lips moving, the eyelids opened wide with a quiver, the light flickering and dying! He died first, standing up, saying something with his pale lips – then fell. And it seemed to me all at once, and for a moment, that I heard a sound of many people marching past, the murmur and hum of a great 'multitude; and softly, softly I was put out of the way, and a voice said, '*Adieu, ma sœur.*' '*Ma sœur!*' who called me '*Ma sœur*'? I have no sister. I cried out, saying I know not what. They told me after that I wept and wrung my hands, and said, 'Not thee, not thee, Marie!' But after that I knew no more.

NINE

The Narrative of Madame Veuve Dupin (née Lepelletier)

TO COMPLETE THE *Procés verbal*, my son wishes me to give my account of the things which happened out of Semur during its miraculous occupation, as it is his desire, in the interests of truth, that nothing should be left out. In this I find a great difficulty for many reasons; in the first place, because I have not the aptitude of expressing myself in writing, and it may well be that the phrases I employ may fail in the correctness which good French requires; and again, because it is my misfortune not to agree in all points with my Martin, though I am proud to think that he is, in every relation of life, so good a man, that the women of his family need not hesitate to follow his advice – but necessarily there are some points which one reserves; and I cannot but feel the closeness of the connection between the late remarkable exhibition of the power of Heaven and the outrage done upon the good Sisters of St Jean by the administration, of which unfortunately my son is at the head. I say unfortunately, since it is the spirit of independence and pride in him which has resisted all the warnings offered by Divine Providence, and which refuses even now to right the wrongs of the Sisters of St Jean; though, if it may be permitted to me to say it, as his mother, it was very fortunate in the late troubles that Martin Dupin found himself at the head of the Commune of Semur – since who else could have kept his self-control as he did? – caring for all things and forgetting nothing; who else would, with so much courage, have entered the city? and what other man, being a person of the world and secular in all his thoughts, as, alas! it is so common for men to be, would have so nobly acknowledged his obligations to the good God when our misfortunes were over? My constant prayers for his conversion do not make me incapable of perceiving the nobility of his conduct. When the evidence has been incontestible he has not hesitated to make a public profession of his gratitude, which all will acknowledge to be the sign of a truly noble mind and a heart of gold.

I have long felt that the times were ripe for some exhibition of the power of God. Things have been going very badly among us. Not only have the powers of darkness triumphed over our holy church, in a manner ever to be wept and mourned by all the faithful, and which might have been expected to bring down fire from Heaven upon our heads, but the corruption of popular manners (as might also have been expected) has been daily arising to a pitch unprecedented. The fêtes may indeed be said to be observed, but in what manner? In the cabarets rather than in the churches; and as for the fasts and the vigils, who thinks of them? who attends to those sacred moments of penitence? Scarcely even a few ladies are found to do so, instead of the whole population, as in duty bound. I have even seen it happen that my daughter-in-law and myself, and her friend Madame de Bois-Sombre, and old Mère Julie from the market, have formed the whole congregation. Figure to yourself the *bon Dieu* and all the blessed saints looking down from heaven to hear – four persons only in our great Cathedral! I trust that I know that the good God does not despise even two or three; but if any one will think of it – the great bells rung, and the candles lighted, and the curé in his beautiful robes, and all the companies of heaven looking on – and only us four! This shows the neglect of all sacred ordinances that was in Semur. While, on the other hand, what grasping there was for money; what fraud and deceit; what foolishness and dissipation! Even the Mère Julie herself, though a devout person, the pears she sold to us on the last market day before these events, were far, very far, as she must have known, from being satisfactory. In the same way Gros-Jean, though a peasant from our own village near La Clairière, and a man for whom we have often done little services, attempted to impose upon me about the wood for the winter's use, the very night before these occurrences. 'It is enough,' I cried out, 'to bring the dead out of their graves.' I did not know – the holy saints forgive me! – how near it was to the moment when this should come true.

And perhaps it is well that I should admit without concealment that I am not one of the women to whom it has been given to see those who came back. There are moments when I will not deny I have asked myself why those others should have been so privileged and never I. Not even in a dream do I see those whom I have lost; yet I think that I too have loved them as well as any have been loved. I have stood by their beds to the last; I have closed their beloved eyes. *Mon Dieu! mon Dieu!* have not I drunk of that cup to the dregs? But never to me, never to me, has it been permitted either to see or to hear. *Bien!* it has been so ordered. Agnès, my daughter-in-law, is a good woman. I have not a word to say against her; and if there are moments when my heart rebels, when I ask myself why she should have her eyes opened and not I, the good God knows that I do not complain against His will – it is in His hand to do as He pleases. And if I receive no privileges, yet have I the privilege which is best, which is, as M. le Maire justly observes, the highest of all – that of doing my duty. In this I thank the good Lord our Seigneur that my Martin has never needed to be ashamed of his mother.

I will also admit that when it was first made apparent to me – not by the sounds of voices which the others heard, but by the use of my reason which I humbly believe is also a gift of God – that the way in which I could best serve both those of the city and my son Martin, who is over them, was to lead the way with the children and all the helpless to La Clairière, thus relieving the watchers, there was for a time a great struggle in my bosom. What were they all to me, that I should desert my Martin, my only son, the child of my old age; he who is as his father, as dear, and yet more dear, because he is his father's son? 'What! (I said in my heart) abandon thee, my child? nay, rather abandon life and every consolation; for what is life to me but thee?' But while my heart swelled with this cry, suddenly it became apparent to me how many there were holding up their hands helplessly to him, clinging to him so that he could not move. To whom else could they turn? He was the one among all who preserved his courage, who neither feared nor failed. When those voices rang out from the walls – which some understood, but which I did not understand, and many more with me – though my heart was wrung with straining my ears to listen if there was not a voice for me too, yet at the same time this thought was working in my heart. There was a poor woman close to me with little children clinging to her; neither did she know what those voices said. Her eyes turned from Semur, all lost in the darkness, to the sky above us and to me beside her, all confused and bewildered; and the children clung to her, all in tears, crying with that wail which is endless – the trouble of childhood which does not know why it is troubled. 'Maman! Maman!' they cried 'let us go home.' 'Oh! be silent, my little ones,' said the poor woman; 'be silent; we will go to M. le Maire – he will not leave us without a friend.' It was then that I saw what my duty was. But it was with a pang – *bon Dieu!* – when I turned my back upon my Martin, when I went away to shelter, to peace, leaving my son thus in face of an offended Heaven and all the invisible powers, do you suppose it was a whole heart I carried in my breast? But no! it was nothing save a great ache – a struggle as of death. But what of that? I had my duty to do, as he had – and as he did not flinch, so did not I; otherwise he would have been ashamed of his mother – and I? I should have felt that the blood was not mine which ran in his veins.

No one can tell what it was, that march to La Clairière. Agnès first was like an angel. I hope I always do Madame Martin justice. She is a saint. She is good to the bottom of her heart. Nevertheless, with those natures which are enthusiast – which are upborne by excitement – there is also a weakness. Though she was brave as the holy Pucelle when we set out, after a while she flagged like another. The colour went out of her face, and though she smiled still, yet the tears came to her eyes, and she would have wept with the other women, and with the wail of the weary children, and all the agitation, and the weariness, and the length of the way, had not I recalled her to herself. 'Courage!' I said to her. 'Courage, *ma fille*! We will throw open all the chambers. I will give up even that one

in which my Martin Dupin, the father of thy husband, died.'
'*Ma mère*,' she said, holding my hand to her bosom, 'he is not
dead – he is in Semur.' Forgive me, dear Lord! It gave me a
pang that she could see him and not I. 'For me,' I cried, 'it is
enough to know that my good man is in heaven: his room,
which I have kept sacred, shall be given up to the poor.' But
oh! the confusion of the stumbling, weary feet; the little
children that dropped by the way, and caught at our skirts,
and wailed and sobbed; the poor mothers with babes upon
each arm, with sick hearts and failing limbs. One cry seemed
to rise round us as we went, each infant moving the others to
sympathy, till it rose like one breath, a wail of '*Maman!
Maman!*' a cry that had no meaning, through having so much
meaning. It was difficult not to cry out too in the excitement,
in the labouring of the long, long, confused, and tedious way.
'*Maman! Maman!*' The Holy Mother could not but hear it. It
is not possible but that she must have looked out upon us, and
heard us, so helpless as we were, where she sits in heaven.

When we got to La Clairière we were ready to sink down
with fatigue like all the rest – nay, even more than the rest, for
we were not used to it, and for my part I had altogether lost
the habitude of long walks. But then you could see what
Madame Martin was. She is slight and fragile and pale, not
strong, as any one can perceive; but she rose above the needs
of the body. She was the one among us who rested not. We
threw open all the rooms, and the poor people thronged in.
Old Léontine, who is the *garde* of the house, gazed upon us
and the crowd whom we brought with us with great eyes full
of fear and trouble. 'But, Madame,' she cried, 'Madame!'
following me as I went above to the better rooms. She pulled
me by my robe. She pushed the poor women with their
children away. '*Allez donc, allez!* – rest outside till these
ladies have time to speak to you,' she said; and pulled me by
my sleeve. Then 'Madame Martin is putting all this *canaille*
into our very chambers,' she cried. She had always distrusted
Madame Martin, who was taken by the peasants for a clerical
and *dévote*, because she was noble. 'The *bon Dieu* be praised
that Madame also is here, who has sense and will regulate
everything.' 'These are no *canaille*,' I said: 'be silent, *ma
bonne* Léontine, here is something which you cannot understand. This is Semur which has come out to us for lodging.'
She let the keys drop out of her hands. It was not wonderful if

she was amazed. All day long she followed me about, her very mouth open with wonder. 'Madame Martin, that understands itself,' she would say. 'She is romanesque – she has imagination – but Madame, Madame has *bon sens* – who would have believed it of Madame?' Léontine had been my *femme de ménage* long before there was a Madame Martin, when my son was young; and naturally it was of me she still thought. But I cannot put down all the trouble we had ere we found shelter for every one. We filled the stables and the great barn, and all the cottages near; and to get them food, and to have something provided for those who were watching before the city, and who had no one but us to think of them, was a task which was almost beyond our powers. Truly it was beyond our powers – but the Holy Mother of heaven and the good angels helped us. I cannot tell to any one how it was accomplished, yet it was accomplished. The wail of the little ones ceased. They slept that first night as if they had been in heaven. As for us, when the night came, and the dews and the darkness, it seemed to us as if we were out of our bodies, so weary were we, so weary that we could not rest. From La Clairière on ordinary occasions it is a beautiful sight to see the lights of Semur shining in all the high windows, and the streets throwing up a faint whiteness upon the sky; but how strange it was now to look down and see nothing but a darkness – a cloud, which was the city! The lights of the watchers in their camp were invisible to us, – they were so small and low upon the broken ground that we could not see them. Our Agnès crept close to me; we went with one accord to the seat before the door. We did not say 'I will go,' but went by one impulse, for our hearts were there; and we were glad to taste the freshness of the night and be silent after all our labours. We leant upon each other in our weariness. '*Ma mère*,' she said, 'where is he now, our Martin?' and wept. 'He is where there is the most to do, be thou sure of that,' I cried, but wept not. For what did I bring him into the world but for this end?

Were I to go day by day and hour by hour over that time of trouble, the story would not please any one. Many were brave and forgot their own sorrows to occupy themselves with those of others, but many also were not brave. There were those among us who murmured and complained. Some would contend with us to let them go and call their husbands, and leave the miserable country where such things could

happen. Some would rave against the priests and the government, and some against those who neglected and offended the
Holy Church. Among them there were those who did not
hesitate to say it was our fault, though how we were answer-
able they could not tell. We were never at any time of the day
or night without a sound of some one weeping or bewailing
herself, as if she were the only sufferer, or crying out against
those who had brought her here, far from all her friends. By
times it seemed to me that I could bear it no longer, that it was
but justice to turn those murmurers (*pleureuses*) away, and let
them try what better they could do for themselves. But in this
point Madame Martin surpassed me. I do not grudge to say it.
She was better than I was, for she was more patient. She wept
with the weeping women, then dried her eyes and smiled
upon them without a thought of anger – whereas I could have
turned them to the door. One thing, however, which I could
not away with, was that Agnès filled her own chamber with
the poorest of the poor. 'How,' I cried, 'thyself and thy friend
Madame de Bois-Sombre, were you not enough to fill it, that
you should throw open that chamber to good-for-nothings, to
va-nu-pieds, to the very rabble?' '*Ma mère*,' said Madame
Martin, 'our good Lord died for them.' 'And surely for thee
too, thou *saint-imbécile!*' I cried out in my indignation. What,
my Martin's chamber which he had adorned for his bride! I
was beside myself. And they have an obstinacy these enthu-
siasts! But for that matter her friend Madame de Bois-Sombre thought the same. She would have been one of the
pleureuses herself had it not been for shame. 'Agnès wishes
to aid the *bon Dieu*, Madame,' she said, 'to make us suffer still
a little more.' The tone in which she spoke, and the contrac-
tion in her forehead, as if our hospitality was not enough for
her, turned my heart again to my daughter-in-law. 'You have
reason, Madame,' I cried; 'there are indeed many ways in
which Agnès does the work of the good God.' The Bois-
Sombres are poor, they have not a roof to shelter them save
that of the old hôtel in Semur, from whence they were sent
forth like the rest of us. And she and her children owed all to
Agnès. Figure to yourself then my resentment when this lady
directed her scorn at my daughter-in-law. I am not myself
noble, though of the *haute bourgeoisie*, which some people
think a purer race.

Long and terrible were the days we spent in this suspense.

For ourselves it was well that there was so much to do – the food to provide for all this multitude, the little children to care for, and to prepare the provisions for our men who were before Semur. I was in the Ardennes during the war, and I saw some of its perils – but these were nothing to what we encountered now. It is true that my son Martin was not in the war, which made it very different to me; but here the dangers were such as we could not understand, and they weighed upon our spirits. The seat at the door, and that point where the road turned, where there was always so beautiful a view of the valley and of the town of Semur – were constantly occupied by groups of poor people gazing at the darkness in which their homes lay. It was strange to see them, some kneeling and praying with moving lips; some taking but one look, not able to endure the sight. I was of these last. From time to time, whenever I had a moment I came out, I know not why, to see if there was any change. But to gaze upon that altered prospect for hours, as some did, would have been intolerable to me. I could not linger nor try to imagine what might be passing there, either among those who were within (as was believed), or those who were without the walls. Neither could I pray as many did. My devotions of every day I will never, I trust, forsake or forget, and that my Martin was always in my mind is it needful to say? But to go over and over all the vague fears that were in me, and all those thoughts which would have broken my heart had they been put into words, I could not do this even to the good Lord Himself. When I suffered myself to think, my heart grew sick, my head swam round, the light went from my eyes. They are happy who can do so, who can take the *bon Dieu* into their confidence, and say all to Him; but me, I could not do it. I could not dwell upon that which was so terrible, upon my home abandoned, my son – Ah? now that it is past, it is still terrible to think of. And then it was all I was capable of, to trust my God and do what was set before me. God, He knows what it is we can do and what we cannot. I could not tell even to Him all the terror and the misery and the darkness there was in me; but I put my faith in Him. It was all of which I was capable. We are not made alike, neither in the body nor in the soul.

And there were many women like me at La Clairière. When we had done each piece of work we would look out with a kind of hope, then go back to find something else to do – not looking at each other, not saying a word. Happily there was a great deal to do. And to see how some of the women, and those the most anxious, would work, never resting, going on from one thing to another, as if they were hungry for more and more! Some did it with their mouths shut close, with their countenances fixed, not daring to pause or meet another's eyes; but some, who were more patient, worked with a soft word, and sometimes a smile, and sometimes a tear; but ever working on. Some of them were an example to us all. In the morning, when we got up, some from beds, some from the floor, – I insisted that all should lie down, by turns at least, for we could not make room for every one at the same hours, – the very first thought of all was to hasten to the window, or, better, to the door. Who could tell what might have happened while we slept? For the first moment no one would speak, – it was the moment of hope – and then there would be a cry, a clasping of the hands, which told – what we all knew. The one of the women who touched my heart most was the wife of Riou of the *octroi*. She had been almost rich for her condition in life, with a good house and a little servant whom she trained admirably, as I have had occasion to know. Her husband and her son were both among those whom we had left under the walls of Semur; but she had three children with her at La Clairière. Madame Riou slept lightly, and so did I. Sometimes I heard her stir in the middle of the night, though so softly that no one woke. We were in the same room, for it may be supposed that to keep a room to one's self was not possible. I did not stir, but lay and watched her as she went to the window, her figure visible against the pale dawning of the light, with an eager quick movement as of expectation – then turning back with slower step and a sigh. She was always full of hope. As the days went on, there came to be a kind of communication between us. We understood each other. When one was occupied and the other free, that one of us who went out to the door to look across the valley where Semur was would look at the other as if to say, 'I go.' When it was Madame Riou who did this, I shook my head, and she gave me a smile which awoke at every repetition (though I knew it was vain) a faint expectation, a little hope. When she came back, it was she who would shake her head, with her eyes full of tears. 'Did I not tell thee?' I said, speaking to her as if she were my daughter. 'It will be for next time,

Madame,' she would say, and smile, yet put her apron to her eyes. There were many who were like her, and there were those of whom I have spoken who were *pleureuses*, never hoping anything, doing little, bewailing themselves and their hard fate. Some of them we employed to carry the provisions to Semur, and this amused them, though the heaviness of the baskets made again a complaint.

As for the children, thank God! they were not disturbed as we were – to them it was a beautiful holiday – it was like Heaven. There is no place on earth that I love like Semur, yet it is true that the streets are narrow, and there is not much room for the children. Here they were happy as the day; they strayed over all our gardens and the meadows, which were full of flowers; they sat in companies upon the green grass, as thick as the daisies themselves, which they loved. Old Sister Mariette, who is called Marie de la Consolation, sat out in the meadow under an acacia-tree and watched over them. She was the one among us who was happy. She had no son, no husband, among the watchers, and though, no doubt, she loved her convent and her hospital, yet she sat all day long in the shade and in the full air, and smiled, and never looked towards Semur. 'The good Lord will do as He wills,' she said, 'and that will be well.' It was true – we all knew it was true; but it might be – who could tell? – that it was His will to destroy our town, and take away our bread, and perhaps the lives of those who were dear to us; and something came in our throats which prevented a reply. '*Ma sœur*,' I said, 'we are of the world, we tremble for those we love; we are not as you are.' Sister Mariette did nothing but smile upon us. 'I have known my Lord these sixty years,' she said, 'and He has taken everything from me.' To see her smile as she said this was more than I could bear. From me He had taken something, but not all. Must we be prepared to give up all if we would be perfected? There were many of the others also who trembled at these words. 'And now He gives me my consolation,' she said, and called the little ones round her, and told them a tale of the Good Shepherd, which is out of the holy Gospel. To see all the little ones round her knees in a crowd, and the peaceful face with which she smiled upon them, and the meadows all full of flowers, and the sunshine coming and going through the branches: and to hear that tale of Him who went forth to seek the lamb that was lost, was like a tale out of a holy book, where all was peace and goodness and joy. But on the other side, not twenty steps off, was the house full of those who wept, and at all the doors and windows anxious faces gazing down upon that cloud in the valley where Semur was. A procession of our women was coming back, many with lingering steps, carrying the baskets which were empty. 'Is there any news?' we asked, reading their faces before they could answer. And some shook their heads, and some wept. There was no other reply.

On the last night before our deliverance, suddenly, in the middle of the night, there was a great commotion in the house. We all rose out of our beds at the sound of the cry, almost believing that some one at the window had seen the lifting of the cloud, and rushed together, frightened, yet all in an eager expectation to hear what it was. It was in the room where the old Mère Julie slept that the disturbance was. Mère Julie was one of the market-women of Semur, the one I have mentioned who was devout, who never missed the *Salut* in the afternoon, besides all masses which are obligatory. But there were other matters in which she had not satisfied my mind, as I have before said. She was the mother of Jacques Richard, who was a good-for-nothing, as is well known. At La Clairière Mère Julie had enacted a strange part. She had taken no part in anything that was done, but had established herself in the chamber allotted to her, and taken the best bed in it, where she kept her place night and day, making the others wait upon her. She had always expressed a great devotion for St Jean; and the Sisters of the Hospital had been very kind to her, and also to her *vaurien* of a son, who was indeed, in some manner, the occasion of all our troubles – being the first who complained of the opening of the chapel into the chief ward, which was closed up by the administration, and thus became, as I and many others think, the cause of all the calamities that have come upon us. It was her bed that was the centre of the great commotion we had heard, and a dozen voices immediately began to explain to us as we entered. 'Mère Julie has had a dream. She has seen a vision,' they said. It was a vision of angels in the most beautiful robes, all shining with gold and whiteness.

'The dress of the Holy Mother which she wears on the great *fêtes* was nothing to them,' Mère Julie told us, when she had composed herself. For all had run here and there at her first cry, and procured for her a *tisane*, and a cup of *bouillon*, and all that was good for an attack of the nerves, which was what it was at first supposed to be. 'Their wings were like the wings of the great peacock on the terrace, but also like those of eagles. And each one had a collar of beautiful jewels about his neck, and robes whiter than those of any bride.' This was the description she gave: and to see the women how they listened, head above head, a cloud of eager faces, all full of awe and attention! The angels had promised her that they would come again, when we had bound ourselves to observe all the functions of the Church, and when all these Messieurs had been converted, and made their submission – to lead us back gloriously to Semur. There was a great tumult in the chamber, and all cried out that they were convinced, that they were ready to promise. All except Madame Martin, who stood and looked at them with a look which surprised me, which was of pity rather than sympathy. As there was no one else to speak, I took the word, being the mother of the present Maire, and wife of the last, and in part mistress of the house. Had Agnès spoken I would have yielded to her, but as she was silent I took my right. 'Mère Julie,' I said, 'and *mes bonnes femmes*, my friends, know you that it is the middle of the night, the hour at which we must rest if we are to be able to do the work that is needful, which the *bon Dieu* has laid upon us? It is not from us – my daughter and myself – who, it is well known, have followed all the functions of the Church, that you will meet with an opposition to your promise. But what I desire is that you should calm yourselves, that you should retire and rest till the time of work, husbanding your strength, since we know not what claim may be made upon it. The holy angels,' I said, 'will comprehend, or if not they, then the *bon Dieu*, who understands everything.'

But it was with difficulty that I could induce them to listen to me, to do that which was reasonable. When, however, we had quieted the agitation, and persuaded the good women to repose themselves, it was no longer possible for me to rest. I promised to myself a little moment of quiet, for my heart longed to be alone. I stole out as quietly as I might, not to disturb any one, and sat down upon the bench outside the door. It was still a kind of half-dark, nothing visible, so that if any one should gaze and gaze down the valley, it was not possible to see what was there: and I was glad that it was not possible, for my very soul was tired. I sat down and leant my back upon the wall of our house, and opened my lips to draw in the air of the morning. How still it was! the very birds not yet begun to rustle and stir in the bushes; the night air hushed, and scarcely the first faint tint of blue beginning to steal into the darkness. When I had sat there a little, closing my eyes, lo, tears began to steal into them like rain when there has been a fever of heat. I have wept in my time many tears, but the time of weeping is over with me, and through all these miseries I had shed none. Now they came without asking, like a benediction refreshing my eyes. Just then I felt a soft pressure upon my shoulder, and there was Agnès coming close, putting her shoulder to mine, as was her way, that we might support each other.

'You weep, *ma mère*,' she said.

'I think it is one of the angels Mère Julie has seen,' said I. 'It is a refreshment – a blessing; my eyes were dry with weariness.'

'Mother,' said Madame Martin, 'do you think it is angels with wings like peacocks and jewelled collars that our Father sends to us? Ah, not so – one of those whom we love has touched your dear eyes,' and with that she kissed me upon my eyes, taking me in her arms. My heart is sometimes hard to my son's wife, but not always – not with my will, God knows! Her kiss was soft as the touch of any angel could be.

'God bless thee, my child,' I said.

'Thanks, thanks, *ma mère*!' she cried. 'Now I am resolved; now will I go and speak to Martin – of something in my heart.'

'What will you do, my child?' I said, for as the light increased I could see the meaning in her face, and that it was wrought up for some great thing. 'Beware, Agnès; risk not my son's happiness by risking thyself; thou art more to Martin than all the world beside.'

'He loves thee dearly, mother,' she said. My heart was comforted. I was able to remember that I too had had my day. 'He loves his mother, thank God, but not as he loves thee. Beware, *ma fille*. If you risk my son's happiness, neither will I forgive you.' She smiled upon me, and kissed my hands.

'I will go and take him his food and some linen, and carry him your love and mine.'

'*You* will go, and carry one of those heavy baskets with the others!'

'Mother,' cried Agnès, 'now you shame me that I have never done it before.'

What could I say? Those whose turn it was were preparing their burdens to set out. She had her little packet made up, besides, of our cool white linen, which I knew would be so grateful to my son. I went with her to the turn of the road, helping her with her basket; but my limbs trembled, what with the long continuance of the trial, what with the agitation of the night. It was but just daylight when they went away, disappearing down the long slope of the road that led to Semur. I went back to the bench at the door, and there I sat down and thought. Assuredly it was wrong to close up the chapel, to deprive the sick of the benefit of the holy mass. But yet I could not but reflect that the *bon Dieu* had suffered still more great scandals to take place without such a punishment. When, however, I reflected on all that has been done by those who have no cares of this world as we have, but are brides of Christ, and upon all they resign by their dedication, and the claim they have to be furthered, not hindered, in their holy work; and when I bethought myself how many and great are the powers of evil, and that, save in us poor women who can do so little, the Church has few friends: then it came back to me how heinous was the offence that had been committed, and that it might well be that the saints out of heaven should return to earth to take the part and avenge the cause of the weak. My husband would have been the first to do it, had he seen with my eyes; but though in the flesh he did not do so, is it to be doubted that in heaven their eyes are enlightened – those who have been subjected to the cleansing fires and have ascended into final bliss? This all became clear to me as I sat and pondered, while the morning light grew around me, and the sun rose and shed his first rays, which are as precious gold, on the summits of the mountains – for at La Clairière we are nearer the mountains than at Semur.

The house was more still than usual, and all slept to a later hour because of the agitation of the past night. I had been seated, like old sister Mariette, with my eyes turned rather towards the hills than to the valley, being so deep in my thoughts that I did not look, as it was our constant wont to look, if any change had happened over Semur. Thus blessings come unawares when we are not looking for them. Suddenly I lifted my eyes – but not with expectation – languidly, as one looks without thought. Then it was that I gave that great cry which brought all crowding to the windows, to the gardens, to every spot from whence that blessed sight was visible; for there before us, piercing through the clouds, were the beautiful towers of Semur, the Cathedral with all its pinnacles, that are as if they were carved out of foam, and the solid tower of St Lambert, and the others, every one. They told me after that I flew, though I am past running, to the farmyard to call all the labourers and servants of the farm, bidding them prepare every carriage and waggon, and even the *charrettes*, to carry back the children, and those who could not walk to the city.

'The men will be wild with privation and trouble,' I said to myself; 'they will want the sight of their little children, the comfort of their wives.'

I did not wait to reason nor to ask myself if I did well; and my son has told me since that he scarcely was more thankful for our great deliverance than, just when the crowd of gaunt and weary men returned into Semur, and there was a moment when excitement and joy were at their highest, and danger possible, to hear the roll of the heavy farm waggons, and to see me arrive, with all the little ones and their mothers, like a new army, to take possession of their homes once more.

TEN

M. le Maire Concludes his Record

THE NARRATIVES WHICH I have collected from the different eyewitnesses during the time of my own absence, will show how everything passed while I, with M. le Curé, was recovering possession of our city. Many have reported to me verbally the occurrences of the last half-hour before my return; and in their accounts there are naturally discrepancies, owing to their different points of view and different ways of regarding the subject. But all are agreed that a strange and universal slumber had seized upon all. M. de Bois-Sombre even admits that he, too, was overcome by this influence.

They slept while we were performing our dangerous and solemn duty in Semur. But when the Cathedral bells began to ring, with one impulse all awoke, and starting from the places where they lay, from the shade of the trees and bushes and sheltering hollows, saw the cloud and the mist and the darkness which had enveloped Semur suddenly rise from the walls. It floated up into the higher air before their eyes, then was caught and carried away, and flung about into shreds upon the sky by a strong wind, of which down below no influence was felt. They all gazed, not able to get their breath, speechless, beside themselves with joy, and saw the walls reappear, and the roofs of the houses, and our glorious Cathedral against the blue sky. They stood for a moment spell-bound. M. de Bois-Sombre informs me that he was afraid of a wild rush into the city, and himself hastened to the front to lead and restrain it; when suddenly a great cry rang through the air, and some one was seen to fall across the high road, straight in front of the Porte St Lambert. M. de Bois-Sombre was at once aware who it was, for he himself had watched Lecamus taking his place at the feet of my wife, who awaited my return there. This checked the people in their first rush towards their homes; and when it was seen that Madame Dupin had also sunk down fainting on the ground after her more than human exertions for the comfort of all, there was but one impulse of tenderness and pity. When I reached the gate on my return, I found my wife lying there in all the pallor of death, and for a moment my heart stood still with sudden terror. What mattered Semur to me, if it had cost me my Agnès? or how could I think of Lecamus or any other, while she lay between life and death? I had her carried back to our own house. She was the first to re-enter Semur; and after a time, thanks be to God, she came back to herself. But Paul Lecamus was a dead man. No need to carry him in, to attempt unavailing cares. 'He has gone, that one; he has marched with the others,' said the old doctor, who had served in his day, and sometimes would use the language of the camp. He cast but one glance at him, and laid his hand upon his heart in passing. 'Cover his face,' was all he said.

It is possible that this check was good for the restraint of the crowd. It moderated the rush with which they returned to their homes. The sight of the motionless figures stretched out by the side of the way overawed them. Perhaps it may seem strange, to any one who has known what had occurred, that the state of the city should have given me great anxiety the first night of our return. The withdrawal of the oppression and awe which had been on the men, the return of everything to its natural state, the sight of their houses unchanged, so that the brain turned round of these common people, who seldom reflect upon anything, and they already began to ask themselves was it all a delusion – added to the exhaustion of their physical condition, and the natural desire for ease and pleasure after the long strain upon all their faculties – produced an excitement which might have led to very disastrous consequences. Fortunately I had foreseen this. I have always been considered to possess great knowledge of human nature, and this has been matured by recent events. I sent off messengers instantly to bring home the women and children, and called around me the men in whom I could most trust. Though I need not say that the excitement and suffering of the past three days had told not less upon myself than upon others, I abandoned all idea of rest. The first thing that I did, aided by my respectable fellow-townsmen, was to take possession of all *cabarets* and wine-shops, allowing indeed the proprietors to return, but preventing all assemblages within them. We then established a patrol of respectable citizens throughout the city, to preserve the public peace. I calculated, with great anxiety, how many hours it would be before my messengers could reach La Clairière, to bring back the women – for in such a case the wives are the best guardians, and can exercise an influence more general and less suspected than that of the magistrates; but this was not to be hoped for for three or four hours at least. Judge, then, what was my joy and satisfaction when the sound of wheels (in itself a pleasant sound, for no wheels had been audible on the high-road since these events began) came briskly to us from the distance; and looking out from the watch tower over the Porte St Lambert, I saw the strangest procession. The wine-carts and all the farm vehicles of La Clairière, and every kind of country waggon, were jolting along the road, all in a tumult and babble of delicious voices; and from under the rude canopies and awnings and roofs of vine branches, made up to shield them from the sun, lo! there were the children like birds in a nest, one little head peeping over the other. And the cries and songs, the laughter, and the shoutings! As they came along the air grew sweet, the world was made new. Many of us, who had borne all the terrors and sufferings of the past without fainting, now felt their strength fail them. Some broke out into tears, interrupted with laughter. Some called out aloud the names of their little ones. We went out to meet them, every man there present, myself at the head. And I will not deny that a sensation of pride came over me when I saw my mother stand up in the first waggon, with all those happy ones fluttering around her. 'My son,' she said, 'I have discharged the trust that was given me. I bring thee back the blessing of God.' 'And God bless thee, my mother!' I cried. The other men, who were fathers, like me, came round me, crowding to kiss her hand. It is not among the women of my family that you will find those who abandon their duties.

And then to lift down in armfuls, those flowers of paradise, all fresh with the air of the fields, all joyous like the birds! We put them down by twos and threes, some of us sobbing with joy. And to see them dispersing hand in hand, running here and there, each to its home, carrying peace, and love, and gladness, through the streets – that was enough to make the most serious smile. No fear was in them, or care. Every haggard man they met – some of them feverish, restless, beginning to think of riot and pleasure after forced abstinence – there was a new shout, a rush of little feet, a shower of soft kisses. The women were following after, some packed into the carts and waggons, pale and worn, yet happy; some walking behind in groups; the more strong, or the more eager, in advance, and a long line of stragglers behind. There was anxiety in their faces, mingled with their joy. How did they know what they might find in the houses from which they had been shut out? And many felt, like me, that in the very return, in the relief, there was danger. But the children feared nothing; they filled the streets with their dear voices, and happiness came back with them. When I felt my little Jean's cheek against mine, then for the first time did I know how much anguish I had suffered – how terrible was parting, and how sweet was life. But strength and prudence melt away when one indulges one's self, even in one's dearest affections. I had to call my guardians together, to put mastery upon myself, that a just vigilance might not be relaxed. M. de Bois-Sombre, though less anxious than myself, and disposed to believe (being a

soldier) that a little licence would do no harm, yet stood by
me; and, thanks to our precautions, all went well.

Before night three parts of the population had returned to
Semur, and the houses were all lighted up as for a great
festival. The Cathedral stood open – even the great west
doors, which are only opened on great occasions – with a glow
of tapers gleaming out on every side. As I stood in the twilight
watching, and glad at heart to think that all was going well,
my mother and my wife – still pale, but now recovered from
her fainting and weakness – came out into the great square,
leading my little Jean. They were on their way to the Cathedral, to thank God for their return. They looked at me, but
did not ask me to go with them, those dear women; they
respect my opinions, as I had always respected theirs. But this
silence moved me more than words; there came into my heart
a sudden inspiration. I was still in my scarf of office, which
had been, I say it without vanity, the standard of authority
and protection during all our trouble; and thus marked out as
representative of all, I uncovered myself, after the ladies of
my family had passed, and, without joining them, silently
followed with a slow and solemn step. A suggestion, a look, is
enough for my countrymen; those who were in the Place with
me perceived in a moment what I meant. One by one they
uncovered, they put themselves behind me. Thus we made
such a procession as had never been seen in Semur. We were
gaunt and worn with watching and anxiety, which only added
to the solemn effect. Those who were already in the Cathedral, and especially M. le Curé, informed me afterwards that
the tramp of our male feet as we came up the great steps gave
to all a thrill of expectation and awe. It was at the moment of
the exposition of the Sacrament that we entered. Instinctively, in a moment, all understood – a thing which could
happen nowhere but in France, where intelligence is swift as
the breath on our lips. Those who were already there yielded
their places to us, most of the women rising up, making as it
were a ring round us, the tears running down their faces.
When the Sacrament was replaced upon the altar, M. le Curé,
perceiving our meaning, began at once in his noble voice to
intone the *Te Deum*. Rejecting all other music, he adopted the
plain song in which all could join, and with one voice, every
man in unison with his brother, we sang with him. The great
Cathedral walls seemed to throb with the sound that rolled

upward, *mâle* and deep, as no song has ever risen from Semur in the memory of man. The women stood up around us, and wept and sobbed with pride and joy.

When this wonderful moment was over, and all the people poured forth out of the Cathedral walls into the soft evening, with stars shining above, and all the friendly lights below, there was such a tumult of emotion and gladness as I have never seen before. Many of the poor women surrounded me, kissed my hand notwithstanding my resistance, and called upon God to bless me; while some of the older persons made remarks full of justice and feeling.

'The *bon Dieu* is not used to such singing,' one of them cried, her old eyes streaming with tears. 'It must have surprised the saints up in heaven!'

'It will bring a blessing,' cried another. 'It is not like our little voices, that perhaps only reach half-way.'

This was figurative language, yet it was impossible to doubt there was much truth in it. Such a submission of our intellects, as I felt in determining to make it, must have been pleasing to heaven. The women, they are always praying; but when we thus presented ourselves to give thanks, it meant something, a real homage; and with a feeling of solemnity we separated, aware that we had contented both earth and heaven.

Next morning there was a great function in the Cathedral, at which the whole city assisted. Those who could not get admittance crowded upon the steps, and knelt halfway across the Place. It was an occasion long remembered in Semur, though I have heard many say not in itself so impressive as the *Te Deum* on the evening of our return. After this we returned to our occupations, and life was resumed under its former conditions in our city.

It might be supposed, however, that the place in which events so extraordinary had happened would never again be as it was before. Had I not been myself so closely involved, it would have appeared to me certain, that the streets, trod once by such inhabitants as those who for three nights and days abode within Semur, would have always retained some trace of their presence; that life there would have been more solemn than in other places; and that those families for whose advantage the dead had risen out of their graves, would have henceforward carried about with them some sign of that interposition. It will seem almost incredible when I now add that nothing of this kind has happened at Semur. The wonderful manifestation which interrupted our existence has passed absolutely as if it had never been. We had not been twelve hours in our houses ere we had forgotten, or practically forgotten, our expulsion from them. Even myself, to whom everything was so vividly brought home, I have to enter my wife's room to put aside the curtain from little Marie's picture, and to see and touch the olive branch which is there, before I can recall to myself anything that resembles the feeling with which I re-entered that sanctuary. My grandfather's bureau still stands in the middle of my library, where I found it on my return; but I have got used to it, and it no longer affects me. Everything is as it was; and I cannot persuade myself that, for a time, I and mine were shut out, and our places taken by those who neither eat nor drink, and whose life is invisible to our eyes. Everything, I say, is as it was – everything goes on as if it would endure for ever. We know this cannot be, yet it does not move us. Why, then, should the other move us? A little time, we are aware, and we, too, shall be as they are – as shadows, and unseen. But neither has the one changed us, and neither does the other. There was, for some time, a greater respect shown to religion in Semur, and a more devout attendance at the sacred functions; but I regret to say this did not continue. Even in my own case – I say it with sorrow – it did not continue. M. le Curé is an admirable person. I know no more excellent ecclesiastic. He is indefatigable in the performance of his spiritual duties; and he has, besides, a noble and upright soul. Since the days when we suffered and laboured together, he has been to me as a brother. Still, it is undeniable that he makes calls upon our credulity, which a man obeys with reluctance. There are ways of surmounting this; as I see in Agnès for one, and in M. de Bois-Sombre for another. My wife does not question, she believes much; and in respect to that which she cannot acquiesce in, she is silent. 'There are many things I hear you talk of, Martin, which are strange to me,' she says, 'of myself I cannot believe in them; but I do not oppose, since it is possible you may have reason to know better than I; and so with some things that we hear from M. le Curé.' This is how she explains herself – but she is a woman. It is a matter of grace to yield to our better judgment. M. de Bois-Sombre has another way. '*Ma foi*,' he says, 'I have not the time for all your delicacies, my good people; I have come to see that these things are for the advantage of the world, and it is not my business to explain them. If M. le Curé attempted to criticise me in military matters, or thee, my excellent Martin, in affairs of business, or in the culture of your vines, I should think him not a wise man; and in like manner, faith and religion, these are his concern.' Félix de Bois-Sombre is an excellent fellow; but he smells a little of the *mousquetaire*. I, who am neither a soldier nor a woman, I have hesitations. Nevertheless, so long as I am Maire of Semur, nothing less than the most absolute respect shall ever be shown to all truly religious persons, with whom it is my earnest desire to remain in sympathy and fraternity, so far as that may be.

It seemed, however, a little while ago as if my tenure of this office would not be long, notwithstanding the services which I am acknowledged, on every hand, to have done to my fellow-townsmen. It will be remembered that when M. le Curé and myself found Semur empty, we heard a voice of complaining from the hospital of St Jean, and found a sick man who had been left there, and who grumbled against the Sisters, and accused them of neglecting him, but remained altogether unaware, in the meantime, of what had happened in the city. Will it be believed that after a time this fellow was put faith in as a seer, who had heard and beheld many things of which we were all ignorant? It must be said that, in the meantime, there had been a little excitement in the town on the subject of the Chapel in the hospital, to which repeated reference has already been made. It was insisted on behalf of these ladies that a promise had been given, taking, indeed, the form of a vow, that, as soon as we were again in possession of Semur, their full privileges should be restored to them. Their advocates even went so far as to send to me a deputation of those who had been nursed in the hospital, the leader of which was Jacques Richard, who since he has been, as he says, 'converted,' thrusts himself to the front of every movement.

'Permit me to speak, M. le Maire,' he said; 'me, who was one of those so misguided as to complain, before the great lesson we have all received. The mass did not disturb any sick person who was of right dispositions. I was then a very bad subject, indeed – as, alas! M. le Maire too well knows. It annoyed me only as all pious observances annoyed me. I am now, thank heaven, of a very different way of thinking—'

But I would not listen to the fellow. When he was a *mauvais sujet* he was less abhorrent to me than now.

The men were aware that when I pronounced myself so distinctly on any subject there was nothing more to be said, for, though gentle as a lamb and open to all reasonable arguments, I am capable of making the most obstinate stand for principle; and to yield to popular superstition, is that worthy of a man who has been instructed? At the same time it raised a great anger in my mind that all that should be thought of was a thing so trivial. That they should have given themselves, soul and body, for a little money; that they should have scoffed at all that was noble and generous, both in religion and in earthly things; all that was nothing to them. And now they would insult the Great God Himself by believing that all He cared for was a little mass in a convent chapel. What desecration! What debasement! When I went to M. le Curé, he smiled at my vehemence. There was pain in his smile, and it might be indignation; but he was not furious like me.

'They will conquer you, my friend,' he said.

'Never,' I cried. 'Before I might have yielded. But to tell me the gates of death have been rolled back, and Heaven revealed, and the great God stooped down from Heaven, in order that mass should be said according to the wishes of the community in the midst of the sick wards! They will never make me believe this, if I were to die for it.'

'Nevertheless, they will conquer,' M. le Curé said.

It angered me that he should say so. My heart was sore as if my friend had forsaken me. And then it was that the worst step was taken in this crusade of false religion. It was from my mother that I heard of it first. One day she came home in great excitement, saying that now indeed a real light was to be shed upon all that had happened to us.

'It appears,' she said, 'that Pierre Plastron was in the hospital all the time, and heard and saw many wonderful things. Sister Géneviève had just told me. It is wonderful beyond anything you could believe. He has spoken with our holy patron himself, St Lambert, and has received instructions for a pilgrimage—'

'Pierre Plastron!' I cried; 'Pierre Plastron saw nothing, *ma mère*. He was not even aware that anything remarkable had occurred. He complained to us of the Sisters that they neglected him: he knew nothing more.'

'My son,' she said, looking upon me with reproving eyes, 'what have the good Sisters done to thee? Why is it that you look so unfavourably upon everything that comes from the community of St Jean?'

'What have I to do with the community?' I cried – 'when I tell thee, Maman, that this Pierre Plastron knows nothing! I heard it from the fellow's own lips, and M. le Curé was present and heard him too. He had seen nothing, he knew nothing. Inquire of M. le Curé, if you have doubts of me.'

'I do not doubt you, Martin,' said my mother with severity, 'when you are not biased by prejudice. And, as for M. le Curé, it is well known that the clergy are often jealous of the good Sisters, when they are not under their own control.'

Such was the injustice with which we were treated. And next day nothing was talked of but the revelation of Pierre Plastron. What he had seen and what he had heard was wonderful. All the saints had come and talked with him, and told him what he was to say to his townsmen. They told him exactly how everything had happened: how St Jean himself had interfered on behalf of the Sisters, and how, if we were not more attentive on the duties of religion, certain among us would be bound hand and foot and cast into the jaws of hell. That I was one, nay the chief, of these denounced persons, no one could have any doubt. This exasperated me; and as soon as I knew that this folly had been printed and was in every house, I hastened to M. le Curé, and entreated him in his next Sunday's sermon to tell the true story of Pierre Plastron, and reveal the imposture. But M. le Curé shook his head. 'It will do no good,' he said.

'But how no good?' said I. 'What good are we looking for? These are lies, nothing but lies. Either he has deceived the poor ladies basely, or they themselves – but this is what I cannot believe.'

'Dear friend,' he said, 'compose thyself. Have you never discovered yet how strong is self-delusion? There will be no lying of which they are aware. Figure to yourself what a stimulus to the imagination to know that he was here, actually here. Even I – it suggests a hundred things to me. The Sisters will have said to him (meaning no evil, nay meaning the edification of the people), "But, Pierre, reflect! You must have seen this and that. Recall thy recollections a little." And by degrees Pierre will have found out that he remembered – more than could have been hoped.'

'*Mon Dieu!*' I cried, out of patience, 'and you know all this, yet you will not tell them the truth – the very truth.'

'To what good?' he said. Perhaps M. le Curé was right: but, for my part, had I stood up in that pulpit, I should have contradicted their lies and given no quarter. This, indeed, was what I did both in my private and public capacity; but the people, though they loved me, did not believe me. They said, 'The best men have their prejudices. M. le Maire is an excellent man; but what will you? He is but human after all.'

M. le Curé and I said no more to each other on this subject. He was a brave man, yet here perhaps he was not quite brave. And the effect of Pierre Plastron's revelations in other quarters was to turn the awe that had been in many minds into mockery and laughter. '*Ma foi*,' said Félix de Bois-Sombre, 'Monseigneur St Lambert had bad taste, *mon ami* Martin, to choose Pierre Plastron for his confidant when he might have had thee.' 'M. de Bois-Sombre does ill to laugh,' said my mother (even my mother! she was not on my side), 'when it is known that the foolish are often chosen to confound the wise.' But Agnès, my wife, it was she who gave me the best consolation. She turned to me with the tears in her beautiful eyes.

'*Mon ami*,' she said, 'let Monseigneur St Lambert say what he will. He is not God that we should put him above all. There were other saints with other thoughts that came for thee and for me!'

All this contradiction was over when Agnès and I together took our flowers on the *jour des morts* to the graves we love. Glimmering among the rest was a new cross which I had not seen before. This was the inscription upon it:—

À PAUL LECAMUS
PARTI
LE 20 JUILLET, 1875
AVEC LES BIEN-AIMÉS

On it was wrought in the marble a little branch of olive. I turned to look at my wife as she laid underneath this cross a handful of violets. She gave me her hand still fragrant with the flowers. There was none of his family left to put up for him any token of human remembrance. Who but she should have done it, who had helped him to join that company and army of the beloved? 'This was our brother,' she said; 'he will tell my Marie what use I made of her olive leaves.'

The Secret Chamber

Dedicated to the inquirers in the Norman Tower

I

CASTLE GOWRIE IS one of the most famous and interesting in all Scotland. It is a beautiful old house, to start with, – perfect in old feudal grandeur, with its clustered turrets and walls that could withstand an army, – its labyrinths, its hidden stairs, its long mysterious passages – passages that seem in many cases to lead to nothing, but of which no one can be too sure what they lead to. The front, with its fine gateway and flanking towers, is approached now by velvet lawns, and a peaceful, beautiful old avenue, with double rows of trees, like a cathedral; and the woods out of which these grey towers rise, look as soft and rich in foliage, if not so lofty in growth, as the groves of the South. But this softness of aspect is all new to the place, – that is, new within the century or two which count for but little in the history of a dwelling-place, some part of which, at least, has been standing since the days when the Saxon Athelings brought such share of the arts as belonged to them to solidify and regulate the original Celtic art which reared incised stones upon rude burial-places, and twined mystic knots on its crosses, before historic days. Even of this primitive decoration there are relics at Gowrie, where the twistings and twinings of Runic cords appear still on some bits of ancient wall, solid as rocks, and almost as everlasting. From these to the graceful French turrets, which recall many a grey chateau, what a long interval of years! But these are filled with stirring chronicles enough, besides the dim, not always decipherable records, which different developments of architecture have left on the old house. The Earls of Gowrie had been in the heat of every commotion that took place on or about the Highland line for more generations than any but a Celtic pen could record. Rebellions, revenges, insurrections, conspiracies, nothing in which blood was shed and lands lost, took place in Scotland, in which they had not had a share; and the annals of the house are very full, and not without many a stain. They had been a bold and vigorous race – with much evil in them, and some good; never insignificant, whatever else they might be. It could not be said, however, that they are remarkable nowadays. Since the first Stuart rising, known in Scotland as 'the Fifteen', they have not done much that has been worth recording; but yet their family history has always been of an unusual kind. The Randolphs could not be called eccentric in themselves: on the contrary, when you know them, they were at bottom a respectable race, full of all the country-gentleman virtues; and yet their public career, such as it was, had been marked by the strangest leaps and jerks of vicissitude. You would have said an impulsive, fanciful family – now making a grasp at some visionary advantage, now rushing into some wild speculation, now making a sudden sally into public life – but soon falling back into mediocrity, not able apparently, even when the impulse was purely selfish and mercenary, to keep it up. But this would not have been at all a true conception of the family character; their actual virtues were not of the imaginative order, and their freaks were a mystery to their friends. Nevertheless these freaks were what the general world was most aware of in the Randolph race. The late Earl had been a representative peer of Scotland (they had no English title), and had made quite a wonderful start, and for a year or two had seemed about to attain a very eminent place in Scotch affairs; but his ambition was found to have made use of some very equivocal modes of gaining influence, and he dropped accordingly at once and for ever from the political firmament. This was quite a common circumstance in the family. An apparently brilliant beginning, a discovery of evil means adopted for ambitious ends, a sudden subsidence, and the curious conclusion at the end of everything that this schemer, this unscrupulous speculator or politician, was a dull, good man after all – unambitious, contented, full of domestic kindness and benevolence. This family peculiarity made the history of the Randolphs a very strange one, broken by the oddest interruptions, and with no consistency in it. There was another circumstance, however, which attracted still more the wonder and observation of the public. For one who can appreciate such a recondite matter as family character, there are hundreds who are interested in a family secret, and this the house of Randolph possessed in perfection. It was a mystery which piqued the imagination and excited the interest of the entire country. The story went, that somewhere hid amid the massive walls and tortuous passages there was a secret chamber in Gowrie Castle. Everybody knew of its existence; but save the Earl, his heir, and one other person, not of the family, but filling a confidential post in their service, no mortal knew where this mysterious hiding-place was. There had been countless guesses made at it, and expedients of all kinds invented to find it out. Every visitor who ever entered the old gateway, nay, even passing travellers who saw the turrets from the road, searched keenly for some trace of this mysterious chamber. But all guesses and researches were equally in vain.

I was about to say that no ghost-story I ever heard of has been so steadily and long believed. But this would be a mistake, for nobody knew even with any certainty that there was a ghost connected with it. A secret chamber was nothing wonderful in so old a house. No doubt they exist in many such old houses, and are always curious and interesting – strange relics, more moving than any history, of the time when a man was not safe in his own house, and when it might be necessary to secure a refuge beyond the reach of spies or traitors at a moment's notice. Such a refuge was a necessity of life to a great medieval noble. The peculiarity about this secret chamber, however, was that some secret connected with the very existence of the family was always understood to be involved in it. It was not only the secret hiding-place for an emergency, a kind of historical possession presupposing the importance of his race, of which a man might be honestly proud; but there was something hidden in it of which assuredly the race could not be proud. It is wonderful how easily a family learns to pique itself upon any distinctive possession. A ghost is a sign of importance not to be despised; a haunted room is worth as much as a small farm to the complacency of the family that owns it. And no doubt the younger branches of the Gowrie family – the light-minded portion of the race – felt this, and were proud of their unfathomable secret, and felt a thrill of

agreeable awe and piquant suggestion go through them, when
they remembered the mysterious something which they did
not know in their familiar home. That thrill ran through the
entire circle of visitors, and children, and servants, when the
Earl peremptorily forbade a projected improvement, or
stopped a reckless exploration. They looked at each other
with a pleasurable shiver. 'Did you hear?' they said. 'He will
not let Lady Gowrie have that closet she wants so much in
that bit of wall. He sent the workmen about their business
before they could touch it, though the wall is twenty feet thick
if it is an inch; ah!' said the visitors, looking at each other; and
this lively suggestion sent tinglings of excitement to their very
finger-points; but even to his wife, mourning the commo-
dious closet she had intended, the Earl made no explanations.
For anything she knew, it might be there, next to her room,
this mysterious lurking-place; and it may be supposed that
this suggestion conveyed to Lady Gowrie's veins a thrill more
keen and strange, perhaps too vivid to be pleasant. But she
was not in the favoured or unfortunate number of those to
whom the truth could be revealed.

I need not say what the different theories on the subject
were. Some thought there had been a treacherous massacre
there, and that the Secret Chamber was blocked by the
skeletons of murdered guests, – a treachery no doubt covering
the family with shame in its day, but so condoned by long
softening of years as to have all the shame taken out of it. The
Randolphs could not have felt their character affected by any
such interesting historical record. They were not so morbidly
sensitive. Some said, on the other hand, that Earl Robert, the
wicked Earl, was shut up there in everlasting penance, playing cards with the devil for his soul. But it would have been
too great a feather in the family cap to have thus got the devil,
or even one of his angels, bottled up, as it were, and safely in
hand, to make it possible that any lasting stigma could be
connected with such a fact as this. What a thing it would be to
know where to lay one's hand upon the Prince of Darkness,
and prove him once for all, cloven foot and everything else, to
the confusion of gainsayers!

So this was not to be received as a satisfactory solution, nor
could any other be suggested which was more to the purpose.
The popular mind gave it up, and yet never gave it up; and
still everybody who visits Gowrie, be it as a guest, be it as a

tourist, be it only as a gazer from a passing carriage, or from the flying railway train which just glimpses its turrets in the distance, daily and yearly spends a certain amount of curiosity, wonderment, and conjecture about the Secret Chamber – the most piquant and undiscoverable wonder which has endured unguessed and undeciphered to modern times.

This was how the matter stood when young John Randolph, Lord Lindores, came of age. He was a young man of great character and energy, not like the usual Randolph strain – for, as we have said, the type of character common in this romantically-situated family, notwithstanding the erratic incidents common to them, was that of dullness and honesty, especially in their early days. But young Lindores was not so. He was honest and honourable, but not dull. He had gone through almost a remarkable course at school and at the university – not perhaps in quite the ordinary way of scholarship, but enough to attract men's eyes to him. He had made more than one great speech at the Union. He was full of ambition, and force, and life, intending all sorts of great things, and meaning to make his position a stepping-stone to all that was excellent in public life. Not for him the country-gentleman existence which was congenial to his father. The idea of succeeding to the family honours and becoming a Scotch peer, either represented or representative, filled him with horror; and filial piety in his case was made warm by all the energy of personal hopes when he prayed that his father might live, if not for ever, yet longer than any Lord Gowrie had lived for the last century or two. He was as sure of his election for the county the next time there was a chance, as anybody can be certain of anything; and in the meantime he meant to travel, to go to America, to go no one could tell where, seeking for instruction and experience, as is the manner of high-spirited young men with parliamentary tendencies in the present day. In former times he would have gone 'to the wars in the Hie Germanie,' or on a crusade to the Holy Land; but the days of the crusaders and of the soldiers of fortune being over, Lindores followed the fashion of his time. He had made all his arrangements for his tour, which his father did not oppose. On the contrary, Lord Gowrie encouraged all those plans, though with an air of melancholy indulgence which his son could not understand. 'It will do you good,' he said, with a sigh. 'Yes, yes, my boy; the best thing for you.' This, no doubt, was true enough; but there was an implied feeling that the young man would require something to do him good – that he would want the soothing of change and the gratification of his wishes, as one might speak of a convalescent or the victim of some calamity. This tone puzzled Lindores, who, though he thought it a fine thing to travel and acquire information, was as scornful of the idea of being done good to as is natural to any fine young fellow fresh from Oxford and the triumphs of the Union. But he reflected that the old school had its own way of treating things, and was satisfied. All was settled accordingly for this journey, before he came home to go through the ceremonial performances of the coming of age, the dinner of the tenantry, the speeches, the congratulations, his father's banquet, his mother's ball. It was in summer, and the country was as gay as all the entertainments that were to be given in his honour. His friend who was going to accompany him on his tour, as he had accompanied him through a considerable portion of his life – Almeric Ffarrington, a young man of the same aspirations – came up to Scotland with him for these festivities. And as they rushed through the night on the Great Northern Railway, in the intervals of two naps, they had a scrap of conversation as to these birthday glories. 'It will be a bore, but it will not last long,' said Lindores. They were both of the opinion that anything that did not produce information or promote culture was a bore.

'But is there not a revelation to be made to you, among all the other things you have to go through?' said Ffarrington. 'Have not you to be introduced to the secret chamber, and all that sort of thing? I should like to be of the party there, Lindores.'

'Ah,' said the heir, 'I had forgotten that part of it,' which, however, was not the case. 'Indeed I don't know if I am to be told. Even family dogmas are shaken nowadays.'

'Oh, I should insist on that,' said Ffarrington, lightly. 'It is not many who have the chance of paying such a visit – better than Home and all the mediums. I should insist upon that.'

'I have no reason to suppose that it has any connection with Home or the mediums,' said Lindores, slightly nettled. He was himself an *esprit fort*; but a mystery in one's own family is not like vulgar mysteries. He liked it to be respected.

'Oh, no offence,' said his companion. 'I have always thought that a railway train would be a great chance for the spirits. If one was to show suddenly in that vacant seat beside you, what a triumphant proof of their existence that would be! but they don't take advantage of their opportunities.'

Lindores could not tell what it was that made him think at that moment of a portrait he had seen in a back room at the castle of old Earl Robert, the wicked Earl. It was a bad portrait – a daub – a copy made by an amateur of the genuine portrait, which, out of horror of Earl Robert and his wicked ways, had been removed by some intermediate lord from its place in the gallery. Lindores had never seen the original – nothing but this daub of a copy. Yet somehow this face occurred to him by some strange link of association – seemed to come into his eyes as his friend spoke. A slight shiver ran over him. It was strange. He made no reply to Ffarrington, but he set himself to think how it could be that the latent presence in his mind of some anticipation of this approaching disclosure, touched into life by his friend's suggestion, should have called out of his memory a momentary realisation of the acknowledged magician of the family. This sentence is full of long words; but unfortunately long words are required in such a case. And the process was very simple when you traced it out. It was the clearest case of unconscious cerebration. He shut his eyes by way of securing privacy while he though it out; and being tired, and not at all alarmed by his unconscious cerebration, before he opened them again fell fast asleep.

And his birthday, which was the day following his arrival at Glenlyon, was a very busy day. He had not time to think of anything but the immediate occupations of the moment. Public and private greetings, congratulations, offerings, poured upon him. The Gowries were popular in this generation, which was far from being usual in the family. Lady Gowrie was kind and generous, with that kindness which comes from the heart, and which is the only kindness likely to impress the keen-sighted popular judgment; and Lord Gowrie had but little of the equivocal reputation of his predecessors. They could be splendid now and then on great occasions, though in general they were homely enough; all which the public likes. It was a bore, Lindores said; but yet the young man did not dislike the honours, and the adulation, and all the hearty speeches and good wishes. It is sweet to a young man to feel himself the centre of all hopes. It seemed very reasonable to him – very natural – that he should be so, and that the farmers should feel a pride of anticipation in thinking of his future speeches in Parliament. He promised to them with the sincerest good faith that he would not disappoint their expectations – that he would feel their interest in him an additional spur. What so natural as that interest and these expectations? He was almost solemnised by his own position – so young, looked up to by so many people – so many hopes depending on him; and yet it was quite natural. His father, however, was still more solemnised than Lindores – and this was strange, to say the least. His face grew graver and graver as the day went on, till it almost seemed as if he were dissatisfied with his son's popularity, or had some painful thought weighing on his mind. He was restless and eager for the termination of the dinner, and to get rid of his guests; and as soon as they were gone, showed an equal anxiety that his son should retire too. 'Go to bed at once, as a favour to me,' Lord Gowrie said. 'You will have a great deal of fatigue – tomorrow.' 'You need not be afraid for me, sir,' said Lindores, half affronted; but he obeyed, being tired. He had not once thought of the secret to be disclosed to him, through all that long day. But when he woke suddenly with a start in the middle of the night, to find the candles all lighted in his room, and his father standing by his bedside, Lindores instantly thought of it, and in a moment felt that the leading event – the chief incident of all that had happened – was going to take place now.

II

Lord Gowrie was very grave, and very pale. He was standing with his hand on his son's shoulder to wake him; his dress was unchanged from the moment they had parted. And the sight of this formal costume was very bewildering to the young man as he started up in his bed. But next moment he seemed to know exactly how it was, and, more than that, to have known it all his life. Explanation seemed unnecessary. At any other moment, in any other place, a man would be startled to be suddenly woke up in the middle of the night. But Lindores had no such feeling; he did not even ask a question, but sprang up, and fixed his eyes, taking in all the strange circumstances, on his father's face.

'Get up, my boy,' said Lord Gowrie, 'and dress as quickly as you can; it is full time. I have lighted your candles, and your things are all ready. You have had a good long sleep.'

Even now he did not ask, What is it? as under any other circumstances he would have done. He got up without a word, with an impulse of nervous speed and rapidity of movement such as only excitement can give, and dressed himself, his father helping him silently. It was a curious scene: the room gleaming with lights, the silence, the hurried toilet, the stillness of deep night all around. The house, though so full, and with the echoes of festivity but just over, was quiet as if there was not a creature within it – more quiet, indeed, for the stillness of vacancy is not half so impressive as the stillness of hushed and slumbering life.

Lord Gowrie went to the table when this first step was over, and poured out a glass of wine from a bottle which stood there, – a rich, golden-coloured, perfumy wine, which sent its scent through the room. 'You will want all your strength,' he said; 'take this before you go. It is the famous Imperial Tokay; there is only a little left, and you will want all your strength.'

Lindores took the wine; he had never drunk any like it before, and the peculiar fragrance remained in his mind, as perfumes so often do, with a whole world of association in them. His father's eyes dwelt upon him with a melancholy sympathy. 'You are going to encounter the greatest trial of your life,' he said; and taking the young man's hand into his, felt his pulse. 'It is quick, but it is quite firm, and you have had a good long sleep.' Then he did what it needs a great deal of pressure to induce an Englishman to do, – he kissed his son on the cheek. ' "God bless you!" ' he said, faltering. 'Come, now, everything is ready, Lindores.'

He took up in his hand a small lamp, which he had apparently brought with him, and led the way. By this time Lindores began to feel himself again, and to wake to the consciousness of all his own superiorities and enlightenments. The simple sense that he was one of the members of a family with a mystery, and that the moment of his personal encounter with this special power of darkness had come, had

been the first thrilling, overwhelming thought. But now as he
followed his father, Lindores began to remember that he
himself was not altogether like other men; that there was that
in him which would make it natural that he should throw
some light, hitherto unthought of, upon this carefully-pre-
served darkness. What secret even there might be in it – secret
of hereditary tendency, of psychic force, of mental conforma-
tion, or of some curious combination of circumstances at once
more and less potent than these – it was for him to find out.
He gathered all his forces about him, reminded himself of
modern enlightenment, and bade his nerves be steel to all
vulgar horrors. He, too, felt his own pulse as he followed his
father. To spend the night perhaps amongst the skeletons of
that old-world massacre, and to repent the sins of his ances-
tors – to be brought within the range of some optical illusion
believed in hitherto by all the generations, and which, no
doubt, was of a startling kind, or his father would not look so
serious, – any of these he felt himself quite strong to encounter. His heart and spirit rose. A young man has but
seldom the opportunity of distinguishing himself so early in
his career; and his was such a chance as occurs to very few. No
doubt it was something that would be extremely trying to the
nerves and imagination. He called up all his powers to
vanquish both. And along with this call upon himself to
exertion, there was the less serious impulse of curiosity: he
would see at last what the Secret Chamber was, where it was,
how it fitted into the labyrinths of the old house. This he tried
to put in its due place as a most interesting object. He said to
himself that he would willingly have gone a long journey at
any time to be present at such an exploration; and there is no
doubt that in other circumstances a secret chamber, with
probably some unthought-of historical interest in it, would
have been a very fascinating discovery. He tried very hard to
excite himself about this; but it was curious how fictitious he
felt the interest, and how conscious he was that it was an effort
to feel any curiosity at all on the subject. The fact was, that the
Secret Chamber was entirely secondary – thrown back, as all
accessories are, by a more pressing interest. The overpowering thought of what was in it drove aside all healthy, natural
curiosity about itself.

It must not be supposed, however, that the father and son
had a long way to go to have time for all these thoughts.

Thoughts travel at lightning speed, and there was abundant leisure for this between the time they had left the door of Lindores' room and gone down the corridor, no further off than to Lord Gowrie's own chamber, naturally one of the chief rooms of the house. Nearly opposite this, a few steps further on, was a little neglected room devoted to lumber, with which Lindores had been familiar all his life. Why this nest of old rubbish, dust, and cob-webs should be so near the bedroom of the head of the house had been a matter of surprise to many people – to the guests who saw it while exploring, and to each new servant in succession who planned an attack upon its ancient stores, scandalised by finding it to have been neglected by their predecessors. All their attempts to clear it out had, however, been resisted, nobody could tell how, or indeed thought it worth while to inquire. As for Lindores, he had been used to the place from his childhood, and therefore accepted it as the most natural thing in the world. He had been in and out a hundred times in his play. And it was here, he remembered suddenly, that he had seen the bad picture of Earl Robert which had so curiously come into his eyes on his journeying here, by a mental movement which he had identified at once as unconscious cerebration. The first feeling in his mind, as his father went to the open door of this lumber-room, was a mixture of amusement and surprise. What was he going to pick up there? some old pentacle, some amulet or scrap of antiquated magic to act as armour against the evil one? But Lord Gowrie, going on and setting down the lamp on the table, turned round upon his son with a face of agitation and pain which barred all further amusement: he grasped him by the hand, crushing it between his own. 'Now my boy, my dear son,' he said, in tones that were scarcely audible. His countenance was full of the dreary pain of a looker-on – one who has no share in the excitement of personal danger, but has the more terrible part of watching those who are in deadliest peril. He was a powerful man, and his large form shook with emotion; great beads of moisture stood upon his forehead. An old sword with a cross handle lay upon a dusty chair among other dusty and battered relics. 'Take this with you,' he said, in the same inaudible, breathless way – whether as a weapon, whether as a religious symbol, Lindores could not guess. The young man took it mechanically. His father pushed open a door which it seemed to him he had never seen before, and led him into another vaulted chamber. Here even the limited powers of speech Lord Gowrie had retained seemed to forsake him, and his voice became a mere hoarse murmur in his throat. For want of speech he pointed to another door in the further corner of this small vacant room, gave him to understand by a gesture that he was to knock there, and then went back into the lumber-room. The door into this was left open, and a faint glimmer of the lamp shed light into this little intermediate place – this debatable land between the seen and the unseen. In spite of himself, Lindores' heart began to beat. He made a breathless pause, feeling his head go round. He held the old sword in his hand, not knowing what it was. Then, summoning all his courage, he went forward and knocked at the closed door. His knock was not loud, but it seemed to echo all over the silent house. Would everybody hear and wake, and rush to see what had happened? This caprice of imagination seized upon him, ousting all the firmer thoughts, the steadfast calm of mind with which he ought to have encountered the mystery. Would they all rush in, in wild *déshabillé*, in terror and dismay, before the door opened? How long it was of opening! He touched the panel with his hand again. – This time there was no delay. In a moment, as if thrown suddenly open by some one within, the door moved. It opened just wide enough to let him enter, stopping half-way as if some one invisible held it, wide enough for welcome, but no more. Lindores stepped across the threshold with a beating heart. What was he about to see? the skeletons of the murdered victims? a ghostly charnel-house full of bloody traces of crime? He seemed to be hurried and pushed in as he made that step. What was this world of mystery into which he was plunged – what was it he saw?

He saw – nothing – except what was agreeable enough to behold, – an antiquated room hung with tapestry, very old tapestry of rude design, its colours faded into softness and harmony; between its folds here and there a panel of carved wood, rude too in design, with traces of half-worn gilding; a table covered with strange instruments, parchments, chemical tubes, and curious machinery, all with a quaintness of form and dimness of material that spoke of age. A heavy old velvet cover, thick with embroidery faded almost out of all colour, was on the table; on the wall above it, something that looked like a very old Venetian mirror, the glass so dim and crusted that it scarcely reflected at all; on the floor an old soft Persian carpet, worn into a vague blending of all colours. This was all that he thought he saw. His heart, which had been thumping so loud as almost to choke him, stopped that tremendous upward and downward motion like a steam piston; and he grew calm. Perfectly still, dim, unoccupied: yet not so dim either; there was no apparent source of light, no windows, curtains of tapestry drawn everywhere – no lamp visible, no fire – and yet a kind of strange light which made everything quite clear. He looked round, trying to smile at his terrors, trying to say to himself that it was the most curious place he had ever seen – that he must show Ffarrington some of that tapestry – that he must really bring away a panel of that carving, – when he suddenly saw that the door was shut by which he had entered – nay, more than shut, undiscernible, covered like all the rest of the walls by that strange tapestry. At this his heart began to beat again in spite of him. He looked round once more, and woke up to more vivid being with a sudden start. Had his eyes been incapable of vision on his first entrance? Unoccupied? Who was that in the great chair?

It seemed to Lindores that he had seen neither the chair nor the man when he came in. There they were, however, solid and unmistakable; the chair carved like the panels, the man seated in front of the table. He looked at Lindores with a calm and open gaze, inspecting him. The young man's heart seemed in his throat fluttering like a bird, but he was brave, and his mind made one final effort to break this spell. He tried to speak, labouring with a voice that would not sound, and with lips too parched to form a word. 'I see how it is,' was what he wanted to say. It was Earl Robert's face that was looking at him; and startled as he was, he dragged forth his philosophy to support him. What could it be but optical delusions, unconscious cerebration, occult seizure by the impressed and struggling mind of this one countenance? But he could not hear himself speak any word as he stood convulsed, struggling with dry lips and choking voice.

The Appearance smiled, as if knowing his thoughts – not unkindly, not malignly – with a certain amusement mingled with scorn. Then he spoke, and the sound seemed to breathe through the room not like any voice that Lindores had ever heard, a kind of utterance of the place, like the rustle of the air or the ripple of the sea. 'You will learn better tonight: this is no phantom of your brain; it is I.'

'In God's name,' cried the young man in his soul; he did not know whether the words ever got into the air or not, if there was any air; – 'in God's name, who are you?'

The figure rose as if coming to him to reply; and Lindores, overcome by the apparent approach, struggled into utterance. A cry came from him – he heard it this time – and even in his extremity felt a pang the more to hear the terror in his own voice. But he did not flinch, he stood desperate, all his strength concentrated in the act; he neither turned nor recoiled. Vaguely gleaming through his mind came the thought that to be thus brought in contact with the unseen was the experiment to be most desired on earth, the final settlement of a hundred questions; but his faculties were not sufficiently under command to entertain it. He only stood firm, that was all.

And the figure did not approach him; after a moment it subsided back again into the chair – subsided, for no sound, not the faintest, accompanied its movements. It was the form of a man of middle age, the hair white, but the beard only crisped with grey, the features those of the picture – a familiar face, more or less like all the Randolphs, but with an air of domination and power altogether unlike that of the race. He was dressed in a long robe of dark colour, embroidered with strange lines and angles. There was nothing repellent or terrible in his air – nothing except the noiselessness, the calm, the absolute stillness, which was as much in the place as in him, to keep up the involuntary trembling of the beholder. His expression was full of dignity and thoughtfulness, and not malignant or unkind. He might have been the kindly patriarch of the house, watching over its fortunes in a seclusion that he had chosen. The pulses that had been beating in Lindores were stilled. What was his panic for? a gleam even of self-ridicule took possession of him, to be standing there like an absurd hero of antiquated romance with the rusty, dusty sword – good for nothing, surely not adapted for use against this noble old magician – in his hand—

'You are right,' said the voice, once more answering his thoughts; 'what could you do with that sword against me, young Lindores? Put it by. Why should my children meet me like an enemy? You are my flesh and blood. Give me your hand.'

A shiver ran through the young man's frame. The hand that was held out to him was large and shapely and white, with a straight line across the palm – a family token upon which the Randolphs prided themselves – a friendly hand; and the face smiled upon him, fixing him with those calm, profound, blue eyes. 'Come,' said the voice. The word seemed to fill the place, melting upon him from every corner, whispering round him with softest persuasion. He was lulled and calmed in spite of himself. Spirit or no spirit, why should not he accept this proferred courtesy? What harm could come of it? The chief thing that retained him was the dragging of the old sword, heavy and useless, which he held mechanically, but which some internal feeling – he could not tell what – prevented him from putting down. Superstition, was it?

'Yes, that is superstition,' said his ancestor, serenely; 'put it down and come.'

'You know my thoughts,' said Lindores; 'I did not speak.'

'Your mind spoke, and spoke justly. Put down that emblem of brute force and superstition together. Here it is the intelligence that is supreme. Come.'

Lindores stood doubtful. He was calm; the power of thought was restored to him. If this benevolent venerable patriarch was all he seemed, why his father's terror? why the secrecy in which his being was involved? His own mind, though calm, did not seem to act in the usual way. Thoughts seemed to be driven across it as by a wind. One of these came to him suddenly now—

> How there looked him in the face,
> An angel beautiful and bright,
> And how he knew it was a fiend.

The words were not ended, when Earl Robert replied suddenly with impatience in his voice, 'Fiends are of the fancy of men; like angels and other follies. I am your father. You know me; and you are mine, Lindores. I have power beyond what you can understand; but I want flesh and blood to reign and to enjoy. Come, Lindores!'

He put out his other hand. The action, the look, were those of kindness, almost of longing, and the face was familiar, the

voice was that of the race. Supernatural! was it supernatural
that this man should live here shut up for ages? and why? and
how? Was there any explanation of it? The young man's brain
began to reel. He could not tell which was real – the life he had
left half an hour ago, or this. He tried to look round him, but
could not; his eyes were caught by those other kindred eyes,
which seemed to dilate and deepen as he looked at them, and
drew him with a strange compulsion. He felt himself yielding,
swaying towards the strange being who thus invited him.
What might happen if he yielded? And he could not turn
away, he could not tear himself from the fascination of those
eyes. With a sudden strange impulse which was half despair
and half a bewildering half-conscious desire to try one potency against another, he thrust forward the cross of the old
sword between him and those appealing hands. 'In the name
of God!' he said.

Lindores never could tell whether it was that he himself grew
faint, and that the dimness of swooning came into his eyes after
this violence and strain of emotion, or if it was his spell that
worked. But there was an instantaneous change. Everything
swam around him for the moment, a giddiness and blindness
seized him, and he saw nothing but the vague outlines of the
room, empty as when he entered it. But gradually his consciousness came back, and he found himself standing on the
same spot as before, clutching the old sword, and gradually, as
though in a dream, recognised the same figure emerging out of
the mist which – was it solely in his own eyes? – had enveloped
everything. But it was no longer in the same attitude. The
hands which had been stretched out to him were busy now with
some of the strange instruments on the table, moving about,
now in the action of writing, now as if managing the keys of a
telegraph. Lindores felt that his brain was all atwist and set
wrong; but he was still a human being of his century. He
thought of the telegraph with a keen thrill of curiosity in the
midst of his reviving sensations. What communication was this
which was going on before his eyes? The magician worked on.
He had his face turned towards his victim, but his hands moved
with unceasing activity. And Lindores, as he grew accustomed
to the position, began to weary – to feel like a neglected suitor
waiting for an audience. To be wound up to such a strain of
feeling, then left to wait, was intolerable; impatience seized
upon him. What circumstances can exist, however horrible, in

which a human being will not feel impatience? He made a great many efforts to speak before he could succeed. It seemed to him that his body felt more fear than he did – that his muscles were contracted, his throat parched, his tongue refusing its office, although his mind was unaffected and undismayed. At last he found an utterance in spite of all resistance of his flesh and blood.

'Who are you?' he said hoarsely. 'You that live here and oppress this house?'

The vision raised its eyes full upon him, with again that strange shadow of a smile, mocking yet not unkind. 'Do you remember me,' he said, 'on your journey here?'

'That was – a delusion.' The young man gasped for breath.

'More like that you are a delusion. You have lasted but one-and-twenty years, and I – for centuries.'

'How? For centuries – and why? Answer me – are you man or demon?' cried Lindores, tearing the words as he felt out of his own throat. 'Are you living or dead?'

The magician looked at him with the same intense gaze as before. 'Be on my side, and you shall know everything, Lindores. I want one of my own race. Others I could have in plenty; but I want *you*. A Randolph, a Randolph! and *you*. Dead! do I seem dead? You shall have everything – more than dreams can give – if you will be on my side.'

Can he give what he has not? was the thought that ran through the mind of Lindores. But he could not speak it. Something that choked and stifled him was in his throat.

'Can I give what I have not? I have everything – power, the one thing worth having; and you shall have more than power, for you are young – my son! Lindores!'

To argue was natural, and gave the young man strength. 'Is this life,' he said, 'here? What is all your power worth – here? To sit for ages, and make a race unhappy?'

A momentary convulsion came across the still face. 'You scorn me,' he cried, with an appearance of emotion, 'because you do not understand how I move the world. Power! 'Tis more than fancy can grasp. And you shall have it!' said the wizard, with what looked like a show of enthusiasm. He seemed to come nearer, to grow larger. He put forth his hand again, this time so close that it seemed impossible to escape. And a crowd of wishes seemed to rush upon the mind of Lindores. What harm to try if this might be true? To try what it meant – perhaps nothing, delusions, vain show, and then there could be no harm; or perhaps there was knowledge to be had, which was power. Try, try, try! the air buzzed about him. The room seemed full of voices urging him. His bodily frame rose into a tremendous whirl of excitement, his veins seemed to swell to bursting, his lips seemed to force a yes, in spite of him, quivering as they came apart. The hiss of the 's' seemed in his ears. He changed it into the name which was a spell too, and cried, 'Help me, God!' not knowing why.

Then there came another pause – he felt as if he had been dropped from something that had held him, and had fallen, and was faint. The excitement had been more than he could bear. Once more everything swam around him, and he did not know where he was. Had he escaped altogether? was the first waking wonder of consciousness in his mind. But when he could think and see again, he was still in the same spot, surrounded by the old curtains and the carved panels – but alone. He felt, too, that he was able to move, but the strangest dual consciousness was in him throughout all the rest of his trial. His body felt to him as a frightened horse feels to a traveller at night – a thing separate from him, more frightened than he was – starting aside at every step, seeing more than its master. His limbs shook with fear and weakness, almost refusing to obey the action of his will, trembling under him with jerks aside when he compelled himself to move. The hair stood upright on his head – every finger trembled as with palsy – his lips, his eyelids, quivered with nervous agitation. But his mind was strong, stimulated to a desperate calm. He dragged himself round the room, he crossed the very spot where the magician had been – all was vacant, silent, clear. Had he vanquished the enemy? This thought came into his mind with an involuntary triumph. The old strain of feeling came back. Such efforts might be produced, perhaps, only by imagination, by excitement, by delusion—

Lindores looked up, by a sudden attraction he could not tell what: and the blood suddenly froze in his veins that had been so boiling and fermenting. Some one was looking at him from the old mirror on the wall. A face not human and life-like, like that of the inhabitant of this place, but ghostly and terrible, like one of the dead; and while he looked, a crowd of other faces came behind, all looking at him, some mournfully, some with a menace in their terrible eyes. The mirror did not change, but within its small dim space seemed to contain an innumerable company, crowded above and below, all with one gaze at him. His lips dropped apart with a gasp of horror. More and more and more! He was standing close by the table when this crowd came. Then all at once there was laid upon him a cold hand. He turned; close to his side, brushing him with his robe, holding him fast by the arm, sat Earl Robert in his great chair. A shriek came from the young man's lips. He seemed to hear it echoing away into unfathomable distance. The cold touch penetrated to his very soul.

'Do you try spells upon me, Lindores? That is a tool of the past. You shall have something better to work with. And are you so sure of whom you call upon? If there is such a one, why should He help you who never called on Him before?'

Lindores could not tell if these words were spoken; it was a communication rapid as the thoughts in the mind. And he felt as if something answered that was not all himself. He seemed to stand passive and hear the argument. 'Does God reckon with a man in trouble, whether he has ever called to Him before? I call now' (now he felt it was himself that said): 'go, evil spirit! – go, dead and cursed! – go, in the name of God!'

He felt himself flung violently against the wall. A faint laugh, stifled in the throat, and followed by a groan, rolled round the room; the old curtains seemed to open here and there, and flutter, as if with comings and goings. Lindores leaned with his back against the wall, and all his senses restored to him. He felt blood trickle down his neck; and in this contact once more with the physical, his body, in its madness of fright, grew manageable. For the first time he felt wholly master of himself. Though the magician was standing in his place, a great, majestic, appalling figure, he did not shrink. 'Liar!' he cried, in a voice that rang and echoed as in natural air – 'clinging to miserable life like a worm – like a reptile; promising all things, having nothing, but this den, unvisited by the light of day. Is this your power – your superiority to men who die? is it for this that you oppress a race, and make a house unhappy? I vow, in God's name, your reign is over! You and your secret shall last no more.'

There was no reply. But Lindores felt his terrible ancestor's eyes getting once more that mesmeric mastery over him which had already almost overcome his powers. He must withdraw his own, or perish. He had a human horror of turning his back upon that watchful adversary: to face him seemed the only safety; but to face him was to be conquered. Slowly, with a pang indescribable, he tore himself from that gaze: it seemed to drag his eyes out of their sockets, his heart out of his bosom. Resolutely, with the daring of desperation, he turned round to the spot where he entered – the spot where no door was, – hearing already in anticipation the step after him – feeling the grip that would crush and smother his exhausted life – but too desperate to care.

III

How wonderful is the blue dawning of the new day before the sun! not rosy-fingered, like that Aurora of the Greeks who comes later with all her wealth; but still, dreamy, wonderful, stealing out of the unseen, abashed by the solemnity of the new birth. When anxious watchers see that first brightness come stealing upon the waiting skies, what mingled relief and renewal of misery is in it! another long day to toil through – yet another sad night over! Lord Gowrie sat among the dust and cobwebs, his lamp flaring idly into the blue morning. He had heard his son's human voice, though nothing more; and he expected to have him brought out by invisible hands, as had happened to himself, and left lying in long deathly swoon outside that mystic door. This was how it had happened to heir after heir, as told from father to son, one after another, as the secret came down. One or two bearers of the name Lindores had never recovered; most of them had been saddened and subdued for life. He remembered sadly the freshness of existence which had never come back to himself; the hopes that had never blossomed again; the assurance with which never more he had been able to go about the world. And now his son would be as himself – the glory gone out of his living – his ambitions, his aspirations wrecked. He had not been endowed as his boy was – he had been a plain, honest man, and nothing more; but experience and life had given him wisdom enough to smile by times at the coquetries of mind in which Lindores indulged. Were they all over now, those freaks of young intelligence, those enthusiasms of the soul? The curse of the house had come upon him – the magnetism of that strange presence, ever living, ever watchful, present in all the family history. His heart was sore for his son; and yet along with this there was a certain consolation to him in having henceforward a partner in the secret – some one to whom he could talk of it as he had not been able to talk since his own father died. Almost all the mental struggles which Gowrie had known had been connected with this mystery; and he had been obliged to hide them in his bosom – to conceal them even when they rent him in two. Now he had a partner in his trouble. This was what he was thinking as he sat through the night. How slowly the moments passed! He was not aware of the daylight coming in. After a while even thought got suspended in listening. Was not the time nearly over? He rose and began to pace about the encumbered space, which was but a step or two in extent. There was an old cupboard in the wall, in which there were restoratives – pungent essences and cordials, and fresh water which he had himself brought – everything was ready; presently the ghastly body of his boy, half dead, would be thrust forth into his care.

But this was not how it happened. While he waited, so intent that his whole frame seemed to be capable of hearing, he heard the closing of the door, boldly shut with a sound that rose in muffled echoes through the house and Lindores himself appeared, ghastly indeed as a dead man, but walking upright and firmly, the lines of his face drawn, and his eyes staring. Lord Gowrie uttered a cry. He was more alarmed by this unexpected return than by the helpless prostration of the swoon which he had expected. He recoiled from his son as if he too had been a spirit. 'Lindores!' he cried; was it Lindores, or some one else in his place? The boy seemed as if he did not see him. He went straight forward to where the water stood on the dusty table, and took a great draught, then turned to the door. 'Lindores!' said his father, in miserable anxiety; 'don't you know me?' Even then the young man only half looked at him, and put out a hand almost as cold as the hand that had clutched himself in the Secret Chamber; a faint smile came upon his face. 'Don't stay here,' he whispered; 'come! come!'

Lord Gowrie drew his son's arm within his own, and felt the thrill through and through him of nerves strained beyond mortal strength. He could scarcely keep up with him as he stalked along the corridor to his room, stumbling as if he could not see, yet swift as an arrow. When they reached his room he turned and closed and locked the door, then laughed as he staggered to the bed. 'That will not keep him out, will it?' he said.

'Lindores,' said his father, 'I expected to find you unconscious. I am almost more frightened to find you like this. I need not ask if you have seen him—'

'Oh, I have seen him. The old liar! Father, promise to expose him, to turn him out – promise to clear out that accursed old nest! It is our own fault. Why have we left such a place shut out from the eye of day? Isn't there something in the Bible about those who do evil hating the light?'

'Lindores! you don't often quote the Bible.'

'No, I suppose not; but there is more truth in – many things than we thought.'

'Lie down,' said the anxious father. 'Take some of this wine – try to sleep.'

'Take it away; give me no more of that devil's drink. Talk to me – that's better. Did you go through it all the same, poor papa? – and hold me fast. You are warm – you are honest!' he cried. He put forth his hands over his father's, warming them with the contact. He put his cheek like a child against his father's arm. He gave a faint laugh, with the tears in his eyes. 'Warm and honest,' he repeated. 'Kind flesh and blood! and did you go through it all the same?'

'My boy!' cried the father, feeling his heart glow and swell over the son who had been parted from him for years by that development of young manhood and ripening intellect which so often severs and loosens the ties of home. Lord Gowrie had felt that Lindores half despised his simple mind and duller imagination; but this childlike clinging overcame him, and tears stood in his eyes. 'I fainted, I suppose. I never knew how it ended. They made what they liked of me. But you, my brave boy, you came out of your own will.'

Lindores shivered. 'I fled!' he said. 'No honour in that. I had not courage to face him longer. I will tell you by-and-by. But I want to know about you.'

What an ease it was to the father to speak! For years and years this had been shut up in his breast. It had made him lonely in the midst of his friends.

'Thank God,' he said, 'that I can speak to you, Lindores. Often and often I have been tempted to tell your mother. But why should I make her miserable? She knows there is something; she knows when I see him, but she knows no more.'

'When you see him?' Lindores raised himself, with a return of his first ghastly look, in his bed. Then he raised his clenched fist wildly, and shook it in the air. 'Vile devil, coward, deceiver!'

'Oh hush, hush, hush, Lindores! God help us! what troubles you may bring!'

'And God help me, whatever troubles I bring,' said the young man. 'I defy him, father. An accursed being like that must be less, not more powerful, than we are – with God to back us. Only stand by me: stand by me—'

'Hush, Lindores! You don't feel it yet – never to get out of hearing of him all your life! He will make you pay for it – if not now, after; when you remember he is there; whatever happens, knowing everything! But I hope it will not be so bad with you as with me, my poor boy. God help you indeed if it is, for you have more imagination and more mind. I am able to forget him sometimes when I am occupied – when in the hunting-field, going across country. But you are not a hunting man, my poor boy,' said Lord Gowrie, with a curious mixture of a regret, which was less serious than the other. Then he lowered his voice. 'Lindores, this is what has happened to me since the moment I gave him my hand.'

'I did not give him my hand.'

'You did not give him your hand? God bless you, my boy! You stood out?' he cried, with tears again rushing to his eyes; 'and they say – they say – but I don't know if there is any truth in it.' Lord Gowrie got up from his son's side, and walked up and down with excited steps. 'If there should be truth in it! Many people think the whole thing is a fancy. If there should be truth in it, Lindores!'

'In what, father?'

'They say, if he is once resisted his power is broken – once refused. *You* could stand against him – you! Forgive me, my boy, as I hope God will forgive me, to have thought so little of His best gifts,' cried Lord Gowrie, coming back with wet eyes; and stooping, he kissed his son's hand. 'I thought you would be more shaken by being more mind than body,' he said, humbly. 'I thought if I could but have saved you from the trial; and *you* are the conqueror!'

'Am I the conqueror? I think all my bones are broken,

father – out of their sockets,' said the young man, in a low
voice. 'I think I shall go to sleep.'

'Yes, rest, my boy. It is the best thing for you,' said the
father, though with a pang of momentary disappointment.
Lindores fell back upon the pillow. He was so pale that there
were moments when the anxious watcher thought him not
sleeping but dead. He put his hand out feebly, and grasped his
father's hand. 'Warm – honest,' he said, with a feeble smile
about his lips, and fell asleep.

The daylight was full in the room, breaking through
shutters and curtains and mocking at the lamp that still flared
on the table. It seemed an emblem of the disorders, mental
and material, of this strange night; and, as such, it affected the
plain imagination of Lord Gowrie, who would have fain got
up to extinguish it, and whose mind returned again and again,
in spite of him, to this symptom of disturbance. By-and-by,
when Lindores' grasp relaxed, and he got his hand free, he got
up from his son's bedside, and put out the lamp, putting it
carefully out of the way. With equal care he put away the wine
from the table, and gave the room its ordinary aspect, softly
opening a window to let in the fresh air of the morning. The
park lay fresh in the early sunshine, still, except for the
twittering of the birds, refreshed with dews, and shining in
that soft radiance of the morning which is over before mortal
cares are stirring. Never, perhaps, had Gowrie looked out
upon the beautiful world around his house without a thought
of the weird existence which was going on so near to him,
which had gone on for centuries, shut up out of sight of the
sunshine. The Secret Chamber had been present with him
since ever he saw it. He had never been able to get free of the
spell of it. He had felt himself watched, surrounded, spied
upon, day after day, since he was of the age of Lindores, and
that was thirty years ago. He turned it all over in his mind, as
he stood there and his son slept. It had been on his lips to tell
it all to his boy, who had now come to inherit the enlightenment of his race. And it was a disappointment to him to
have it all forced back again, and silence imposed upon him
once more. Would he care to hear it when he woke? would he
not rather, as Lord Gowrie remembered to have done himself, thrust the thought as far as he could away from him, and
endeavour to forget for the moment – until the time came
when he would not be permitted to forget? He had been like

that himself, he recollected now. He had not wished to hear his own father's tale. 'I remember,' he said to himself; 'I remember' – turning over everything in his mind – if Lindores might only be willing to hear the story when he woke! But then he himself had not been willing when he was Lindores, and he could understand his son, and could not blame him; but it would be a disappointment. He was thinking this when he heard Lindores' voice calling him. He went back hastily to his bedside. It was strange to see him in his evening dress with his worn face, in the fresh light of the morning, which poured in at every crevice. 'Does my mother know?' said Lindores; 'what will she think?'

'She knows something; she knows you have some trial to go through. Most likely she will be praying for us both; that's the way of women,' said Lord Gowrie, with the tremulous tenderness which comes into a man's voice sometimes when he speaks of a good wife. 'I'll go and ease her mind, and tell her all is well over—'

'Not yet. Tell me first,' said the young man, putting his hand upon his father's arm.

What an ease it was! 'I was not so good to my father,' he thought to himself, with sudden penitence for the long-past, long-forgotten fault, which, indeed, he had never realised as a fault before. And then he told his son what had been the story of his life – how he had scarcely ever sat alone without feeling, from some corner of the room, from behind some curtain, those eyes upon him; and how, in the difficulties of his life, that secret inhabitant of the house had been present, sitting by him and advising him. 'Whenever there has been anything to do: when there has been a question between two ways, all in a moment I have seen him by me: I feel when he is coming. It does not matter where I am – here or anywhere – as soon as ever there is a question of family business; and always he persuades me to the wrong way, Lindores. Sometimes I yield to him, how can I help it? He makes everything so clear; he makes wrong seem right. If I have done unjust things in my day—'

'You have not, father.'

'I have: there were these Highland people I turned out. I did not mean to do it, Lindores; but he showed me that it would be better for the family. And my poor sister that married Tweedside and was wretched all her life. It was his doing, that marriage; he said she would be rich, and so she was, poor thing, poor thing! and died of it. And old Macalister's lease – Lindores, Lindores! when there is any business it makes my heart sick. I know he will come, and advise wrong, and tell me – something I will repent after.'

'The thing to do is to decide beforehand, that, good or bad, you will not take his advice.'

Lord Gowrie shivered. 'I am not strong like you, or clever; I cannot resist. Sometimes I repent in time and don't do it; and then! But for your mother and you children, there is many a day I would not have given a farthing for my life.'

'Father,' said Lindores, springing from his bed, 'two of us together can do many things. Give me your word to clear out this cursed den of darkness this very day.'

'Lindores, hush, hush, for the sake of heaven!'

'I will not, for the sake of heaven! Throw it open – let everybody who likes see it – make an end of the secret – pull down everything, curtains, walls. What do you say? – sprinkle holy water? Are you laughing at me?'

'I did not speak,' said Earl Gowrie, growing very pale, and grasping his son's arm with both his hands. 'Hush, boy; do you think he does not hear?'

And then there was a low laugh close to them – so close that both shrank; a laugh no louder than a breath.

'Did you laugh – father?'

'No, Lindores.' Lord Gowrie had his eyes fixed. He was as pale as the dead. He held his son tight for a moment; then his gaze and his grasp relaxed, and he fell back feebly in a chair.

'You see!' he said; 'whatever we do it will be the same; we are under his power.'

And then there ensued the blank pause with which baffled men confront a hopeless situation. But at that moment the first faint stirrings of the house – a window being opened, a bar undone, a movement of feet, and subdued voices – became audible in the stillness of the morning. Lord Gowrie roused himself at once. 'We must not be found like this,' he said; 'we must not show how we have spent the night. It is over, thank God! and oh, my boy, forgive me! I am thankful there are two of us to bear it; it makes the burden lighter – though I ask your pardon humbly for saying so. I would have saved you if I could, Lindores.'

'I don't wish to have been saved; but *I* will not bear it. I will end it,' the young man said, with an oath out of which his emotion took all profanity. His father said, 'Hush, hush.' With a look of terror and pain, he left him; and yet there was a thrill of tender pride in his mind. How brave the boy was! even after he had been *there*. Could it be that this would all come to nothing, as every other attempt to resist had done before?

'I suppose you know all about it now, Lindores,' said his friend Ffarrington, after breakfast; 'luckily for us who are going over the house. What a glorious old place it is!'

'I don't think that Lindores enjoys the glorious old place today,' said another of the guests under his breath. 'How pale he is! He doesn't look as if he had slept.'

'I will take you over every nook where I have ever been,' said Lindores. He looked at his father with almost command in his eyes. 'Come with me, all of you. We shall have no more secrets here.'

'Are you mad?' said his father in his ear.

'Never mind,' cried the young man. 'Oh, trust me; I will do it with judgment. Is everybody ready?' There was an excitement about him that half frightened, half roused the party. They all rose, eager, yet doubtful. His mother came to him and took his arm.

'Lindores! you will do nothing to vex your father; don't make him unhappy. I don't know your secrets, you two; but look, he has enough to bear.'

'I want you to know our secrets, mother. Why should we have secrets from you?'

'Why, indeed?' she said, with tears in her eyes. 'But, Lindores, my dearest boy, don't make it worse for *him*.'

'I give you my word, I will be wary,' he said; and she left him to go to his father, who followed the party, with an anxious look upon his face.

'Are you coming, too?' he asked.

'I? No; I will not go: but trust him – trust the boy, John.'

'He can do nothing; he will not be able to do anything,' he said.

And thus the guests set out on their round – the son in advance, excited and tremulous, the father anxious and watchful behind. They began in the usual way, with the old state-rooms and picture-gallery; and in a short time the party had half forgotten that there was anything unusual in the inspection. When, however, they were half-way down the gallery, Lindores stopped short with an air of wonder. 'You have had it put back then?' he said. He was standing in front of the vacant space where Earl Robert's portrait ought to have been. 'What is it?' they all cried, crowding upon him, ready for any marvel. But as there was nothing to be seen, the strangers smiled among themselves. 'Yes, to be sure, there is nothing so suggestive as a vacant place,' said a lady who was of the party. 'Whose portrait ought to be there, Lord Lindores?'

He looked at his father, who made a slight assenting gesture, then shook his head drearily.

'Who put it there?' Lindores said, in a whisper.

'It is not there; but you and I see it,' said Lord Gowrie, with a sigh.

Then the strangers perceived that something had moved the father and the son, and, notwithstanding their eager curiosity, obeyed the dictates of politeness, and dispersed into groups looking at the other pictures. Lindores set his teeth and clenched his hands. Fury was growing upon him – not the awe that filled his father's mind. 'We will leave the rest of this to another time,' he cried, turning to the others, almost fiercely. 'Come, I will show you something more striking now.' He made no further pretence of going systematically over the house. He turned and went straight upstairs, and along the corridor. 'Are we going over the bedrooms?' some one said. Lindores led the way straight to the old lumber-room, a strange place for such a gay party. The ladies drew their dresses about them. There was not room for half of them. Those who could get in began to handle the strange things that lay about, touching them with dainty fingers, exclaiming how dusty they were. The window was half blocked up by old armour and rusty weapons; but this did not hinder the full summer daylight from penetrating in a flood of light. Lindores went in with fiery determination on his face. He went straight to the wall, as if he would go through, then paused with a blank gaze. 'Where is the door?' he said.

'You are forgetting yourself,' said Lord Gowrie, speaking over the heads of the others. 'Lindores! you know very well there never was any door there; the wall is very thick; you can see by the depth of the window. There is no door there.'

The young man felt it over with his hand. The wall was smooth, and covered with the dust of ages. With a groan he turned away. At this moment a suppressed laugh, low, yet distinct, sounded close by him. 'You laughed?' he said, fiercely, to Ffarrington, striking his hand upon his shoulder.

'I – laughed! Nothing was farther from my thoughts,' said his friend, who was curiously examining something that lay upon an old carved chair. 'Look here! what a wonderful sword, cross-hilted! Is it an Andrea? What's the matter, Lindores?'

Lindores had seized it from his hands; he dashed it against the wall with a suppressed oath. The two or three people in the room stood aghast.

'Lindores!' his father said, in a tone of warning. The young man dropped the useless weapon with a groan. 'Then God help us!' he said; 'but I will find another way.'

'There is a very interesting room close by,' said Lord Gowrie, hastily – 'this way! Lindores has been put out by – some changes that have been made without his knowledge,' he said, calmly. 'You must not mind him. He is disappointed. He is perhaps too much accustomed to have his own way.'

But Lord Gowrie knew that no one believed him. He took them to the adjoining room, and told them some easy story of an apparition that was supposed to haunt it. 'Have you ever seen it?' the guests said, pretending interest. 'Not I; but we don't mind ghosts in this house,' he answered, with a smile. And then they resumed their round of the old noble mystic house.

I cannot tell the reader what young Lindores has done to carry out his pledged word and redeem his family. It may not be known, perhaps, for another generation, and it will not be for me to write that concluding chapter: but when, in the ripeness of time, it can be narrated, no one will say that the mystery of Gowrie Castle has been a vulgar horror, though there are some who are disposed to think so now.

Earthbound

I

THERE WAS BUT a small party for Christmas at Daintrey. The
family were in mourning, which meant more than it usually
means, and the whole life of the place was subdued. Nevertheless, the brothers and sisters were young, and were beginning to rise above the impression of the grief which had come
upon them. The gloom had lightened a little; they began to
forget the details of death, and regard the image of their
brother in an aspect more familiar. It was not long since the
news had come, and yet already this change had taken place,
as was inevitable. The father and mother were less easily
cheered; but life must go on even though death interrupts.
The girls and boys could not be made to sit like mutes around
a grave. They had to rise up again, and go on with their
individual existence. Lady Beresford, who was a wise mother,
felt and acknowledged this, though her heart was still bleeding. Christmas was coming; and though there could be no
Christmas festivities in the ordinary sense of the word, one or
two old friends and connections were invited. Sir Robert, for
his part, was opposed to the appearance of strangers. He was
never very fond of visitors. 'What do you want with people
here?' he said, with a kind of growl, in which he disguised his
grief. 'Surely once in a way the girls might get through
Christmas without visitors. Christmas! the very idea of these
horrible merry Christmases that we shall have to go through
makes me ill!'

'I should do without them only too gladly, Robert: but the
girls and the boys are too young to be cooped up. Grief is so
monotonous, and they are so young. It is not that they love
him the less; but they must live – for that matter, we must all
go on living,' she said, keeping with an effort the tears in her
eyes. A mother who cannot give herself over to her sorrow,

who must work through all her little daily round of duties all
the same, and think of the girls' bonnets, and the boots and
flannels of the boys at school, and only now and then in a
spare moment can shut her door or turn her face to the wall
and weep a little over her dead, the tears that have been
gathering slowly while she has smiled and talked and kept
everything going through the long day – has a hard task when
her troubles come; but Lady Beresford bore her burden as
sweetly as a woman could, holding up as long as was possible,
then stopping to have her cry out, and rising and going on
again. Sir Robert became morose with his grief; but she had
no time for self-indulgence. And naturally she had her way,
and the few were invited whom it had seemed to her good to
invite. One of them was Edmund Coventry, who had been a
ward of Sir Robert, and now in his manhood calculated upon
being a member of the Daintrey party at all those periods
which are specially dedicated to home. He was a young man of
excellent character and very fair fortune; and, if the truth
must be told, the heads of the house at Daintrey had concluded that he would be a very convenient match for Maud,
who was the second girl. Perhaps it would be better to say that
one of the heads of the house had already perceived and
accepted this view. A matchmaking mother is a thing that is
supposed on English soil to be extremely objectionable; and
yet if she does not think of the welfare of her girls, who is to do
it? The French mother considers it her first duty. Lady
Beresford was a high-minded Englishwoman, and not a
scheming mamma; but she could not shut her eyes to the
fact that Edmund Coventry was exactly suited to Maud. And
so, among the few who came to spend a very quiet Christmas
at Daintrey, and 'cheer a sad house,' which was what she said
in her invitations, Edmund was one of the first of whom she
thought.

'Poor boy!' she said, 'he has always come here. He has no
other place where he will care to go. Of course he will know
that it will not be lively. But he is a good boy. I do not think he
will mind.'

'I am sure, mamma, he will not mind,' said Susan, who was
the eldest. Susan was going to make a by no means brilliant
marriage. She was to marry a young man who was in the
diplomatic service, but had no money, and was scarcely the
sort of man to be a diplomat; so that the prizes of that

profession seemed improbable to him. And she thought it very desirable that Maud and Edmund Coventry should see a good deal of each other. 'He will be glad to be with us in our trouble,' she said; 'he was always fond of Willie.' Thus the invitation was given half in love and tender certainty of sympathy, yet half with a certain calculation too.

The other guests were of a very quiet kind – a brother of Sir Robert's, a lonely bachelor; a widowed sister of Lady Beresford's with her little boy and girl; the former clergyman of the parish, who had been Willie's tutor once upon a time; a nephew who was an orphan, and had no home to spend his Christmas in; and Edmund. 'He will be the only little bit of liveliness. He will help to cheer us up,' Susan said. Her attaché was to come too, but only for a few days. He was one of those to whom social duties were important, and he had a great many visits to pay. But for this mourning they would have been married before now.

Edmund Coventry was a young man who was very well off, and very greatly esteemed. He was twenty-seven – no longer a boy. He had a very nice estate, and a house in town, and no relations to speak of. He was very well-looking, without being handsome, which is perhaps the sort of compromise with nature which is most approved in England. There are a great many people who do not care for unusually handsome men. Beauty is an extravagance, they feel, in the male portion of the world. But Edmund's good looks did not go the length of beauty. He was not a tall, muscular, well-developed hero, but slight, and not more than of middle stature. With all he was an ingratiating, lovable young man, very gentle in manners, very tender in his friendships; no doubt he would make an excellent husband. There was no need to explain to him the position of affairs in the house. He knew all about it, and he sympathised with them in every point. 'Mamma hesitated to ask you,' said Maud, 'because we were to be so quiet.' 'Could I wish to be anything but quiet?' he said, with a tender half-reproach. 'Do you think, after all the happy times here, that I have no feeling?' But, indeed, no one had thought that, as Maud made haste to say.

The carols were sung, but with tears in them. The house was dressed as usual with holly and all the decorations of the time; and there was at least a great deal of conversation which lightened the gloom and silence of the previous period. Even

Sir Robert was glad to talk to Mr Lightfoot, who had been the rector in former times. On Christmas night the attempt at games was somewhat doleful as it will be, alas! this Christmas in many a sorrowing and many an anxious house; but the talk and the little bustle of renewed movement did everybody good. The commonplace ghost-stories which are among the ordinary foolishness of Christmas did not suit with the more serious tone in which their thoughts flowed; but there was some talk among the older people about those sensations and presentiments that seem sometimes to convey a kind of prophecy, only understood after the event, of sorrow on the way; and the young ones amused themselves after a sort with discussions of those new-fangled fancies which have replaced that old favourite lore. They talked about what is called spiritualism, and of many things, both in that fantastic faith and in the older ghostly traditions, which we are all half glad to think cannot be explained. The older people, indeed, unhesitatingly rejected all mediums and supernatural operators of every kind as impostors; but even on this point various members of the party had things to tell which they did not know how to explain. 'Is not there some tradition of a ghost about Daintrey?' Mr Lightfoot, the old rector, said, as they all sat in a wide circle round the great glowing fire just before the moment should arrive for bed-candles and general good-nights. There was not very much light in the room, but, large as it was, it was all ruddy and brilliant with the blaze of the great cheerful fire.

'Nothing of the sort,' said Sir Robert emphatically. It was he who was most strong as to the whole thing being an imposition, and who 'did not believe a word' of the stories he was told.

'I believe there is something – very vague,' said Lady Beresford. But there was a meaning look exchanged between them, and the talk suddenly came to an end.

And by and by the ladies went all flocking out of the room, carrying their lights, like a procession of the wise virgins in the parable. But their black dresses made that procession a sad one, though the soft bloom of the young faces came out with even more effect when the light found nothing else to dwell upon. The young men found a little relief from the gravity of the conversation in the smoking-room, where Mr Beresford the elder, the uncle of the party, discoursed upon

town and its charms, and congratulated himself that he was
not like his brother Robert, the head of the family, and
compelled to pass his winters in the middle of those damp
acres of park. 'It would kill me in a year,' Mr Beresford said.
On the whole they were all glad that the worst was over, and
Christmas got safely done with for that year.

II

Edmund showed no inclination to cut his visit short; he
stayed on after Uncle Reginald had returned to his dear club
and his rooms in St James's Street, and the attaché had gone
on upon his round of visits, and young Beresford, the cousin,
had returned to his work. The eldest of the sons at home was
over twenty; the other two were boys at school. And Susan
and Maud and little Edie were the girls. It could not be a very
sad house, after all, with all that youth in it; and on the whole
Daintrey began to turn round as it were, like the earth when a
new day is breaking, turning itself to meet the light. Edmund
was very much at home and very comfortable, and he was
pleased to think that he was doing them good, as Lady
Beresford told him with a smile of tender gratitude. It had
not yet occurred to him that of all people in the world Maud
was the one who would suit him most exactly for a wife. But
he was in a very promising way for making that discovery,
which had already faintly gleamed upon the consciousness of
Maud herself as neither unlikely nor unpleasant. They saw a
great deal of each other, though not a bit too much. They
were like brother and sister, Lady Beresford said; which was
quite true: and yet there was always a possibility of something
more.

Daintrey was a handsome house of no particular period,
built almost due east and west like a church. The front
entrance was by a square court shut in by a screen-wall built
between the two wings. At the back the wings were very
shallow, projecting but slightly from the *corps de logis*. On the
south side of the house was a green terrace, as high as the
windows of the sitting-rooms, ascended by handsome marble
steps ornamented with vases as in an Italian garden and
separated by the brilliant parterres of the flower-garden from

the house. Running along the upper end of the garden and connecting it with the west end of the house was the Lime-tree Walk, a noble bit of avenue at right angles with the terrace. Both of these were beautiful – but the little square corner which connected them was not beautiful. Here, for no apparent reason at all, a wall had been built, of the date of some hundred years back, a high brick wall, quite out of place, screening in a square and rather gloomy angle of grass, in the midst of which stood a high pedestal surmounted by a large stone vase. Whether this was meant to commemorate anything, or whether it was merely supposed to be orna-mental, in the days of George III, nobody could tell; but that it was very funereal and ugly was certain. In the side of this wall farthest from the house was a door which opened into the byway through the park. Perhaps the wall had been built to stop some right of way; perhaps – but there is little use in multiplying peradventures. There stood the wall built to shut out no one knew what; there loomed aloft the funeral urn upon its pedestal raised to commemorate no one knew what. Sometimes the door would be locked by a sulky gardener, and the key had to be hunted for in the house and out of it, high and low. At such moments Sir Robert, especially if he had himself to wait, would vow that he would throw down the wall and abolish both urn and door. But Sir Robert was an absolute Tory in action, though something of a Liberal in politics; and threatened walls live long, especially when there is no reason why they should live.

Edmund had gone out with the intention of walking to the village one of these wintry afternoons. There had been talk of skating, but the ice was not quite solid enough for skating, and his errands to the village were manifold. He was going to see about Maud's skates, which wanted something done to them. He was going to the Rectory to tell the new rector, who was young and a great athlete, to join the party at the pond to-morrow if the frost 'held'; and he had other little commissions to do. When there is nothing better to be done it is something for a man to have commissions in the village – it gives him a reason for his walk; it makes him feel that he is not absolutely without an occupation. The boys were all about the pond, helping it to freeze, as the keeper said – watching, at least, with the most anxious eyes, how this process went on. Edmund came out at the western door of the house facing a low red sun, which shone into his eyes, casting long level gleams of light across the grass and dyeing it orange. He was very lighthearted today, with a feeling that poor Willie Beresford had died long ago, and that life had begun again, and that the prospects of existence were opening out. Perhaps it was Maud, whose sweetness and pleasant society had suggested to him long stretches of happy life to come. He went out, glad even of the sharpness of the air, pleased to hear the crackling under his feet which betokened the frost, and admiring the fairy whiteness in which the great trees had robed themselves. All lit up with those red rays, with warm and gorgeous belts of colour upon the sky, and every prospect of cold and fine weather, the things most desirable when there is a frost and it is Christmas, the prospect round him was of itself exhilarating. How foolish, he thought, of the girls not to come out, to get the benefit of the smart walk through the park, and the keen fresh air which made his countenance glow. Talk of summer! The park at Daintrey was lovely always, but it never was more beautiful than it was now, with that red sunshine lighting up all those stately white giants in their robes of rime. He started lightly, closing the door after him with a cheerful bang, and turning his steps towards the lime-tree walk, through which one great beam of sunshine like red gold had pierced in the opening between the two greatest trees. This looked like a golden bridge cutting the little avenue in two; beyond it there was the shadow of the wall already described which thrust itself straight in front of the low sun.

While Edmund admired this great broad blaze of light he was startled by seeing something move beyond it in the darker part – something white, which he could not make out so long as he was himself in the sun. But when he had crossed that bridge of light he was still more surprised to see in front of him, at the end of the avenue, a woman, a lady, walking along with the most composed and gentle tread. The road was not exactly a private road – all the people from the village, almost everybody who came to Daintrey on foot, used it. But Edmund thought he knew all the people about, and he certainly did not know anyone whose appearance was at all like that of the lady who preceded him to the door in the wall – unless it were one of the girls masquerading; but he had just left the girls with their mother round the fire, and he could not entertain this idea. The dress, too, struck him with great surprise. It was a white dress, with a black mantle round the shoulders, and a large hat: not unlike the kind of costume which people in aesthetic circles begin to affect, but far more real and natural, it seemed to him – though how he could judge at this distance and with only the lady's back visible it would be difficult to tell. The curious thing was that the moment Edmund saw this pretty figure in front of him his heart began to beat. He had the same feeling which a man sometimes has when he suddenly meets a lovely face and says to himself that, please God, this woman is the one woman for him. But such a thing would be absurd when you consider that it was only her back he saw. Yet it made his heart beat; he was seized with a great desire to follow, to 'get a good look' at her, to know what she could be doing here and who she was. What had she been doing there? Surely a creature of so much grace, moving like that, dressed like that, could not possibly have been visiting the servants' hall; and that she had not been in the drawing-room he was sure. If she only would turn round at the sound of his step – but she did not turn round. She moved on as if she heard nothing – across the curious little square, straight to the door in the wall. Come, Edmund said to himself, if she is going to the village I must overtake her. And he did not hurry, feeling sure she could not escape him. He was pleased by the little mystery – Who could it be? But he must find out before he returned, for unknown ladies do not walk about in a park in the country, or go to and fro between the village and the great house, without being easily traceable. What a pretty walk she had! so light that her step was not audible – no creaking and crunching upon fallen twigs and stones and frostbound sod as with him. He was charmed with the pretty graceful figure – certainly a little like Maud, slimmer and not quite so straight, with a pretty droop in it of fragility and dependence, but yet certainly like – younger perhaps, though Maud was but nineteen. He followed her softly, promising to himself to quicken his steps as soon as she should have passed the door in the wall to which she was leading the way. Presently, about two minutes before him, she reached the door; he was so near that he could see her half turn round as if to look who was behind: but, though she must have perceived him, she closed the door upon him as she passed through – not very civil, he thought; but perhaps she was *espiègle*, and could not resist a little merry affront to him, innocently provocative, as is the fashion of girls. He hurried along the few intervening steps of the way, and opened the door. Perhaps after all she knew him; perhaps it *was* Maud, who was very fond of fun in the old days. The smile was almost a laugh on his mouth when he stepped out of the park and let the door swing carelessly behind him – not shutting it elaborately, as she had taken the trouble to do.

Strange, very strange! There was nobody to be seen on the other side of the door; certainly it must be Maud or one of the girls. She had slipped behind a bush, no doubt, to bewilder him. There were several byways running in different directions – one towards the deserted cricket-ground, another towards the keeper's cottage, beside the straight road which led to the village. Probably she had tucked up her dress and made a dart among the brushwood out of sight. He stood for a moment looking after her, now one way, now another, but he could see no one. 'I know you,' he cried, 'I know you; where are you, Maud?' But there was no answer from among the brushwood. Finally, he had to make up his mind that the trick had been successful, that she had got away, and that if he was to execute his commissions in the village he must not lose any time. But he went along with only half the spirit with which he had started, his mind quite absorbed in this adventure. As he resumed his way he met one of the keepers coming in the opposite direction, whom he stopped to ask if he had met a lady on his way. The man looked at him as if he thought him mad, but answered. No, he had met no one. 'A lady in a white dress and a black mantle,' said Edmund. 'Lord bless you, sir,' said the keeper, 'a white dress!' – and then it occurred to Edmund for the first time how entirely inappropriate such a garb was to the season. It must have been one of the girls who had 'dressed up,' as they used to be so fond of doing in the old days, to give him a fright. And yet in his heart he did not in the least believe this explanation he had given to himself. Even Maud, though he liked her so much, had never excited that sudden and causeless emotion in his heart. It was someone new – someone who had never crossed his path before, and who was destined to work he knew not what commotion in it. But then, who could it be?

'Did you go out after I went out?' he asked when he went

back to Daintrey. 'Tell me, did you or anyone take a run into the park?'

'Oh, no; mother would not let us go. She said we could not go to skate tomorrow if we went out so late today.'

'Or has anyone been here? Did you have any visitors?' Edmund asked, though he knew very well that this could not explain the presence of the lady who must have left the house before he did. Maud looked up at him with her soft blue eyes. 'We have had no one,' she said. 'We did not stir all the afternoon. Mother had a headache, and we did not wish to leave her. After you went out we sat and talked till the dressing-bell rang. That was all; but why do you suppose we must have had visitors?' Edmund felt – he could scarcely tell why – a little shyness and unwillingness to explain himself.

'Because I met a lady in the park,' he said, 'and could not make out who she was. Have you any new neighbours since I have been gone?'

Maud shook her head. 'Nobody,' she said. Nobody had been calling. Nobody had intruded into the neighbourhood. She looked earnestly at the young man, who, for his part, was a little excited by his own questions, but not at all unpleasantly excited.

'I thought for a moment you were playing me a trick. She looked a little like you – that is, her figure looked like you. I did not see her face.'

'Like me?' Maud was half pleased, but more surprised. '*I* play you a trick? I don't think,' she said, with a sad look, 'that I shall ever do that again.'

'But I hope you will a hundred times,' said the young man; and this pleased her, though she could not have told why. 'But help me to find out who it is,' he went on. 'I feel annoyed that I don't know everybody, as I used to do. She was dressed in white with a—'

'In white! You must have been dreaming,' said Maud, in amazement.

He stopped short again. 'That's why I thought it must be you,' he said, yet with a little conscious jesuitry, for he had not thought so – indeed, had assured himself that the little stir of his being which he had experienced could only mean that this was some one of a different kind from any he had met before: a new woman, a creature born to influence him. 'But it is quite true, and I was not dreaming. She had on a white gown. Something black over her shoulders like the thing ladies have been wearing lately: I forget how you call it – not a cloak nor a scarf – something put round and knotted behind like this,' said Edmund, doing his best to show how, upon himself with his hands.

'A fichu, you mean,' said Maud, suffering herself to be betrayed into a smile.

'A fichu, that's the thing; and a large broad hat. But she did not look like art-needlework – she looked quite natural.'

'What an interest you must have taken in this lady! When did you meet her? It could not have been anyone coming here, for no one has been here all day.'

'I met her – but I did not meet her – I followed her along the Lime-tree Walk and out by the little corner door.'

'How very strange! I cannot think who it can have been. And where did she go after?'

'That is the strangest of all,' said Edmund. 'She disappeared somewhere. That was another reason why I thought it must have been you. I cannot tell where she went. Down by the keeper's cottage, I suppose; but I saw her no more.'

'I'll tell you who it was,' said Maud, just a little piqued – 'it must have been the keeper's niece, who has come for a little change. She is in a dressmaker's in London. Of course she will dress nicely – though to wear *white* on a winter's afternoon, trailing across the damp grass—' She laughed again but not so sweetly as before. 'This must have been your lady, Edmund, I fear.'

'I do not believe it. I cannot believe it,' he said, much vexed; but after a good deal of resistance he was brought to allow that as he had only seen her back, and that at a little distance, he could not have any such certainty as he had supposed that she was a lady.

'Besides,' said Maud, with a little gentle triumph, 'a girl like that may walk like a lady and dress like a lady. She has got to be among ladies most of her time, and to see the best people. Unless you talked to her and found she dropped her h's, or had vulgar ideas, how could you tell? Indeed, sometimes they talk even, just as nicely as we do,' said the young lady, more just than many of her kind. This seemed to make an end of the question. At least Edmund could find no more to say; and Lady Beresford, who had observed the long and interesting conversation in which he had been engaged with Maud, gave him a still kinder smile than usual when she bade him good night.

III

Next day the frost held; the pond was bearing, and the whole house turned out to skate – even Sir Robert. Lady Beresford looked on with that indulgent wonder with which a woman regards a man's delight in outdoor amusements, and the charm they exercise over him. She was unfeignedly glad that her husband should be roused from that growling seclusion in the library, which looked like temper and meant grief – glad to the bottom of her heart; and yet there was a wondering in her mind, a sensation of half-grieved, half-smiling surprise. She was glad to get them all out of the house, and said 'Thank God!' fervently, that here was something which would take off the strain, which would bring in a little amusement, and help the convalescence of grief which was working itself so quickly in these young people; and then she went up to her own room and shut her door, feeling as if she, who had the best right to it, had got that faithful sorrow all to herself, and uncovered his picture, and read his last letter, and wept out all the tears that had been gathering and gathering. Meanwhile, the rest had got out of the shadow for the moment, and the pond was a merry scene. Sir Robert skated about very solemnly at first, taking long turns round the island that lay at one end of the long piece of water; but by and by he began to help little Edie and give directions to Tom. This diversion filled up the whole day and the next. Edmund had been half vexed, half irritated by the supposed discovery that his white lady was the keeper's niece, especially as Maud had already given him several little playful reminders and he determined, accordingly, that he would not allow himself to think any more of the little figure which had so charmed him. Of course it was mere imagination, nothing else – a girl's back, in a black fichu and white gown. What could anyone make of that? There was in his mind a lurking purpose of coming home from the ice some evening by the keeper's cottage, just to see; but even that he did not carry out for those two days. On the third afternoon, however, by some chance, he was left to come home alone. The others had set out before he was ready. He heard their voices sounding cheerily through the frosty night air, a good way on, upon the path before him, when he completed his last long whirl round the island, during which Sir Robert had got impatient, and summoned all his flock about him. They had all lingered to the last moment possible, as there were signs of the frost breaking. It was dark, so dark that Edmund could scarcely see to take his skates off, and all the hollows of the park were full of mist, and the sky overspread and blurred, and covered with clouds. It was clearer in the east, however, and there an early pale-eyed young moon, with a certain eagerness about her, as though full of impatience to see what was going on in the earth, had got up hastily in a bit of blue. She touched the mists, and made them poetical, gradually lightening over the milky expanse of the park, in which the trees stood up like bands of shadows.

Suddenly it came into Edmund's head that this was the very moment to carry out his intention. He took up his skates hastily, and walked round by the other end of the pond towards the cottage of Ferney the keeper. The moon, getting brighter every moment, threw the whole little settlement of this small habitation in the midst of the park and woods, into brilliant relief. There was a sound of dogs and human voices populating the stillness, and the cluster of low red roofs, the smoke from the chimneys, the cheerful blaze of firelight out of the uncovered windows, seemed to cheer and warm the whole landscape. Half ashamed of his own artifice, Edmund stopped at the door to give some message to the keeper. In the room beyond he saw a young woman seated at a table sewing, the light of a candle throwing a full light upon her. She was dressed in black, with the usual white collar and little locket – a handsome, pale girl; and as Edmund stared in, forgetful of politeness in his curiosity, she got up, with a reserve that was in itself coquettish, and walked to the other end of the room. When he saw this movement he had almost laughed aloud. That the lady of the lime-walk! They might as well have told him that good Mrs Ferney, with her stout, matronly bulk, and white apron, was the lady he had met. He went off, pleased with his own discrimination, pleased that he had not been mistaken, wondering if he should ever meet her again anywhere. He felt sure that he would know her, wherever he might see her, by her figure and by her walk.

He asked the keeper some trivial question to justify his pause at the house, then walked on, whistling, with cheerful speed, till he came to the little corner door, as it was called; but he had scarcely got within, when he checked himself abruptly. The moon was shining full across the green terrace and the empty beds of the flower-garden, streaming upon this little forlorn angle and its big ugly urn. Full in its light, softly crossing in front of the big pedestal, her pretty figure relieved against it, within half a dozen paces of him, coming towards him, was the lady he had seen before. Her dress was the same, dead white, with the black fichu, all frills and fringe, tied behind; a broad hat, thrown back a little from her face. His heart gave a great jump when he saw that in a moment he must pass close, and that she could not in any way conceal herself from him. He almost stopped short, but she came on softly without embarrassment, without alarm. Certainly she was like Maud: a tender little pensive face, with soft, very large eyes – which must be blue, Edmund felt – a pensive half-smile about the mouth. She was neither startled by the sight of him nor did she take a single step out of his way, but went on at the same composed pace. She had almost passed him, when he bethought himself to pull off his hat. This seemed to give her a little movement of surprise. She half turned her head to look at him, and the half-smile on her delicate lips brightened a little. It was too slight, too evanescent, to be called pleasure; and yet it was something like pleasure that lighted up the gentle face. Then she passed on, and in another moment had gone out by the door. He had not opened it for her, as politeness required. He had been too much taken by surprise – bewildered by the sudden appearance. Even now he stood still, dazed, not knowing what to do, puzzled how to address a lady whom he did not know, to intrude into an acquaintance whether she wished it or not, but yet feeling it impossible to let her go like this. He stood – was it for a moment, or longer? – hesitating, wondering: then rushed after her, meaning to say that she could not possibly cross the park at this hour alone, that she must permit him to accompany her. In his haste he made a dash at the door, threw it open, plunged out into the wide white desert where she had gone. The moon shone full upon all the breadth of the park.

The ground was higher here, and there was less mist; the pathway wound along for a hundred yards or so fully visible; but no one was there. 'Again!' he cried, speaking the word aloud in his confusion and annoyance. The bushes indeed clustered thick upon the way to the keeper's cottage. Could this be a second niece, a daughter, another young woman living there? He was so vexed, so disappointed, so tantalised, that he did not know what to do or say.

'Has Ferney a daughter as well as a niece?' he said to Maud, singling her out again, her mother remarked, from all the rest.

'A daughter? Oh, no; nobody but Jane. They brought her up; but that is all. Why do you take so much interest in the Ferneys, Edmund? You have always known them, ever since you first came here.'

Then Edmund told his story. How once more he had seen the strange lady: how she had passed through the door, and once more gone down the keeper's way; or, at least, so he supposed. Had she gone to the village he must have seen her. This time Maud became excited, too. She took her mother into council. 'Mother, do you know anyone who has lately come to the village, or to any of the houses about? I should think she must be a crazy person. Edmund has met her twice in the Lime-tree Walk, in a white dress—'

'Edmund must have been dreaming,' Lady Beresford said.

'Not any more than I am now. I saw her quite plain to-night. There is something in her air, generally, that reminds me of Maud. I thought it was Maud herself playing me a trick the first time I saw her.'

'And dressed in white. Such an extraordinary thing!' said Maud. 'Who can it be?'

This incident of the dress moved the ladies more than it did the man. He had to explain to them exactly what kind of a dress it was that she wore. 'Though I daresay he has not a notion,' said Lady Beresford. 'Probably it is only some light colour. Men never know—'

A slight look of uneasiness got into her face. She listened as the dress was described with reluctance, trying to change the subject; but the others were very much interested. 'A dress not like anything you ladies wear now,' Edmund said.

'A dress, I should say, very like what the art people wear. It must be some artistic person who has taken lodgings in the village,' said Mrs Cole, who was Lady Beresford's sister.

'Depend upon it that is what she is, an art-student, not rich, living in some little rooms, studying the effects of a winter landscape, or something of that sort. Perhaps Ferney has let her his parlour. Hasn't he got a parlour? That is what this strange visitor must be.'

This was not quite so objectionable to Edmund's feelings as the other guess, and the talk got quite animated about his lady. Only Lady Beresford did not quite like it. 'Please not to say anything about her to Sir Robert,' she said; 'he is not fond of strangers about.' And she was visibly uneasy. But no one could tell why.

As for Edmund himself, his mind was very much occupied with this pretty vision. He thought, with a thrill all through him, of the soft look of surprised pleasure that had come over her face as he took off his hat. Why should she be surprised? It was a thing any gentleman ought to have done, meeting her there, all alone, a stranger in the place, where he was himself at home. The thing he regretted was that he had not been a little quicker, that he had not followed her out, and asked her to let him see her safely across the park. Perhaps she would not have liked that. Perhaps the suggestion that it was not safe to walk about alone might have offended her. But she did not look at all like one of those women who assert a right to walk alone, and to do whatever pleases them. Anyhow, he would not let her escape him so another time; and no doubt he would meet her again. After this he was continually haunting the Lime-tree Walk. The last day of the skating he made an excuse to return early, but she was not there; and, indeed, he did not see her again till his heart had been sick with disappointment on two or three occasions. The frost broke up; then came a day or two of rain, and all the bondage of the ice melted, and the paths ran in little torrents, and a few feeble spikes of snowdrops began to come up in the empty flower-beds. The weather grew mild all of a sudden. And one day the hounds met near Daintrey, and all the party went out. They came back in the afternoon, tired, and damp, and soiled with the mud; but when the others went in to be warmed and dried, and made comfortable, having had enough of air and exercise for the day, Edmund lingered outside, as he now always did, as long as he could get any excuse for doing so. And this time he was rewarded. In the middle of the Lime-tree Walk he saw her suddenly coming towards him. One moment there had seemed to be nobody about. He turned his head to see what was meant by some little stir behind him; and when he turned again she was there, walking towards him, with her soft, gentle, composed tread. Her hands were clasped before her. Her white dress trailed a little behind her, but seemed to have no stain upon it, or mark of the wet. Her head was a little thrown back. Ah, yes! surely they were blue, those eyes; they could not have been anything but blue. And she had very little colour in her face, just enough to make it lifelike, and give an appearance of health and perfection; no sickliness, no incompleteness, was in the hue. The soft little half-smile was still upon the lips – lips that were like rose-coral, not very red, but warm and soft. She came on without paying any attention to Edmund, as if, indeed, she did not see him. And this piqued him a little. But his heart leaped so at the sight of her that he was not capable of cool judgment or criticism. This time his mind was made up. If it was rude, he was very sorry, but he must speak to her, whatever happened. He stopped suddenly when they met, and once more took off his hat. And then, in a moment, like the sun rising, that expression of pleasure came to her face. The smile grew brighter. She stopped, too, and looked at him with such satisfaction, such a tender interest in her eyes, that he was utterly confounded, and stood gazing at her, the words that he had meant to say failing him. Rude! no, evidently she did not think him rude. A gentle delight seemed to spread over her – affectionate pleasure, as if of a happiness she had vainly expected, and for which she was thankful beyond words. After all, it was she who spoke first. She said, in the softest little musical voice, a little thin, but sweet, like the cooing of a dove; and what she said was as remarkable in its simplicity as the fact that she was the first to begin the acquaintance. 'So you see me!' was, in tones of gentle pleasure, what she said.

'See you! – indeed this is now the third time that I have the pleasure of seeing you,' said Edmund eagerly. 'The last night I could not forgive myself for not asking if I might walk home with you. It was very late for you to walk alone across the park.'

To this she answered nothing, but looked at him with the softest caressing looks, as if it were a pleasure to her to hear his voice; and yet the perfect modesty, simplicity, and in-nocence of the virginal countenance uplifted to him, made every thought but those of respect and even reverence impossible to Edmund. At the same time he was slightly abashed by this steadfast look, which might have made a vain man complacent, but for something in it of unapproachable purity and isolation which gave the beholder a sense of awe. Edmund did not know how to go on. It was more difficult than could be told to proceed in the conversation. Phrases about the happiness of making her acquaintance – about the desire of the ladies at Daintrey to know if they could be of service to the stranger, which he had (though totally without authority) conned and prepared, no longer seemed within his power of utterance. He stammered forth something about 'Lady Beresford – would be glad to see you – to be of use.' To which she shook her head half sadly, half with a kind of shadowy amusement. 'You have come to the neighbourhood lately?' he said at last.

'No; oh, no; I have been here – about Daintrey – a long, long time.' These strange words were interrupted by a little faint laugh like an echo, like a laugh in music, the most spiritual liquid roll of soft words. 'I have been a long time here.'

Edmund grew more and more confused. 'If that was so I must have seen you,' he said; 'but perhaps you think a little time long. It would be natural, you are so young.'

'Nineteen,' she said; 'I never was any more than nineteen; but it is a long, long time ago.'

Then it began to dawn upon Edmund, though it was an idea he received with the greatest reluctance, that this tender, beautiful creature must be, not mad – that was too harsh a word – but like Ophelia, distraught. 'Do you come out alone?' he said, gently. 'Is there no one with you in these winter nights? it is dreary and cold in the park. I don't think you ought to be alone.'

She smiled upon him, again not saying anything for a moment. Then she said suddenly and very low, 'I am always about here.'

'You mean you are fond of this walk,' Edmund said.

Again she smiled. 'I go all about,' she said, very softly, 'sometimes into the house; but no one sees me. That is what made me so glad when you spoke. I have seen you often, but you are confused with the other ones. So many, so many I have seen. Now that you have spoken to me I will always remember which is you.'

Certainly she must be distraught. He was very sorry for her, very much touched by her, but also, though why he could not tell, a little alarmed, his heart beating very unsteadily and plunging in his breast.

'I hope,' he said, 'not out of any intrusive or impertinent feeling, but for safety, I hope you will let me see you home.'

Again he heard the little roll of the laugh, so utterly soft and distant; but she made no reply. 'I have seen a great many, a great many,' she said; 'they all come and go, but they do not see me. That is the punishment I have. The house is altered. But I take a great interest in it: I was always fond of it.' Then the innocent little laugh was succeeded by a gentle, scarcely audible sigh.

All this time the evening had been darkening, the sun had set, the mists were creeping up once more in all the hollows. Edmund felt a chill run through him. 'It is getting late,' he said, 'and cold. If you are going to the village it is a long walk. Forgive me, but I think you should let me take you home.'

She looked at him almost mocking, but with such a tender version of mockery; then turned and went towards the door in the wall. Her movements were so gentle and light that Edmund felt himself noisy, stumbling, awkward in every step he took. Her little feet seemed scarcely to touch the earth. He walked on beside her confused, trembling, afraid, yet full of a strange happiness; and the moon, which had been rising all the time, came shining upon them through the lofty, slender lime branches. It seemed to him, in his bewildered condition, that it was like some poem he had read, or some dream he had dreamt, to walk thus in this measured soft cadence, with the moon upon their heads all broken and chequered by the anatomy of the great trees, like dark lines traced upon the sky. Then they came into the full moonlight, in the corner where the urn stood upon its pedestal. It seemed to Edmund that she went more slowly, as if lingering. 'This is a gloomy corner,' he said, forcing himself to speak. For the charm of the silence had come over him, and words seemed hard things to disturb those soft moments as they flowed away.

'Not gloomy to me. I was always fond of it. When it was put up we were all pleased. That was what was wrong in me. You know,' she said, with her little soft laugh, 'I was so fond of the house and the trees, and everything that was our own. I thought there was nothing better, nothing so good. I was all for the earth, and nothing more. That is why I am here so much.' She paused, and gave a little sigh: but then added, brightening, 'It is not hard: when you are used to it, when now and then you meet with someone who sees you, it is not so hard. I am a little sad sometimes, but very happy now.'

And again she looked at him with that look of tender pleasure – enough to turn any man's head. Edmund's went round and round – he could say nothing more, but stammer, repeating himself, 'It is a long walk; you must let me see you safely home across the park.'

She answered him only by that low laugh, but even softer, sweeter, than before. Then he opened the door for her. As she passed through she smiled upon him with a little wave of her hand. For his part he had put his foot on a soft piece of turf sodden with the rain, and it took him a minute to extricate the heel of his boot which had sunk into it. A minute, scarcely so much as a minute, but when he stepped out eagerly after her, his head full of that walk across the park, she was nowhere to be seen. One minute, not so much. Where was she? How had she managed to elude him? He was wild with disappointment and anger. Once more he made a hurried search behind all the bushes, in every little clump of brushwood. There was not a trace of her; though he thought once he heard her low melodious laugh. Was it a trick she was playing him? What was the meaning of it? But when he had walked about for nearly an hour, Edmund had to go back to the house disappointed. Once more she had escaped him; his head was giddy, his heart beating loud, his whole being full of agitation and excitement. What did it mean? and who was she, this mysterious girl?

Edmund felt like a man in a dream as he came downstairs, and sat among the party at table, where the meal went on amid cheerful conversation. For himself he seemed quite incapable of taking any share in it. It flowed round him like something in which he had no voice. Afterwards the ladies asked him in the drawing-room, their voices coming to him faintly as out of a cloud, whether he had seen the white lady again. But it was impossible to him to speak of her tonight. He answered briefly, saying no, though it was not true; and pretended to have letters to write, that universal excuse for pre-occupation. But when he escaped from the circle on this pretence, he did not write any letters. He sat in his room, opening his window, though the night was not so balmy as to make this desirable; and with his head supported by his hands, gazed out upon the great darkness round. The moon set early, and the skies were veiled with clouds, and nothing was discernible but the dark outlines of the trees, and a great dimness of space and air. Now and then he almost thought he saw her below, a flicker of white moving about, as if it might have been her dress; and it was only by strenuous resolution that he kept himself from rushing wildly into the night, with a kind of mad hope of meeting her. Then he gathered together in his mind all that she had said, which was so sweet, so tender, and yet, God help him, so wild. 'When you meet with someone who sees you' – 'I was nineteen – but it is long, long ago.' What could it mean? Was it, indeed, the sweet bells jangled out of tune, of some lovely nature? Edmund's eyes filled with tears. He said to himself that if it was so, he would take more care of her than anyone; he would be her tender protector, her keeper to preserve her from everything that could hurt her innocence. What a strange fatal charm was it that had fallen upon him thus unawares? He could think of nothing else. Ophelia – but far more sweet in her madness – pure as a vision, with that dear look of happiness in her face. Could anything be more sweet than that she should be happy when he spoke to her, her face full of pleasure at the sound of his voice? Edmund's heart melted altogether at this thought. But those sweet fairy-tricks should not suffice her another day. He would find her, whatever might happen; he would secure her beyond all possibility of escape. Her reason, what did it matter about her reason. Love would supply the place. And thus he spent the evening in a kind of soft delirium, able to think of nothing, to see and hear nothing, but his new-born yet all-absorbing love.

IV

Edmund did not sleep all night. He rose excited and restless, in the dim cold dawn of the winter morning; he was silent as a ghost at the cheerful breakfast table; he excused himself from all the occupations of the day. He had 'things to do,' he said;

and in fact he was impatient and unhappy until he found an opportunity to steal out unseen by anyone. He went hastily through the Lime-tree Walk, following exactly the course he had taken the previous evening with *her*. There he contemplated the park in the clear daylight with wondering and anxious scrutiny. The little road down by the back of the green terrace, which led to the keeper's cottage, was the only one by which she could possibly have gone. A little plantation of young trees was at the corner, and as it wound downwards, though the declivity was slight, there were various scattered bushes, furze and broom, and a few old knotted hawthorn thickets, darned out and in with pendants of brambles, showing here and there a red leaf still. There any mischievous girl could have played hide-and-seek with a petulant lover for hours together. Edmund felt a little lightening of the anxiety which possessed him as he saw these interruptions of the way. But if it was indeed by this way she had gone, she could not have afterwards emerged into the park without passing at least by Ferney's cottage. Perhaps, as someone had suggested, she was a lodger there after all. He went slowly towards it, examining every corner of the way, and every bit of cover. His search was so slow and minute that it took him a long time. He emerged upon Ferney's little enclosure almost before he was aware.

When his step was heard on the gravel, someone came to the window to see who it was and Edmund heard a little exclamation. 'Aunt! here's that gentleman again.' Was he, then, coming to some real elucidation of all his wonderings? Mrs Ferney came to the half-open door in answer to his summons. He thought she looked a little disturbed. He spoke peremptorily, to leave her no room for thought, or settling beforehand what she was to say. 'I want to know if you have a lodger – a lady living in your house?'

Mrs Ferney's countenance grew more disturbed than ever. 'Well, sir—, no, Mr Edmund, I've got no lodger. There's Ferney's niece staying on a visit.'

'Is that your niece sitting in the room on the right hand?' When Edmund said this, a chair was hastily drawn back out of his range of vision, and a voice said, 'La!'

'I mean a totally different person,' he cried, with a little impatience; 'a lady; very young; very slight; with blue eyes; in a white dress, and something black round her shoulders.'

Mrs Ferney was gazing at him with wide open eyes, but a visible air of relief. 'No, indeed, sir; nothing of the sort. Not a soul lives here but Ferney and me, and, for the present, Ada Jane.'

'Where, then, can she live?' he said half to himself. Mrs Ferney thought he had taken leave of his senses. She stood and gazed at him with bewildered looks, making a curtsey, and much relieved to see that he was not 'after' Ada Jane. Edmund walked away without so much as a glance at the window where Ada Jane was lurking expectant. He went to the village, where he walked about not knowing what to do, looking in at every window. He could not stop everybody he met there to ask them did they know where he could find a lady with blue eyes and in a white gown? He did the only other thing that was practicable in the circumstances. He went to see the Rector, whom he asked that question, and to whom he told his little story. The Rector was a young man, and he was sympathetic. He thought of all the ladies within twenty miles, and described them, without finding any one who at all resembled the lady whom Edmund sought. 'Besides,' the young enquirer had still so much reason left in him as to say, 'what would it advantage me if Miss Ingestre, who lives fifteen miles off, were like her? Miss Ingestre would not come here and wander about Lime-tree Walk.' So that nothing was to be made of it in any direction. When he left the Rectory the short afternoon was beginning to wane. He saw nobody along all the length of the way, and when he came to the door in the wall found it locked; evidently she had not passed that way today.

It was again a misty afternoon; the sun veiled in clouds. Edmund went down by the path that led towards Ferney's, and got across the brook and round by the corner of the house, which was a way practicable to one who had been a boy there, and knew all about the surroundings and byways of the place. What he meant was to hurry round to the conservatories, in which he was likely to find the head gardener, and get the key from him. What if she should come to her favourite walk and find it closed against her? He was breathless with haste scrambling up the bank, rushing along at his most rapid pace, lest this foolish obstacle should prevent their meeting: when suddenly, in the midst of his excitement, all at once his heart stood still. In spite of the locked door, she was standing there. It was earlier than he had ever seen her before. His heart stopped short, then leapt into wilder beating than ever. He did not ask himself how she got through. Why should he think of any such trivial obstacle? She was there, that was all he thought of; and this time it was evident that she was looking for him. She waved her hand to him with the prettiest gesture. She was standing against the pedestal, her white dress standing out from that background. He noticed for the first time how white and pure was the fulness of the flounce where it fell upon the grass, without a mark on it of the wetness around. This seemed to him quite natural, an exquisite quality, somehow, in herself, which kept everything about her white and pure.

'I was going,' he said, flushed and eager, 'to get the key. I thought you would wonder to find it shut. But you came through before it was shut, I suppose.'

She smiled. It seemed to be a rule with her to answer none of his questions. She looked at him with a sort of innocent admiration, mixed with the pleasure in her face. 'It is so long since I have spoken to anyone – since I have seen anyone run to meet me,' she said. 'I wonder how it is that you, out of them all—'

'Yes,' he said, taking up her words, 'that is what I cannot understand, how I, of all the people in Daintrey, should have been so happy as to meet you. We are like old friends now, are we not? we have seen each other so often. I am Edmund Coventry, once Sir Robert's ward, and free of the house. Might I ask your name?'

There was no embarrassment in her face. From first to last she was never embarrassed, but always full of sweet composure: and her smile seemed to express a hundred different feelings. There was amusement in it, and a little regret, and always that affectionate pleasure. 'I was Maud,' she said, quite simply. Edmund could not understand why she should put her name in the past tense, and it gave him a subtle, little thrill of pain, he could scarcely tell why.

'Maud – it is the very sweetest name,' he said, with a half-adoring passion; 'but what else? You will not let me say Maud. Tell me your other name.'

What a strange smile it was! It seemed to go on like an accompaniment in music, confusing the listener who was so anxious to gather every word that came from her lips. He did not seem to know that she had not said anything, so full was the air of that sweet influence. A little while after he began again to speak himself.

'These meetings have made a change in my life,' he said. 'I was taking the future quite easily, not thinking what it was to bring forth; but now I see that one ought to select one's path, to settle, to take up the more serious part of life. All this I have learned since I have known you; since I have loved you,' he added, very low, looking earnestly in her face.

She took the confession quite calmly; not a tinge of additional colour, not the slightest shyness or confusion appeared in her. She kept her quiet, sweet, ease of manner undisturbed. And what was Edmund to say more? He felt somehow baffled, helpless, before this invulnerable calm.

'Won't you say anything to me?' he cried; 'I don't know who you are, or where you are living, but I love you, Maud. Do not be angry.'

'Oh, no! Not angry,' she said, in her soft voice; 'only you cannot understand. I am not here to make friends, though I have always wished that someone might see me and speak. And before you spoke I had noticed you; I thought to myself, This one surely – this one surely! There was something about you; but there had been so many, so many before,' she said, with an innocent, wistful look, like the unconscious protest against neglect, yet acquiescence of a child.

'But you will give me an answer, Maud? I love you, sweet. I do not know,' said Edmund, with passion, 'what has happened to you; what it is that makes you wander like this; but I will not mind, whatever it is. I will take care of you; I will watch over you; it will make no difference to me. Do you not understand me, dear?' He put out his hand to take hers, to secure her attention, to show her how serious he was. And then Edmund felt as if the whole misty heaven and earth were going round about him. He could not find the hand he sought. It was as if some spell prevented him from touching her. He felt again more baffled, more confounded, and hopelessly kept back, than words could say.

'You must not ask me questions,' she made answer, softly, after a pause. 'It is not permitted to answer questions. I am here – for a time. I have been here no one could tell how long. We do not count as you do. If I told you more than this you would not understand.'

'I will understand if it is about you. But, Maud, Maud, answer me first. Give me your hand. Won't you give me your hand?'

A look of trouble came into her face; yet so soft, so shadowy, that it did not seem pain. The smile did not go out of her eyes. She shook her head gently, standing so near him, her hands crossed, clasping each other. He had only to put out his arms and take her into them, but he could not. She was close, close to him, and yet – what was it that stood between? Not the mild refusal with which she shook her head; something that chilled his blood in its ardour, and made his heart contract with awe. He put out his hands beseeching, but seemed to come no nearer; and yet she did not draw back, nor move away from him. Edmund did not seem to himself to know what he was saying, what was happening, and yet he heard and meant every word that rushed to his lips. 'Sweet! I will understand anything; I know there must be something strange. Whatever it is I accept it, I accept it! Say you will love me, Maud! Say you will – marry me!'

What happened? One of the Beresford boys, as Edmund dimly perceived, had been approaching, rushing along towards the door; but somehow the intruder had made no difference to him, and had not stopped him in his impassioned suit. At this moment, however, the boy rushed headlong past, dashing against her, touching Edmund's coat as he plunged along. The lovely, gentle figure was straight in his way. Edmund caught him by the throat with a fury beyond words.

'The lady!' he stammered out; 'you brute, do you not see the lady?' and flung him wildly to a distance upon the wet ground.

Fred Beresford was altogether taken by surprise. He was not a boy of patient temper, and he was in a hurry; but the wildness of the other bewildered him. He picked himself up, and came forward wondering, to where Edmund stood, pale as death, and gazing wildly about him. Fred's wrath was entirely quailed at this sight. 'What is it?' he asked, quite timidly and softly laying his hand on Edmund's arm.

The young man was trembling in every limb; he did not seem able to move. His eyes were staring wildly here and there. There was no softening dusk as yet to conceal anything; all was white daylight, cold and pale and clear. When he felt

Fred's touch he turned upon him for one second, furious, violently thrusting him away. 'You have killed her!' he said; and then clutching the boy again, 'Where is she? where is she? where is she?' Edmund cried. Fred felt the whole trembling weight of his companion upon him. His boyish strength swayed under the burden.

'Are you ill, old fellow?' he said, alarmed. 'What is the matter? I thought you were saying poetry. I don't know what you mean about a lady.'

'You have killed her,' he said, wildly clutching the boy's throat; then, all in a moment, he softened, and burst into a transport of cries. 'Where is she? where is she? Maud! Maud! come back to me,' cried the young man, with a voice of despair. There was nothing to be seen, Fred swore afterwards, nothing, except the big stone pedestal with the urn upon it, and behind, the mossy old wall.

'I say – you are ill,' said the boy. 'Come in, that's the best thing to do; come in to mother. Maud's there with her, if it's Maud you want. Edmund, come along.'

Edmund broke from him, pushing him away. He went all round the pedestal, wandering about it, feeling it with his hands. Then he held out those hands piteously, appealing, into the empty air. 'Maud! Maud!' he cried. 'Don't laugh at me; don't play with me,' as if he were talking to somebody, the astonished boy described. Fred at last ran in alarmed to the library where Sir Robert was sitting. 'I wish you'd come out, father, into the Lime-tree Walk to Edmund – he's gone mad,' the boy cried.

When Sir Robert went out, Edmund was standing leaning against one of the lime trees, gazing at the green space which contained the pedestal and the urn. When he was entreated to come in, he answered quite gently, that if he only waited patiently she would be sure to come back. 'This is where she always comes. She is fond of this place,' he said. 'There are things I don't understand about her, but she will come. I am sure she will come if you will only let me wait.' 'Tell me, my good fellow, all about it,' Sir Robert said. He was a kind man when his attention was fully roused, and now he remembered that his wife had told him something of a strange lady whom Edmund had seen in the park. Edmund told him the whole story, standing there with his back against the tree. He asked Sir Robert first to stand close to him, almost behind him, that nothing might interfere with his clear vision round. And then he told him all. 'She always tricks me,' he said, with an attempt at a laugh. 'She is so innocent – like a child. How she got away this time I cannot tell. There seems nothing to hide behind here. But she always does it. I confess, sir,' he added, with great candour and gravity, 'there are many things about her I do not understand; but whatever they are, I am ready to accept them all.'

'Have you ever seen her more than once in the same day?' asked Sir Robert. 'No? Then come with me, Edmund, it is of no use waiting. I think I can tell you something about her.' Sir Robert put his arm into that of the young man. He scarcely knew himself what he meant; but it was clear that something must be done. No, he had never seen her twice the same day; and to know about her, was not that what he wanted most in the world? He suffered himself, after one long glance around, to be led away.

Sir Robert took him upstairs to an old gallery which he remembered very well as a child, which had been given up to the children's romps on wet days, a place full of pictures, the accumulations of an old house – all kinds of grim portraits of early Beresfords. There were some good pictures among them, he had always remembered to have heard said, and so long as Edmund could recollect there had been an intention expressed of disinterring these treasures. 'I don't know where it is exactly; I don't know if it is still here. It was by a pupil of Sir Joshua's, and with something of his feeling. I have always intended to bring it downstairs,' Sir Robert said, rummaging as he spoke among old dusty canvasses. Edmund stood by listless, in the lull of reaction after his great excitement. It was not here, he thought, that anything would be told him about *her*. He did not understand what his companion meant. He was only waiting, feeling hazily that he had some further trial of patience to go through, not very anxious now for anything but the end of the day, and that another might dawn, on which, perhaps, he might see her again.

'Was she like this?' said Sir Robert, at last. Edmund went after him slowly, languidly, to the square of light in front of the great window whither he was dragging a picture in an old-fashioned black frame. Then the young man gave a great cry.

There she stood looking out of the old canvas with the smile he knew so well – her blue eyes looking upwards, the soft curves about her mouth, her hands clasped before her, and every detail exactly as he had seen her an hour ago; the white dress with its flounce, the black scarf with all its little frills. Then he fell down on his knees before the beautiful little figure, with a cry which was half alarm and half joy.

Sir Robert drew his breath quick; in fact, he had not been prepared for such success to his experiment. He was confounded by the explanation he had himself suggested. 'Do you mean that this is – the person,' he said, in a husky voice, and glanced round him with a certain shrinking. His ruddy countenance paled. 'I should prefer,' he said, with a little difficulty, 'to tell you the story in my own room. But turn first to the back of the picture and look at the date. Now come along. I don't like this vacant old place.'

Edmund looked at the date; it did not convey any particular idea to his mind.

'Seven, seven, seven,' he said to himself; seven is one of the numbers of perfection. It must be that the painter had meant. Otherwise it made no impression upon him. He went down to the library, having first placed the picture carefully in the light where he could come and worship it again. Sir Robert sat down in his usual chair, looking pale. 'Sit down, Edmund,' he said, 'my poor boy. I am afraid you are not in your usual health. You must see the doctor; you must try a change of scene.'

'What has that to do with it?' said Edmund, astonished. 'You were to tell me who she is – that is of far more importance to me than my health, which is excellent, all the same. Who is she? You gave me your promise—'

'Is—?' said Sir Robert. 'Edmund, my dear fellow, you must have heard the story, though you don't remember it. It must have excited your imagination. Did you notice the date on the picture? I told you to look at it.'

'The date! What has that to do with it? Seven, seven, I forget what it was.'

'Seventeen hundred and seventy-seven,' said Sir Robert, solemnly. 'Seventeen hundred and seventy-seven – nearly a hundred years ago.'

There was no intelligence in Edmund's eyes. 'I knew there must be something strange about her,' he said; 'it would be vain to conceal that from one's self. There are many things I don't understand – but I am willing to accept – anything. Sir Robert—'

'Edmund!' cried Sir Robert, almost wildly, 'command yourself. You don't seem to see. My dear fellow, this is all a delusion. You have seen no lady. It has been your imagination working. How in the name of all that is reasonable could you see a woman who has been dead for a hundred years?'

The young man looked up startled. Confusion seemed to envelop everything round him. 'A hundred years,' he said to himself, wondering; then laughed, and repeated, 'I saw no lady? I am going to marry her, Sir Robert.'

'God bless us all!' said Sir Robert, with a voice of terror. 'Edmund, my dear fellow – Edmund, see a doctor, see a clergyman. I'll send for old Parkins and for the Rector. You can't, you can't go on like this, you know.'

Edmund's brain was still too much confused to take in any impression from what was said. 'A hundred years,' he repeated to himself, with a smile. 'It is strange; but I always felt there was something strange. I told you there were many things I did not understand. But what may be the meaning – this hundred years? Is that all you have to tell me, sir?' he continued, trying to wake up from the confused sense of mystery, yet almost of pleasure, which the picture brought him. He did not understand it – but then in the whole matter there was so little that he could understand.

'All,' Sir Robert said. He was in great excitement and distress. 'I don't want the ladies to know if we can help it. Don't say anything to them, I entreat of you. And, my dear boy, if you would go and lie down, I will send for Parkins to come directly. I'll have the Rector up in half an hour. It will yield to remedies – it will yield to remedies,' Sir Robert said.

'I am quite well,' said Edmund. To him it seemed that Sir Robert was going out of his senses. 'But I will not keep you longer, and I will say nothing to the ladies. In the meantime,' he added, in his confusion, 'I have got – some letters to write.'

'The very best thing you can do; occupy yourself – occupy yourself, my dear fellow,' said Sir Robert, patting him on the shoulder. Edmund felt that his guardian was glad to be rid of him. Perhaps it was not wonderful that Sir Robert did not understand him; he did not understand himself. His head was confused as if the fog had got into it. To some things he seemed to attach no importance at all, while others were quite clear to him, and had all their natural weight. 'Seventeen, seven, seven.' He repeated this over to himself with a smile, but whether it was a charm, or a fact, or what it was, he could not tell; on the other hand, he thought the precaution about the ladies was quite right. And he could not appear without betraying that something had happened to him. He sent word downstairs by his servant that he had caught a cold and was going to keep to his room; and there he received the visit of old Dr Parkins with much conscious amusement, but would not say a word to him of what had befallen him, and utterly confounded the old doctor, who could say nothing but that his pulse was excited, and that it would be necessary for him to keep quiet for a day or two. Then the Rector came, much abashed, as a man called upon to minister to a mind diseased, and knowing nothing about it, was likely to be. When they were gone Edmund spent the night alone. He wrote a long letter to – he did not know whom – giving an account of the whole, so little as there was of it, and so much. 'I know there is something strange,' he wrote, 'but nothing to prevent me taking the charge of her, taking care of her. An hour a day of her will be more to me than twenty-four of any other. I know there are things which I can't understand.' When he had done this it was late, and all the family had gone to bed. He heard them going one by one – a sound of steps in the long passages, mounting the stairs, a little gleam of the passing lights under his door. By and by silence fell upon everything. There was no sound or stir anywhere – all silent, all dark, the doors shut fast, soft waves of quiet breathing going through the house. He came out with his light in his hand and stood for a moment on the threshold of his door – an adventurer bound upon a last voyage, a sailor setting out into unknown seas. Then he went up, up to the upper part of the house, past all the closed doors, moving quietly through lines of unseen sleepers on every side. The great house was as silent as the grave.

The moon was shining full from the west, just about to set, as she had risen, early. There was a large west window in the gallery, and this was full of silvery light pouring in, making all white and dazzling. The portrait, which had been drawn towards this window to get the evening light, stood there still, receiving the white illumination of the moonlight. Edmund walked up – holding in his hand a candle, which flamed yellow and earthly in that radiance from heaven – through the whiteness, a sort of milky way, with the annals of the past on every side of him. He came to the picture of his love, and threw himself down beside it on the floor. There she stood before him, shadowed in the moonlight – the same, and yet not the same. Something disappointing, narrower, smaller, was in the pictured countenance. As he gazed at it the confusion grew in his mind; all that was real seemed to die away from him. In the vehemence of this sense of loss, he began to speak to her, tears filling his eyes, and her face shining more and more like life through that tremulous medium. 'Maud! Maud! I do not understand you; I do not know you; but I love you,' he said in a rapture, not knowing that he said it. Then he came to himself with a gasp. There, close to the frame of the picture, her shoulder touching it, stood the original. He held up his candle, like a yellow flaming torch. For the moment, in the silent moonlight, with all the world asleep around, alone with these two – were they two? – his reason went from him. He raised himself to his knees, and knelt like a devotee before a shrine – his arms widely opened, his face raised, wild with worship: were they two, standing side by side, comparing themselves each to each, or were they one?

'You have come to me at last – you have come to me – Maud!'

She looked at him as before with her soft smile. There was no reply in her to his passion. 'I did wrong to speak to you,' she said; 'you do not understand. I was so pleased that you saw me. No one sees me. I come and go, sometimes out, sometimes in. I go to their rooms and they do not see me. Then when I find one that will speak – that will smile, I am glad.' There came from her, mingled together, the soft laugh and the sigh, that made his heart stand still. 'But no more – but no more,' she said.

And there seemed to creep about him a chill. He had never felt it before. When he had seen her first all had been soft as her looks, delightful as the bloom on her face. The bloom was still on her face, but shaded as by a mist. Nor could he see as he did before. The moonlight confused the soft features – or perhaps it was his yellow flaming human candle, not everlasting like the other light, ready to burn out and extinguish itself. His strength and his senses seemed to fail.

'I do not understand,' he cried; 'I do not understand! but whatever it is, I accept – I accept. Dead or living, Maud,

Maud, come with me – let us be together! Come!' he said, stretching his arms wildly.

She did not draw back nor move, but neither did he touch her with his longing arms. Did fear seize them half-way extended? He could not tell. They dropped down by his side, and his heart dropped, sinking within him. She stood before him unmoved – always the same calm, the half smile on her lips, her blue eyes pleased and tender. Then she shook her head slowly, gently.

'It is not permitted. I told you I had loved the earth and all that was on it: and now I am earthbound. I could not go if I would, and I would not if I could. What we have to do, that is what we love best. But I never thought that you would mistake so much – that you would not understand. Now I know why there are so few that see us. It is to keep them from harm,' she said with a soft sigh. 'Ah me! when the only thing we long for, it is sometimes to speak – but I will never wish for it more—'

'Maud!' He threw himself at her feet again with a great cry. 'Touch me – mark me, that I may be yours always. If not in life, yet in death. Say we shall meet when I die.'

Once more she shook her head. 'How can I tell? I do not know you in the soul. You will do what is appointed; but do not be sorry, you will like to do it,'[2] she said, with her sweet look of tender pleasure. 'Good-bye, brother – good-bye!'

'I will not let you go!' he cried; 'I will not let you go!' and seized her in his arms.

Then in Edmund's head was a roaring of echoes, a clanging of noises, a blast as of great trumpets and music; and he knew no more.

'Edmund is not in his room; his bed has not been slept in,' said Lady Beresford, coming hastily upstairs next morning immediately after she had gone down. Sir Robert had not yet left his dressing-room. She was pale and full of alarm. 'His door was open; there is no trace of him. I have sent out over all the park. He must have left the house last night. And Fred tells me the strangest story. What is it, Robert?' Sir Robert was very much disturbed himself, but he would make no certain reply.

'I daresay he will be found wandering about somewhere. He has got some nonsense in his head.' Then he hurried down to the Lime-tree Walk, and out to the park, looking under the bushes and trees. If he had found Edmund there lying white and stark, Sir Robert would not have been surprised. They searched for him all the morning, but found no trace anywhere. Later in the day, Sir Robert suddenly bethought himself of another possibility. He hurried up to the old gallery, calling his eldest son to go with him. And there, indeed, they found Edmund – lying on the floor. But not dead, nor raving; pale enough, pale as a ghost, but asleep; his candle long ago burnt out to the socket, and the soft little face he had loved, placidly watching over him from the picture, as unmoved, though not so sweet, as the vision he had seen.

It cannot be said that Edmund Coventry was well enough to leave Daintrey that day, nor for several days. But he went away as soon as it was possible, going off from the great door, and by the drive, not approaching the Lime-tree Walk. He had no brain-fever, nor any other kind of fever. Various changes were perceptible, the Beresfords thought, in his life; but other people were unconscious of them. He had always been a gentle soul, friendly, and charitable, and true. More than a year after, when he met his former guardian and family in town, the old intercourse was renewed, and that came to pass which Lady Beresford had always thought would be so very suitable. He married Maud, and made her a very good husband. But he would never go to Daintrey again. And though there have been a great many versions of the story scattered abroad, and the Beresfords, once so silent on the subject, have become in their hearts a little proud of it – though it is supposed against their will that it should be known – no one else, so far as we have ever heard, has been again accosted by the gentle little lady who was earthbound. Perhaps her time of willing punishment is over, and she is earthbound no more.

The Open Door

I TOOK THE house of Brentwood on my return from India in
18——, for the temporary accommodation of my family, until
I could find a permanent home for them. It had many
advantages which made it peculiarly appropriate. It was
within reach of Edinburgh, and my boy Roland, whose
education had been considerably neglected, could go in
and out to school, which was thought to be better for him
than either leaving home altogether or staying there always
with a tutor. The first of these expedients would have seemed
preferable to me, the second commended itself to his mother.
The doctor, like a judicious man, took the midway between.
'Put him on his pony and let him ride into the Academy every
morning; it will do him all the good in the world,' Dr Simson
said; 'and when it is bad weather there is the train.' His
mother accepted this solution of the difficulty more easily
than I could have hoped; and our pale-faced boy, who had
never known anything more invigorating than Simla, began
to encounter the brisk breezes of the North in the subdued
severity of the month of May. Before the time of the vacation
in July we had the satisfaction of seeing him begin to acquire
something of the brown and ruddy complexion of his schoolfellows. The English system did not commend itself to Scotland in these days. There was no little Eton at Fettes; nor do I
think, if there had been, that a genteel exotic of that class
would have tempted either my wife or me. The lad was
doubly precious to us, being the only one left us of many;
and he was fragile in body, we believed, and deeply sensitive
in mind. To keep him at home, and yet to send him to school –
to combine the advantages of the two systems – seemed to be
everything that could be desired. The two girls also found at
Brentwood everything they wanted. They were near enough
to Edinburgh to have masters and lessons as many as they
required for completing that never-ending education which

the young people seem to require nowadays. Their mother married me when she was younger than Agatha, and I should like to see them improve upon their mother! I myself was then no more than twenty-five – an age at which I see the young fellows now groping about them, with no notion what they are going to do with their lives. However, I suppose every generation has a conceit of itself which elevates it, in its own opinion, above that which comes after it. Brentwood stands on that fine and wealthy slope of country, one of the richest in Scotland, which lies between the Pentland Hills and the Firth. In clear weather you could see the blue gleam – like a bent bow, embracing the wealthy fields and scattered houses – of the great estuary on one side of you; and on the other the blue heights, not gigantic like those we had been used to, but just high enough for all the glories of the atmosphere, the play of clouds, and sweet reflections, which give to a hilly country an interest and a charm which nothing else can emulate. Edinburgh, with its two lesser heights – the Castle and the Calton Hill – its spires and towers piercing through the smoke, and Arthur's Seat, lying crouched behind, like a guardian no longer very needful, taking his repose beside the well-beloved charge, which is now, so to speak, able to take care of itself without him – lay at our right hand. From the lawn and drawing-room windows we could see all these varieties of landscape. The colour was sometimes a little chilly, but sometimes, also, as animated and full of vicissitude as a drama. I was never tired of it. Its colour and freshness revived the eyes which had grown weary of arid plains and blazing skies. It was always cheery, and fresh, and full of repose.

The village of Brentwood lay almost under the house, on the other side of the deep little ravine, down which a stream – which ought to have been a lovely, wild, and frolicsome little river – flowed between its rocks and trees. The river, like so many in that district, had, however, in its earlier life been sacrificed to trade, and was grimy with paper-making. But this did not affect our pleasure in it so much as I have known it to affect other streams. Perhaps our water was more rapid – perhaps less clogged with dirt and refuse. Our side of the dell was charmingly *accidenté*, and clothed with fine trees, through which various paths wound down to the river-side and to the village bridge which crossed the stream. The village lay in the hollow, and climbed, with very prosaic houses, the other side. Village architecture does not flourish in Scotland. The blue slates and the grey stone are sworn foes to the picturesque; and though I do not, for my own part, dislike the interior of an old-fashioned pewed and galleried church, with its little family settlements on all sides, the square box outside, with its bit of a spire like a handle to lift it by, is not an improvement to the landscape. Still a cluster of houses on differing elevations, with scraps of garden coming in between, a hedgerow with clothes laid out to dry, the opening of a street with its rural sociability, the women at their doors, the slow waggon lumbering along – gives a centre to the landscape. It was cheerful to look at, and convenient in a hundred ways. Within ourselves we had walks in plenty, the glen being always beautiful in all its phases, whether the woods were green in the spring or ruddy in the autumn. In the park which surrounded the house were the ruins of the former mansion of Brentwood, a much smaller and less important house than the solid Georgian edifice which we inhabited. The ruins were picturesque, however, and gave importance to the place. Even we, who were but temporary tenants, felt a vague pride in them, as if they somehow reflected a certain consequence upon ourselves. The old building had the remains of a tower, an indistinguishable mass of mason-work, overgrown with ivy, and the shells of walls attached to this were half filled up with soil. I had never examined it closely, I am ashamed to say. There was a large room, or what had been a large room, with the lower part of the windows still existing, on the principal floor, and underneath other windows, which were perfect, though half filled up with fallen soil, and waving with a wild growth of brambles and chance growths of all kinds. This was the oldest part of all. At a little distance were some very commonplace and disjointed fragments of building, one of them suggesting a certain pathos by its very commonness and the complete wreck which it showed. This was the end of a low gable, a bit of grey wall, all encrusted with lichens, in which was a common doorway. Probably it had been a servants' entrance, a back-door, or opening into what are called 'the offices' in Scotland. No offices remained to be entered – pantry and kitchen had all been swept out of being; but there stood the doorway open and vacant, free to all the winds, to the rabbits, and every wild creature. It struck my eye, the first time I went to Brentwood, like a melancholy comment upon a life that was over. A door that led to nothing – closed once, perhaps, with anxious care, bolted and guarded, now void of any meaning. It impressed me, I remember, from the first; so perhaps it may be said that my mind was prepared to attach to it an importance which nothing justified.

The summer was a very happy period of repose for us all. The warmth of Indian suns was still in our veins, and we did not feel the cold. It seemed to us that we could never have enough of the greenness, the dewiness, the freshness of the northern landscape. Even its mists were pleasant to us, taking all the fever out of us, and pouring in vigour and refreshment. In autumn we followed the fashion of the time, and went away for change, which we did not in the least require. It was when the family had settled down for the winter, when the days were short and dark, and the rigorous reign of frost upon us, that the incidents occurred which alone could justify me in intruding upon the world my private affairs. These incidents were, however, of so curious a character, that I hope my inevitable references to my own family and pressing personal interests will meet with a general pardon.

I was absent in London when these events began. In London an old Indian plunges back into the interests with which all his previous life has been associated, and meets old friends at every step. I had been circulating among some half-dozen of these – enjoying the return of my former life in shadow, though I had been so thankful in substance to throw it aside – and had missed some of my home letters, what with going down from Friday to Monday to old Benbow's place in the country, and stopping on the way back to dine and sleep at Sellar's, and to take a look into Cross's stables, which occupied another day. It is never safe to miss one's letters. In this transitory life, as the Prayer-book says, how can one ever be certain what is going to happen? All was perfectly well at home. I knew very well (I thought) what they would have to say to me: 'The weather has been so fine, that Roland has not once gone by train, and he enjoys the ride beyond anything.' 'Dear papa, be sure that you don't forget anything, but bring us so-and-so, and so-and-so' – a list as long as my arm. Dear girls and dearer mother! I would not for the world have forgotten their commissions, or given the sight of their little letters, for all the Benbows and Crosses in the world.

But I was confident in my home-comfort and peacefulness. When I got back to my club, however, three or four letters were lying for me, upon some of which I noticed the 'immediate', 'urgent', which old-fashioned people and anxious people still believe will influence the post-office and quicken the speed of the mails. I was about to open one of these, when the club porter brought me two telegrams, one of which, he said, had arrived the night before. I opened, as was to be expected, the last first, and this was what I read: 'Why don't you come or answer? For God's sake, come. He is much worse.' This was a thunderbolt to fall upon a man's head who had one only son, and he the light of his eyes! The other telegram, which I opened with hands trembling so much that I lost time by my haste, was to much the same purport: 'No better; doctor afraid of brain-fever. Calls for you day and night. Let nothing detain you.' The first thing I did was to look up the time-tables to see if there was any way of getting off sooner than by the night-train, though I knew well enough there was not; and then I read the letters, which furnished, alas! too clearly, all the details. They told me that the boy had been pale for some time, with a scared look. His mother had noticed it before I left home, but would not say anything to alarm me. This look had increased day by day; and soon it was observed that Roland came home at a wild gallop through the park, his pony panting and in foam, himself 'as white as a sheet', but with the perspiration streaming from his forehead. For a long time he had resisted all questioning, but at length had developed such strange changes of mood, showing a reluctance to go to school, a desire to be fetched in the carriage at night – which was a ridiculous piece of luxury – an unwillingness to go out in the grounds, and nervous start at every sound, that his mother had insisted upon an explanation. When the boy – our boy Roland, who had never known what fear was – began to talk to her of voices he had heard in the park, and shadows that had appeared to him among the ruins, my wife promptly put him to bed and sent for Dr Simson – which, of course, was the only thing to do.

I hurried off that evening, as may be supposed, with an anxious heart. How I got through the hours before the starting of the train, I cannot tell. We must all be thankful for the quickness of the railway when in anxiety; but to have thrown myself into a post-chaise as soon as horses could be put to, would have been a relief. I got to Edinburgh very early in the blackness of the winter morning, and scarcely dared look the man in the face, at whom I gasped 'What news?' My wife had sent the brougham for me, which I concluded, before the man spoke, was a bad sign. His answer was that stereotyped answer which leaves the imagination so wildly free – 'Just the same.' Just the same! What might that mean? The horses seemed to me to creep along the long dark country-road. As we dashed through the park, I thought I heard some one moaning among the trees, and clenched my fist at them (whoever they might be) with fury. Why had the fool of a woman at the gate allowed any one to come in to disturb the quiet of the place? If I had not been in such hot haste to get home, I think I should have stopped the carriage and got out to see what tramp it was that had made an entrance, and chosen my grounds, of all places in the world, – when my boy was ill! – to grumble and groan in. But I had no reason to complain of our slow pace here. The horses flew like lightning along the intervening path, and drew up at the door all panting, as if they had run a race. My wife stood at the open door with a pale face, and a candle in her hand, which made her look paler still as the wind blew the flame about. 'He is sleeping,' she said in a whisper, as if her voice might wake him. And I replied, when I could find my voice, also in a whisper, as though the jingling of the horses' furniture and the sound of their hoofs must not have been more dangerous. I stood on the steps with her a moment, almost afraid to go in, now that I was here; and it seemed to me that I saw without observing, if I may say so, that the horses were unwilling to turn round, though their stables lay that way, or that the men were unwilling. These things occurred to me afterwards, though at the moment I was not capable of anything but to ask questions and to hear of the condition of the boy.

I looked at him from the door of his room, for we were afraid to go near, lest we should disturb that blessed sleep. It looked like actual sleep – not the lethargy into which my wife told me he would sometimes fall. She told me everything in the next room, which communicated with his, rising now and then and going to the door of communication; and in this there was much that was very startling and confusing to the mind. It appeared that ever since the winter began, since it was early dark, and night had fallen before his return from school, he had been hearing voices among the ruins – at first only a groaning, he said, at which his pony was as much alarmed as he was, but by degrees a voice. The tears ran down my wife's cheeks as she described to me how he would start up in the night and cry out, 'Oh, mother, let me in! oh, mother, let me in!' with a pathos which rent her heart. And she sitting there all the time, only longing to do everything his heart could desire! But though she would try to soothe him, crying, 'You are at home, my darling. I am here. Don't you know me? Your mother is here!' he would only stare at her, and after a while spring up again with the same cry. At other times he would be quite reasonable, she said, asking eagerly when I was coming, but declaring that he must go with me as soon as I did so, 'to let them in.' 'The doctor thinks his nervous system must have received a shock,' my wife said. 'Oh, Henry, can it be that we have pushed him on too much with his work – a delicate boy like Roland? – and what is his work in comparison with his health? Even you would think little of honours or prizes if it hurt the boy's health.' Even I! as if I were an inhuman father sacrificing my child to my ambition. But I would not increase her trouble by taking any notice. After a while they persuaded me to lie down, to rest, and to eat – none of which things had been possible since I received their letters. The mere fact of being on the spot, of course, in itself was a great thing; and when I knew that I could be called in a moment, as soon as he was awake and wanted me, I felt capable, even in the dark, chill morning twilight, to snatch an hour or two's sleep. As it happened, I was so worn out with the strain of anxiety, and he so quieted and consoled by knowing I had come, that I was not disturbed till the afternoon, when the twilight had again settled down. There was just daylight enough to see his face when I went to him; and what a change in a fortnight! He was paler and more worn, I thought, than even in those dreadful days in the plains before we left India. His hair seemed to me to have grown long and lank; his eyes were like blazing lights projecting out of his white face. He got hold of my hand in a cold and tremulous clutch, and waved to everybody to go away. 'Go away – even mother,' he said, – 'go away.' This went to her heart, for she did not like that even I should have more of the boy's confidence than herself; but my wife has never been a woman to think of herself, and she left us alone. 'Are they all gone?' he said, eagerly. 'They would not let me speak. The doctor treated me as if I was a fool. You know I am not a fool, papa.'

'Yes, yes, my boy, I know; but you are ill, and quiet is so necessary. You are not only not a fool, Roland, but you are reasonable and understand. When you are ill you must deny yourself; you must not do everything that you might do being well.'

He waved his thin hand with a sort of indignation. 'Then, father, I am not ill,' he cried. 'Oh, I thought when you came you would not stop me, – you would see the sense of it! What do you think is the matter with me, all of you? Simson is well enough, but he is only a doctor. What do you think is the matter with me? I am no more ill than you are. A doctor, of course, he thinks you are ill the moment he looks at you – that's what he's there for – and claps you into bed.'

'Which is the best place for you at present, my dear boy.'

'I made up my mind,' cried the little fellow, 'that I would stand it till you came home. I said to myself, I won't frighten mother and the girls. But now, father,' he cried, half jumping out of bed, 'it's not illness, – it's a secret.'

His eyes shone so wildly, his face was so swept with strong feeling, that my heart sank within me. It could be nothing but fever that did it, and fever had been so fatal. I got him into my arms to put him back into bed. 'Roland,' I said, humouring the poor child, which I knew was the only way, 'if you are going to tell me this secret to do any good, you know you must be quite quiet, and not excite yourself. If you excite yourself, I must not let you speak.'

'Yes, father,' said the boy. He was quiet directly, like a man, as if he quite understood. When I had laid him back on his pillow, he looked up at me with that grateful sweet look with which children, when they are ill, break one's heart, the water coming into his eyes in his weakness. 'I was sure as soon as you were here you would know what to do,' he said.

'To be sure, my boy. Now keep quiet, and tell it all out like a man.' To think I was telling lies to my own child! for I did it only to humour him, thinking, poor little fellow, his brain was wrong.

'Yes, father. Father, there is some one in the park, – some one that has been badly used.'

'Hush, my dear; you remember, there is to be no excitement. Well, who is this somebody, and who has been ill-using him? We will soon put a stop to that.'

'Ah,' cried Roland, 'but it is not so easy as you think. I don't know who it is. It is just a cry. Oh, if you could hear it! It gets into my head in my sleep. I heard it as clear – as clear; – and they think that I am dreaming – or raving perhaps,' the boy said, with a sort of disdainful smile.

This look of his perplexed me; it was less like fever than I thought. 'Are you quite sure you have not dreamt it, Roland!' I said.

'Dreamt? – that!' He was springing up again when he suddenly bethought himself, and lay down flat with the same sort of smile on his face. 'The pony heard it too,' he said. 'She jumped as if she had been shot. If I had not grasped at the reins, – for I was frightened, father—'

'No shame to you, my boy,' said I, though I scarcely knew why.

'If I hadn't held to her like a leech, she'd have pitched me over her head, and never drew breath till we were at the door. Did the pony dream it?' he said, with a soft disdain, yet indulgence for my foolishness. Then he added slowly: 'It was only a cry the first time, and all the time before you went away. I wouldn't tell you, for it was so wretched to be frightened. I thought it might be a hare or a rabbit snared, and I went in the morning and looked, but there was nothing. It was after you went I heard it really first, and this is what it says.' He raised himself on his elbow close to me, and looked me in the face. ' "Oh, mother, let me in! oh, mother, let me in!" ' As he said the words a mist came over his face, the mouth quivered, the soft features all melted and changed, and when he had ended these pitiful words, dissolved in a shower of heavy tears.

Was it a hallucination? Was it the fever of the brain? Was it the disordered fancy caused by great bodily weakness? How could I tell? I thought it wisest to accept it as if it were all true.

'This is very touching, Roland,' I said.

'Oh, if you had just heard it, father! I said to myself, if father heard it he would do something; but mamma, you know, she's given over to Simson, and that fellow's a doctor, and never thinks of anything but clapping you into bed.'

'We must not blame Simson for being a doctor, Roland.'

'No, no,' said my boy, with delightful toleration and indulgence; 'oh no; that's the good of him – that's what he's for; I know that. But you – you are different; you are just father, and you'll do something, – directly, papa, directly, – this very night.'

'Surely,' I said. 'No doubt it is some little lost child.'

He gave me a sudden, swift look, investigating my face as if to see if, after all, this was everything my eminence as 'father' came to, – no more than that? Then he got hold of my shoulder, clutching it with his thin hand: 'Look here,' he said, with a quiver in his voice; 'suppose it wasn't living at all!'

'My dear boy, how then could you have heard it?' I said.

He turned away from me with a pettish exclamation – 'As if you didn't know better than that!'

'Do you want to tell me it is a ghost?' I said.

Roland withdrew his hand; his countenance assumed an aspect of great dignity and gravity; a slight quiver remained about his lips. 'Whatever it was – you always said we were not to call names. It was something – in trouble. Oh, father, in terrible trouble!'

'But, my boy,' I said – I was at my wits' end – 'if it was a child that was lost, or any poor human creature – but, Roland, what do you want me to do?'

'I should know if I was you,' said the child, eagerly. 'That is what I always said to myself – Father will know. Oh, papa, papa, to have to face it night after night, in such terrible, terrible trouble! and never to be able to do it any good. I don't want to cry; it's like a baby, I know; but I can't help it; – out there all by itself in the ruin, and nobody to help it. I can't bear it, I can't bear it!' cried my generous boy. And in his weakness he burst out, after many attempts to restrain it, into a great childish fit of sobbing and tears.

I do not know that I ever was in a greater perplexity in my life; and afterwards, when I thought of it, there was something comic in it too. It is bad enough to find your child's mind possessed with the conviction that he has seen – or heard – a ghost. But that he should require you to go instantly and help that ghost, was the most bewildering experience that had ever come my way. I am a sober man myself, and not superstitious – at least any more than everybody is superstitious. Of course I do not believe in ghosts; but I don't deny any more than other people, that there are stories, which I cannot pretend to understand. My blood got a sort of chill in my veins at the idea that Roland should be a ghost-seer; for that generally means a hysterical temperament and weak health, and all that men most hate and fear for their children. But that I should take up his ghost and right its wrongs, and save it from its trouble, was such a mission as was enough to confuse any man. I did my best to console my boy without giving any promise of this astonishing kind; but he was too sharp for me. He would have none of my caresses. With sobs breaking in at intervals upon his voice, and the rain-drops hanging on his eyelids, he yet returned to the charge.

'It will be there now – it will be there all the night. Oh, think, papa, think, if it was me! I can't rest for thinking of it. Don't!' he cried, putting away my hand – 'don't! You go and help it, and mother can take care of me.'

'But, Roland, what can I do?'

My boy opened his eyes, which were large with weakness and fever, and gave me a smile such, I think, as sick children only know the secret of. 'I was sure you would know as soon as you came. I always said – Father will know: and mother,' he cried, with a softening of repose upon his face, his limbs relaxing, his form sinking with a luxurious repose in his bed – 'mother can come and take care of me.'

I called her, and saw him turn to her with the complete dependence of a child, and then I went away and left them, as perplexed a man as any in Scotland. I must say, however, I had this consolation, that my mind was greatly eased about Roland. He might be under a hallucination, but his head was clear enough, and I did not think him so ill as everybody else did. The girls were astonished even at the ease with which I took his illness. 'How do you think he is?' they said in a breath, coming round me, laying hold of me. 'Not half so ill as I expected,' I said; 'not very bad at all.' 'Oh, papa, you are a darling!' cried Agatha, kissing me, and crying upon my shoulder; while little Jeanie, who was as pale as Roland, clasped both her arms round mine, and could not speak at all. I knew nothing about it, not half so much as Simson, but they believed in me; they had a feeling that all would go right now. God is very good to you when your children look to you like that. It makes one humble, not proud. I was not worthy of it; and then I recollected that I had to act the part of a father to Roland's ghost, which made me almost laugh, though I might just as well have cried. It was the strangest mission that ever was intrusted to mortal man.

It was then I remembered suddenly the looks of the men when they turned to take the brougham to the stables in the dark that morning: they had not liked it, and the horses had not liked it. I remembered that even in my anxiety about Roland I had heard them tearing along the avenue back to the stables, and had made a memorandum mentally that I must speak of it. It seemed to me that the best thing I could do was to go to the stables now and make a few inquiries. It is impossible to fathom the minds of rustics; there might be some deviltry of practical joking, for anything I knew; or they might have some reason in getting up a bad reputation for the Brentwood avenue. It was getting dark by the time I went out, and nobody who knows the country will need to be told how black is the darkness of a November night under high laurel-bushes and yew-trees. I walked into the heart of the shrub-beries two or three times, not seeing a step before me, till I came out upon the broader carriage-road, where the trees opened a little, and there was a faint grey glimmer of sky visible, under which the great limes and elms stood darkling like ghosts; but it grew black again as I approached the corner where the ruins lay. Both eyes and ears were on the alert, as may be supposed; but I could see nothing in the absolute gloom, and, so far as I can recollect, I heard nothing. Never-theless there came a strong impression upon me that some-body was there. It is a sensation which most people have felt. I have seen when it has been strong enough to awake you out of sleep, the sense of some one looking at you. I suppose my imagination had been affected by Roland's story; and the mystery of the darkness is always full of suggestions. I stamped my feet violently on the gravel to rouse myself, and called out sharply, 'Who's there?' Nobody answered, nor did I expect any one to answer, but the impression had been made. I was so foolish that I did not like to look back, but went sideways, keeping an eye on the gloom behind. It was with great relief that I spied the light in the stables, making a sort of oasis in the darkness. I walked very quickly into the midst of that lighted and cheerful place, and thought the clank of the groom's pail one of the pleasantest sounds I had ever heard. The coachman was the head of this little colony, and it was to his house I went to pursue my investigations. He was a native of the district, and had taken care of the place in the absence of the family for years; it was impossible but that he must know everything that was going on, and all the traditions of the place. The men, I could see, eyed me anxiously when I thus appeared at such an hour among them, and followed me with their eyes to Jarvis's house, where he lived alone with his old wife, their children being all married and out in the world. Mrs Jarvis met me with anxious questions. How was the poor young gentleman? but the others knew, I could see by their faces, that not even this was the foremost thing in my mind.

'Noises? – ou ay, there'll be noises – the wind in the trees, and the water soughing down the glen. As for tramps, Cornel, no, there's little o' that kind o' cattle about here; and Merran at the gate's a careful body.' Jarvis moved about with some embarrassment from one leg to another as he spoke. He kept in the shade, and did not look at me more than he could help. Evidently his mind was perturbed, and he had reasons for keeping his own counsel. His wife sat by, giving him a quick look now and then, but saying nothing. The kitchen was very snug, and warm, and bright – as different as could be from the chill and mystery of the night outside.

'I think you are trifling with me, Jarvis,' I said.

'Triflin', Cornel? no me. What would I trifle for? If the deevil himsel was in the auld hoose, I have no interest in't one way or another—'

'Sandy, hold your peace!' cried his wife, imperatively.

'And what am I to hold my peace for, wi' the Cornel standing there asking a' thae questions? I'm saying, if the deevil himsel—'

'And I'm telling ye hold your peace!' cried the woman, in great excitement. 'Dark November weather and lang nichts, and us that ken a' we ken. How daur ye name – a name that shouldna be spoken?' She threw down her stocking and got up, also in great agitation. 'I tellt ye you never could keep it. It's no a thing that will hide; and the haill toun kens as weel as you or me. Tell the Cornel straight out, or see, I'll do it. I dinna hold wi' your secrets: and a secret that the haill toun kens!' She snapped her fingers with an air of large disdain. As for Jarvis, ruddy and big as he was, he shrank to nothing before this decided woman. He repeated to her two or three times her own adjuration, 'Hold your peace!' then, suddenly changing his tone, cried out, 'Tell him then, confound ye! I'll wash my hands o't. If a' the ghosts in Scotland were in the auld hoose, is that ony concern o' mine?'

After this I elicited without much difficulty the whole story. In the opinion of the Jarvises, and of everybody about, the certainty that the place was haunted was beyond all doubt. As Sandy and his wife warmed to the tale, one tripping up another in their eagerness to tell everything, it gradually developed as distinct a superstition as I ever heard, and not without poetry and pathos. How long it was since the voice had been heard first, nobody could tell with certainty. Jarvis's opinion was that his father, who had been coachman at Brentwood before him, had never heard anything about it, and that the whole thing had arisen within the last ten years, since the complete dismantling of the old house: which was a wonderfully modern date for a tale so well authenticated. According to these witnesses, and to several whom I questioned afterwards, and who were all in perfect agreement, it was only in the months of November and December that 'the visitation' occurred. During these months, the darkest of the year, scarcely a night passed without the recurrence of these inexplicable cries. Nothing, it was said, had ever been seen – at least nothing that could be identified. Some people, bolder or more imaginative than the others, had seen the darkness moving, Mrs. Jarvis said, with unconscious poetry. It began when night fell, and continued, at intervals, till day broke. Very often it was only an inarticulate cry and moaning, but sometimes the words which had taken possession of my poor boy's fancy had been distinctly audible – 'Oh, mother, let me in!' The Jarvises were not aware that there had ever been any investigation into it. The estate of Brentwood had lapsed into the hands of a distant branch of the family, who had lived but little there; and of the many people who had taken it, as I had done, few had remained through two Decembers. And nobody had taken the trouble to make a very close examination into the facts. 'No, no,' Jarvis said, shaking his head, 'no, no, Cornel. Wha wad set themsels up for a laughin'-stock to a' the country-side, making a wark about a ghost? Naebody believes in ghosts. It bid to be the wind in the trees, the last gentleman said, or some effec' o' the water wrastlin' among the rocks. He said it was a' quite easy explained: but he gave up the hoose.

And when you cam, Cornel, we were awfu' anxious you should never hear. What for should I have spoiled the bargain and hairmed the property for nothing?'

'Do you call my child's life nothing?' I said in the trouble of the moment, unable to restrain myself. 'And instead of telling this all to me, you have told it to him – to a delicate boy, a child unable to sift evidence, or judge for himself, a tender-hearted young creature—'

I was walking about the room with an anger all the hotter that I felt it to be most likely quite unjust. My heart was full of bitterness against the stolid retainers of a family who were content to risk other people's children and comfort rather than let a house lie empty. If I had been warned I might have taken precautions, or left the place, or sent Roland away, a hundred things which now I could not do; and here I was with my boy in brain-fever, and his life, the most precious life on earth, hanging in the balance, dependent on whether or not I could get to the reason of a *banal*, commonplace ghost-story! I paced about in high wrath, not seeing what I was to do; for, to take Roland away, even if he were able to travel, would not settle his agitated mind; and I feared even that a scientific explanation of refracted sound, or reverberation, or any other of the easy certainties with which we elder men are silenced, would have very little effect upon the boy.

'Cornel,' said Jarvis, solemnly, 'and *she'll* bear me witness – the young gentleman never heard a word from me – no, nor from either groom or gardener; I'll gie ye my word for that. In the first place, he's no a lad that invites ye to talk. There are some that are, and some that arena. Some will draw ye on, till ye've tellt them a' the clatter of the toun, and a' ye ken, and whiles mair. But Maister Roland, his mind's fu' of his books. He's aye civil and kind, and a fine lad; but no that sort. And ye see it's for a' our interest, Cornel, that you should stay at Brentwood. I took it upon me mysel to pass the word – "No a syllable to Maister Roland, nor to the young leddies – no a syllable." The women-servants, that have little reason to be out at night, ken little or nothing about it. And some think it grand to have a ghost so long as they're no in the way of coming across it. If you had been tellt the story to begin with, maybe ye would have thought so yoursel?'

This was true enough, though it did not throw any light upon my perplexity. If we had heard of it to start with, it is

possible that all the family would have considered the possession of a ghost a distinct advantage. It is the fashion of the
times. We never think what a risk it is to play with young
imaginations, but cry out, in the fashionable jargon, 'A ghost!
– nothing else was wanted to make it perfect.' I should not
have been above this myself. I should have smiled, of course,
at the idea of the ghost at all, but then to feel that it was mine
would have pleased my vanity. Oh yes, I claim no exemption.
The girls would have been delighted. I could fancy their
eagerness, their interest, and excitement. No; if we had been
told, it would have done no good – we should have made the
bargain all the more eagerly, the fools that we are. 'And there
has been no attempt to investigate it,' I said, 'to see what it
really is?'

'Eh, Cornel,' said the coachman's wife, 'wha would investigate, as ye call it, a thing that nobody believes in? Ye
would be the laughin'-stock of a' the country-side, as my
man says.'

'But you believe in it,' I said, turning upon her hastily. The
woman was taken by surprise. She made a step backward out
of my way.

'Lord, Cornel, how ye frichten a body! Me! – there's awfu'
strange things in this world. An unlearned person doesna ken
what to think. But the minister and the gentry they just laugh
in your face. Inquire into the thing that is not! Na, na, we just
let it be—'

'Come with me, Jarvis,' I said, hastily, 'and we'll make an
attempt at least. Say nothing to the men or to anybody. I'll
come back after dinner, and we'll make a serious attempt to
see what it is, if it is anything. If I hear it – which I doubt –
you may be sure I shall never rest till I make it out. Be ready
for me about ten o'clock.'

'Me, Cornel!' Jarvis said, in a faint voice. I had not been
looking at him in my own preoccupation, but when I did
so, I found that the greatest change had come over the fat
and ruddy coachman. 'Me, Cornel!' he repeated, wiping
the perspiration from his brow. His ruddy face hung in
flabby folds, his knees knocked together, his voice seemed
half extinguished in his throat. Then he began to rub his
hands and smile upon me in a deprecating, imbecile way.
'There's no-thing I wouldna do to pleasure ye, Cornel,'
taking a step further back. 'I'm sure, *she* kens I've aye said

I never had to do with a mair fair, weel-spoken gentle-man—' Here Jarvis came to a pause, again looking at me, rubbing his hands.

'Well?' I said.

'But eh, sir!' he went on, with the same imbecile yet insinuating smile, 'if ye'll reflect that I am no used to my feet. With a horse atween my legs, or the reins in my hand, I'm maybe nae worse than other men; but on fit, Cornel— It's no the – bogles;—but I've been cavalry, ye see,' with a little hoarse laugh, 'a' my life. To face a thing ye didna understan' – on your feet, Cornel.'

'Well, sir, if *I* do it,' said I, tartly, 'why shouldn't you?'

'Eh, Cornel, there's an awfu' difference. In the first place, ye tramp about the haill country-side, and think naething of it, but a walk tires me mair than a hunard miles' drive: and then ye're a gentleman, and do your ain pleasure; and you're no so auld as me; and it's for your ain bairn, ye see, Cornel; and then—'

'He believes in it, Cornel, and you dinna believe in it,' the woman said.

'Will you come with me?' I said, turning to her.

She jumped back, upsetting her chair in her bewilderment. 'Me!' with a scream, and then fell into a sort of hysterical laugh. 'I wouldna say but what I would go; but what would the folk say to hear of Cornel Mortimer with an auld silly woman at his heels?'

The suggestion made me laugh too, though I had little inclination for it. 'I'm sorry you have so little spirit, Jarvis,' I said. 'I must find some one else, I suppose.'

Jarvis, touched by this, began to remonstrate, but I cut him short. My butler was a soldier who had been with me in India, and was not supposed to fear anything – man or devil, – certainly not the former; and I felt that I was losing time. The Jarvises were too thankful to get rid of me. They attended me to the door with the most anxious courtesies. Outside, the two grooms stood close by, a little confused by my sudden exit. I don't know if perhaps they had been listening – at least standing as near as possible, to catch any scrap of the conversation. I waved my hand to them as I went past, in answer to their salutations, and it was very apparent to me that they also were glad to see me go.

And it will be thought very strange, but it would be weak

not to add, that I myself, though bent on the investigation I have spoken of, pledged to Roland to carry it out, and feeling that my boy's health, perhaps his life, depended on the result of my inquiry, – I felt the most unaccountable reluctance to pass these ruins on my way home. My curiosity was intense; and yet it was all my mind could do to pull my body along. I daresay the scientific people would describe it the other way, and attribute my cowardice to the state of my stomach. I went on; but if I had followed my impulse I should not have gone on; I should have turned and bolted. Everything in me seemed to cry out against it; my heart thumped, my pulses all began, like sledge-hammers, beating against my ears and every sensitive part. It was very dark, as I have said; the old house, with its shapeless tower, loomed a heavy mass through the darkness, which was only not entirely so solid as itself. On the other hand, the great dark cedars of which we were so proud seemed to fill up the night. My foot strayed out of the path in my confusion and the gloom together, and I brought myself up with a cry as I felt myself knock against something solid. What was it? The contact with hard stone and lime, and prickly bramble-bushes, restored me a little to myself. 'Oh, it's only the old gable,' I said aloud, with a little laugh to reassure myself. The rough feeling of the stones reconciled me. As I groped about thus, I shook off my visionary folly. What so easily explained as that I should have strayed from the path in the darkness? This brought me back to common existence, as if I had been shaken by a wise hand out of all the silliness of superstition. How silly it was, after all! What did it matter which path I took? I laughed again, this time with better heart – when suddenly, in a moment, the blood was chilled in my veins, a shiver stole along my spine, my faculties seemed to forsake me. Close by me at my side, at my feet, there was a sigh. No, not a groan, not a moaning, not anything so tangible – a perfectly soft, faint, inarticulate sigh. I sprung back, and my heart stopped beating. Mistaken! no, mistake was impossible. I heard it as clearly as I hear myself speak; a long, soft, weary sigh, as if drawn to the utmost, and empty-ing out a load of sadness that filled the breast. To hear this in the solitude, in the dark, in the night (though it was still early), had an effect which I cannot describe. I feel it now – something cold creeping over me, up into my hair, and down to my feet, which refused to move. I cried out, with a trembling voice, 'Who is there?' as I had done before – but there was no reply.

I got home I don't quite know how; but in my mind there was no longer any indifference as to the thing, whatever it was, that haunted these ruins. My scepticism disappeared like a mist. I was as firmly determined that there was something as Roland was. I did not for a moment pretend to myself that it was possible I could be deceived; there were movements and noises which I understood all about, cracklings of small branches in the frost, and little rolls of gravel on the path, such as have a very eerie sound sometimes, and perplex you with wonder as to who has done it, *when there is no real mystery*; but I assure you all these little movements of nature don't affect you one bit *when there is something*. I understood *them*. I did not understand the sigh. That was not simple nature; there was meaning in it – feeling, the soul of a creature invisible. This is the thing that human nature trembles at – a creature invisible, yet with sensations, feelings, a power somehow of expressing itself. I had not the same sense of unwillingness to turn my back upon the scene of the mystery which I had experienced in going to the stables; but I almost ran home, impelled by eagerness to get everything done that had to be done, in order to apply myself to finding it out. Bagley was in the hall as usual when I went in. He was always there in the afternoon, always with the appearance of perfect occupation, yet, so far as I know, never doing anything. The door was open, so that I hurried in without any pause, breathless; but the sight of his calm regard, as he came to help me off with my overcoat, subdued me in a moment. Anything out of the way, anything incomprehensible, faded to nothing in the presence of Bagley. You saw and wondered how *he* was made: the parting of his hair, the tie of his white neckcloth, the fit of his trousers, all perfect as works of art; but you could see how they were done, which makes all the difference. I flung myself upon him, so to speak, without waiting to note the extreme unlikeness of the man to anything of the kind I meant. 'Bagley,' I said, 'I want you to come out with me tonight to watch for—'

'Poachers, Colonel,' he said, a gleam of pleasure running all over him.

'No, Bagley; a great deal worse,' I cried.

'Yes, Colonel; at what hour, sir?' the man said; but then I had not told him what it was.

It was ten o'clock when we set out. All was perfectly quiet indoors. My wife was with Roland, who had been quite calm, she said, and who (though the fever of course must run its course) had been better ever since I came. I told Bagley to put on a thick greatcoat over his evening coat, and did the same myself – with strong boots; for the soil was like a sponge, or worse. Talking to him, I almost forgot what we were going to do. It was darker even than it had been before, and Bagley kept very close to me as we went along. I had a small lantern in my hand, which gave us partial guidance. We had come to the corner where the path turns. On one side was the bowling-green, which the girls had taken possession of for their croquet-lawn – a wonderful enclosure surrounded by high hedges of holly, three hundred years old and more; on the other, the ruins. Both were black as night; but before we got so far, there was a little opening in which we could just discern the trees and the lighter line of the road. I thought it best to pause there and take breath. 'Bagley,' I said, 'there is something about these ruins I don't understand. It is there I am going. Keep your eyes open and your wits about you. Be ready to pounce upon any stranger you see – anything, man or woman. Don't hurt, but seize – anything you see.' 'Colonel,' said Bagley, with a little tremor in his breath, 'they do say there's things there – as is neither man nor woman.' There was no time for words. 'Are you game to follow me, my man? that's the question,' I said. Bagley fell in without a word, and saluted. I knew then I had nothing to fear.

We went, so far as I could guess, exactly as I had come, when I heard that sigh. The darkness, however, was so complete that all marks, as of trees or paths, disappeared. One moment we felt our feet on the gravel, another sinking noiselessly into the slippery grass, that was all. I had shut up my lantern, not wishing to scare any one, whoever it might be. Bagley followed, it seemed to me, exactly in my footsteps as I made my way, as I supposed, towards the mass of the ruined house. We seemed to take a long time groping along seeking this; the squash of the wet soil under our feet was the only thing that marked our progress. After a while I stood still to see, or rather feel, where we were. The darkness was very still, but no stiller than is usual in a winter's night. The sounds I have mentioned – the crackling of twigs, the roll of a pebble, the sound of some rustle in the dead leaves, or creeping creature on the grass – were audible when you listened, all mysterious enough when your mind is disengaged, but to me cheering now as signs of the livingness of nature, even in the death of the frost. As we stood still there came up from the trees in the glen the prolonged hoot of an owl. Bagley started with alarm, being in a state of general nervousness, and not knowing what he was afraid of. But to me the sound was encouraging and pleasant, being so comprehensible. 'An owl,' I said, under my breath. 'Y—es, Colonel,' said Bagley, his teeth chattering. We stood still about five minutes, while it broke into the still brooding of the air, the sound widening out in circles, dying upon the darkness. This sound, which is not a cheerful one, made me almost gay. It was natural, and relieved the tension of the mind. I moved on with new courage, my nervous excitement calming down.

When all at once, quite suddenly, close to us, at our feet, there broke out a cry. I made a spring backwards in the first moment of surprise and horror, and in doing so came sharply against the same rough masonry and brambles that had struck me before. This new sound came upwards from the ground – a low, moaning, wailing voice, full of suffering and pain. The contrast between it and the hoot of the owl was indescribable; the one with a wholesome wildness and naturalness that hurt nobody – the other, a sound that made one's blood curdle, full of human misery. With a great deal of fumbling – for in spite of everything I could do to keep up my courage my hands shook, I managed to remove the slide of my lantern. The light leaped out like something living, and made the place visible in a moment. We were what would have been inside the ruined building had anything remained but the gable-wall which I have described. It was close to us, the vacant doorway in it going out straight into the blackness outside. The light showed the bit of wall, the ivy glistening upon it in clouds of dark green, the bramble branches waving, and below, the open door – a door that led to nothing. It was from this the voice came which died out just as the light flashed upon this strange scene. There was a moment's silence, and then it broke forth again. The sound was so near, so penetrating, so pitiful, that, in the nervous start I gave, the light fell out of my hand. As I groped for it in the dark my hand was clutched by Bagley, who I think must have dropped upon his knees; but I was too much perturbed myself to think much of this. He clutched at me in the confusion of his terror, forgetting all his usual decorum. 'For God's sake, what is it, sir?' he gasped. If I yielded, there was evidently an end of both of us. 'I can't tell,' I said, 'any more than you; that's what we've got to find out: up, man, up!' I pulled him to his feet. 'Will you go round and examine the other side, or will you stay here with the lantern?' Bagley gasped at me with a face of horror. 'Can't we stay together, Colonel?' he said – his knees were trembling under him. I pushed him against the corner of the wall, and put the light into his hands. 'Stand fast till I come back; shake yourself together, man; let nothing pass you,' I said. The voice was within two or three feet of us, of that there could be no doubt.

I went myself to the other side of the wall, keeping close to it. The light shook in Bagley's hand, but, tremulous though it was, shone out through the vacant door, one oblong block of light marking all the crumbling corners and hanging masses of foliage. Was that something dark huddled in a heap by the side of it? I pushed forward across the light in the doorway, and fell upon it with my hands; but it was only a juniper-bush growing close against the wall. Meanwhile, the sight of my figure crossing the doorway had brought Bagley's nervous excitement to a height: he flew at me, gripping my shoulder. 'I've got him, Colonel! I've got him!' he cried, with a voice of sudden exultation. He thought it was a man, and was at once relieved. But at that moment the voice burst forth again between us, at our feet – more close to us than any separate being could be. He dropped off from me, and fell against the wall, his jaw dropping as if he were dying. I suppose, at the same moment, he saw that it was I whom he had clutched. I, for my part, had scarcely more command of myself. I snatched the light out of his hand, and flashed it all about me wildly. Nothing, – the juniper-bush, which I thought I had never seen before, the heavy growth of the glistening ivy, the brambles waving. It was close to my ears now, crying, crying, pleading as if for life. Either I heard the same words Roland had heard, or else, in my excitement, his imagination got possession of mine. The voice went on, growing into distinct articulation, but waving about, now from one point, now from another, as if the owner of it were moving slowly back and forward. 'Mother! mother!' and then an outburst of wailing. As my mind steadied, getting accustomed (as one's mind gets accustomed to anything), it seemed to me as if some uneasy, miserable creature was pacing up and down before a closed door. Sometimes – but that must have been excitement – I thought I heard a sound like knocking, and then another burst, 'Oh, mother! mother!' All this close, close to the space where I was standing with my lantern – now before me, now behind me: a creature restless, unhappy, moaning, crying, before the vacant doorway, which no one could either shut or open more.

'Do you hear it, Bagley? do you hear what it is saying?' I cried, stepping in through the doorway. He was lying against the wall – his eyes glazed, half dead with terror. He made a motion of his lips as if to answer me, but no sounds came; then lifted his hand with a curious imperative movement as if ordering me to be silent and listen. And how long I did so I cannot tell. It began to have an interest, an exciting hold upon me, which I could not describe. It seemed to call up visibly a scene any one could understand – a something shut out, restlessly wandering to and fro; sometimes the voice dropped, as if throwing itself down – sometimes wandered off a few paces, growing sharp and clear. 'Oh, mother, let me in! oh, mother, mother, let me in! oh, let me in!' every word was clear to me. No wonder the boy had gone wild with pity. I tried to steady my mind upon Roland, upon his conviction that I could do something, but my head swam with the excitement, even when I partially overcame the terror. At last the words died away, and there was a sound of sobs and moaning. I cried out, 'In the name of God who are you?' with a kind of feeling in my mind that to use the name of God was profane, seeing that I did not believe in ghosts or anything supernatural; but I did it all the same, and waited, my heart giving a leap of terror lest there should be a reply. Why this should have been I cannot tell, but I had a feeling that if there was an answer it would be more than I could bear. But there was no answer; the moaning went on, and then, as if it had been real, the voice rose a little higher again, the words recommenced, 'Oh, mother, let me in! oh, mother, let me in!' with an expression that was heart-breaking to hear.

As if it had been real! What do I mean by that? I suppose I got less alarmed as the thing went on. I began to recover the use of my senses – I seemed to explain it all to myself by saying that this had once happened, that it was a recollection of a real scene. Why there should have seemed something quite satisfactory and composing in this explanation I cannot tell, but so it was. I began to listen almost as if it had been a play, forgetting Bagley, who, I almost think, had fainted, leaning against the wall. I was startled out of this strange spectatorship that had fallen upon me by the sudden rush of something which made my heart jump once more, a large black figure in the doorway waving its arms. 'Come in! come in! come in!' it shouted out hoarsely at the top of a deep bass voice, and then poor Bagley fell down senseless across the threshold. He was less sophisticated than I, – he had not been able to bear it any longer. I took him for something supernatural, as he took me, and it was some time before I awoke to the necessities of the moment. I remembered only after, that from the time I began to give my attention to the man, I heard the other voice no more. It was some time before I brought him to. It must have been a strange scene; the lantern making a luminous spot in the darkness, the man's white face lying on the black earth, I over him, doing what I could for him. Probably I should have been thought to be murdering him had any one seen us. When at last I succeeded in pouring a little brandy down his throat, he sat up and looked about him wildly. 'What's up?' he said; then recognising me, tried to struggle to his feet with a faint 'Beg your pardon, Colonel.' I got him home as best I could, making him lean upon my arm. The great fellow was as weak as a child. Fortunately he did not for some time remember what had happened. From the time Bagley fell the voice had stopped, and all was still.

'You've got an epidemic in your house, Colonel,' Simson said to me next morning. 'What's the meaning of it all? Here's your butler raving about a voice. This will never do, you know; and so far as I can make out, you are in it too.'

'Yes, I am in it, doctor. I thought I had better speak to you. Of course you are treating Roland all right – but the boy is not raving, he is as sane as you or I. It's all true.'

'As sane as – I – or you. I never thought the boy insane. He's got cerebral excitement, fever. I don't know what you've got. There's something very queer about the look of your eyes.'

'Come,' said I, 'you can't put us all to bed, you know. You had better listen and hear the symptoms in full.'

The doctor shrugged his shoulders, but he listened to me patiently. He did not believe a word of the story, that was clear; but he heard it all from beginning to end. 'My dear fellow,' he said, 'the boy told me just the same. It's an epidemic. When one person falls a victim to this sort of thing, it's as safe as can be – there's always two or three.'

'Then how do you account for it?' I said.

'Oh, account for it! – that's a different matter; there's no accounting for the freaks our brains are subject to. If it's delusion; if it's some trick of the echoes or the winds – some phonetic disturbance or other—'

'Come with me tonight, and judge for yourself,' I said.

Upon this he laughed aloud, then said, 'That's not such a bad idea; but it would ruin me for ever if it were known that John Simson was ghost-hunting.'

'There it is,' said I; 'you dart down on us who are unlearned with your phonetic disturbances, but you daren't examine what the thing really is for fear of being laughed at. That's science!'

'It's not science – it's common-sense,' said the doctor. 'The thing has delusion on the front of it. It is encouraging an unwholesome tendency even to examine. What good could come of it? Even if I am convinced, I shouldn't believe.'

'I should have said so yesterday; and I don't want you to be convinced or to believe,' said I. 'If you prove it to be a delusion, I shall be very much obliged too, for one. Come; somebody must go with me.'

'You are cool,' said the doctor. 'You've disabled this poor fellow of yours, and made him – on that point – a lunatic for life; and now you want to disable me. But for once, I'll do it. To save appearance, if you'll give me a bed, I'll come over after my last rounds.'

It was agreed that I should meet him at the gate, and that we should visit the scene of last night's occurrences before we came to the house, so that nobody might be the wiser. It was scarcely possible to hope that the cause of Bagley's sudden illness should not somehow steal into the knowledge of the servants at least, and it was better that all should be done as quietly as possible. The day seemed to me a very long one. I had to spend a certain part of it with Roland, which was a terrible ordeal for me – for what could I say to the boy? The improvement continued, but he was still in a very precarious state, and the trembling vehemence with which he turned to me when his mother left the room, filled me with alarm. 'Father?' he said, quietly. 'Yes, my boy; I am giving my best attention to it – all is being done that I can do. I have not come to any conclusion – yet. I am neglecting nothing you said,' I cried. What I could not do was to give his active mind any encouragement to dwell upon the mystery. It was a hard predicament, for some satisfaction had to be given him. He looked at me very wistfully, with the great blue eyes which gazed so large and brilliant out of his white and worn face. 'You must trust me,' I said. 'Yes, father. Father knows – father knows,' he said to himself, as if to soothe some inward doubt. I left him as soon as I could. He was about the most precious thing I had on earth, and his health my first thought; but yet somehow, in the excitement of this other subject, I put it aside, and preferred not to dwell upon Roland, which was the most curious part of it all.

That night at eleven I met Simson at the gate. He had come by train, and I let him in gently myself. I had been so much absorbed in the coming experiment that I passed the ruins in going to meet him, almost without thought, if you can understand that. I had my lantern; and he showed me a coil of taper which he had ready for use. 'There is nothing like light,' he said, in his scoffing tone. It was a very still night, scarcely a sound, but not so dark. We could keep the path without difficulty as we went along. As we approached the spot we could hear a low moaning, broken occasionally by a bitter cry. 'Perhaps that is your voice,' said the doctor; 'I thought it must be something of the kind. That's a poor brute caught in some of these infernal traps of yours; you'll find it among the bushes somewhere.' I said nothing. I felt no particular fear, but a triumphant satisfaction in what was to follow. I led him to the spot where Bagley and I had stood on the previous night. All was silent as a winter night could be – so silent that we heard far off the sound of the horses in the stables, the shutting of a window at the house. Simson lighted his taper and went peering about, poking into all the corners. We looked like two conspirators lying in wait for some unfortunate traveller; but not a sound broke the quiet. The moaning had stopped before we came up; a star or two shone over us in the sky, looking down as if surprised at our strange proceedings. Dr Simson did nothing but utter subdued laughs under his breath. 'I thought as much,' he said. 'It is just the same with tables and all other kinds of ghostly apparatus; a sceptic's presence stops everything. When I am present nothing ever comes off. How long do you think it will be necessary to stay here? Oh, I don't complain; only, when *you* are satisfied, *I* am – quite.'

I will not deny that I was disappointed beyond measure by this result. It made me look like a credulous fool. It gave the doctor such a pull over me as nothing else could. I should point all his morals for years to come, and his materialism, his scepticism would be increased beyond endurance. 'It seems, indeed,' I said, 'that there is to be no—' 'Manifestation', he said, laughing; 'that is what all the mediums say. No manifestations, in consequence of the presence of an unbeliever.' His laugh sounded very uncomfortable to me in the silence; and it was now near midnight. But that laugh seemed the signal; before it died away the moaning we had heard before was resumed. It started from some distance off, and came towards us, nearer and nearer, like some one walking along and moaning to himself. There could be no idea now that it was a hare caught in a trap. The approach was slow, like that of a weak person with little halts and pauses. We heard it coming along the grass straight towards the vacant doorway. Simson had been a little startled by the first sound. He said hastily, 'That child has no business to be out so late.' But he felt, as well as I, that this was no child's voice. As it came nearer, he grew silent, and, going to the doorway with his taper, stood looking out towards the sound. The taper being unprotected blew about in the night air, though there was scarcely any wind. I threw the light of my lantern steady and white across the same space. It was in a blaze of light in the midst of the blackness. A little icy thrill had gone over me at the first sound, but as it came close, I confess that my only feeling was satisfaction. The scoffer could scoff no more. The light 'touched his own face, and showed a very perplexed countenance. If he was afraid, he concealed it with great success, but he was perplexed. And then all that had happened on the previous night was enacted once more. It fell strangely upon me with a sense of repetition. Every cry, every sob seemed the same as before. I listened almost without any emotion at all in my own person, thinking of its effect upon Simson. He maintained a very bold front on the whole. All that coming and going of the voice was, if our ears could be trusted, exactly in front of the vacant, blank doorway, blazing full of light, which caught and shone in the glistening leaves of the great hollies at a little distance. Not a rabbit could have crossed the turf without being seen; – but there was nothing. After a time, Simson, with a certain caution and bodily reluctance, as it seemed to me, went out with his roll of taper into this space. His figure showed against the holly in full outline. Just at this moment the voice sank, as was its custom, and seemed to fling itself down at the door. Simson recoiled violently, as if some one had come up against him, then turned, and held his taper low as if examining something. 'Do you see anybody?' I cried in a whisper, feeling the chill of nervous panic steal over me at this action. 'It's nothing but a – confounded juniper-bush,' he said. This I knew very well to be nonsense, for the juniper-bush was on the other side. He went about after this round and round, poking his taper everywhere, then returned to me on the inner side of the wall. He scoffed no longer; his face was contracted and pale. 'How long does this go on?' he whispered to me, like a man who does not wish to interrupt some one who is speaking. I had become too much perturbed myself to remark whether the successions and changes of the voice were the same as last night. It suddenly went out in the air almost as he was speaking, with a soft reiterated sob dying away. If there had been anything to be seen, I should have said that the person was at that moment crouching on the ground close to the door.

We walked home very silent afterwards. It was only when we were in sight of the house that I said, 'What do you think of it?' 'I can't tell what to think of it,' he said quickly. He took – though he was a very temperate man – not the claret I was going to offer him, but some brandy from the tray, and swallowed it almost undiluted. 'Mind you, I don't believe a word of it,' he said, when he had lighted his candle; 'but I can't tell what to think of it,' he turned round to add, when he was half-way upstairs.

All of this, however, did me no good with the solution of my problem. I was to help this weeping, sobbing thing, which was already to me as distinct a personality as anything I knew – or what should I say to Roland? It was on my heart that my boy would die if I could not find some way of helping this creature. You may be surprised that I should speak of it in this way. I did not know if it was man or woman; but I no more doubted that it was a soul in pain than I doubted my own being; and it was my business to soothe this pain – to deliver it, if that was possible. Was ever such a task given to an anxious father trembling for his only boy? I felt in my heart, fantastic as it may appear, that I must fulfil this somehow, or part with my child; and you may conceive that rather than do that I was ready to die. But even my dying would not have advanced me – unless by bringing me into the same world with that seeker at the door.

Next morning Simson was out before breakfast, and came in with evident signs of the damp grass on his boots, and a look of worry and weariness, which did not say much for the night he had passed. He improved a little after breakfast, and visited his two patients, for Bagley was still an invalid. I went out with him on his way to the train, to hear what he had to say about the boy. 'He is going on very well,' he said; 'there are no complications as yet. But mind you, that's not a boy to be trifled with, Mortimer. Not a word to him about last night.' I had to tell him then of my last interview with Roland, and of the impossible demand he had made upon me – by which, though he tried to laugh, he was much discomposed, as I could see. 'We must just perjure ourselves all round,' he said, 'and swear you exorcised it;' but the man was too kind-hearted to be satisfied with that. 'It's frightfully serious for you, Mortimer. I can't laugh as I should like to. I wish I saw a way out of it, for your sake. By the way,' he added shortly, 'didn't you notice that juniper-bush on the left-hand side?' 'There was one on the right hand of the door. I noticed you made that mistake last night.' 'Mistake!' he cried, with a curious low laugh, pulling up the collar of his coat as though he felt the cold, – 'there's no juniper there this morning, left or right. Just go and see.' As he stepped into the train a few minutes after, he looked back upon me and beckoned me for a parting word. 'I'm coming back tonight,' he said.

I don't think I had any feeling about this as I turned away from that common bustle of the railway which made my private preoccupations feel so strangely out of date. There had been a distinct satisfaction in my mind before that his scepticism had been so entirely defeated. But the more serious part of the matter pressed upon me now. I went straight from the railway to the manse, which stood on a little plateau on the side of the river opposite to the woods of Brentwood. The minister was one of a class which is not so common in Scotland as it used to be. He was a man of good family, well educated in the Scotch way, strong in philosophy, not so strong in Greek, strongest of all in experience, – a man who had 'come across', in the course of his life, most people of note that had ever been in Scotland – and who was said to be very sound in doctrine, without infringing the toleration to which old men, who are good men, so often come. He was old-fashioned; perhaps he did not think so much about the troublous problems of theology as many of the young men, nor ask himself any hard questions upon the Confession of Faith – but he understood human nature, which is perhaps better. He received me with a cordial welcome. 'Come away, Colonel Mortimer,' he said; 'I'm all the more glad to see you, that I feel it's a good sign for the boy. He's doing well? – God be praised – and the Lord bless him and keep him. He has many a poor body's prayers – and that can do nobody harm.'

'He will need them all, Dr Moncrieff,' I said, 'and your counsel too.' And I told him the story – more than I had told Simson. The old clergyman listened to me with many suppressed exclamations, and at the end the water stood in his eyes.

'That's just beautiful,' he said. 'I do not mind to have heard anything like it; it's as fine as Burns when he wished deliverance to one – that is prayed for in no kirk. Ay, ay! so he would have you console the poor lost spirit? God bless the boy! There's something more than common in that, Colonel Mortimer. And also the faith of him in his father! – I would like to put that into a sermon.' Then the old gentleman gave me an alarmed look, and said, 'No, no; I was not meaning a sermon; but I must write it down for the "Children's Record."' I saw the thought that passed through his mind. Either he thought, or he feared I would think, of a funeral sermon. You may believe this did not make me more cheerful.

I can scarcely say that Dr Moncrieff gave me any advice. How could any one advise on such a subject? But he said, 'I think I'll come too. I'm an old man; I'm less liable to be frighted than those that are further off the world unseen. It behoves me to think of my own journey there. I've no cut-

and-dry beliefs on the subject. I'll come too: and maybe at the moment the Lord will put it into our heads what to do.'

This gave me a little comfort – more than Simson had given me. To be clear about the cause of it was not my grand desire. It was another thing that was in my mind – my boy. As for the poor soul at the open door, I had no more doubt, as I have said, of its existence than I had of my own. It was no ghost to me. I knew the creature, and it was in trouble. That was my feeling about it, as it was Roland's. To hear it first was a great shock to my nerves, but not now; a man will get accustomed to anything. But to do something for it was the great problem; how was I to be serviceable to a being that was invisible, that was mortal no longer? 'Maybe at the moment the Lord will put it into our heads.' This is very old-fashioned phraseology, and a week before, most likely, I should have smiled (though always with kindness) at Dr Moncrieff's credulity; but there was a great comfort, whether rational or otherwise I cannot say, in the mere sound of the words.

The road to the station and the village lay through the glen – not by the ruins; but though the sunshine and the fresh air, and the beauty of the trees, and the sound of the water were all very soothing to the spirits, my mind was so full of my own subject that I could not refrain from turning to the right hand as I got to the top of the glen, and going straight to the place which I may call the scene of all my thoughts. It was lying full in the sunshine, like all the rest of the world. The ruined gable looked due east, and in the present aspect of the sun the light streamed down through the doorway as our lantern had done, throwing a flash of light upon the damp grass beyond. There was a strange suggestion in the open door – so futile, a kind of emblem of vanity – all free around, so that you could go where you pleased, and yet that semblance of an enclosure – that way of entrance, unnecessary, leading to nothing. And why any creature should pray and weep to get in – to nothing: or be kept out – by nothing! You could not dwell upon it, or it made your brain go round. I remembered, however, what Simson said about the juniper, with a little smile on my own mind as to the inaccuracy of recollection, which even a scientific man will be guilty of. I could see now the light of my lantern gleaming upon the wet glistening surface of the spiky leaves at the right hand – and he ready to go to the stake for it that it was the left! I went round to make sure. And then I saw what he had said. Right or left there was no juniper at all. I was confounded by this, though it was entirely a matter of detail: nothing at all: a bush of brambles waving, the grass growing up to the very walls. But after all, though it gave me a shock for a moment, what did that matter? There were marks as if a number of footsteps had been up and down in front of the door; but these might have been our steps; and all was bright, and peaceful, and still. I poked about the other ruin – the larger ruins of the old house – for some time, as I had done before. There were marks upon the grass here and there, I could not call them footsteps, all about; but that told for nothing one way or another. I had examined the ruined rooms closely the first day. They were half filled up with soil and *débris*, without brackens and bramble – no refuge for any one there. It vexed me that Jarvis should see me coming from that spot when he came up to me for his orders. I don't know whether my nocturnal expeditions had got wind among the servants. But there was a significant look in his face. Something in it I felt was like my own sensations when Simson in the midst of his scepticism was struck dumb. Jarvis felt satisfied that his veracity had been put beyond question. I never spoke to a servant of mine in such a peremptory tone before. I sent him away 'with a flea in his lug', as the man described it afterwards. Interference of every kind was intolerable to me at such a moment.

But what was strangest of all was, that I could not face Roland. I did not go up to his room as I would have naturally done at once. This the girls could not understand. They saw there was some mystery in it. 'Mother has gone to lie down,' Agatha said; 'he has had such a good night.' 'But he wants you so, papa!' cried little Jeanie, always with her two arms embracing mine in a pretty way she had. I was obliged to go at last – but what could I say? I could only kiss him, and tell him to keep still – that I was doing all I could. There is something mystical about the patience of a child. 'It will come all right, won't it, father?' he said. 'God grant it may! I hope so, Roland.' 'Oh yes, it will come all right.' Perhaps he understood that in the midst of my anxiety I could not stay with him as I should have done otherwise. But the girls were more surprised than it is possible to describe. They looked at me with wondering eyes. 'If I were ill, papa, and you only stayed with me a moment, I should break my heart,' said

Agatha. But the boy had a sympathetic feeling. He knew that of my own will I would not have done it. I shut myself up in the library, where I could not rest, but kept pacing up and down like a caged beast. What could I do? and if I could do nothing, what would become of my boy? These were the questions that, without ceasing, pursued each other through my mind.

Simson came out to dinner, and when the house was all still, and most of the servants in bed, we went out and met Dr Moncrieff, as we had appointed, at the head of the glen. Simson, for his part, was disposed to scoff at the Doctor. 'If there are to be any spells, you know, I'll cut the whole concern,' he said. I did not make him any reply. I had not invited him; he could go or come as he pleased. He was very talkative, far more so than suited my humour, as we went on. 'One thing is certain, you know, there must be some human agency,' he said. 'It is all bosh about apparitions. I never have investigated the laws of sound to any great extent, and there's a great deal in ventriloquism that we don't know much about.' 'If it's the same to you,' I said, 'I wish you'd keep all that to yourself, Simson, it doesn't suit my state of mind.' 'Oh, I hope I know how to respect idiosyncrasy,' he said. The very tone of his voice irritated me beyond measure. These scientific fellows, I wonder people put up with them as they do, when you have no mind for their cold-blooded confidence. Dr Moncrieff met us about eleven o'clock, the same time as on the previous night. He was a large man, with a venerable countenance and white hair – old, but in full vigour, and thinking less of a cold night walk than many a younger man. He had his lantern as I had. We were fully provided with means of lighting the place, and we were all of us resolute men. We had a rapid consultation as we went up, and the result was that we divided to different posts. Dr Moncrieff remained inside the wall – if you can call that inside where there was no wall but one. Simson placed himself on the side next the ruins, so as to intercept any communication with the old house, which was what his mind was fixed upon. I was posted on the other side. To say that nothing could come near without being seen was self-evident. It had been so also on the previous night. Now, with our three lights in the midst of the darkness, the whole place seemed illuminated. Dr Moncrieff's lantern, which was a large one, without any means of shutting up – an old-fashioned lantern with a pierced and ornamental top – shone steadily, the rays shooting out of it upward into the gloom. He placed it on the grass, where the middle of the room, if this had been a room, would have been. The usual effect of the light streaming out of the doorway was prevented by the illumination which Simson and I on either side supplied. With these differences, everything seemed as on the previous night.

And what occurred was exactly the same, with the same air of repetition, point for point, as I had formerly remarked. I declare that it seemed to me as if I were pushed against, put aside, by the owner of the voice as he paced up and down in his trouble, – though these are perfectly futile words, seeing that the stream of light from my lantern, and that from Simson's taper, lay broad and clear, without a shadow, without the smallest break, across the entire breadth of the grass. I had ceased even to be alarmed, for my part. My heart was rent with pity and trouble – pity for the poor suffering human creature that moaned and pleaded so, and trouble for myself and my boy. God! if I could not find any help – and what help could I find? – Roland would die.

We were all perfectly still till the first outburst was exhausted, as I knew (by experience) it would be. Dr Moncrieff, to whom it was new, was quite still on the other side of the wall, as we were in our places. My heart had remained almost at its usual beating during the voice. I was used to it; it did not rouse all my pulses as it did at first. But just as it threw itself sobbing at the door (I cannot use other words), there suddenly came something which sent the blood coursing in my veins and my heart into my mouth. It was a voice inside the wall – the minister's well-known voice. I would have been prepared for it in any kind of adjuration, but I was not prepared for what I heard. It came out with a sort of stammering, as if too much moved for utterance. 'Willie, Willie! Oh, God preserve us! is it you?'

These simple words had an effect upon me that the voice of the invisible creature had ceased to have. I thought the old man, whom I had brought into this danger, had gone mad with terror. I made a dash round to the other side of the wall, half crazed myself with the thought. He was standing where I had left him, his shadow thrown vague and large upon the grass by the lantern which stood at his feet. I lifted my own light to see his face as I rushed forward. He was very pale, his eyes wet and glistening, his mouth quivering with parted lips. He neither saw nor heard me. We that had gone through this experience before, had crouched towards each other to get a little strength to bear it. But he was not even aware that I was there. His whole being seemed absorbed in anxiety and tenderness. He held out his hands, which trembled, but it seemed to me with eagerness, not fear. He went on speaking all the time. 'Willie, if it is you – and it's you, if it is not a delusion of Satan, – Willie, lad! why come ye here frighting them that know you not? Why came ye not to me?'

He seemed to wait for an answer. When his voice ceased, his countenance, every line moving, continued to speak. Simson gave me another terrible shock, stealing into the open doorway with his light, as much awestricken, as wildly curious, as I. But the minister resumed, without seeing Simson, speaking to some one else. His voice took a tone of expostulation—

'Is this right to come here? Your mother's gone with your name on her lips. Do you think she would ever close her door on her own lad? Do ye think the Lord will close the door, ye faint-hearted creature? No! – I forbid ye! I forbid ye!' cried the old man. The sobbing voice had begun to resume its cries. He made a step forward, calling out the last words in a voice of command. 'I forbid ye! Cry out no more to man. Go home, ye wandering spirit! go home! Do you hear me? – me that christened ye, that have struggled with ye, that have wrestled for ye with the Lord!' Here the loud tones of his voice sank into tenderness. 'And her too, poor woman! poor woman! her you are calling upon. She's no here. You'll find her with the Lord. Go there and seek her, not here. Do you hear me, lad? go after her there. He'll let you in, though it's late. Man, take heart! if you will lie and sob and greet, let it be at heaven's gate, and no your poor mother's ruined door.'

He stopped to get his breath: and the voice had stopped, not as it had done before, when its time was exhausted and all its repetitions said, but with a sobbing catch in the breath as if overruled. Then the minister spoke again. 'Are you hearing me, Will? Oh, laddie, you've liked the beggarly elements all your days. Be done with them now. Go home to the Father – the Father! Are you hearing me?' Here the old man sank down upon his knees, his face raised upwards, his hands held up with a tremble in them, all white in the light in the midst of the darkness. I resisted as long as I could, though I cannot tell why, – then I, too, dropped upon my knees. Simson all the time stood in the doorway, with an expression in his face such as words could not tell, his underlip dropped, his eyes wild, staring. It seemed to be to him, that image of blank ignorance and wonder, that we were praying. All the time the voice, with a low arrested sobbing, lay just where he was standing, as I thought.

'Lord,' the minister said – 'Lord, take him into Thy everlasting habitations. The mother he cries to is with Thee. Who can open to him but Thee? Lord, when is it too late for Thee, or what is too hard for Thee? Lord, let that woman there draw him inower! Let her draw him inower!'

I sprang forward to catch something in my arms that flung itself wildly within the door. The illusion was so strong, that I never paused till I felt my forehead graze against the wall and my hands clutch the ground – for there was nobody there to save from falling, as in my foolishness I thought. Simson held out his hand to me to help me up. He was trembling and cold, his lower lip hanging, his speech almost inarticulate. 'It's gone,' he said, stammering, – 'it's gone!' We leant upon each other for a moment, trembling so much both of us that the whole scene trembled as if it were going to dissolve and disappear; and yet as long as I live I will never forget it – the shining of the strange lights, the blackness all round, the kneeling figure with all the whiteness of the light concentrated on its white venerable head and uplifted hands. A strange solemn stillness seemed to close all round us. By intervals a single syllable, 'Lord! Lord!' came from the old minister's lips. He saw none of us, nor thought of us. I never knew how long we stood, like sentinels guarding him at his prayers, holding our lights in a confused dazed way, not knowing what we did. But at last he rose from his knees, and standing up at his full height, raised his arms, as the Scotch manner is at the end of a religious service, and solemnly gave the apostolical benediction – to what? to the silent earth, the dark woods, the wide breathing atmosphere – for we were but spectators gasping an Amen!

It seemed to me that it must be the middle of the night, as we all walked back. It was in reality very late. Dr Moncrieff put his arm into mine. He walked slowly, with an air of exhaustion. It was as if we were coming from a death-bed. Something hushed and solemnised the very air. There was that sense of relief in it which there always is at the end of a death-struggle. And nature, persistent, never daunted, came back in all of us, as we returned into the ways of life. We said nothing to each other, indeed, for a time; but when we got clear of the trees and reached the opening near the house, where we could see the sky, Dr Moncrieff himself was the first to speak. 'I must be going,' he said; 'it's very late, I'm afraid. I will go down the glen, as I came.'

'But not alone. I am going with you, Doctor.'

'Well, I will not oppose it. I am an old man, and agitation wearies more than work. Yes; I'll be thankful of your arm. Tonight, Colonel, you've done me more good turns than one.'

I pressed his hand on my arm, not feeling able to speak. But Simson, who turned with us, and who had gone along all this time with his taper flaring, in entire unconsciousness, came to himself, apparently at the sound of our voices, and put out that wild little torch with a quick movement, as if of shame. 'Let me carry your lantern,' he said; 'it is heavy.' He recovered with a spring, and in a moment, from the awestricken spectator he had been, became himself, sceptical and cynical. 'I should like to ask you a question,' he said. 'Do you believe in Purgatory, Doctor? It's not in the tenets of the Church; so far as I know.'

'Sir,' said Dr Moncrieff, 'an old man like me is sometimes not very sure what he believes. There is just one thing I am certain of – and that is the loving-kindness of God.'

'But I thought that was in this life. I am no theologian—'

'Sir,' said the old man again, with a tremor in him which I could feel going over all his frame, 'if I saw a friend of mine within the gates of hell, I would not despair but his Father would find him still – if he cried like *yon*.'

'I allow it is very strange – very strange. I cannot see through it. That there must be human agency, I feel sure. Doctor, what made you decide upon the person and the name?'

The minister put out his hand with the impatience which a man might show if he were asked how he recognised his brother. 'Tuts!' he said, in familiar speech – then more solemnly, 'how should I not recognise a person that I know better – far better – than I know you?'

'Then you saw the man?'

Dr Moncrieff made no reply. He moved his hand again with a little impatient movement, and walked on, leaning heavily on my arm. And we went on for a long time without another word, threading the dark paths, which were steep and slippery with the damp of the winter. The air was very still – not more than enough to make a faint sighing in the branches, that mingled with the sound of the water to which we were descending. When we spoke again, it was about different matters – about the height of the river, and the recent rains. We parted with the minister at his own door, where his old housekeeper appeared in great perturbation, waiting for him. 'Eh me, minister! the young gentleman will be worse?' she cried.

'Far from that – better. God bless him!' Dr Moncrieff said. I think if Simson had begun again to me with his questions, I should have pitched him over the rocks as we returned up the glen; but he was silent, by a good inspiration. And the sky was clearer than it had been for many nights, shining high over the trees, with here and there a star faintly gleaming through the wilderness of dark and bare branches. The air, as I have said, was very soft in them, with a subdued and peaceful cadence. It was real, like every natural sound, but came to us like a hush of peace and relief. I thought there was a sound in it as of the breath of a sleeper, and it seemed clear to me that Roland must be sleeping, satisfied and calm. We went up to his room when we went in. There we found the complete hush of rest. My wife looked up out of a doze, and gave me a smile; 'I think he is a great deal better: but you are very late,' she said in a whisper, shading the light with her hand that the doctor might see his patient. The boy had got back something like his own colour. He woke as we stood all round his bed. His eyes had the happy half-awakened look of childhood, glad to shut again, yet pleased with the interruption and glimmer of the light. I stooped over him and kissed his forehead, which was moist and cool. 'It is all well, Roland,' I said. He looked up at me with a glance of pleasure, and took my hand and laid his cheek upon it, and so went to sleep.

For some nights after, I watched among the ruins, spending all the dark hours up to midnight patrolling about the bit of wall which was associated with so many emotions; but I heard nothing, and saw nothing beyond the quiet course of nature: nor, so far as I am aware, has anything been heard again. Dr Moncrieff gave me the history of the youth, whom he never hesitated to name. I did not ask, as Simson did, how he recognised him. He had been a prodigal – weak, foolish, easily imposed upon, and 'led away', as people say. All that we had heard had passed actually in life, the doctor said. The young man had come home thus a day or two after his mother died – who was no more than the housekeeper in the old house – and distracted with the news, had thrown himself down at the door and called upon her to let him in. The old man could scarcely speak of it for tears. To me it seemed as if – Heaven help us, how little do we know about anything! – a scene like that might impress itself somehow upon the hidden heart of nature. I do not pretend to know how, but the repetition had struck me at the time as, in its terrible strangeness and incomprehensibility, almost mechanical – as if the unseen actor could not exceed or vary, but was bound to re-enact the whole. One thing that struck me, however, greatly, was the likeness between the old minister and my boy in the manner of regarding these strange phenomena. Dr Moncrieff was not terrified, as I had been myself, and all the rest of us. It was no 'ghost', as I fear we all vulgarly considered it, to him – but a poor creature whom he knew under these conditions, just as he had known him in the flesh, having no doubt of his identity. And to Roland it was the same. This spirit in pain – if it was a spirit – this voice out of the unseen – was a poor fellow-creature in misery, to be succoured and helped out of his trouble, to my boy. He spoke to me quite frankly about it when he got better. 'I knew father would find out some way,' he said. And this was when he was strong and well, and all idea that he would turn hysterical or become a seer of visions had happily passed away.

I must add one curious fact which does not seem to me to have any relation to the above, but which Simson made great use of, as the human agency which he was determined to find somehow. We had examined the ruins very closely at the time of these occurrences; but afterwards, when all was over, as we went casually about them one Sunday afternoon in the idleness of that unemployed day, Simson with his stick penetrated an old window which had been entirely blocked up with fallen soil. He jumped down into it in great excitement, and called me to follow. There we found a little hole – for it was more a hole than a room – entirely hidden under the ivy and ruins, in which there was a quantity of straw laid in a corner, as if some one had made a bed there, and some remains of crusts about the floor. Some one had lodged there, and not very long before, he made out; and that this unknown being was the author of all the mysterious sounds we heard he is convinced. 'I told you it was human agency,' he said triumphantly. He forgets, I suppose, how he and I stood with our lights seeing nothing while the space between us was audibly traversed by something that could speak, and sob, and suffer. There is no argument with men of this kind. He is ready to get up a laugh against me on this slender ground. 'I was puzzled myself – I could not make it out – but I always felt convinced human agency was at the bottom of it. And here it is – and a clever fellow he must have been,' the doctor says.

Bagley left my service as soon as he got well. He assured me it was no want of respect; but he could not stand 'them kind of things'. And the man was so shaken and ghastly that I was glad to give him a present and let him go. For my own part, I made a point of staying out the time, two years, for which I had taken Brentwood; but I did not renew my tenancy. By that time we had settled, and found for ourselves a pleasant home of our own.

I must add that when the doctor defies me, I can always bring back gravity to his countenance, and a pause in his railing, when I remind him of the juniper-bush. To me that was a matter of little importance. I could believe I was mistaken. I did not care about it one way or other; but on his mind the effect was different. The miserable voice, the spirit in pain, he could think of as the result of ventriloquism, or reverberation, or – anything you please: an elaborate prolonged hoax executed somehow by the tramp that had found a lodging in the old tower. But the juniper-bush staggered him. Things have effects so different on the minds of different men.

Old Lady Mary

SHE WAS VERY old, and therefore it was very hard for her to make up her mind to die.

I am aware that this is not at all the general view, but that it is believed, as old age must be near death, that it prepares the soul for that inevitable event. It is not so, however, in many cases. In youth we are still so near the unseen out of which we came, that death is rather pathetic than tragic – a thing that touches all hearts, but to which, in many cases, the young hero accommodates himself sweetly and courageously. And amid the storms and burdens of middle life there are many times when we would fain push open the door that stands ajar, and behind which there is ease for all our pains, or at least rest, if nothing more. But Age, which has gone through both these phases, is apt, out of long custom and habit, to regard the matter from a different view. All things that are violent have passed out of its life, – no more strong emotions, such as rend the heart – no great labours, bringing after them the weariness which is unto death, but the calm of an existence which is enough for its needs, which affords the moderate amount of comfort and pleasure for which its being is now adapted, and of which there seems no reason that there should ever be any end. To passion, to joy, to anguish, an end must come; but mere gentle living, determined by a framework of gentle rules and habits – why should that ever be ended? When a soul has got to this retirement and is content in it, it becomes very hard to die: hard to accept the necessity of dying, and to accustom one's self to the idea, and still harder to consent to carry it out.

The woman who is the subject of the following narrative was in this position. She had lived through almost everything that is to be found in life. She had been beautiful in her youth,

and had enjoyed all the triumphs of beauty; had been in-
toxicated with flattery, and triumphant in conquest, and mad
with jealousy and the bitterness of defeat when it became
evident that her day was over. She had never been a bad
woman, or false, or unkind; but she had thrown herself with
all her heart into these different stages of being, and had
suffered as much as she enjoyed, according to the unfailing
usage of life. Many a day during these storms and victories,
when things went against her, when delights did not satisfy
her, she had thrown out a cry into the wide air of the universe
and wished to die. And then she had come to the higher table-
land of life, and had borne all the spites of fortune, – had been
poor and rich, and happy and sorrowful; had lost and won a
hundred times over; had sat at feasts and kneeled by death-
beds, and followed her best-loved to the grave, often, often
crying out to God above to liberate her, to make an end of her
anguish, for that her strength was exhausted and she could
bear no more. But she had borne it and lived through all – and
now had arrived at a time when all strong sensations are over,
when the soul is no longer either triumphant or miserable,
and when life itself, and comfort, and ease, and the warmth of
the sun, and of the fireside, and the mild beauty of home were
enough for her, and she required no more. That is, she
required very little more, – a useful routine of hours and
rules, a play of reflected emotion, a pleasant exercise of
faculty, making her feel herself still capable of the best things
in life – of interest in her fellow-creatures, kindness to them,
and a little gentle intellectual occupation, with books and men
around. She had not forgotten anything in her life – not the
excitements and delights of her beauty, nor love, nor grief,
nor the higher levels she had touched in her day. She did not
forget the dark day when her first-born was laid in the grave,
nor that triumphant and brilliant climax of her life when
every one pointed to her as the mother of a hero. All these
things were like pictures hung in the secret chambers of her
mind, to which she could go back in silent moments, in the
twilight seated by the fire, or in the balmy afternoon, when
languor and sweet thoughts are over the world. Sometimes at
such moments there would be heard from her a faint sob,
called forth, it was quite as likely, by the recollections of the
triumph as by that of the deathbed. With these pictures to go
back upon at her will she was never dull, but saw herself

moving through the various scenes of her life with a continual sympathy, feeling for herself in all her troubles – sometimes approving, sometimes judging that woman who had been so pretty, so happy, so miserable, and had gone through everything that life can go through. How much that is looking back upon it! passages so hard that the wonder was how she could survive them – pangs so terrible that the heart would seem at its last gasp, but yet would revive and go on.

Besides these, however, she had many mild pleasures. She had a pretty house full of things which formed a graceful *entourage* suitable, as she felt, for such a woman as she was, and in which she took pleasure for their own beauty – soft chairs and couches, a fireplace and lights which were the perfection of tempered warmth and illumination. She had a carriage, very comfortable and easy, in which, when the weather was suitable, she went out; and a pretty garden and lawns, in which, when she preferred staying at home, she could have her little walk or sit out under the trees. She had books in plenty, and all the newspapers and everything that was needful to keep her within the reflection of the busy life which she no longer cared to encounter in her own person. The post rarely brought her painful letters; for all those impassioned interests which bring pain had died out, and the sorrows of others, when they were communicated to her, gave her a luxurious sense of sympathy yet exemption. She was sorry for them; but such catastrophes could touch her no more: and often she had pleasant letters, which afforded her something to talk and think about, and discuss as if it concerned her – and yet did not concern her, – business which could not hurt her if it failed, which would please her if it succeeded. Her letters, her papers, her books, each coming at its appointed hour, were all instruments of pleasure. She came downstairs at a certain hour, which she kept to as if it had been of the utmost importance, although it was of no importance at all: she took just so much good wine, so many cups of tea. Her repasts were as regular as clockwork – never too late, never too early. Her whole life went on velvet, rolling smoothly along, without jar or interruption, blameless, pleasant, kind. People talked of her old age as a model of old age, with no bitterness or sourness in it. And, indeed, why should she have been sour or bitter? It suited her far better to be kind. She was in reality kind to everybody, liking to see pleasant faces about her. The poor had no reason to complain of her; her servants were very comfortable; and the one person in her house who was nearer to her own level, who was her companion and most important minister, was very comfortable too.

This was a young woman about twenty, a very distant relation, with 'no claim', everybody said, upon her kind mistress and friend – the daughter of a distant cousin. How very few think anything at all of such a tie! but Lady Mary had taken her young namesake when she was a child, and she had grown up as it were at her godmother's footstool, in the conviction that the measured existence of the old was the rule of life, and that her own trifling personality counted for nothing, or next to nothing, in its steady progress. Her name was Mary too – always called 'little Mary' as having once been little, and not yet very much in the matter of size. She was one of the pleasantest things to look at of all the pretty things in Lady Mary's rooms, and she had the most sheltered, peaceful, and pleasant life that could be conceived. The only little thorn in her pillow was, that whereas in the novels, of which she read a great many, the heroines all go and pay visits and have adventures, she had none, but lived constantly at home. There was something much more serious in her life, had she known, which was that she had nothing, and no power of doing anything for herself; that she had all her life been accustomed to a modest luxury which would make poverty very hard to her; and that Lady Mary was over eighty, and had made no will. If she did not make any will, her property would all go to her grandson, who was so rich already that her fortune would be but as a drop in the ocean to him; or to some great-grandchildren of whom she knew very little – the descendants of a daughter long ago dead who had married an Austrian, and who were therefore foreigners both in birth and name. That she should provide for little Mary was therefore a thing which nature demanded, and which would hurt nobody. She had said so often; but she deferred the doing of it as a thing for which there was 'no hurry'. For why should she die? There seemed no reason or need for it. So long as she lived, nothing could be more sure, more happy and serene, than little Mary's life; and why should she die? She did not perhaps put this into words; but the meaning of her smile, and the manner in which she put aside every suggestion about the chances of the hereafter away from her, said it more clearly than words. It was not that she had any superstitious fear about the making of a will. When the doctor or the vicar or her man of business, the only persons who ever talked to her on the subject, ventured periodically to refer to it, she assented pleasantly, – Yes, certainly, she must do it – some time or other.

'It is a very simple thing to do,' the lawyer said. 'I will save you all trouble; nothing but your signature will be wanted – and that you give every day.'

'Oh, I should think nothing of the trouble!' she said.

'And it would liberate your mind from all care, and leave you free to think of things more important still,' said the clergyman.

'I think I am very free of care,' she replied.

Then the doctor added, bluntly, 'And you will not die an hour the sooner for having made your will.'

'Die!' said Lady Mary, surprised. And then she added, with a smile, 'I hope you don't think so little of me as to believe I would be kept back by that?'

These gentlemen all consulted together in despair, and asked each other what should be done. They thought her an egotist – a cold-hearted old woman, holding at arm's-length any idea of the inevitable. And so she did; but not because she was cold-hearted – because she was so accustomed to living, and had survived so many calamities, and gone on so long – so long; and because everything was so comfortably arranged about her – all her little habits so firmly established, as if nothing could interfere with them. To think of the day arriving which should begin with some other formula than that of her maid's entrance drawing aside the curtains, lighting the cheerful fire, bringing her a report of the weather; and then the little tray, resplendent with snowy linen and shining silver and china, with its bouquet of violets or a rose in the season, the newspaper carefully dried and cut, the letters, – every detail was so perfect, so unchanging, regular as the morning. It seemed impossible that it should come to an end. And then when she came downstairs, there were all the little articles upon her table always ready to her hand; a certain number of things to do, each at the appointed hour; the slender refreshments it was necessary for her to take, in which there was a little exquisite variety – but never any change in the fact that at eleven and at three and so forth something had to be taken. Had a woman wanted to abandon the peaceful life which was thus supported and carried on, the very framework itself would have resisted. It was impossible (almost) to contemplate the idea that at a given moment the whole machinery must stop. She was neither without heart nor without religion, but on the contrary a good woman, to whom many gentle thoughts had been given at various portions of her career. But the occasion seemed to have passed for that as well as other kinds of emotion. The mere fact of living was enough for her. The little exertion which it was well she was required to make produced a pleasant weariness. It was a duty much enforced upon her by all around her, that she should do nothing which would exhaust or fatigue. 'I don't want you to think,' even the doctor would say; 'you have done enough of thinking in your time.' And this she accepted with great composure of spirit. She had thought and felt and done much in her day; but now everything of the kind was over. There was no need for her to fatigue herself; and day followed day, all warm and sheltered and pleasant. People died, it is true, now and then out of doors; but they were mostly young people, whose death might have been prevented had proper care been taken – who were seized with violent maladies, or caught sudden infections, or were cut down by accident – all things which seemed natural. Her own contemporaries were very few, and they were like herself – living on in something of the same way. At eighty-five all people under seventy are young; and one's contemporaries are very, very few.

Nevertheless these men did disturb her a little about her will. She had made more than one will in the former days during her active life; but all those to whom she had bequeathed her possessions were dead. She had survived them all, and inherited from many of them, which had been a hard thing in its time. One day the lawyer had been more than ordinarily pressing. He had told her stories of men who had died intestate, and left trouble and penury behind them to those whom they would have most wished to preserve from all trouble. It would not have become Mr Furnival to say brutally to Lady Mary – 'This is how you will leave your godchild when you die.' But he told her story after story, many of them piteous enough.

'People think it is so troublesome a business,' he said,

'when it is nothing at all – the most easy matter in the world. We are getting so much less particular nowadays about formalities. So long as the testator's intentions are made quite apparent – that is the chief matter, and a very bad thing for us lawyers.'

'I daresay,' said Lady Mary, 'it is unpleasant for a man to think of himself as "the testator". It is a very abstract title, when you come to think of it.'

'Pooh!' said Mr Furnival, who had no sense of humour.

'But if this great business is so very simple,' she went on, 'one could do it, no doubt, for one's self?'

'Many people do – but it is never advisable,' said the lawyer. 'You will say it is natural for me to tell you that. When they do, it should be as simple as possible. I give all my real property, or my personal property, or my shares in so-and-so, or my jewels, or so forth, to – whoever it may be. The fewer words the better, so that nobody may be able to read between the lines, you know; and the signature attested by two witnesses; but they must not be witnesses that have any interest – that is, that have anything left to them by the document they witness.'

Lady Mary put up her hand defensively, with a laugh. It was still a most delicate hand, like ivory, a little yellowed with age, but fine, the veins standing out a little upon it, the finger-tips still pink. 'You speak,' she said, 'as if you expected me to take the law in my own hands. No, no, my old friend; never fear, you shall have the doing of it.'

'Whenever you please, my dear lady – whenever you please. Such a thing cannot be done an hour too soon. Shall I take your instructions now?'

Lady Mary laughed, and said, 'You were always a very keen man for business. I remember your father used to say, Robert would never neglect an opening.'

'No,' he said, with a peculiar look. 'I have always looked after my six-and-eightpences; and in that case it is true the pounds take care of themselves.'

'Very good care,' said Lady Mary; and then she bade her young companion bring that book she had been reading, where there was something she wanted to show Mr Furnival. 'It is only a case in a novel – but I am sure it is bad law; give me your opinion,' she said.

He was obliged to be civil, very civil. Nobody is rude to the

Lady Marys of life; and besides, she was old enough to have an additional right to every courtesy. But while he sat over the novel, and tried with unnecessary vehemence to make her see what very bad law it was, and glanced from her smiling attention to the innocent sweetness of the girl beside her, who was her loving attendant, the good man's heart was sore. He said many hard things of her in his own mind as he went away.

'She will die,' he said, bitterly. 'She will go off in a moment when nobody is looking for it, and that poor child will be left destitute.'

It was all he could do not to go back and take her by her fragile old shoulders and force her to sign and seal at once. But then he knew very well that as soon as he found himself in her presence, he would of necessity be obliged to subdue his impatience, and be once more civil, very civil, and try to suggest and insinuate the duty which he dared not force upon her. And it was very clear that till she pleased she would take no hint. He supposed it must be that strange reluctance to part with their power which is said to be common to old people, or else that horror of death, and determination to keep it at arm's-length, which is also common. Thus he did as spectators are so apt to do, he forced a meaning and motive into what had no motive at all, and imagined Lady Mary, the kindest of women, to be of purpose and intention risking the future of the girl whom she had brought up, and whom she loved – not with passion, indeed, or anxiety, but with tender benevolence: a theory which was as false as anything could be.

That evening in her room, Lady Mary, in a very cheerful mood, sat by a little bright unnecessary fire, with her writing-book before her, waiting till she should be sleepy. It was the only point in which she was a little hard upon her maid, who in every other respect was the best-treated of servants. Lady Mary, as it happened, had often no inclination for bed till the night was far advanced. She slept little, as is common enough at her age. She was in her warm wadded dressing-gown, an article in which she still showed certain traces (which were indeed visible in all she wore) of her ancient beauty, with her white hair becomingly arranged under a cap of cambrics and lace. At the last moment, when she had been ready to step into bed, she had changed her mind, and told Jervis that she would write a letter or two first. And she had written her letters, but still felt no inclination to sleep. Then there fluttered across her memory somehow the conversation she had held with Mr Furnival in the morning. It would be amusing, she thought, to cheat him out of some of those six-and-eightpences he pretended to think so much of. It would be still more amusing, next time the subject of her will was recurred to, to give his arm a little tap with her fan, and say, 'Oh, that is all settled, months ago.' She laughed to herself at this, and took out a fresh sheet of paper. It was a little jest that pleased her.

'Do you think there is any one up yet, Jervis, except you and me?' she said to the maid. Jervis hesitated a little, and then said that she believed Mr Brown had not gone to bed yet: for he had been going over the cellar, and was making up his accounts. Jervis was so explanatory that her mistress divined what was meant. 'I suppose I have been spoiling sport, keeping you here,' she said, good-humouredly; for it was well known that Miss Jervis and Mr Brown were engaged, and that they were only waiting (everybody knew but Lady Mary, who never suspected it) the death of their mistress to set up a lodging-house in Jermyn Street, where they fully intended to make their fortune. 'Then go,' Lady Mary said, 'and call Brown. I have a little business paper to write, and you must both witness my signature.' She laughed to herself a little as she said this, thinking how she would steal a march on Mr Furnival. 'I give and bequeath,' she said to herself playfully, after Jervis had hurried away. She fully intended to leave both of these good servants something, but then she recollected that people who are interested in a will cannot sign as witnesses. 'What does it matter?' she said to herself gaily; 'if it should ever be wanted, Mary would see to that.' Accordingly she dashed off in her pretty old-fashioned handwriting, which was very angular and pointed, as was the fashion in her day, and still very clear, though slightly tremulous, a few lines, in which, remembering playfully Mr Furnival's recommendation of 'few words', she left to little Mary all she possessed, adding, by the prompting of that recollection about the witnesses, 'She will take care of the servants.' It filled one side only of the large sheet of note-paper, which was what Lady Mary habitually used. Brown, introduced timidly by Jervis, and a little overawed by the solemnity of the bedchamber, came in and painted solidly his large signature after the spidery lines of his mistress. She had folded down the paper, so that neither saw what it was.

'Now I will go to bed,' Lady Mary said, when Brown had left the room. 'And Jervis, you must go to bed too.'

'Yes, my lady,' said Jervis.

'I don't approve of courtship at this hour.'

'No, my lady,' Jervis replied, deprecating and disappointed.

'Why cannot he tell his tale in daylight?'

'Oh, my lady, there's no tale to tell,' cried the maid. 'We are not of the gossiping sort, my lady, neither me nor Mr Brown.' Lady Mary laughed, and watched while the candles were put out: the fire made a pleasant flicker in the room – it was autumn and still warm, and it was 'for company' and cheerfulness that the little fire was lit; she liked to see it dancing and flickering upon the walls, – and then closed her eyes amid an exquisite softness of comfort and luxury, life itself bearing her up as softly, filling up all crevices as warmly, as the downy pillow upon which she rested her still beautiful old head.

If she had died that night! The little sheet of paper that meant so much lay openly, innocently, in her writing-book, along with the letters she had written, and looking of as little importance as they. There was nobody in the world who grudged old Lady Mary one of those pretty placid days of hers. Brown and Jervis, if they were sometimes a little impatient, consoled each other that they were both sure of something in her will, and that in the meantime it was a very good place. And all the rest would have been very well content that Lady Mary should live for ever. But how wonderfully it would have simplified everything, and how much trouble and pain it would have saved to everybody, herself included, could she have died that night!

But naturally there was no question of dying on that night. When she was about to go downstairs next day, Lady Mary, giving her letters to be posted, saw the paper which she had forgotten lying beside them. She had forgotten all about it, but the sight of it made her smile. She folded it up and put it in an envelope while Jervis went downstairs with the letters; and then, to carry out her joke, she looked round her to see where she would put it. There was an old Italian cabinet in the room with a secret drawer, which it was a little difficult to open, almost impossible for any one who did not know the secret. Lady Mary looked round her, smiled, hesitated a little, and then walked across the room and put the envelope in the secret drawer. She was still fumbling with it when Jervis came back, but there was no connection in Jervis's mind then, or ever after, between the paper she had signed and this old cabinet, which was one of the old lady's toys. She arranged Lady Mary's shawl, which had dropped off her shoulders a little in her unusual activity, and took up her book and her favourite cushion, and all the little paraphernalia that moved with her, and gave her lady her arm to go downstairs; where little Mary had placed her chair just at the right angle, and arranged the little table, on which there were so many little necessaries and conveniences, and was standing smiling, the prettiest object of all, the climax of the gentle luxury and pleasantness, to receive her godmother, who had been her providence all her life.

But what a pity! oh, what a pity, that she had not died that night!

II

Life went on after this without any change. There was never any change in that delightful house; and if it was years or months, or even days, the youngest of its inhabitants could scarcely tell, and Lady Mary could not tell at all. This was one of her little imperfections – a little mist which hung like the lace about her head over her memory. She could not remember how time went, or that there was any difference between one day and another. There were Sundays, it was true, which made a kind of gentle measure of the progress of time; but she said, with a smile, that she thought it was always Sunday – they came so close upon each other. And Time flew on gentle wings, that made no sound and left no reminders. She had her little ailments like anybody, but in reality less than anybody, seeing there was nothing to fret her, nothing to disturb the even tenor of her days. Still there were times when she took a little cold, or got a chill, in spite of all precautions, as she went from one room to another. She came to be one of the marvels of the time – an old lady who had seen everybody worth seeing for generations back – who remembered as distinctly as if they had happened yesterday, great events that had taken place before the present age began at all, before the great statesmen of our time were born. And in full possession of all her faculties, as everybody said, her mind as clear as ever, her intelligence as active, reading everything, interested in everything, and still beautiful in extreme old age. Everybody about her, and in particular all the people who helped to keep the thorns from her path, and felt themselves to have a hand in her preservation, were proud of Lady Mary: and she was perhaps a little, a very little, delightfully, charmingly proud of herself. The doctor, beguiled by professional vanity, feeling what a feather she was in his cap, quite confident that she would reach her hundredth birthday, and with an ecstatic hope that even, by grace of his admirable treatment and her own beautiful constitution she might (almost) solve the problem and live for ever, gave up troubling about the will which at a former period he had taken so much interest in. 'What is the use?' he said; 'she will see us all out.' And the vicar, though he did not give in to this, was overawed by the old lady, who knew everything that could be taught her, and to whom it seemed an impertinence to utter commonplaces about duty, or even to suggest subjects of thought. Mr Furnival was the only man who did not cease his representations, and whose anxiety about the young Mary, who was so blooming and sweet in the shadow of the old, did not decrease. But the recollection of the bit of paper in the secret drawer of the cabinet, fortified his old client against all his attacks. She had intended it only as a jest, with which some day or other to confound him, and show how much wiser she was than he supposed. It became quite a pleasant subject of thought to her, at which she laughed to herself. Some day, when she had a suitable moment, she would order him to come with all his formalities, and then produce her bit of paper, and turn the laugh against him. But oddly, the very existence of that little document kept her indifferent even to the laugh. It was too much trouble; she only smiled at him, and took no more notice, amused to think how astonished he would be – when, if ever, he found it out.

It happened, however, that one day in the early winter the wind changed when Lady Mary was out for her drive: at least they all vowed the wind changed. It was in the south, that genial quarter, when she set out, but turned about in some uncomfortable way, and was a keen north-easter when she came back. And in the moment of stepping from the carriage she caught a chill. It was the coachman's fault, Jervis said, who allowed the horses to make a step forward when Lady Mary was getting out, and kept her exposed, standing on the step of the carriage, while he pulled them up; and it was Jervis's fault, the footman said, who was not clever enough to get her lady out, or even to throw a shawl round her, when she perceived how the weather had changed. It is always some one's fault, or some unforeseen unprecedented change, that does it at the last. Lady Mary was not accustomed to be ill, and did not bear it with her usual grace. She was a little impatient at first, and thought they were making an unnecessary fuss. But then there passed a few uncomfortable feverish days, when she began to look forward to the doctor's visit as the only thing there was any comfort in. Afterwards she passed a night of a very agitating kind. She dozed and dreamed, and awoke and dreamed again. Her life seemed all to run into dreams – a strange confusion was about her, through which she could define nothing. Once waking up, as she supposed, she saw a group round her bed, the doctor with a candle in his hand (how should the doctor be there in the middle of the night?), holding her hand or feeling her pulse: little Mary at one side crying – why should the child cry? and Jervis very anxious, pouring something into a glass. There were other faces there which she was sure must have come out of a dream, so unlikely was it that they should be collected in her bedchamber; and all with a sort of halo of feverish light about them, a magnified and mysterious importance. This strange scene, which she did not understand, seemed to make itself visible all in a moment out of the darkness, and then disappeared again as suddenly as it came.

III

When she woke again it was morning; and her first waking consciousness was, that she must be much better. The choking sensation in her throat was altogether gone. She had no desire to cough – no difficulty in breathing. She had a fancy, however, that she must be still dreaming, for she felt sure that some one had called her by her name, 'Mary'. Now all who could call her by her Christian name were dead years ago – therefore it must be a dream. However, in a short time it was repeated, – 'Mary, Mary! get up; there is a great deal to do.' This voice confused her greatly. Was it possible that all that was past had been mere fancy; that she had but dreamed those long, long years – maturity and motherhood, and trouble and triumph, and old age at the end of all? It seemed to her possible that she might have dreamed the rest, for she had been a girl much given to visions; but she said to herself that she never could have dreamed old age. And then with a smile she mused and thought that it must be the voice that was a dream; for how could she get up without Jervis, who had never appeared yet to draw the curtains or make the fire? Jervis perhaps had sat up late. She remembered now to have seen her that time in the middle of the night by her bedside, so that it was natural enough, poor thing, that she should be late. Get up! who was it that was calling to her so? She had not been so called to, she who had always been a great lady, since she was a girl by her mother's side. 'Mary, Mary!' It was a very curious dream. And what was more curious still, was, that by-and-by she could not keep still any longer, but got up without thinking any more of Jervis, and going out of her room came all at once into the midst of a company of people all very busy – whom she was much surprised to find at first, but whom she soon accustomed herself to, finding the greatest interest in their proceedings, and curious to know what they were doing. They, for their part, did not seem at all surprised by her appearance, nor did any one stop to explain, as would have been natural; but she took this with great composure, somewhat astonished perhaps, being used, wherever she went, to a great many observances and much respect, but soon, very soon, becoming used to it. Then some one repeated what she had heard before. 'It was time you got up – for there is a great deal to do.'

'To do,' she said, 'for me?' and then she looked round upon them with that charming smile which had subjugated so many. 'I am afraid,' she said, 'you will find me of very little use. I am too old now, if ever I could have done much, for work.'

'Oh no, you are not old, – you will do very well,' some one said.

'Not old!' – Lady Mary felt a little offended in spite of
herself. 'Perhaps I like flattery as well as my neighbours,' she
said with dignity, 'but then it must be reasonable. To say I am
anything but a very old woman—'

Here she paused a little, perceiving for the first time with
surprise that she was standing and walking without her stick
or the help of any one's arm, quite freely and at her ease, and
that the place in which she was had expanded into a great
place like a gallery in a palace, instead of the room next her
own into which she had walked a few minutes ago; but this
discovery did not at all affect her mind, or occupy her except
with the most passing momentary surprise.

'The fact is, I feel a great deal better and stronger,' she said.

'Quite well, Mary, and stronger than ever you were before?'

'Who is it that calls me Mary? I have had nobody for a long
time to call me Mary; the friends of my youth are all dead. I
think that you must be right, although the doctor, I feel sure,
thought me very bad last night. I should have got alarmed if I
had not fallen asleep again.'

'And then woke up well?'

'Quite well: it is wonderful, but quite true. You seem to
know a great deal about me?'

'I know everything about you. You have had a very pleasant life, and do you think you have made the best of it? Your
old age has been very plcasant.'

'Ah! you acknowledge that I am old, then?' cried Lady
Mary, with a smile.

'You are old no longer, and you are a great lady no longer.
Don't you see that something has happened to you? It is
seldom that such a great change happens without being found
out.'

'Yes; it is true I have got better all at once. I feel an
extraordinary renewal of strength. I seem to have left home
without knowing it; none of my people seem near me. I feel
very much as if I had just awakened from a long dream. Is it
possible,' she said, with a wondering look, 'that I have
dreamed all my life, and after all am just a girl at home?'
The idea was ludicrous, and she laughed. 'You see I am very
much improved indeed,' she said.

She was still so far from perceiving the real situation, that
some one came towards her out of the group of people about –
some one whom she recognised – with the evident intention of

explaining to her how it was. She started a little at the sight of him, and held out her hand, and cried: 'You here! I am very glad to see you – doubly glad, since I was told a few days ago that you had – died.'

There was something in this word as she herself pronounced it that troubled her a little. She had never been one of those who are afraid of death. On the contrary, she had always taken a great interest in it, and liked to hear everything that could be told her on the subject. It gave her now, however, a curious little thrill of sensation, which she did not understand: she hoped it was not superstition.

'You have guessed rightly,' he said – 'quite right. That is one of the words with a false meaning, which is to us a mere symbol of something we cannot understand. But you see what it means now.'

It was a great shock, it need not be concealed. Otherwise she had been quite pleasantly occupied with the interest of something new, into which she had walked so easily out of her own bedchamber, without any trouble, and with the delightful new sensation of health and strength. But when it flashed upon her that she was not to go back to her bedroom again, nor have any of those cares and attentions which had seemed necessary to existence, she was very much startled and shaken. Died! Was it possible that she personally had died? She had known it was a thing that happened to everybody; but yet. – And it was a solemn matter, to be prepared for, and looked forward to, whereas – 'If you mean that I too—' she said, faltering a little; and then she added, 'it is very surprising,' with a trouble in her mind which yet was not all trouble. 'If that is so, it is a thing well over. And it is very wonderful how much disturbance people give themselves about it – if this is all.'

'This is not all, however,' her friend said; 'you have an ordeal before you which you will not find pleasant. You are going to think about your life, and all that was imperfect in it, and which might have been done better.'

'We are none of us perfect,' said Lady Mary, with a little of that natural resentment with which one hears one's self accused – however ready one may be to accuse one's self.

'Permit me,' said he, and took her hand and led her away without further explanation. The people about were so busy with their own occupations, that they took very little notice;

neither did she pay much attention to the manner in which
they were engaged. Their looks were friendly when they met
her eye, and she too felt friendly, with a sense of brotherhood.
But she had always been a kind woman. She wanted to step
aside and help, on more than one occasion, when it seemed to
her that some people in her way had a task above their powers;
but this her conductor would not permit. And she endeavoured to put some questions to him as they went along with
still less success.

'The change is very confusing,' she said; 'one has no
standard to judge by. I should like to know something about
– the kind of people – and the – manner of life.'

'For a time,' he said, 'you will have enough to do, without
troubling yourself about that.'

This naturally produced an uneasy sensation in her mind.
'I suppose,' she said rather timidly, 'that we are not in – what
we have been accustomed to call heaven?'

'That is a word,' he said, 'which expresses rather a condition than a place.'

'But there must be a place – in which that condition can
exist.' She had always been fond of discussions of this kind,
and felt encouraged to find that they were still practicable. 'It
cannot be the – Inferno, that is clear at least,' she added with
the sprightliness which was one of her characteristics; 'perhaps – Purgatory? since you infer that I have something to
endure.'

'Words are interchangeable,' he said: 'that means one thing
to one of us which to another has a totally different signification.' There was something so like his old self in this, that she
laughed with an irresistible sense of amusement.

'You were always fond of the oracular,' she said. She was
conscious that on former occasions, if he had made such a
speech to her, though she would have felt the same amusement, she would not have expressed it so frankly. But he did
not take it at all amiss. And her thoughts went on in other
directions. She felt herself saying over to herself the words of
the old north-country dirge, which came to her recollection
she knew not how—

> If hosen and shoon thou gavest nane,
> The whins shall prick thee intill the bane.

When she saw that her companion heard her, she asked, 'Is that true?'

He shook his head a little. 'It is too matter of fact,' he said, 'as I need hardly tell you. Hosen and shoon are good, but they do not always sufficiently indicate the state of the heart.'

Lady Mary had a consciousness, which was pleasant to her, that so far as the hosen and shoon went, she had abundant means of preparing herself for the pricks of any road, however rough; but she had no time to indulge this pleasing reflection, for she was shortly introduced into a great building full of innumerable rooms, in one of which her companion left her.

IV

The door opened, and she felt herself free to come out. How long she had been there, or what passed there, is not for any one to say. She came out tingling and smarting – if such words can be used – with an intolerable recollection of the last act of her life. So intolerable was it that all that had gone before, and all the risings up of old errors and visions long dead, were forgotten in the sharp and keen prick of this, which was not over and done like the rest. No one had accused her, or brought before her Judge the things that were against her. She it was who had done it all – she whose memory did not spare her one fault, who remembered everything. But when she came to that last frivolity of her old age, and saw for the first time how she had played with the future of the child whom she had brought up, and abandoned to the hardest fate – for nothing, for folly, for a jest – the horror and bitterness of the thought filled her mind to overflowing. In the first anguish of that recollection she had to go forth, receiving no word of comfort in respect to it, meeting only with a look of sadness and compassion, which went to her very heart. She came forth as if she had been driven away, but not by any outward influence, by the force of her own miserable sensations. 'I will write,' she said to herself, 'and tell them – I will go—' And then she stopped short, remembering that she could neither go nor write – that all communication with the world she had left was closed. Was it all closed? Was there no way in which a message could reach those who remained behind? She caught the first passer-by whom she passed, and addressed him piteously. 'Oh, tell me – you have been longer here than I – cannot one send a letter, a message, if it were only a single word?'

'Where?' he said, stopping and listening; so that it began to seem possible to her that some such expedient might still be within her reach.

'It is to England,' she said, thinking he meant to ask as to which quarter of the world.

'Ah,' he said, shaking his head, 'I fear that is impossible.'

'But it is to set something right, which out of mere inadvertence, with no ill meaning—' No, no (she repeated to herself), no ill meaning – none! 'Oh sir, for charity! tell me how I can find a way. There must – there must be some way.'

He was greatly moved by the sight of her distress. 'I am but a stranger here,' he said; 'I may be wrong. There are others who can tell you better; but' – and he shook his head sadly – 'most of us would be so thankful, if we could, to send a word, if it were only a single word, to those we have left behind, that I fear, I fear—'

'Ah!' cried Lady Mary, 'but that would be only for tenderness; whereas this is for justice and for pity, and to do away with a great wrong which I did before I came here.'

'I am very sorry for you,' he said; but shook his head once more as he went away. She was more careful next time, and chose one who had the look of much experience and knowledge of the place. He listened to her very gravely, and answered Yes, that he was one of the officers, and could tell her whatever she wanted to know; but when she told him what she wanted, he too shook his head. 'I do not say it cannot be done,' he said. 'There are some cases in which it has been successful, but very few. It has often been attempted. There is no law against it. Those who do it do it at their own risk. They suffer much, and almost always they fail.'

'No, oh no. You said there were some who succeeded. No one can be more anxious than I. I will give – anything – everything I have in the world!—'

He gave her a smile, which was very grave nevertheless, and full of pity. 'You forget,' he said, 'that you have nothing to give; and if you had, that there is no one here to whom it would be of any value.'

Though she was no longer old and weak, yet she was still a

woman, and she began to weep, in the terrible failure and contrariety of all things; but yet she would not yield. She cried: 'There must be some one here who would do it for love. I have had people who loved me in my time. I must have some here who have not forgotten. Ah! I know what you would say. I lived so long I forgot them all, and why should they remember me?'

Here she was touched on the arm, and looking round, saw close to her the face of one whom, it was very true, she had forgotten. She remembered him but dimly, after she had looked long at him. A little group had gathered about her, with grieved looks, to see her distress. He who had touched her was the spokesman of them all.

'There is nothing I would not do,' he said, 'for you and for love.' And then they all sighed, surrounding her, and added, 'But it is impossible – impossible!'

She stood and gazed at them, recognising by degrees faces that she knew, and seeing in all that look of grief and sympathy which makes all human souls brothers. Impossible was not a word that had been often said to be in her life; and to come out of a world in which everything could be changed, everything communicated in the twinkling of an eye, and find a dead blank before her and around her, through which not a word could go, was more terrible than can be said in words. She looked piteously upon them, with that anguish of helplessness which goes to every heart, and cried, 'What is impossible? To send a word – only a word – to set right what is wrong? Oh, I understand,' she said, lifting up her hands. 'I understand! that to send messages of comfort must not be; that the people who love you must bear it, as we all have done in our time, and trust to God for consolation. But I have done a wrong! Oh, listen, listen to me, my friends. I have left a child, a young creature, unprovided for – without any one to help her. And must that be? Must she bear it, and I bear it, for ever, and no means, no way of setting it right? Listen to me! I was there last night, – in the middle of the night I was still there, – and here this morning. So it must be easy to come – only a short way; and two words would be enough, – only two words!'

They gathered closer and closer round her, full of compassion. 'It is easy to come,' they said, 'but not to go.'

And one added, 'It will not be for ever; comfort yourself. When she comes here, or to a better place, that will seem to you only as a day.'

'But to her,' cried Lady Mary, – 'to her it will be long years – it will be trouble and sorrow; and she will think I took no thought for her: and she will be right,' the penitent said, with a great and bitter cry.

It was so terrible that they were all silent, and said not a word; except the man who had loved her, who put his hand upon her arm, and said, 'We are here for that; this is the fire that purges us, – to see at last what we have done, and the true aspect of it, and to know the cruel wrong, yet never be able to make amends.'

She remembered then that this was a man who had neglected all lawful affections, and broken the hearts of those who trusted him for her sake; and for a moment she forgot her own burden in sorrow for his.

It was now that he who had called himself one of the officers came forward again, – for the little crowd had gathered round her so closely that he had been shut out. He said, 'No one can carry your message for you; that is not permitted. But there is still a possibility. You may have permission to go yourself. Such things have been done, though they have not often been successful. But if you will—'

She shivered when she heard him; and it became apparent to her why no one could be found to go, – for all her nature revolted from that step which it was evident must be the most terrible which could be thought of. She looked at him with troubled, beseeching eyes, and the rest all looked at her, pitying and trying to soothe her.

'Permission will not be refused,' he said, 'for a worthy cause.'

Upon which the others all spoke together, entreating her. 'Already,' they cried, 'they have forgotten you living. You are to them one who is dead. They will be afraid of you if they can see you. Oh, go not back! Be content to wait – to wait; it is only a little while. The life of man is nothing; it appears for a little time, and then it vanishes away. And when she comes here she will know – or in a better place.' They sighed as they named the better place; though some smiled too, feeling perhaps more near to it.

Lady Mary listened to them all, but she kept her eyes upon

the face of him who offered her this possibility. There passed through her mind a hundred stories she had heard of those who had *gone back*. But not one that spoke of them as welcome, as received with joy, as comforting those they loved. Ah no! was it not rather a curse upon the house to which they came? The rooms were shut up, the houses abandoned, where they were supposed to appear. Those whom they had loved best feared and fled them. They were a vulgar wonder, – a thing that the poorest laughed at, yet feared. Poor banished souls! it was because no one would listen to them that they had to linger and wait, and come and go. She shivered, and, in spite of her longing and her repentance, a cold dread and horror took possession of her. She looked round upon her companions for comfort, and found none.

'Do not go,' they said; 'do not go. We have endured like you. We wait till all things are made clear.'

And another said, 'All will be made clear. It is but for a time.'

She turned from one to another, and back again to the first speaker, – he who had authority.

He said, 'It is very rarely successful; it retards the course of your penitence. It is an indulgence, and it may bring harm and not good; but if the meaning is generous and just, permission will be given, and you may go.'

Then all the strength of her nature rose in her. She thought of the child forsaken, and of the dark world round her, where she would find so few friends; and of the home shut up in which she had lived her young and pleasant life; and of the thoughts that must rise in her heart, as though she were forsaken and abandoned of God and man. Then Lady Mary turned to the man who had authority. She said, 'If He whom I saw today will give me His blessing, I will go—' and they all pressed round her, weeping and kissing her hands.

'He will not refuse His blessing,' they said; 'but the way is terrible, and you are still weak. How can you encounter all the misery of it? He commands no one to try that dark and dreadful way.'

'I will try,' Lady Mary said.

V

The night which Lady Mary had been conscious of, in a momentary glimpse full of the exaggeration of fever, had not indeed been so expeditious as she believed. The doctor, it is true, had been pronouncing her death-warrant when she saw him holding her wrist and wondered what he did there in the middle of the night; but she had been very ill before this, and the conclusion of her life had been watched with many tears. Then there had risen up a wonderful commotion in the house, of which little Mary, her godchild, was very little sensible. Had she left any will, any instructions, the slightest indication of what she wished to be done after her death? Mr Furnival, who had been very anxious to be allowed to see her, even in the last days of her illness, said emphatically, No. She had never executed any will, never made any disposition of her affairs, he said, almost with bitterness, in the tone of one who is ready to weep with vexation and distress. The vicar took a more hopeful view. He said it was impossible that so considerate a person could have done this, and that there must, he was sure, be found somewhere, if close examination was made, a memorandum, a letter – something which should show what she wished; for she must have known very well, notwithstanding all flatteries and compliments upon her good looks, that from day to day her existence was never to be calculated upon. The doctor did not share this last opinion. He said that there was no fathoming the extraordinary views that people took of their own case; and that it was quite possible, though it seemed incredible, that Lady Mary might really be as little expectant of death, on the way to ninety, as a girl of seventeen; but still he was of opinion that she might have left a memorandum somewhere. These three gentlemen were in the foreground of affairs; because she had no relations to step in and take the management. The Earl, her grandson, was abroad, and there were only his solicitors to interfere on his behalf – men to whom Lady Mary's fortune was quite unimportant, although it was against their principles to let anything slip out of their hands that could aggrandise their client; but who knew nothing about the circumstances – about little Mary, about the old lady's peculiarities, in any way. Therefore the persons who had surrounded her in her life, and Mr Furnival, her man of business, were the persons who really had the management of everything. Their wives interfered a little too, or rather the one wife who only could do so – the wife of the vicar, who came in beneficently at once, and took poor little Mary, in her first desolation, out of the melancholy house. Mrs Vicar did this without any hesitation, knowing very well that, in all probability, Lady Mary had made no will, and consequently that the poor girl was destitute. A great deal is said about the hardness of the world, and the small consideration that is shown for a destitute dependant in such circumstances. But this is not true; and, as a matter of fact, there is never, or very rarely, such profound need in the world, without a great deal of kindness and much pity. The three gentlemen all along had been entirely in Mary's interest. They had not expected legacies from the old lady, or any advantage to themselves. It was of the girl that they had thought. And when now they examined everything and inquired into all her ways and what she had done, it was of Mary they were thinking. But Mr Furnival was very certain of his point. He knew that Lady Mary had made no will; time after time he had pressed it upon her. He was very sure, even while he examined her writing-table, and turned out all the drawers, that nothing would be found. The little Italian cabinet had *chiffons* in its drawers, fragments of old lace, pieces of ribbon, little nothings of all sorts. Nobody thought of the secret drawer; and if they had thought of it, where could a place have been found less likely? If she had ever made a will, she could have had no reason for concealing it. To be sure they did not reason in this way, being simply unaware of any place of concealment at all. And Mary knew nothing about this search they were making. She did not know how she was herself 'left'. When the first misery of grief was exhausted, she began, indeed, to have troubled thoughts in her own mind, – to expect that the vicar would speak to her, or Mr Furnival send for her, and tell her what she was to do. But nothing was said to her. The vicar's wife had asked her to come for a long visit; and the anxious people, who were for ever talking over this subject and consulting what was best for her, had come to no decision as yet, as to what must be said to the person chiefly concerned. It was too heartrending to have to put the real state of affairs before her.

The doctor had no wife; but he had an anxious mother,

who, though she would not for the world have been unkind to
the poor girl, yet was very anxious that she should be disposed
of and out of her son's way. It is true that the doctor was forty
and Mary only eighteen, – but what then? Matches of that
kind were seen every day, and his heart was so soft to the child
that his mother never knew from one day to another what
might happen. She had naturally no doubt at all that Mary
would seize the first hand held out to her, and as time went on
held many an anxious consultation with the vicar's wife on the
subject. 'You cannot have her with you for ever,' she said.
'She must know one time or another how she is left, and that
she must learn to do something for herself.'

'Oh,' said the vicar's wife, 'how is she to be told? It is
heartrending to look at her and to think, – nothing but luxury
all her life, and now, in a moment, destitution. I am very glad
to have her with me; she is a dear little thing, and so nice with
the children. And if some good man would only step in—'

The doctor's mother trembled; for that a good man should
step in was exactly what she feared. 'That is a thing that can
never be depended upon,' she said; 'and marriages made out
of compassion are just as bad as mercenary marriages. Oh no,
my dear Mrs Bowyer, Mary has a great deal of character. You
should put more confidence in her than that. No doubt she
will be much cast down at first, but when she knows, she will
rise to the occasion and show what is in her.'

'Poor little thing! what is in a girl of eighteen, and one that
has lain on the roses and fed on the lilies all her life? Oh, I
could find it in my heart to say a great deal about old Lady
Mary that would not be pleasant! Why did she bring her up so
if she did not mean to provide for her? I think she must have
been at heart a wicked old woman.'

'Oh no – we must not say that. I daresay, as my son says,
she always meant to do it some time—'

'Some time! how long did she expect to live, I wonder?'

'Well,' said the doctor's mother, 'it is wonderful how little
old one feels sometimes within one's self, even when one is
well up in years.' She was of the faction of the old, instead of
being like Mrs Bowyer, who was not much over thirty, of the
faction of the young. She could make excuses for Lady Mary;
but she thought that it was unkind to bring the poor little girl
here in ignorance of her real position, and in the way of men –
who, though old enough to know bettter, were still capable of

folly, as what man is not when a girl of eighteen is concerned?
'I hope,' she added, 'that the Earl will do something for her.
Certainly he ought to, when he knows all that his grand-
mother did, and what her intentions must have been. He
ought to make her a little allowance – that is the least he can
do. Not, to be sure, such a provision as we all hoped Lady
Mary was going to make for her, but enough to live upon. Mr
Furnival, I believe, has written to him to that effect.'

'Hush!' cried the vicar's wife; indeed she had been making
signs to the other lady, who stood with her back to the door, for
some moments. Mary had come in while this conversation was
going on. She had not paid any attention to it; and yet her ear had
been caught by the names of Lady Mary and the Earl and Mr
Furnival. For whom was it that the Earl should make an
allowance enough to live upon? whom Lady Mary had not
provided for, and whom Mr Furnival had written about? When
she sat down to the needlework in which she was helping Mrs
Vicar, it was not to be supposed that she should not ponder these
words – for some time very vaguely, not perceiving the meaning
of them; and then with a start she woke up to perceive that there
must be something meant, some one – even some one she knew.
And then the needle dropped out of the girl's hand, and the
pinafore she was making fell on the floor. Some one! it must be
herself they meant! Who but she could be the subject of that
earnest conversation? She began to remember a great many
conversations as earnest, which had been stopped when she
came into the room, and the looks of pity which had been bent
upon her. She had thought in her innocence that this was
because she had lost her godmother, her protectress – and
had been very grateful for the kindness of her friends. But
now another meaning came into everything. Mrs Bowyer had
accompanied her visitor to the door, still talking, and when she
returned her face was very grave. But she smiled when she met
Mary's look, and said cheerfully, 'How kind of you, my dear, to
make all those pinafores for me! The little ones will not know
themselves. They never were so fine before.'

'Oh, Mrs Bowyer,' cried the girl, 'I have guessed something, and I want you to tell me! Are you keeping me for
charity, and is it I that am left – without any provision? and
that Mr Furnival has written—'

She could not finish her sentence; for it was very bitter to
her, as may be supposed.

'I don't know what you mean, my dear,' cried the vicar's wife. 'Charity, – well, I suppose that is the same as love – at least it is so in the 13th chapter of 1st Corinthians. You are staying with us, I hope, for love, if that is what you mean.'

Upon which she took the girl in her arms and kissed her, and cried as women must. 'My dearest,' she said, 'as you have guessed the worst, it is better to tell you. Lady Mary – I don't know why, – oh, I don't wish to blame her, – has left no will: and, my dear, my dear, you who have been brought up in luxury, you have not a penny.' Here the vicar's wife gave Mary a closer hug, and kissed her once more. 'We love you all the better – if that was possible,' she said.

How many thoughts will fly through a girl's mind while her head rests on some kind shoulder, and she is being consoled for the first calamity that has touched her life! She was neither ungrateful nor unresponsive; but as Mrs Bowyer pressed her close to her kind breast and cried over her, Mary did not cry but thought, seeing in a moment a succession of scenes, and realising in a moment so complete a new world, that all her pain was quelled by the hurry and rush in her brain as her forces rallied to sustain her. She withdrew from her kind support after a moment with eyes tearless and shining, the colour mounting to her face, and not a sign of discouragement in her, nor yet of sentiment, though she grasped her kind friend's hands with a pressure which her innocent small fingers seemed incapable of giving. 'One has read of such things – in books,' she said, with a faint courageous smile; 'and I suppose they happen – in life.'

'Oh, my dear, too often in life. Though how people can be so cruel, so indifferent, so careless of the happiness of those they love—'

Here Mary pressed her friend's hands till they hurt, and cried, 'Not cruel, not indifferent. I cannot hear a word—'

'Well, dear, it is like you to feel so – I knew you would; and I will not say a word. Oh, Mary, if she ever thinks of such things now—'

'I hope she will not – I hope she cannot!' cried the girl, with once more a vehement pressure of her friend's hands.

'What is that?' Mrs Bowyer said, looking round. 'It is somebody in the next room, I suppose. No, dear; I hope so too, for she would not be happy if she remembered. Mary, dry your eyes, my dear. Try not to think of this. I am sure there is some one in the next room. And you must try not to look wretched, for all our sakes—'

'Wretched!' cried Mary, springing up. 'I am not wretched.' And she turned with a countenance glowing and full of courage to the door. But there was no one there – no visitor lingering in the smaller room as sometimes happened.

'I thought I heard some one come in,' said the vicar's wife. 'Didn't you hear something, Mary? I suppose it is because I am so agitated with all this, but I could have sworn I heard some one come in.'

'There is nobody,' said Mary, who, in the shock of the calamity which had so suddenly changed the world to her, was perfectly calm. She did not feel at all disposed to cry or 'give way'. It went to her head with a thrill of pain, which was excitement as well, like a strong stimulant suddenly applied; and she added, 'I should like to go out a little, if you don't mind, just to get used to the idea.' 'My dear, I will get my hat in a moment—'

'No, please. It is not unkindness; but I must think it over by myself – by myself,' Mary cried. She hurried away, while Mrs Bowyer took another survey of the outer room, and called the servant to know who had been calling. Nobody had been calling, the maid said; but her mistress still shook her head.

'It must have been some one who does not ring, who just opens the door,' she said to herself. 'That is the worst of the country. It might be Mrs Blunt, or Sophia Blackburn, or the curate, or half-a-dozen people – and they have just gone away when they heard me crying. How could I help crying? But I wonder how much they heard, whoever it was.'

VI

It was winter, and snow was on the ground.

Lady Mary found herself on the road that led through her own village going home. It was like a picture of a wintry night – like one of those pictures that please the children at Christmas. A little snow sprinkled on the roofs, just enough to define them, and on the edges of the roads; every cottage window showing a ruddy glimmer in the twilight; the men coming home from their work; the children, tied up in comforters and caps, stealing in from the slides, and from the pond where they were forbidden to go; and, in the distance, the trees of the great House standing up dark, turning the twilight into night. She had a curious enjoyment in it, simple like that of a child, and a wish to talk to some one out of the fulness of her heart. She overtook, her step being far lighter and quicker than his, one of the men going home from his work, and spoke to him, telling him with a smile not to be afraid; but he never so much as raised his head, and went plodding on with his heavy step, not knowing that she had spoken to him. She was startled by this; but said to herself that the men were dull, that their perceptions were confused, and that it was getting dark – and went on, passing him quickly. His breath made a cloud in the air as he walked, and his heavy plodding steps sounded into the frosty night. She perceived that her own were invisible and inaudible, with a curious momentary sensation half of pleasure, half of pain. She felt no cold, and she saw through the twilight as clearly as if it had been day. There was no fatigue or sense of weakness in her; but she had the strange, wistful feeling of an exile returning after long years, not knowing how he may find those he had left. At one of the first houses in the village there was a woman standing at her door, looking out for her children – one who knew Lady Mary well. She stopped quite cheerfully to bid her good evening, as she had done in her vigorous days, before she grew old. It was a little experiment, too. She thought it possible that Catherine would scream out, and perhaps fly from her; but surely would be easily reassured when she heard the voice she knew, and saw by her one who was no ghost, but her own kind mistress. But Catherine took no notice when she spoke; she did not so much as turn her head. Lady Mary stood by her patiently, with more and more of that wistful desire to be recognised. She put her hand timidly upon the woman's arm, who was thinking of nothing but her boys, and calling to them, straining her eyes in the fading light. 'Don't be afraid – they are coming, they are safe,' she said, pressing Catherine's arm. But the woman never moved. She took no notice. She called to a neighbour who was passing to ask if she had seen the children, and the two stood and talked in the dim air, not conscious of the third who stood between them, looking from one to another, astonished, paralysed. Lady Mary had not been prepared for this; she

could not believe it even now. She repeated their names more
and more anxiously, and even plucked at their sleeves to call
their attention. She stood as a poor dependant sometimes
stands, wistful, civil, trying to say something that will please,
while they talked and took no notice; and then the neighbour
passed on, and Catherine went into her house. It is hard to be
left out in the cold when others go into their cheerful houses;
but to be thus left outside of life, to speak and not be heard, to
stand, unseen, astounded, unable to secure any attention! She
had thought they would be frightened, but it was not they
who were frightened. A great panic seized the woman who
was no more of this world. She had almost rejoiced to find
herself back walking so lightly, so strongly, finding everything easy that had been so hard; and yet but a few minutes
had passed, and she knew, never more to be deceived, that she
was no longer of this world. What if she should be condemned
to wander for ever among familiar places that knew her no
more, appealing for a look, a word, to those who could no
longer see her, or hear her cry, or know of her presence?
Terror seized upon her, a chill and pang of fear beyond
description. She felt an impulse to fly wildly into the dark,
into the night, like a lost creature; to find again somehow, she
could not tell how, the door out of which she had come, and
beat upon it wildly with her hands, and implore to be taken
home. For a moment she stood looking round her, lost and
alone in the wide universe; no one to speak to her, no one to
comfort her – outside of life altogether. Other rustic figures,
slow-stepping, leisurely, at their ease, went and came, one at a
time; but in this place, where every stranger was an object of
curiosity, no one cast a glance at her. She was as if she had
never been.

Presently she found herself entering her own house.

It was all shut up and silent, – not a window lighted along
the whole front of the house which used to twinkle and glitter
with lights. It soothed her somewhat to see this, as if in
evidence that the place had changed with her. She went in
silently, and the darkness was as day to her. Her own rooms
were all shut up, yet were open to her steps, which no external
obstacle could limit. There was still the sound of life below
stairs, and in the housekeeper's room a cheerful party gathered round the fire. It was there that she turned first with
some wistful human attraction towards the warmth and light

rather than to the still places in which her own life had been passed. Mrs Prentiss, the housekeeper, had her daughter with her on a visit and the daughter's baby lay asleep in a cradle placed upon two chairs outside the little circle of women round the table – one of whom was Jervis, Lady Mary's maid. Jervis sat and worked and cried, and mixed her words with little sobs. 'I never thought as I should have had to take another place,' she said. 'Brown and me, we made sure of a little something to start upon. He's been here for twenty years, and so have you, Mrs Prentiss; and me, as nobody can say I wasn't faithful night and day.'

'I never had that confidence in my lady to expect anything,' Prentiss said.

'Oh, mother, don't say that: many and many a day you've said, when my lady dies—'

'And we've all said it,' said Jervis. 'I can't think how she did it, nor why she did it; for she was a kind lady, though appearances is against her.'

'She was one of them, and I've known a many, as could not abide to see a gloomy face,' said the housekeeper. 'She kept us all comfortable for the sake of being comfortable herself, but no more.'

'Oh, you are hard upon my lady!' cried Jervis, 'and I can't bear to hear a word against her, though it's been an awful disappointment to me.'

'What's you or me, or any one,' cried Mrs Prentiss, 'in comparison of that poor little thing that can't work for her living like we can; that is left on the charity of folks she don't belong to? I'd have forgiven my lady anything if she'd done what was right by Miss Mary. You'll get a place, and a good place; and me, they'll leave me here when the new folks come as have taken the house. But what will become of her, the darling? and not a penny, nor a friend, nor one to look to her? Oh, you selfish old woman! oh, you heart of stone! I just hope you are feeling it where you're gone,' the housekeeper cried.

But as she said this, the woman did not know who was looking at her with wide wistful eyes, holding out her hands in appeal, receiving every word as if it had been a blow. Though she knew it was useless, Lady Mary could not help it. She cried out to them, 'Have pity upon me! have pity upon me! I am not cruel, as you think,' with a keen anguish in her voice, which seemed to be sharp enough to pierce the very air and go up to the skies. And so, perhaps, it did; but never touched the human atmosphere in which she stood a stranger. Jervis was threading her needle when her mistress uttered that cry, but her hand did not tremble, nor did the thread deflect a hair's-breadth from the straight line. The young mother alone seemed to be moved by some faint disturbance. 'Hush!' she said; 'is he waking?' looking towards the cradle. But as the baby made no further sound, she too returned to her sewing; and they sat bending their heads over their work round the table, and continued their talk. The room was very comfortable, bright, and warm, as Lady Mary had liked all her rooms to be. The warm firelight danced upon the walls; the women talked in cheerful tones. She stood outside their circle, and looked at them with a wistful face. Their notice would have been more sweet to her as she stood in that great humiliation, than in other times the look of a queen.

'But what is the matter with baby?' the mother said, rising hastily.

It was with no servile intention of securing a look from that little prince of life that she who was not of this world had stepped aside forlorn, and looked at him in his cradle. Though she was not of this world, she was still a woman, and had nursed her children in her arms. She bent over the infant by the soft impulse of nature, tenderly, with no interested thought. But the child saw her; was it possible? He turned his head towards her, and flickered his baby hands, and cooed with that indescribable voice that goes to every woman's heart. Lady Mary felt such a thrill of pleasure go through her, as no incident had given her for long years. She put out her arms to him as the mother snatched him from his little bed; and he, which was more wonderful, stretched towards her in his innocence, turning away from them all.

'He wants to go to some one,' cried the mother. 'Oh look, look, for God's sake! who is there that the child sees?'

'There's no one there – not a soul. Now dearie, dearie, be reasonable. You can see for yourself there's not a creature,' said the grandmother.

'Oh, my baby, my baby! He sees something we can't see,' the young woman cried. 'Something has happened to his father, or he's going to be taken from me!' she said, holding the child to her in a sudden passion. The other women rushed to her to console her – the mother with reason and Jervis with poetry. 'It's the angels whispering, like the song says.' Oh the pang that was in the heart of the other whom they could not hear! She stood wondering how it could be – wondering with an amazement beyond words, how all that was in her heart, the love and the pain, and the sweetness and bitterness, could all be hidden – all hidden by that air in which the women stood so clear! She held out her hands, she spoke to them, telling who she was, but no one paid any attention; only the little dog Fido, who had been basking by the fire, sprang up, looked at her, and, retreating slowly backwards till he reached the wall, sat down there and looked at her again, with now and then a little bark of inquiry. The dog saw her. This gave her a curious pang of humiliation, yet pleasure. She went away out of that little centre of human life in a great excitement and thrill of her whole being. The child had seen her and the dog; but, oh heavens! how was she to work out her purpose by such auxiliaries as these?

She went up to her old bedchamber with unshed tears heavy about her eyes, and a pathetic smile quivering on her mouth. It touched her beyond measure that the child should have that confidence in her. 'Then God is still with me,' she said to herself. Her room, which had been so warm and bright, lay desolate in the stillness of the night; but she wanted no light, for the darkness was no darkness to her. She looked round her for a little, wondering to think how far away from her now was this scene of her old life, but feeling no pain in the sight of it – only a kind indulgence for the foolish simplicity which had taken so much pride in all these infantile elements of living. She went to the little Italian cabinet which stood against the wall, feeling now at least that she could do as she would, – that here there was no blank of human unconsciousness to stand in her way. But she was met by something that baffled and vexed her once more. She felt the polished surface of the wood under her hand, and saw all the pretty ornamentation, the inlaid work, the delicate carvings, which she knew so well. They swam in her eyes a little, as if they were part of some phantasmagoria about her, existing only in her vision. Yet the smooth surface resisted her touch; and when she withdrew a step from it, it stood before her solidly and square, as it had stood always, a glory to the place. She put forth her hands upon it, and could have traced the waving lines of the exquisite work, in which some artist soul had worked itself out in the old times; but though she thus saw it and felt, she could not with all her endeavours find the handle of the drawer, the richly wrought knob of ivory, the little door that opened into the secret place. How long she stood by it, attempting again and again to find what was as familiar to her as her own hand. What was before her, visible in every line, what she felt with fingers which began to tremble, she could not tell. Time did not count with her as with common men. She did not grow weary, or require refreshment or rest, like those who were still of this world. But at length her head grew giddy and her heart failed. A cold despair took possession of her soul. She could do nothing then – nothing; neither by help of man, neither by use of her own faculties, which were greater and clearer than ever before. She sank down upon the floor at the foot of that old toy, which had pleased her in the softness of her old age, to which she had trusted the fortunes of another; by which, in wantonness and folly, she had sinned, she had sinned! And she thought she saw standing round her companions in the land she had left, saying, 'It is impossible, impossible!' with infinite pity in their eyes; and the face of Him who had given her permission to come, yet who had said no word to her to encourage her in what was against nature. And there came into her heart a longing to fly, to get home, to be back in the land where her fellows were, and her appointed place. A child lost, how pitiful that is! without power to reason and divine how help will come; but a soul lost, outside of one method of existence, withdrawn from the other, knowing no way to retrace its steps, nor how help can come! There had been no bitterness in the passing from earth to the land where she had gone; but now there came upon her soul, in all the power of her new faculties, the bitterness of death. The place which was hers she had forsaken and left, and the place that had been hers knew her no more.

VII

Mary, when she left her kind friend in the vicarage, went out and took a long walk. She had received a shock so great that it took all sensation from her, and threw her into the seething

and surging of an excitement altogether beyond her control.
She could not think until she had got familiar with the idea,
which indeed had been vaguely shaping itself in her mind
ever since she had emerged from the first profound gloom and
prostration of the shadow of death. She had never definitely
thought of her position before – never even asked herself what
was to become of her when Lady Mary died. She did not see,
any more than Lady Mary did, why she should ever die; and
girls, who have never wanted anything in their lives, who
have had no sharp experience to enlighten them, are slow to
think upon such subjects. She had not expected anything; her
mind had not formed any idea of inheritance: and it had not
surprised her to hear of the Earl, who was Lady Mary's
natural heir; nor to feel herself separated from the house in
which all her previous life had been passed. But there had
been gradually dawning upon her a sense that she had come to
a crisis in her life, and that she must soon be told what was to
become of her. It was not so urgent as that she should ask any
questions; but it began to appear very clearly in her mind that
things were not to be with her as they had been. She had
heard the complaints and astonishment of the servants, to
whom Lady Mary had left nothing, with resentment. Jervis,
who could not marry and take her lodging-house, but must
wait until she had saved more money, and wept to think, after
all her devotion, of having to take another place; and Mrs
Prentiss, the housekeeper, who was cynical, and expounded
Lady Mary's kindness to her servants to be the issue of a
refined selfishness; and Brown, who had sworn subdued
oaths, and had taken the liberty of representing himself to
Mary as 'in the same box' with herself. Mary had been angry,
very angry at all this; and she had not by word or look given
any one to understand that she felt herself 'in the same box'.
But yet she had been vaguely anxious, curious, desiring to
know. And she had not even begun to think what she should
do. That seemed a sort of affront to her godmother's memory,
at all events, until some one had made it clear to her. But now,
in a moment, with her first consciousness of the importance of
this matter in the sight of others, a consciousness of what it
was to herself, came into her mind. A change of everything – a
new life – a new world; and not only so, but a severance from
the old world, – a giving up of everything that had been most
dear and pleasant to her.

These thoughts were driven through her mind like the snowflakes in a storm. The year had slid on since Lady Mary's death. Winter was beginning to yield to spring; the snow was over and the great cold. And other changes had taken place. The great house had been let, and the family who had taken it had been about a week in possession. Their coming had inflicted a wound upon Mary's heart; but everybody had urged upon her the idea that it was much better the house should be let for a time 'till everything was settled'. When all was settled things would be different. Mrs Vicar did not say, 'You can then do what you please,' but she did convey to Mary's mind somehow a sort of inference that she would have something to do it with. And when Mary had protested, 'It shall never be let again with my will,' the kind woman had said tremulously, 'Well, my dear!' and had changed the subject. All these things now came to Mary's mind. They had been afraid to tell her; they had thought it would be so much to her – so important, such a crushing blow. To have nothing – to be destitute; to be written about by Mr Furnival to the Earl; to have her case represented – Mary felt herself stung by such unendurable suggestions into an energy – a determination – of which her soft young life had known nothing. No one should write about her, or ask charity for her, she said to herself. She had gone through the woods and round the park, which was not large, and now she could not leave these beloved precincts without going to look at the house. Up to this time she had not had the courage to go near the house; but to the commotion and fever of her mind every violent sensation was congenial, and she went up the avenue now almost gladly, with a little demonstration to herself of energy and courage. Why not that as well as all the rest?

It was once more twilight, and the dimness favoured her design. She wanted to go there unseen, to look up at the windows with their alien lights, and to think of the time when Lady Mary sat behind the curtains, and there was nothing but tenderness and peace throughout the house. There was a light in every window along the entire front, a lavishness of firelight and lamplight which told of a household in which there were many inhabitants. Mary's mind was so deeply absorbed, and perhaps her eyes so dim with tears that she could scarcely see what was before her, when the door opened suddenly and a lady came out. 'I will go myself,' she said in an agitated tone to some one behind her. 'Don't get yourself laughed at,' said a voice from within. The sound of the voices roused the young spectator. She looked with a little curiosity, mixed with anxiety, at the lady who had come out of the house, and who started, too, with a gesture of alarm, when she saw Mary move in the dark. 'Who are you?' she cried out in a trembling voice, 'and what do you want here?'

Then Mary made a step or two forward and said, 'I must ask your pardon if I am trespassing. I did not know there was any objection—' This stranger to make an objection! It brought something like a tremulous laugh to Mary's lips.

'Oh, there is no objection,' said the lady, 'only we have been a little put out. I see now: you are the young lady who – you are the young lady that; – you are the one that – suffered most.'

'I am Lady Mary's goddaughter,' said the girl. 'I have lived here all my life.'

'Oh, my dear, I have heard all about you,' the lady cried. The people who had taken the house were merely rich people; they had no other characteristic; and in the vicarage, as well as in the other houses about, it was said when they were spoken of, that it was a good thing they were not people to be visited, since nobody could have had the heart to visit strangers in Lady Mary's house. And Mary could not but feel a keen resentment to think that her story, such as it was, the story which she had only now heard in her own person, should be discussed by such people. But the speaker had a look of kindness, and, so far as could be seen, of perplexity and fretted anxiety in her face, and had been in a hurry, but stopped herself in order to show her interest. 'I wonder,' she said impulsively, 'that you can come here and look at the place again after all that has passed.'

'I never thought,' said Mary, 'that there could be – any objection.'

'Oh, how can you think I mean that? how can you pretend to think so?' cried the other impatiently. 'But after you have been treated so heartlessly, so unkindly, – and left, poor thing! they tell me, without a penny, without any provision—'

'I don't know you,' cried Mary, breathless with quick-rising passion. 'I don't know what right you can have to meddle with my affairs.'

The lady stared at her for a moment without speaking, and

then she said, all at once, 'That is quite true – but it is rude as
well; for though I have no right to meddle with your affairs, I
did it in kindness, because I took an interest in you from all I
have heard.'

Mary was very accessible to such a reproach and argument.
Her face flushed with a sense of her own churlishness. 'I beg
your pardon,' she said; 'I am sure you mean to be kind.'

'Well,' said the stranger, 'that is perhaps going too far on
the other side, for you can't even see my face to know what I
mean. But I do mean to be kind, and I am very sorry for you.
And though I think you've been treated abominably, all the
same I like you better for not allowing any one to say so. And
now, do you know where I was going? I was going to the
vicarage, – where you are living, I believe, – to see if the vicar,
or his wife, or you, or all of you together, could do a thing for
me.'

'Oh, I am sure Mrs Bowyer—' said Mary, with a voice
much less assured than her words.

'You must not be too sure, my dear. I know she doesn't
mean to call upon me, because my husband is a City man.
That is just as she pleases. I am not very fond of City men
myself. But there's no reason why I should stand on ceremony when I want something, is there? Now, my dear, I want
to know – Don't laugh at me. I am not superstitious, so far as I
am aware; but – Tell me, in your time was there ever any
disturbance, any appearances you couldn't understand, any—
Well, I don't like the word ghosts. It's disrespectful, if there's
anything of the sort; and it's vulgar if there isn't. But you
know what I mean. Was there anything – of that sort – in your
time?'

In your time! Poor Mary had scarcely realised yet that her
time was over. Her heart refused to allow it when it was thus
so abruptly brought before her; but she obliged herself to
subdue these rising rebellions, and to answer, though with
some *hauteur*. 'There is nothing of the kind that I ever heard
of. There is no superstition or ghost in our house.'

She thought it was the vulgar desire of new people to find a
conventional mystery, and it seemed to Mary that this was a
desecration of her home. Mrs Turner, however (for that was
her name), did not receive the intimation as the girl expected,
but looked at her very gravely, and said, 'That makes it a great
deal more serious,' as if to herself. She paused, and then

added, 'You see, the case is this. I have a little girl who is our
youngest, who is just my husband's idol. She is a sweet little
thing, though perhaps I should not say it. Are you fond of
children? Then I almost feel sure you would think so too. Not
a moping child at all, or too clever, or anything to alarm one.
Well, you know, little Connie, since ever we came in, has seen
an old lady walking about the house—'

'An old lady!' said Mary, with an involuntary smile.

'Oh yes. I laughed too, the first time. I said it would be old
Mrs Prentiss, or perhaps the charwoman, or some old lady
from the village that had been in the habit of coming in the
former people's time. But the child got very angry. She said it
was a real lady. She would not allow me to speak. Then we
thought perhaps it was some one who did not know the house
was let, and had walked in to look at it; but nobody would go
on coming like that with all the signs of a large family in the
house. And now the doctor says the child must be low, that
the place perhaps doesn't agree with her, and that we must
send her away. Now, I ask you, how could I send little Connie
away, the apple of her father's eye? I should have to go with
her, of course, and how could the house get on without me?
Naturally we are very anxious. And this afternoon she has
seen her again, and sits there crying because she says the dear
old lady looks so sad. I just seized my hat, and walked out, to
come to you and your friends at the vicarage to see if you
could help me. Mrs Bowyer may look down upon a City
person – I don't mind that; but she is a mother, and surely she
would feel for a mother,' cried the poor lady vehemently,
putting up her hands to her wet eyes.

'Oh indeed, indeed she would! I am sure now that she will
call directly. We did not know what a—' Mary stopped
herself in saying, 'what a nice woman you are,' which she
thought would be rude, though poor Mrs Turner would have
liked it. But then she shook her head and added, 'What could
any of us do to help you? I have never heard of any old lady.
There never was anything—I know all about the house,
everything that has ever happened, and Prentiss will tell
you. There is nothing of that kind – indeed, there is nothing.
You must have—' But here Mary stopped again; for to
suggest that a new family, a city family, should have brought
an apparition of their own with them, was too ridiculous an
idea to be entertained.

'Miss Vivian,' said Mrs Turner, 'will you come back with me and speak to the child?'

At this Mary faltered a little. 'I have never been there – since the – funeral,' she said.

The good woman laid a kind hand upon her shoulder, caressing and soothing. 'You were very fond of her – in spite of the way she has used you?'

'Oh, how dare you, or any one, to speak of her so? She used me as if I had been her dearest child. She was more kind to me than a mother. There is no one in the world like her!' Mary cried.

'And yet she left you without a penny. Oh, you must be a good girl to feel for her like that. She left you without – What are you going to do, my dear? I feel like a friend. I feel like a mother to you, though you don't know me. You mustn't think it is only curiosity. You can't stay with your friends for ever, – and what are you going to do?'

There are some cases in which it is more easy to speak to a stranger than to one's dearest and oldest friend. Mary had felt this when she rushed out, not knowing how to tell the vicar's wife that she must leave her, and find some independence for herself. It was, however, strange to rush into such a discussion with so little warning, and Mary's pride was very sensitive. She said, 'I am not going to burden my friends,' with a little indignation; but then she remembered how forlorn she was, and her voice softened. 'I must do something – but I don't know what I am good for,' she said, trembling, and on the verge of tears.

'My dear, I have heard a great deal about you,' said the stranger; 'it is not rash, though it may look so. Come back with me directly, and see Connie. She is a very interesting little thing, though I say it – it is wonderful sometimes to hear her talk. You shall be her governess, my dear. Oh, you need not teach her anything – that is not what I mean. I think, I am sure, you will be the saving of her, Miss Vivian; and such a lady as you are, it will be everything for the other girls to live with you. Don't stop to think, but just come with me. You shall have whatever you please, and always be treated like a lady. Oh, my dear, consider my feelings as a mother, and come; oh, come to Connie! I know you will save her; it is an inspiration. Come back! Come back with me!'

It seemed to Mary too like an inspiration. What it cost her

to cross that threshold and walk in, a stranger, to the house which had been all her life as her own, she never said to any one. But it was independence; it was deliverance from entreaties and remonstrances without end. It was a kind of setting right, so far as could be, of the balance which had got so terribly wrong. No writing to the Earl now; no appeal to friends, – anything in all the world, much more honest service and kindness, must be better than that.

VIII

'Tell the young lady all about it, Connie,' said her mother.

But Connie was very reluctant to tell. She was very shy, and clung to her mother, and hid her face in her ample dress; and though presently she was beguiled by Mary's voice, and in a short time came to her side, and clung to her as she had clung to Mrs Turner, she still kept her secret to herself. They were all very kind to Mary, the elder girls, standing round in a respectful circle looking at her, while their mother exhorted them to 'take a pattern' by Miss Vivian. The novelty, the awe which she inspired, the real kindness about her, ended by overcoming in Mary's young mind the first miserable impression of such a return to her home. It gave her a kind of pleasure to write to Mrs Bowyer that she had found employment, and had thought it better to accept it at once. 'Don't be angry with me: and I think you will understand me,' she said. And then she gave herself up to the strange new scene.

The 'ways' of the large simple-minded family, homely yet kindly, so transformed Lady Mary's graceful old rooms that they no longer looked the same place. And when Mary sat down with them at the big heavy-laden table, surrounded with the hum of so large a party, it was impossible for her to believe that everything was not new about her. In no way could the saddening recollections of a home from which the chief figure had disappeared have been more completely broken up. Afterwards Mrs Turner took her aside, and begged to know which was Mary's old room, 'for I should like to put you there, as if nothing had happened.' 'Oh, do not put me there!' Mary cried, 'so much has happened.' But this seemed a refinement to the kind woman, which it was far better for her young guest not to 'yield' to. The room Mary had occupied had been next to her godmother's, with a door between, and when it turned out that Connie, with an elder sister, was in Lady Mary's room, everything seemed perfectly arranged in Mrs Turner's eyes. She thought it was providential, with a simple belief in Mary's powers that in other circumstances would have been amusing. But there was no amusement in Mary's mind when she took possession of the old room 'as if nothing had happened'. She sat by the fire for half the night, in an agony of silent recollection and thought, going over the last days of her godmother's life, calling up everything before her, and realising, as she had never realised till now, the lonely career on which she was setting out, the subjection to the will and convenience of strangers in which henceforth her life must be passed. This was a kind woman who had opened her doors to the destitute girl; but notwithstanding, however great the torture to Mary, there was no escaping this room, which was haunted by the saddest recollections of her life. Of such things she must no longer complain – nay, she must think of nothing but thanking the mistress of the house for her thoughtfulness, for the wish to be kind which so often exceeds the performance.

The room was warm and well lighted; the night was very calm and sweet outside. Nothing had been touched or changed of all her little decorations, the ornaments which had been so delightful to her girlhood. A large photograph of Lady Mary held the chief place over the mantelpiece, representing her in the fulness of her beauty, – a photograph which had been taken from the picture painted ages ago by a Royal Academician. It was fortunately so little like Lady Mary in her old age that, save as a thing which had always hung there, and belonged to her happier life, it did not affect the girl; but no picture was necessary to bring before her the well-remembered figure. She could not realise that the little movements she heard on the other side of the door were any other than those of her mistress, her friend, her mother, for all these names Mary lavished upon her in the fulness of her heart. The blame that was being cast upon Lady Mary from all sides made this child of her bounty but more deeply her partisan, more warm in her adoration. She would not, for all the inheritances of the world, have acknowledged even to herself that Lady Mary was in fault. Mary felt that she would rather a thousand times be poor and have to gain her daily bread, than that she who had nourished and cherished her should have been forced in her cheerful old age to think, before she chose to do so, of parting and farewell and the inevitable end.

She thought, like every young creature in strange and painful circumstances, that she would be unable to sleep, and did indeed lie awake and weep for an hour or more, thinking of all the changes that had happened; but sleep overtook her before she knew, while her mind was still full of these thoughts; and her dreams were endless, confused, full of misery and longing. She dreamed a dozen times over that she heard Lady Mary's soft call through the open door – which was not open, but shut closely and locked by the sisters who now inhabited the next room; and once she dreamed that Lady Mary came to her bedside and stood there looking at her earnestly with the tears flowing from her eyes. Mary struggled in her sleep to tell her benefactress how she loved her, and approved of all she had done, and wanted nothing – but felt herself bound as by a nightmare, so that she could not move or speak, or even put out a hand to dry those tears which it was intolerable to her to see; and woke with the struggle, and the miserable sensation of seeing her dearest friend weep and being unable to comfort her. The moon was shining into the room, throwing part of it into a cold full light, while blackness lay in all the corners. The impression of her dream was so strong that Mary's eyes turned instantly to the spot where in her dream her godmother had stood. To be sure there was nobody there; but as her consciousness returned, and with it the sweep of painful recollection, the sense of change, the miserable contrast between the present and the past, sleep fled from her eyes. She fell into the vividly awake condition which is the alternative of broken sleep, and gradually, as she lay, there came upon her that mysterious sense of another presence in the room, which is so subtle and indescribable. She neither saw anything nor heard anything, and yet she felt that some one was there.

She lay still for some time and held her breath, listening for a movement, even for the sound of breathing, scarcely alarmed, yet sure that she was not alone. After a while she raised herself on her pillow, and in a low voice asked, 'Who is there? is any one there?' There was no reply, no sound of any description, and yet the conviction grew upon her. Her heart began to beat, and the blood to mount to her head. Her own being made so much sound, so much commotion, that it seemed to her she could not hear anything save those beatings and pulsings. Yet she was not afraid. After a time, however, the oppression became more than she could bear. She got up and lit her candle, and searched through the familiar room; but she found no trace that any one had been there. The furniture was all in its usual order. There was no hiding-place where any human thing could find refuge. When she had satisfied herself, and was about to return to bed, suppressing a sensation which must, she said to herself, be altogether fantastic, she was startled by a low knocking at the door of communication. Then she heard the voice of the elder girl. 'Oh, Miss Vivian – what is it? Have you seen anything?' A new sense of anger, disdain, humiliation, swept through Mary's mind. And if she had seen anything, she said to herself, what was that to those strangers? She replied. 'No, nothing; what should I see?' in a tone which was almost haughty in spite of herself.

'I thought it might be – the ghost. Oh, please, don't be angry. I thought I heard this door open, but it is locked. Oh! perhaps it is very silly, but I am so frightened, Miss Vivian.'

'Go back to bed,' said Mary; 'there is no – ghost. I am going to sit up and write some – letters. You will see my light under the door.'

'Oh, thank you,' cried the girl.

Mary remembered what a consolation and strength in all wakefulness had been the glimmer of the light under her godmother's door. She smiled to think that she herself, so desolate as she was, was able to afford this innocent comfort to another girl, and then sat down and wept quietly, feeling her solitude and the chill about her, and the dark and the silence. The moon had gone behind a cloud. There seemed no light but her small, miserable candle in earth and heaven. And yet that poor little speck of light kept up the heart of another – which made her smile again in the middle of her tears. And by-and-by the commotion in her head and heart calmed down, and she too fell asleep.

Next day she heard all the floating legends that were beginning to rise in the house. They all arose from Connie's questions about the old lady whom she had seen going upstairs before her, the first evening after the new family's arrival. It was in the presence of the doctor – who had come to see the child, and whose surprise at finding Mary there was almost ludicrous – that she heard the story, though much against his will.

'There can be no need for troubling Miss Vivian about it,' he said, in a tone which was almost rude. But Mrs Turner was not sensitive.

'When Miss Vivian has just come, like a dear, to help us with Connie!' the good woman cried. 'Of course she must hear it, doctor; for otherwise, how could she know what to do?'

'Is it true that you have come here – *here*? to help – Good heavens, Miss Mary, *here*?'

'Why not here?' Mary said, smiling as best she could. 'I am Connie's governess, doctor.'

He burst out into that suppressed roar which serves a man instead of tears, and jumped up from his seat, clenching his fist. The clenched fist was to the intention of the dead woman whose fault this was; and if it had ever entered the doctor's mind, as his mother supposed, to marry this forlorn child, and thus bestow a home upon her whether she would or no, no doubt he would now have attempted to carry out that plan. But as no such thing had occurred to him, the doctor only showed his sense of the intolerable by look and gesture. 'I must speak to the vicar. I must see Furnival. It can't be permitted,' he cried.

'Do you think I shall not be kind to her, doctor?' cried Mrs Turner. 'Oh, ask her! She is one that understands. She knows far better than that. We're not fine people, doctor, but we're kind people. I can say that for myself. There is nobody in this house but will be good to her, and admire her, and take an example by her. To have a real lady with the girls, that is what I would give anything for; and as she wants taking care of, poor dear, and petting, and an 'ome—'

Mary, who would not hear any more, got up hastily, and took the hand of her new protectress, and kissed her, partly out of gratitude and kindness, partly to stop her mouth, and prevent the saying of something which it might have been still more difficult to support. 'You are a real lady yourself, dear Mrs Turner,' she cried. (And this notwithstanding the one deficient letter: but many people who are much more dignified than Mrs Turner – people who behave themselves very well in every other respect – say ''ome.')

'Oh, my dear, I don't make any pretensions,' the good woman cried, but with a little shock of pleasure which brought the tears to her eyes.

And then the story was told. Connie had seen the lady walk upstairs, and had thought no harm. The child supposed it was some one belonging to the house. She had gone into the room which was now Connie's room, but as that had a second door, there was no suspicion caused by the fact that she was not found there a little time after, when the child told her mother what she had seen. After this Connie had seen the same lady several times, and once had met her face to face. The child declared that she was not at all afraid. She was a pretty old lady, with white hair and dark eyes. She looked a little sad, but smiled when Connie stopped and stared at her – not angry at all, but rather pleased – and looked for a moment as if she would speak. That was all. Not a word about a ghost was said in Connie's hearing. She had already told it all to the doctor, and he had pretended to consider which of the old ladies in the neighbourhood this could be. In Mary's mind, occupied as it was by so many important matters, there had been up to this time no great question about Connie's apparition: now she began to listen closely, not so much from real interest as from a perception that the doctor, who was her friend, did not want her to hear. This naturally aroused her attention at once. She listened to the child's description with growing eagerness, all the more because the doctor opposed.

'Now that will do, Miss Connie,' he said; 'it is one of the old Miss Murchisons, who are always so fond of finding out about their neighbours. I have no doubt at all on that subject. She wants to find you out in your pet naughtiness, whatever it is, and tell me.'

'I am sure it is not for that,' cried Connie. 'Oh, how can you be so disagreeable? I know she is not a lady who would tell. Besides, she is not thinking at all about me. She was either looking for something she had lost, or – oh, I don't know what it was! – and when she saw me she just smiled. She is not dressed like any of the people here. She had got no cloak on, or bonnet, or anything that is common, but a beautiful white shawl and a long dress, and it gives a little sweep when she walks – oh no! not like your rustling, mamma; but all soft, like water – and it looks like lace upon her head, tied here,' said Connie, putting her hands to her chin, 'in such a pretty, large, soft knot.'

Mary had gradually risen as this description went on, starting a little at first, looking up, getting upon her feet. The colour went altogether out of her face – her eyes grew to twice their natural size. The doctor put out his hand without looking at her, and laid it on her arm with a strong emphatic pressure. 'Just like some one you have seen a picture of,' he said.

'Oh no. I never saw a picture that was so pretty,' said the child.

'Doctor, why do you ask her any more? don't you see, don't you see, the child has seen—?'

'Miss Mary, for God's sake, hold your tongue; it is folly, you know. Now, my little girl, tell me. I know this old lady is the very image of that pretty old lady with the toys for good children, who was in the last Christmas number?'

'Oh!' said Connie, pausing a little. 'Yes, I remember; it was a very pretty picture – mamma put it up in the nursery. No, she is not like that, not at all, much prettier; and then *my* lady is sorry about something – except when she smiles at me. She has her hair put up like this, and this,' the child went on, twisting her own bright locks.

'Doctor! I can't bear any more.'

'My dear! you are mistaken, it is all a delusion. She has seen a picture. I think now, Mrs Turner, that my little patient had better run away and play. Take a good run through the woods, Miss Connie, with your brother, and I will send you some physic which will not be at all nasty, and we shall hear no more of your old lady. My dear Miss Vivian, if you will but hear reason! I have known such cases a hundred times. The child has seen a picture, and it has taken possession of her imagination. She is a little below par, and she has a lively imagination: and she has learned something from Prentiss, though probably she does not remember that. And there it is! a few doses of quinine, and she will see visions no more.'

'Doctor,' cried Mary, 'how can you speak so to me? You dare not look me in the face. You know you dare not: as if you did not know as well as I do! Oh, why does that child see her, and not me?'

'There it is,' he said, with a broken laugh; 'could anything show better that it is a mere delusion? Why, in the name of all that is reasonable, should this stranger child see her, if it was anything, and not you?'

Mrs Turner looked from one to another with wondering eyes. 'You know what it is?' she said. 'Oh, you know who it is? Doctor, doctor, is it because my Connie is so delicate? is it a warning? is it—?'

'Oh, for heaven's sake! you will drive me mad, you ladies. Is it this, and is it that? It is nothing, I tell you. The child is out of sorts, and she has seen some picture that has caught her fancy – and she thinks she sees – I'll send her a bottle,' he cried, jumping up; 'that will put an end to all that.'

'Doctor, don't go away: tell me rather what I must do – if she is looking for something! Oh, doctor, think if she were unhappy, if she were kept out of her sweet rest!'

'Miss Mary! for God's sake, be reasonable. You ought never to have heard a word.'

'Doctor, think! if it should be anything we can do. Oh, tell me, tell me! don't go away and leave me! perhaps we can find out what it is.'

'I will have nothing to do with your findings out. It is mere delusion. Put them both to bed, Mrs Turner – put them all to bed! As if there was not trouble enough!'

'What is it?' cried Connie's mother; 'is it a warning! Oh, for the love of God, tell me, is that what comes before a death?'

When they were all in this state of agitation, the Vicar and his wife were suddenly shown into the room. Mrs Bowyer's eyes flew to Mary, but she was too well-bred a woman not to pay her respects first to the lady of the house, and there were a number of politenesses exchanged, very breathlessly on Mrs Turner's part, before the newcomers were free to show the real occasion of their visit. 'Oh, Mary, what did you mean by taking such a step all in a moment? How could you come here of all places in the world? and how could you leave me without a word?' the Vicar's wife said, with her lips against Mary's cheek. She had already perceived, without dwelling upon it, the excitement in which all the party were. This was said while the Vicar was still making his bow to his new parishioner – who knew very well that her visitors had not intended to call: for the Turners were dissenters, to crown all their misdemeanours, besides being city people and *nouveaux riches*.

'Don't ask me any questions just now,' said Mary, clasping almost hysterically her friend's hand. 'It was providential. Come and hear what the child has seen.' Mrs Turner, though she was so anxious, was too polite not to make a fuss about getting chairs for all her visitors. She postponed her own trouble to this necessity, and trembling, sought the most comfortable seat for Mrs Bowyer, the largest and most imposing for the Vicar himself. When she had established them in a little circle, and done her best to draw Mary too into a chair, she sat down quietly, her mind divided between the cares of courtesy and the alarms of an anxious mother. Mary stood at the table and waited till the commotion was over. The newcomers thought she was going to explain her conduct in leaving them; and Mrs Bowyer, at least, who was critical in point of manners, shivered a little, wondering if perhaps (though she could not find it in her heart to blame Mary) her proceedings were in perfect taste.

'The little girl,' Mary said, beginning abruptly. She had been standing by the table, her lips apart, her countenance utterly pale, her mind evidently too much absorbed to notice anything. 'The little girl – has seen several times a lady going upstairs. Once she met her and saw her face, and the lady smiled at her; but her face was sorrowful, and the child thought she was looking for something. The lady was old, with white hair done up upon her forehead, and lace upon her head. She was dressed,' – here Mary's voice began to be interrupted from time to time by a brief sob, – 'in a long dress that made a soft sound when she walked, and a white shawl, and the lace tied under her chin in a large soft knot—'

'Mary, Mary!' Mrs Bowyer had risen, and stood behind the girl, in whose slender throat the climbing sorrow was almost visible, supporting her, trying to stop her. 'Mary, Mary!' she cried; 'oh, my darling, what are you thinking of? Francis! doctor! make her stop, make her stop—'

'Why should she stop?' said Mrs Turner, rising, too, in her agitation. 'Oh, is it a warning, is it a warning? for my child has seen it – Connie has seen it.'

'Listen to me, all of you,' said Mary, with an effort. 'You all know – who that is. And she has seen her – the little girl—'

Now the others looked at each other, exchanging a startled look.

'My dear people,' cried the doctor, 'the case is not the least unusual. No, no, Mrs Turner, it is no warning – it is nothing of the sort. Look here, Bowyer; you'll believe me. The child is very nervous and sensitive. She has evidently seen a picture somewhere of our dear old friend. She has heard the story somehow – oh, perhaps in some garbled version from Prentiss, or – of course they've all been talking of it. And the child is one of those creatures with its nerves all on the surface – and a little below par in health, in need of iron and quinine, and all that sort of thing. I've seen a hundred such cases,' cried the doctor – 'a thousand such; but now, of course, we'll have a fine story made of it, now that it's come into the ladies' hands.'

He was much excited with this long speech; but it cannot be said that any one paid much attention to him. Mrs Bowyer was holding Mary in her arms, uttering little cries and sobs over her, and looking anxiously at her husband. The vicar sat down suddenly in his chair, with the air of a man who has judgment to deliver without the least idea what to say; while Mary, freeing herself unconsciously from her friend's re-straining embrace, stood facing them all with a sort of trembling defiance: and Mrs Turner kept on explaining nervously that – 'no, no, her Connie was not excitable, was not over-sensitive, never had known what a delusion was.'

'This is very strange,' the Vicar said.

'Oh, Mr Bowyer,' cried Mary, 'tell me what I am to do! – think if she cannot rest, if she is not happy, she that was so good to everybody, that never could bear to see any one in trouble. Oh, tell me, tell me what I am to do! It is you that have disturbed her with all you have been saying. Oh, what can I do, what can I do to give her rest?'

'My dear Mary! My dear Mary!' they all cried in different tones of consternation; and for a few minutes no one could speak. Mrs Bowyer, as was natural, said something, being unable to endure the silence; but neither she nor any of the others knew what it was she said. When it was evident that the Vicar must speak, all were silent, waiting for him; and though it had now become imperative that something in the shape of a judgment must be delivered, yet he was as far as ever from knowing what to say.

'Mary,' he said, with a little tremulousness of voice, 'it is quite natural that you should ask me; but, my dear, I am not at all prepared to answer. I think you know that the doctor, who ought to know best about such matters—'

'Nay, not I. I only know about the physical; the other – if there is another – that's your concern.'

'Who ought to know best,' repeated Mr Bowyer; 'for everybody will tell you, my dear, that the mind is so dependent upon the body. I suppose he must be right. I suppose it is just the imagination of a nervous child working upon the data which has been given – the picture; and then, as you justly remind me, all we have been saying—'

'How could the child know what we have been saying, Francis?'

'Connie has heard nothing that any one has been saying; and there is no picture.'

'My dear lady, you hear what the doctor says. If there is no picture, and she has heard nothing, I suppose, then, your premises are gone, and the conclusion falls to the ground.'

'What does it matter about premises?' cried the Vicar's wife; 'here is something dreadful that has happened. Oh, what nonsense that is about imagination; children have no imagination. A dreadful thing has happened. In heaven's name, Francis, tell this poor child what she is to do.'

'My dear,' said the Vicar again, 'you are asking me to believe in purgatory, – nothing less. You are asking me to contradict the Church's teaching. Mary, you must compose yourself. You must wait till this excitement has passed away.'

'I can see by her eyes she did not sleep last night,' the doctor said, relieved. 'We shall have her seeing visions too, if we don't take care.'

'And, my dear Mary,' said the Vicar, 'if you will think of it, it is derogatory to the dignity of the – of our dear friends who have passed away. How can we suppose that one of the blessed would come down from heaven, and walk about her own house, which she had just left, and show herself to a – to a – little child who had never seen her before.'

'Impossible,' said the doctor. 'I told you so – a stranger – that had no connection with her; knew nothing about her—'

'Instead of,' said the Vicar, with a slight tremor, 'making herself known, if that was permitted, to – to me, for example; or our friend here.'

'That sounds reasonable, Mary,' said Mrs Bowyer; 'don't you think so, my dear? If she had come to one of us, or to yourself, my darling, I should never have wondered, after all that has happened. But to this little child—'

'Whereas there is nothing more likely – more consonant with all the teachings of science – than that the little thing should have this hallucination, of which you ought never to have heard a word. You are the very last person—'

'That is true,' said the Vicar, 'and all the associations of the place must be overwhelming. My dear, we must take her away with us. Mrs Turner, I am sure, is very kind, but it cannot be good for Mary to be here.'

'No, no! I never thought so,' said Mrs Bowyer; 'I never intended – dear Mrs Turner, we all appreciate your motives. I hope you will let us see much of you, and that we may become very good friends. But, Mary – it is her first grief, don't you know?' said the Vicar's wife, with the tears in her eyes; 'she has always been so much cared for, so much thought of all her life, – and then all at once! You will not think that we misunderstand your kind motives; but it is more than she can bear. She made up her mind in a hurry without thinking. You must not be annoyed if we take her away.'

Mrs Turner had been looking from one to another while this dialogue went on. She said now, a little wounded, 'I wished only to do what was kind; but, perhaps, I was thinking most of my own child. Miss Vivian must do what she thinks best.'

'You are all kind – too kind,' Mary cried; 'but no one must say another word, please. Unless Mrs Turner should send me away, until I know what this all means, it is my place to stay here.'

IX

It was Lady Mary who had come into the vicarage that afternoon when Mrs Bowyer supposed some one had called. She wandered about to a great many places in these days, but always returned to the scenes in which her life had been passed, and where alone her work could be done, if it were done at all. She came in and listened while the tale of her own carelessness and heedlessness was told, and stood by while her favourite was taken to another woman's bosom for comfort, and heard everything and saw everything. She was used to it by this time: but to be nothing is hard, even when you are accustomed to it; and though she knew that they would not hear her, what could she do but cry out to them as she stood there unregarded? 'Oh, have pity upon me!' Lady Mary said; and the pang in her heart was so great that the very atmosphere was stirred, and the air could scarcely contain her and the passion of her endeavour to make herself known, but thrilled like a harp-string to her cry. Mrs Bowyer heard the jar and tingle in the inanimate world; but she thought only that it was some charitable visitor who had come in, and gone softly away again at the sound of tears.

And if Lady Mary could not make herself known to the poor cottagers who had loved her, or to the women who wept for her loss while they blamed her, how was she to reveal herself and her secret to the men who, if they had seen her, would have thought her a hallucination? Yes, she tried all, and even went a long journey over land and sea to visit the Earl who was her heir, and awake in him an interest in her child. And she lingered about all these people in the silence of the night, and tried to move them in dreams, since she could not move them waking. It is more easy for one who is no more of this world, to be seen and heard in sleep; for then those who are still in the flesh stand on the borders of the unseen, and see and hear things which, waking, they do not understand. But alas! when they woke, this poor wanderer discovered that her friends remembered no more what she had said to them in their dreams.

Presently, however, when she found Mary re-established in her old home, in her own room, there came to her a new hope. For there is nothing in the world so hard to believe, or to be convinced of, as that no effort, no device, will ever make you known and visible to those you love. Lady Mary being little altered in her character, though so much in her being, still believed that if she could but find the way, in a moment, in the twinkling of an eye, all would be revealed and understood. She went to Mary's room with this new hope strong in her heart. When they were alone together, in that nest of comfort which she had herself made beautiful for her child, – two hearts so full of thought for each other, – what was there in earthly bonds which could prevent them from meeting? She went into the silent room, which was so familiar and dear, and waited like a mother long separated from her child, with a faint doubt trembling on the surface of her mind, yet a quaint joyful confidence underneath in the force of nature. A few words would be enough, – a moment, and all would be right. And then she pleased herself with fancies of how, when that was done, she would whisper to her darling what has never been told to flesh and blood; and so go home proud, and satisfied, and happy in the accomplishment of all that she had hoped.

Mary came in with her candle in her hand, and closed the door between her and all external things. She looked round wistful with that strange consciousness which she had already experienced that some one was there. The other stood so close to her that the girl could not move without touching her. She held up her hands, imploring, to the child of her love. She called to her, 'Mary, Mary!' putting her hands upon her, and gazed into her face with an intensity and anguish of eagerness which might have drawn the stars out of the sky. And a strange tumult was in Mary's bosom. She stood looking blankly round her, like one who is blind with open eyes, and saw nothing; and strained her ears, like a deaf man, but heard nothing. All was silence, vacancy, an empty world about her. She sat down at her little table, with a heavy sigh. 'The child can see her, but she will not come to me,' Mary said, and wept.

Then Lady Mary turned away with a heart full of despair. She went quickly from the house, out into the night. The pang of her disappointment was so keen, that she could not endure it. She remembered what had been said to her in the place from whence she came, and how she had been entreated to be patient and wait. Oh, had she but waited and been patient! She sat down upon the ground, a soul forlorn, outside of life, outside of all things, lost in a world which had no place for her. The moon shone, but she made no shadow in it; the rain fell upon her, but did not hurt her; the little night-breeze blew without finding any resistance in her. She said to herself, 'I have failed. What am I that I should do what they all said was impossible? It was my pride, because I have had my own way all my life. But now I have no way and no place on earth, and what I have to tell them will never, never be known. Oh my little Mary, a servant in her own house! And a word would make it right! – but never, never can she hear that word. I am wrong to say never; she will know when she is in heaven. She will not live to be old and foolish, like me. She will go up there early, and then she will know. But I, what will become of me? – for I am nothing here, and I cannot go back to my own place.'

A little moaning wind rose up suddenly in the middle of the dark night, and carried a faint wail, like the voice of some one lost, to the windows of the sleeping house. It woke the children, and Mary, who opened her eyes quickly in the dark, wondering if perhaps now the vision might come to her. But the vision had come when she could not see it, and now returned no more.

X

On the other side, however, visions which had nothing sacred in them began to be heard of, and Connie's ghost, as it was called in the house, had various vulgar effects. A housemaid became hysterical, and announced that she too had seen the lady, of whom she gave a description, exaggerated from Connie's, which all the household were ready to swear she had never heard. The lady, whom Connie had only seen passing, went to Betsy's room in the middle of the night, and told her, in a hollow and terrible voice, that she could not rest, opening a series of communications by which it was evident all the secrets of the unseen world would soon be disclosed. And following upon this, there came a sort of panic in the house – noises were heard in various places, sounds of footsteps pacing, and of a long robe sweeping about the passages; and Lady Mary's costume, and the head-dress which was so peculiar, which all her friends had recognised in Connie's description, grew into something portentous under the heavier hand of the foot-boy and the kitchen-maid. Mrs Prentiss, who had remained as a special favour to the new people, was deeply indignant and outraged by this treatment of her mistress. She appealed to Mary with mingled anger and tears.

'I would have sent the hussy away at an hour's notice, if I had the power in my hands,' she cried; 'but, Miss Mary, it is easily seen who is a real lady and who is not. Mrs Turner interferes herself in everything, though she likes it to be supposed that she has a housekeeper.'

'Dear Prentiss, you must not say Mrs Turner is not a lady. She has far more delicacy of feeling than many ladies,' cried Mary.

'Yes, Miss Mary, dear, I allow that she is very nice to you; but who could help that? and to hear my lady's name – that might have her faults, but who was far above anything of the sort – in every mouth, and her costoome, that they don't know how to describe, and to think that *she* would go and talk to the like of Betsy Barnes about what is on her mind! I think sometimes I shall break my heart, or else throw up my place, Miss Mary,' Prentiss said, with tears.

'Oh, don't do that; oh, don't leave me, Prentiss!' Mary said, with an involuntary cry of dismay.

'Not if you mind, not if you mind, dear,' the housekeeper cried. And then she drew close to the young lady with an anxious look. 'You haven't seen anything?' she said. 'That would be only natural, Miss Mary. I could well understand she couldn't rest in her grave – if she came and told it all to you.'

'Prentiss, be silent,' cried Mary; 'that ends everything between you and me if you say such a word. There has been too much said already – oh, far too much! as if I only loved her for what she was to leave me.'

'I did not mean that, dear,' said Prentiss; 'but—'

'There is no but; and everything she did was right,' the girl cried with vehemence. She shed hot and bitter tears over this wrong which all her friends did to Lady Mary's memory. 'I am *glad* it was so,' she said to herself when she was alone, with youthful extravagance. 'I am glad it was so; for now no one can think that I loved her for anything but herself.'

The household, however, was agitated by all these rumours and inventions. Alice, Connie's elder sister, declined to sleep any longer in that which began to be called the haunted room. She, too, began to think she saw something, she could not tell what, gliding out of the room as it began to get dark, and to hear sighs and moans in the corridors. The servants, who all wanted to leave, and the villagers, who avoided the grounds after nightfall, spread the rumour far and near that the house was haunted.

XI

In the meantime Connie herself was silent, and said no more
of the Lady. Her attachment to Mary grew into one of those
visionary passions which little girls so often form for young
women. She followed her so-called governess wherever she
went, hanging upon her arm when she could, holding her
dress when no other hold was possible – following her everywhere, like her shadow. The vicarage, jealous and annoyed at
first, and all the neighbours indignant too, to see Mary
metamorphosed into a dependant of the city family, held
out as long as possible against the good-nature of Mrs Turner, and were revolted by the spectacle of this child claiming
poor Mary's attention wherever she moved. But by-and-by
all these strong sentiments softened, as was natural. The only
real drawback was, that amid all these agitations Mary lost her
bloom. She began to droop and grow pale under the observation of the watchful doctor, who had never been otherwise
than dissatisfied with the new position of affairs, and betook
himself to Mrs Bowyer for sympathy and information. 'Did
you ever see a girl so fallen off?' he said. 'Fallen off, doctor! I
think she is prettier and prettier every day.' 'Oh,' the poor
man cried, with a strong breathing of impatience, 'you ladies
think of nothing but prettiness! was I talking of prettiness?
She must have lost a stone since she went back there. It is all
very well to laugh,' the doctor added, growing red with
suppressed anger, 'but I can tell you that is the true test.
That little Connie Turner is as well as possible; she has
handed over her nerves to Mary Vivian. I wonder now if
she ever talks to you on that subject.'

'Who? Little Connie?'

'Of course I mean Miss Vivian, Mrs Bowyer. Don't you
know the village is all in a tremble about the ghost at the Great
House?'

'Oh yes, I know; and it is very strange. I can't help
thinking, doctor—'

'We had better not discuss that subject. Of course I don't
put a moment's faith in any such nonsense. But girls are full
of fancies. I want you to find out for me whether she has

begun to think she sees anything. She looks like it; and if something isn't done she will soon do so, if not now.'

'Then you do think there is something to see,' said Mrs Bowyer, clasping her hands; 'that has always been my opinion: what so natural—?'

'As that Lady Mary, the greatest old aristocrat in the world, should come and make private revelations to Betsy Barnes, the under housemaid—?' said the doctor, with a sardonic grin.

'I don't mean that, doctor; but if she could not rest in her grave, poor old lady—'

'You think then, my dear,' said the vicar, 'that Lady Mary, our old friend, who was as young in her mind as any of us, lies body and soul in that old dark hole of a vault?'

'How you talk, Francis! what can a woman say between you horrid men? I say if she couldn't rest – wherever she is – because of leaving Mary destitute, it would be only natural – and I should think the more of her for it,' Mrs Bowyer cried.

The vicar had a gentle professional laugh over the confusion of his wife's mind. But the doctor took the matter more seriously. 'Lady Mary is safely buried and done with. I am not thinking of her,' he said; 'but I am thinking of Mary Vivian's senses, which will not stand this much longer. Try and find out from her if she sees anything: if she has come to that, whatever she says we must have her out of there.'

But Mrs Bowyer had nothing to report when this conclave of friends met again. Mary would not allow that she had seen anything. She grew paler every day, her eyes grew larger, but she made no confession. And Connie bloomed and grew, and met no more old ladies upon the stairs.

XII

The days passed on, and no new event occurred in this little history. It came to be summer – balmy and green – and everything around the old house was delightful, and its beautiful rooms became more pleasant than ever in the long days and soft brief nights. Fears of the Earl's return and of the possible end of the Turner's tenancy began to disturb the household, but no one so much as Mary, who felt herself to cling as she had never done before to the old house. She had never got over the impression that a secret presence, revealed to no one else, was continually near her, though she saw no one. And her health was greatly affected by this visionary double life.

This was the state of affairs on a certain soft wet day when the family were all within doors. Connie had exhausted all her means of amusement in the morning. When the afternoon came, with its long, dull, uneventful hours, she had nothing better to do than to fling herself upon Miss Vivian, upon whom she had a special claim. She came to Mary's room, disturbing the strange quietude of that place, and amused herself looking over all the trinkets and ornaments that were to be found there, all of which were associated to Mary with her godmother. Connie tried on the bracelets and brooches which Mary in her deep mourning had not worn, and asked a hundred questions. The answer which had to be so often repeated, 'That was given to me by my godmother,' at last called forth the child's remark, 'How fond your godmother must have been of you, Miss Vivian! she seems to have given you everything—'

'Everything!' cried Mary, with a full heart.

'And yet they all say she was not kind enough,' said little Connie – 'what do they mean by that? for you seem to love her very much still, though she is dead. Can one go on loving people when they are dead?'

'Oh yes, and better than ever,' said Mary; 'for often you do not know how you loved them, or what they were to you, till they are gone away.'

Connie gave her governess a hug and said, 'Why did not she leave you all her money, Miss Vivian? everybody says she was wicked and unkind to die without—'

'My dear,' cried Mary, 'do not repeat what ignorant people say, because it is not true.'

'But mamma said it, Miss Vivian.'

'She does not know, Connie – you must not say it. I will tell your mamma she must not say it; for nobody can know so well as I do – and it is not true—'

'But they say,' cried Connie, 'that that is why she can't rest in her grave. You must have heard. Poor old lady, they say she cannot rest in her grave because—'

Mary seized the child in her arms with a pressure that hurt

Connie. 'You must not! you must not!' she cried, with a sort of panic. Was she afraid that some one might hear? She gave Connie a hurried kiss, and turned her face away, looking out into the vacant room. 'It is not true! it is not true!' she cried, with a great excitement and horror, as if to stay a wound. 'She was always good, and like an angel to me. She is with the angels. She is with God. She cannot be disturbed by anything – anything! Oh let us never say, or think, or imagine—!' Mary cried. Her cheeks burned, her eyes were full of tears. It seemed to her that something of wonder and anguish and dismay was in the room round her – as if some one unseen had heard a bitter reproach, an accusation undeserved, which must wound to the very heart.

Connie struggled a little in that too tight hold. 'Are you frightened, Miss Vivian? what are you frightened for? No one can hear; and if you mind it so much, I will never say it again.'

'You must never, never say it again. There is nothing I mind so much,' Mary said.

'Oh!' said Connie, with mild surprise. Then as Mary's hold relaxed, she put her arms round her beloved companion's neck. 'I will tell them all you don't like it. I will tell them they must not – Oh!' cried Connie again, in a quick astonished voice. She clutched Mary round the neck, returning the violence of the grasp which had hurt her, and with her other hand pointed to the door. 'The lady! the lady! Oh, come and see where she is going!' Connie cried.

Mary felt as if the child in her vehemence lifted her from her seat. She had no sense that her own limbs or her own will carried her in the impetuous rush with which Connie flew. The blood mounted to her head. She felt a heat and throbbing as if her spine were on fire. Connie, holding by her skirts, pushing her on, went along the corridor to the other door, now deserted, of Lady Mary's room. 'There, there! don't you see her? She is going in,' the child cried, and rushed on, clinging to Mary, dragging her on, her light hair streaming, her little white dress waving.

Lady Mary's room was unoccupied and cold – cold, though it was summer, with the chill that rests in uninhabited apartments. The blinds were drawn down over the windows; a sort of blank whiteness, greyness, was in the place, which no one ever entered. The child rushed on with eager gestures, crying 'Look! look!' turning her lively head from side to side.

Mary, in a still and passive expectation, seeing nothing, looking mechanically where Connie told her to look, moving like a creature in a dream, against her will, followed. There was nothing to be seen. The blank, the vacancy went to her heart. She no longer thought of Connie or her vision. She felt the emptiness with a desolation such as she had never felt before. She loosed her arm with something like impatience from the child's close clasp. For months she had not entered the room which was associated with so much of her life. Connie and her cries and warnings passed from her mind like the stir of a bird or a fly. Mary felt herself alone with her dead, alone with her life, with all that had been and that never could be again. Slowly, without knowing what she did, she sank upon her knees. She raised her face in the blank of desolation about her to the unseen heaven. Unseen! unseen! whatever we may do. God above us, and those who have gone from us, and He who has taken them, who has redeemed them, who is ours and theirs, our only hope; but all unseen, unseen, concealed as much by the blue skies as by the dull blank of that roof. Her heart ached and cried into the unknown. 'O God,' she cried, 'I do not know where she is, but Thou art everywhere. O God, let her know that I have never blamed her, never wished it otherwise, never ceased to love her, and thank her, and bless her. God! God!' cried Mary, with a great and urgent cry, as if it were a man's name. She knelt there for a moment before her senses failed her, her eyes shining as if they would burst from their sockets, her lips dropping apart, her countenance like marble—.

XIII

'And *she* was standing there all the time,' said Connie, crying and telling her little tale after Mary had been carried away – 'standing with her hand upon that cabinet, looking and looking, oh, as if she wanted to say something and couldn't. Why couldn't she, mamma? Oh, Mr Bowyer, why couldn't she, if she wanted so much? Why wouldn't God let her speak?'

XIV

Mary had a long illness, and hovered on the verge of death. She said a great deal in her wanderings about some one who had looked at her. 'For a moment, a moment,' she would cry; 'only a moment! and I had so much to say.' But as she got better nothing was said to her about this face she had seen. And perhaps it was only the suggestion of some feverish dream. She was taken away, and was a long time getting up her strength; and in the meantime the Turners insisted that the drains should be thoroughly seen to, which were not at all in a perfect state. And the Earl coming to see the place, took a fancy to it, and determined to keep it in his own hands. He was a friendly person, and his ideas of decoration were quite different from those of his grandmother. He gave away a great deal of her old furniture, and sold the rest.

Among the articles given away was the Italian cabinet which the vicar had always had a fancy for; and naturally it had not been in the vicarage a day before the boys insisted on finding out the way of opening the secret drawer. And there the paper was found in the most natural way, without any trouble or mystery at all.

XV

They all gathered to see the wanderer coming back. She was not as she had been when she went away. Her face, which had been so easy, was worn with trouble; her eyes were deep with things unspeakable. Pity and knowledge were in the lines which time had not made. It was a great event in that place to see one come back who did not come by the common way. She was received by the great officer who had given her permission to go, and her companions who had received her at the first all came forward, wondering, to hear what she had to say: because it only occurs to those wanderers who have gone back to earth of their own will to return when they have accomplished what they wished, or it is judged above that there is nothing possible more. Accordingly the question was on all their lips, 'You have set the wrong right – you have done what you desired?'

'Oh,' she said, stretching out her hands, 'how well one is in one's own place! how blessed to be at home! I have seen the trouble and sorrow in the earth till my heart is sore, and sometimes I have been near to die.'

'But that is impossible,' said the man who had loved her.

'If it had not been impossible, I should have died,' she said. 'I have stood among people who loved me, and they have not seen me nor known me, nor heard my cry. I have been outcast from all life, for I belonged to none. I have longed for you all, and my heart has failed me. Oh how lonely it is in the world when you are a wanderer, and can be known of none—'

'You were warned,' said he who was in authority, 'that it was more bitter than death.'

'What is death?' she said. And no one made any reply. Neither did any one venture to ask her again whether she had been successful in her mission. But at last, when the warmth of her appointed home had melted the ice about her heart, she smiled once more and spoke.

'The little children knew me; they were not afraid of me; they held out their arms. And God's dear and innocent creatures—' She wept a few tears, which were sweet after the ice-tears she had shed upon the earth. And then some one, more bold than the rest, asked again, 'And did you accomplish what you wished?'

She had come to herself by this time, and the dark lines were melting from her face. 'I am forgiven,' she said, with a low cry of happiness. 'She whom I wronged loves me and blessed me; and we saw each other face to face. I know nothing more.'

'There is no more,' said all together. For everything is included in pardon and love.

The Portrait

AT THE PERIOD when the following incidents occurred I was living with my father at The Grove, a large old house in the immediate neighbourhood of a little town. This had been his home for a number of years; and I believe I was born in it. It was a kind of house which, notwithstanding all the red and white architecture, known at present by the name of Queen Anne, builders nowadays have forgotten how to build. It was straggling and irregular, with wide passage, wide staircases, broad landings; the rooms large but not very lofty; the arrangements leaving much to be desired, with no economy of space; a house belonging to a period when land was cheap, and, so far as that was concerned, there was no occasion to economise. Though it was so near the town, the clump of trees in which it was environed was a veritable grove. In the grounds in spring the primroses grew as thickly as in the forest. We had a few fields for the cows, and an excellent walled garden. The place is being pulled down at this moment to make room for more streets of mean little houses, – the kind of thing, and not a dull house of faded gentry, which perhaps the neighbourhood requires. The house was dull, and so were we, its last inhabitants; and the furniture was faded, even a little dingy, – nothing to brag of. I do not, however, intend to convey a suggestion that we were faded gentry, for that was not the case. My father, indeed, was rich, and had no need to spare any expense in making his life and his house bright if he pleased; but he did not please, and I had not been long enough at home to exercise any special influence of my own. It was the only home I had ever known; but except in my earliest childhood, and in my holidays as a schoolboy, I had in reality known but little of it. My mother had died at my birth, or shortly after, and I had grown up in the gravity and silence of a house without women. In my infancy, I believe, a sister of my father's had lived with us, and taken charge of the household and of me; but she, too, had died long, long ago, my mourning for her being one of the first things I could recollect. And she had no successor. There was, indeed, a housekeeper and some maids, – the latter of whom I only saw disappearing at the end of a passage, or whisking out of a room when one of 'the gentlemen' appeared. Mrs Weir, indeed, I saw nearly every day; but a curtsey, a smile, a pair of nice round arms which she caressed while folding them across her ample waist, and a large white apron, were all I knew of her. This was the only female influence in the house. The drawing-room I was aware of only as a place of deadly good order, into which nobody ever entered. It had three long windows opening on the lawn, and communicated at the upper end, which was rounded like a great bay, with the conservatory. Sometimes I gazed into it as a child from without, wondering at the needlework on the chairs, the screens, the looking-glasses which never reflected any living face. My father did not like the room, which probably was not wonderful, though it never occurred to me in those early days to inquire why.

I may say here, though it will probably be disappointing to those who form a sentimental idea of the capabilities of children, that it did not occur to me either, in these early days, to make any inquiry about my mother. There was no room in life, as I knew it, for any such person; nothing suggested to my mind either the fact that she must have existed, or that there was need of her in the house. I accepted, as I believe most children do, the facts of existence, on the basis with which I had first made acquaintance with them, without question or remark. As a matter of fact. I was aware that it was rather dull at home; but neither by comparison with the books I read, nor by the communications received from my schoolfellows, did this seem to me anything remarkable. And I was possibly somewhat dull too by nature, for I did not mind. I was fond of reading, and for that there was unbounded opportunity. I had a little ambition in respect to work, and that too could be prosecuted undisturbed. When I went to the university, my society lay almost entirely among men; but by that time and afterwards, matters had of course greatly changed with me, and though I recognised women as part of the economy of nature, and did not indeed by any means dislike or avoid them, yet the idea of connecting them at all with my own home never entered into my head. That continued to be as it had always been, when at intervals I descended upon the cool, grave, colourless place, in the midst of my traffic with the world: always very still, well-ordered, serious – the cooking very good, the comfort perfect – old Morphew, the butler, a little older (but very little older, perhaps on the whole less old, since in my childhood I had thought him a kind of Methuselah), and Mrs Weir, less active, covering up her arms in sleeves, but folding and caressing them just as always. I remember looking in from the lawn through the windows upon that deadly-orderly drawing-room, with a humorous recollection of my childish admiration and wonder, and feeling that it must be kept so for ever and ever, and that to go into it would break some sort of amusing mock mystery, some pleasantly ridiculous spell.

But it was only at rare intervals that I went home. In the long vacation, as in my school holidays, my father often went abroad with me, so that we had gone over a great deal of the Continent together very pleasantly. He was old in proportion to the age of his son, being a man of sixty when I was twenty, but that did not disturb the pleasure of the relations between us. I don't know that they were ever very confidential. On my side there was but little to communicate, for I did not get into scrapes nor fall in love, the two predicaments which demand sympathy and confidences. And as for my father himself, I was never aware what there could be to communicate on his side. I knew his life exactly – what he did almost at every hour of the day; under what circumstances of the temperature he would ride and when walk; how often and with what guests he would indulge in the occasional break of a dinner-party, a serious pleasure, – perhaps, indeed, less a pleasure than a duty. All this I knew as well as he did, and also his views on public matters, his political opinions, which naturally were different from mine. What ground, then, remained for confidence? I did not know any. We were both of us of a reserved nature, not apt to enter into our religious feelings, for instance. There are many people who think reticence on such subjects a sign of the most reverential way of contemplating them. Of this I am far from being sure; but, at all events, it was the practice most congenial to my own mind.

And then I was for a long time absent, making my own way in the world. I did not make it very successfully. I accomplished the natural fate of an Englishman, and went out to the Colonies; then to India in a semi-diplomatic position; but returned home after seven or eight years, invalided, in bad health and not much better spirits, tired and disappointed with my first trial of life. I had, as people say, 'no occasion' to insist on making my way. My father was rich, and had never given me the slightest reason to believe that he did not intend me to be his heir. His allowance to me was not illiberal, and though he did not oppose the carrying out of my own plans, he by no means urged me to exertion. When I came home he received me very affectionately, and expressed his satisfaction in my return. 'Of course,' he said, 'I am not glad that you are disappointed, Philip, or that your health is broken; but otherwise it is an ill wind, you know, that blows nobody good – and I am very glad to have you at home. I am growing an old man—'

'I don't see any difference, sir,' said I; 'everything here seems exactly the same as when I went away—'

He smiled, and shook his head. 'It is true enough,' he said, 'after we have reached a certain age we seem to go on for a long time on a plane, and feel no great difference from year to year; but it is an inclined plane – and the longer we go on, the more sudden will be the fall at the end. But at all events it will be a great comfort to me to have you here.'

'If I had known that,' I said, 'and that you wanted me, I should have come in any circumstances. As there are only two of us in the world—'

'Yes,' he said, 'there are only two of us in the world; but still I should not have sent for you, Phil, to interrupt your career.'

'It is as well, then, that it has interrupted itself,' I said, rather bitterly; for disappointment is hard to bear.

He patted me on the shoulder, and repeated, 'It is an ill wind that blows nobody good,' with a look of real pleasure which gave me a certain gratification too; for, after all, he was an old man, and the only one in all the world to whom I owed any duty. I had not been without dreams of warmer affections, but they had come to nothing – not tragically, but in the ordinary way. I might perhaps have had love which I did not want, but not that which I did want, – which was not a thing to make any unmanly moan about, but in the ordinary course of events. Such disappointments happen every day; indeed, they are more common than anything else, and sometimes it is apparent afterwards that it is better it was so.

However, here I was at thirty stranded – yet wanting for nothing, in a position to call forth rather envy than pity from the greater part of my contemporaries, – for I had an assured and comfortable existence, as much money as I wanted, and the prospect of an excellent fortune for the future. On the other hand, my health was still low, and I had no occupation. The neighbourhood of the town was a drawback rather than an advantage. I felt myself tempted, instead of taking the long walk into the country which my doctor recommended, to take a much shorter one through the High Street, across the river, and back again, which was not a walk but a lounge. The country was silent and full of thoughts – thoughts not always very agreeable – whereas there were always the humours of the little urban population to glance at, the news to be heard, all those petty matters which so often make up life in a very impoverished version for the idle man. I did not like it, but I felt myself yielding to it, not having energy enough to make a stand. The rector and the leading lawyer of the place asked me to dinner. I might have glided into the society, such as it was, had I been disposed for that – everything about me began to close over me as if I had been fifty, and fully contented with my lot.

It was possibly my own want of occupation which made me observe with surprise, after a while, how much occupied my father was. He had expressed himself glad of my return; but now that I had returned, I saw very little of him. Most of his time was spent in his library, as had always been the case. But on the few visits I paid him there, I could not but perceive that the aspect of the library was much changed. It had acquired the look of a business-room, almost an office. There were large business-like books on the table, which I could not associate with anything he could naturally have to do; and his correspondence was very large. I thought he closed one of those books hurriedly as I came in, and pushed it away, as if he did not wish me to see it. This surprised me at the moment, without arousing any other feeling; but afterwards I remembered it with a clearer sense of what it meant. He was more absorbed altogether than I had been used to see him. He was visited by men sometimes not of very prepossessing appearance. Surprise grew in my mind without any very distinct idea of the reason of it; and it was not till after a chance conversation with Morphew that my vague uneasiness began to take definite shape. It was begun without any special intention on my part. Morphew had informed me that master was very busy, on some occasion when I wanted to see him. And I was a little annoyed to be thus put off. 'It appears to me that my father is always busy,' I said, hastily. Morphew then began very oracularly to nod his head in assent.

'A deal too busy, sir, if you take my opinion,' he said.

This startled me much, and I asked hurriedly, 'What do you mean?' without reflecting that to ask for private information from a servant about my father's habits was as bad as investigating into a stranger's affairs. It did not strike me in the same light.

'Mr Philip,' said Morphew, 'a thing 'as 'appened as 'appens more often than it ought to. Master has got awful keen about money in his old age.'

'That's a new thing for him,' I said.

'No, sir, begging your pardon, it ain't a new thing. He was once broke of it, and that wasn't easy done; but it's come back, if you'll excuse me saying so. And I don't know as he'll ever be broke of it again at his age.'

I felt more disposed to be angry than disturbed by this. 'You must be making some ridiculous mistake,' I said. 'And if you were not so old a friend as you are, Morphew, I should not have allowed my father to be so spoken of to me.'

The old man gave me a half-astonished, half-contemptuous look. 'He's been my master a deal longer than he's been your father,' he said, turning on his heel. The assumption was so comical that my anger could not stand in face of it. I went out, having been on my way to the door when this conversation occurred, and took my usual lounge about, which was not a satisfactory sort of amusement. Its vanity and emptiness appeared to be more evident than usual today. I met half-a-dozen people I knew, and had as many pieces of news confided to me. I went up and down the length of the High Street. I made a small purchase or two. And then I turned homeward – despising myself, yet finding no alternative within my reach. Would a long country walk have been more virtuous? – it would at least have been more wholesome – but that was all that could be said. My mind did not dwell on Morphew's communication. It seemed without sense or meaning to me; and after the excellent joke about his superior interest in his master to mine in my father, was dismissed lightly enough from my mind. I tried to invent some way of telling this to my father without letting him perceive that Morphew had been finding faults in him, or I listening; for it seemed a pity to lose so good a joke. However, as I returned home, something happened which put the joke entirely out of my head. It is curious when a new subject of trouble or anxiety has been suggested to the mind in an unexpected way, how often a second advertisement follows immediately after the first, and gives to that a potency which in itself it had not possessed.

I was approaching our own door, wondering whether my father had gone, and whether, on my return, I should find him at leisure – for I had several little things to say to him – when I noticed a poor woman lingering about the closed gates. She had a baby sleeping in her arms. It was a spring night, the stars shining in the twilight, and everything soft and dim; and the woman's figure was like a shadow, flitting about, now here, now there, on one side or another of the gate. She stopped when she saw me approaching, and hesitated for a moment, then seemed to take a sudden resolution. I watched her without knowing, with a prevision that she was going to address me, though with no sort of idea as to the subject of her address. She came up to me doubtfully, it seemed, yet certainly, as I felt, and when she was close to me, dropped a sort of hesitating curtsy, and said, 'It's Mr Philip?' in a low voice.

'What do you want with me?' I said.

Then she poured forth suddenly, without warning or preparation, her long speech – a flood of words which must have been all ready and waiting at the doors of her lips for utterance. 'Oh, sir, I want to speak to you! I can't believe you'll be so hard, for you're young; and I can't believe he'll be so hard if so be as his own son, as I've always heard he had but one, 'll speak up for us. Oh, gentleman, it is easy for the likes of you, that, if you ain't comfortable in one room, can just walk into another; but if one room is all you have, and every bit of furniture you have taken out of it, and nothing but the four walls left – not so much as the cradle for the child, or a chair for your man to sit down upon when he comes from his work, or a saucepan to cook him his supper—'

'My good woman,' I said, 'who can have taken all that from you? surely nobody can be so cruel?'

'You say it's cruel!' she cried with a sort of triumph. 'Oh, I knowed you would, or any true gentleman that don't hold with screwing poor folks. Just go and say that to him inside there, for the love of God. Tell him to think what he's doing, driving poor creatures to despair. Summer's coming, the Lord be praised, but yet it's bitter cold at night with your counterpane gone; and when you've been working hard all day, and nothing but four bare walls to come home to, and all your poor little sticks of furniture that you've saved up for, and got together one by one, all gone – and you no better than when you started, or rather worse, for then you was young. Oh, sir!' the woman's voice rose into a sort of passionate wail. And then she added, beseechingly, recovering herself – 'Oh, speak for us – he'll not refuse his own son—'

'To whom am I to speak? who is it that has done this to you?' I said.

The woman hesitated again, looking keenly in my face – then repeated with a slight faltering, 'It's Mr Philip?' as if that made everything right.

'Yes; I am Philip Canning,' I said; 'but what have I to do with this? and to whom am I to speak?'

She began to whimper, crying and stopping herself. 'Oh, please sir! it's Mr Canning as owns all the house property about – it's him that our court and the lane and everything belongs to. And he's taken the bed from under us, and the baby's cradle, although it's said in the Bible as you're not to take poor folks's bed.'

'My father!' I cried in spite of myself – 'then it must be some agent, some one else in his name. You may be sure he knows nothing of it. Of course I shall speak to him at once.'

'Oh, God bless you, sir,' said the woman. But then she added, in a lower tone – 'It's no agent. It's one as never knows trouble. It's him that lives in that grand house.' But this was said under her breath, evidently not for me to hear.

Morphew's words flashed through my mind as she spoke. What was this? Did it afford an explanation of the much occupied hours, the big books, the strange visitors? I took the poor woman's name, and gave her something to procure a few comforts for the night, and went indoors disturbed and troubled. It was impossible to believe that my father himself

would have acted thus; but he was not a man to brook
interference, and I did not see how to introduce the subject,
what to say. I could but hope that, at the moment of broach-
ing it, words would be put into my mouth, which often
happens in moments of necessity, one knows not how, even
when one's theme is not so all-important as that for which
such help has been promised. As usual, I did not see my
father till dinner. I have said that our dinners were very good,
luxurious in a simple way, everything excellent in its kind,
well cooked, well served, the perfection of comfort without
show – which is a combination very dear to the English heart.
I said nothing till Morphew, with his solemn attention to
everything that was going, had retired – and then it was with
some strain of courage that I began.

'I was stopped outside the gate today by a curious sort of
petitioner – a poor woman, who seems to be one of your
tenants, sir, but whom your agent must have been rather too
hard upon.'

'My agent? who is that?' said my father, quietly.

'I don't know his name, and I doubt his competence. The
poor creature seems to have had everything taken from her –
her bed, her child's cradle.'

'No doubt she was behind with her rent.'

'Very likely, sir. She seemed very poor,' said I.

'You take it coolly,' said my father, with an upward glance,
half-amused, not in the least shocked by my statement. 'But
when a man, or a woman either, takes a house, I suppose you
will allow that they ought to pay rent for it.'

'Certainly, sir,' I replied, 'when they have got anything to
pay.'

'I don't allow the reservation,' he said. But he was not
angry, which I had feared he would be.

'I think,' I continued, 'that your agent must be too severe.
And this emboldens me to say something which has been in
my mind for some time' – (these were the words, no doubt,
which I had hoped would be put into my mouth; they were
the suggestion of the moment, and yet as I said them it was
with the most complete conviction of their truth) – 'and that is
this: I am doing nothing; my time hangs heavy on my hands.
Make me your agent. I will see for myself, and save you from
such mistakes; and it will be an occupation—'

'Mistakes? What warrant have you for saying these are

mistakes?' he said testily; then after a moment: 'This is a strange proposal from you, Phil. Do you know what it is you are offering? – to be a collector of rents, going about from door to door, from week to week; to look after wretched little bits of repairs, drains, etc.; to get paid, which, after all, is the chief thing, and not to be taken in by tales of poverty.'

'Not to let you be taken in by men without pity,' I said.

He gave me a strange glance, which I did not very well understand, and said, abruptly, a thing which, so far as I remember, he had never in my life said before, 'You've become a little like your mother, Phil—'

'My mother!' The reference was so unusual – nay, so unprecedented – that I was greatly startled. It seemed to me like the sudden introduction of a quite new element in the stagnant atmosphere, as well as a new party to our conversation. My father looked across the table, as if with some astonishment at my tone of surprise.

'Is that so very extraordinary?' he said.

'No; of course it is not extraordinary that I should resemble my mother. Only – I have heard very little of her – almost nothing.'

'That is true.' He got up and placed himself before the fire, which was very low, as the night was not cold – had not been cold heretofore at least; but it seemed to me now that a little chill came into the dim and faded room. Perhaps it looked more dull from the suggestion of a something brighter, warmer, that might have been. 'Talking of mistakes,' he said, 'perhaps that was one: to sever you entirely from her side of the house. But I did not care for the connection. You will understand how it is that I speak of it now when I tell you—' He stopped here, however, said nothing more for a minute or so, and then rang the bell. Morphew came, as he always did, very deliberately, so that some time elapsed in silence, during which my surprise grew. When the old man appeared at the door – 'Have you put the lights in the drawing-room, as I told you?' my father said.

'Yes, sir; and opened the box, sir; and it's a – it's a speaking likeness—'

This the old man got out in a great hurry, as if afraid that his master would stop him. My father did so with a wave of his hand.

'That's enough. I asked no information. You can go now.'

The door closed upon us, and there was again a pause. My subject had floated away altogether like a mist, though I had been so concerned about it. I tried to resume, but could not. Something seemed to arrest my very breathing: and yet in this dull respectable house of ours, where everything breathed good character and integrity, it was certain that there could be no shameful mystery to reveal. It was some time before my father spoke, not from any purpose that I could see, but apparently because his mind was busy with probably un-accustomed thoughts.

'You scarcely know the drawing-room, Phil,' he said at last.

'Very little. I have never seen it used. I have a little awe of it, to tell the truth.'

'That should not be. There is no reason for that. But a man by himself, as I have been for the greater part of my life, has no occasion for a drawing-room. I always, as a matter of preference, sat among my books; however, I ought to have thought of the impression on you.'

'Oh, it is not important,' I said; 'the awe was childish. I have not thought of it since I came home.'

'It never was anything very splendid at the best,' said he. He lifted the lamp from the table with a sort of abstraction, not remarking even my offer to take it from him, and led the way. He was on the verge of seventy, and looked his age: but it was a vigorous age, with no symptoms of giving way. The circle of light from the lamp lit up his white hair, and keen blue eyes, and clear complexion; his forehead was like old ivory, his cheek warmly coloured: an old man, yet a man in full strength. He was taller than I was, and still almost as strong. As he stood for a moment with the lamp in his hand, he looked like a tower in his great height and bulk. I reflected as I looked at him that I knew him intimately, more intimately than any other creature in the world, – I was familiar with every detail of his outward life; could it be that in reality I did not know him at all?

The drawing-room was already lighted with a flickering array of candles upon the mantelpiece and along the walls, produ-cing the pretty starry effect which candles give without very much light. As I had not the smallest idea what I was about to see, for Morphew's 'speaking likeness' was very hurriedly said, and only half comprehensible in the bewilderment of my faculties, my first glance was at this very unusual illumination, for which I could assign no reason. The next showed me a large full-length portrait, still in the box in which apparently it had travelled, placed upright, supported against a table in the centre of the room. My father walked straight up to it, motioned to me to place a smaller table close to the picture on the left side, and put his lamp upon that. Then he waved his hand towards it, and stood aside that I might see.

It was a full-length portrait of a very young woman – I might say a girl, scarcely twenty – in a white dress, made in a very simple old fashion, though I was too little accustomed to female costume to be able to fix the date. It might have been a hundred years old, or twenty, for aught I knew. The face had an expression of youth, candour, and simplicity more than any face I had ever seen, – or so, at least, in my surprise, I thought. The eyes were a little wistful, with something which was almost anxiety – which at least was not content – in them; a faint, almost imperceptible, curve in the lids. The complexion was of a dazzling fairness, the hair light, but the eyes dark, which gave individuality to the face. It would have been as lovely had the eyes been blue – probably more so – but their darkness gave a touch of character, a slight discord, which made the harmony finer. It was not, perhaps, beautiful in the highest sense of the word. The girl must have been too young, too slight, too little developed for actual beauty; but a face which so invited love and confidence I never saw. One smiled at it with instinctive affection. 'What a sweet face!' I said. 'What a lovely girl! Who is she? Is this one of the relations you were speaking of on the other side?'

My father made me no reply. He stood aside, looking at it as if he knew it too well to require to look, – as if the picture was already in his eyes. 'Yes,' he said, after an interval, with a longdrawn breath, 'she was a lovely girl, as you say.'

'Was? – then she is dead. What a pity!' I said; 'what a pity! so young and so sweet!'

We stood gazing at her thus, in her beautiful stillness and calm – two men, the younger of us full grown and conscious of many experiences, the other an old man – before this impersonation of tender youth. At length he said, with a slight tremulousness in his voice, 'Does nothing suggest to you who she is, Phil?'

I turned round to look at him with profound astonishment,

but he turned away from my look. A sort of quiver passed over his face. 'That is your mother,' he said, and walked suddenly away, leaving me there.

My mother!

I stood for a moment in a kind of consternation before the white-robed innocent creature, to me no more than a child; then a sudden laugh broke from me, without any will of mine: something ludicrous, as well as something awful, was in it. When the laugh was over, I found myself with tears in my eyes, gazing, holding my breath. The soft features seemed to melt, the lips to move, the anxiety in the eyes to become a personal inquiry. Ah, no! nothing of the kind; only because of the water in mine. My mother! oh, fair and gentle creature, scarcely woman – how could any man's voice call her by that name! I had little idea enough of what it meant, – had heard it laughed at, scoffed at, reverenced, but never had learned to place it even among the ideal powers of life. Yet, if it meant anything at all, what it meant was worth thinking of. What did she ask, looking at me with those eyes? what would she have said if 'those lips had language'? If I had known her only as Cowper did – with a child's recollection – there might have been some thread, some faint but comprehensible link, between us; but now all that I felt was the curious incongruity. Poor child! I said to myself; so sweet a creature: poor little tender soul! as if she had been a little sister, a child of mine, – but my mother! I cannot tell how long I stood looking at her, studying the candid, sweet face, which surely had germs in it of everything that was good and beautiful; and sorry, with a profound regret, that she had died and never carried these promises to fulfilment. Poor girl! poor people who had loved her! These were my thoughts: with a curious vertigo and giddiness of my whole being in the sense of a mysterious relationship, which it was beyond my power to understand.

Presently my father came back: possibly because I had been a long time unconscious of the passage of the minutes, or perhaps because he was himself restless in the strange disturbance of his habitual calm. He came in and put his arm within mine, leaning his weight partially upon me, with an affectionate suggestion which went deeper than words. I pressed his arm to my side: it was more between us two grave Englishmen than any embracing.

'I cannot understand it,' I said.

'No. I don't wonder at that; but if it is strange to you, Phil, think how much more strange to me! That is the partner of my life. I have never had another – or thought of another. That – girl! If we are to meet again, as I have always hoped we should meet again, what am I to say to her – I, an old man? Yes; I know what you mean. I am not an old man for my years; but my years are threescore and ten, and the play is nearly played out. How am I to meet that young creature? We used to say to each other that it was for ever, that we never could be but one, that it was for life and death. But what – what am I to say to her, Phil, when I meet her again, that – that angel? No, it is not her being an angel that troubles me; but she is so young! She is like my – my granddaughter,' he cried, with a burst of what was half sobs, half laughter; 'and she is my wife, – and I am an old man – an old man! And so much has happened that she could not understand.'

I was too much startled by this strange complaint to know what to say. It was not my own trouble, and I answered it in the conventional way.

'They are not as we are, sir,' I said; 'they look upon us with larger, other eyes than ours.'

'Ah! you don't know what I mean,' he said quickly; and in the interval he had subdued his emotion. 'At first, after she died, it was my consolation to think that I should meet her again – that we never could be really parted. But, my God, how I have changed since then! I am another man – I am a different being. I was not very young even then – twenty years older than she was: but her youth renewed mine. I was not an unfit partner; she asked no better: and knew as much more than I did in some things – being so much nearer the source – as I did in others that were of the world. But I have gone a long way since then, Phil – a long way; and there she stands just where I left her.'

I pressed his arm again. 'Father,' I said, which was a title I seldom used, 'we are not to suppose that in a higher life the mind stands still.' I did not feel myself qualified to discuss such topics, but something one must say.

'Worse, worse!' he replied; 'then she too will be like me, a different being, and we shall meet as what? as strangers, as people who have lost sight of each other, with a long past between us – we who parted, my God! with – with—'

His voice broke and ended for a moment: then while,

surprised and almost shocked by what he said, I cast about in my mind what to reply, he withdrew his arm suddenly from mine, and said in his usual tone, 'Where shall we hang the picture, Phil? It must be here in this room. What do you think will be the best light?'

This sudden alteration took me still more by surprise, and gave me almost an additional shock; but it was evident that I must follow the changes of his mood, or at least the sudden repression of sentiment which he originated. We went into that simpler question with great seriousness, consulting which would be the best light. 'You know I can scarcely advise,' I said; 'I have never been familiar with this room. I should like to put off, if you don't mind, till daylight.'

'I think,' he said, 'that this would be the best place.' It was on the other side of the fireplace, on the wall which faced the windows, – not the best light, I knew enough to be aware, for an oil-painting. When I said so, however, he answered me with a little impatience, – 'It does not matter very much about the best light. There will be nobody to see it but you and me. I have my reasons—' There was a small table standing against the wall at this spot, on which he had his hand as he spoke. Upon it stood a little basket in very fine lace-like wickerwork. His hand must have trembled, for the table shook, and the basket fell, its contents turning out upon the carpet, – little bits of needlework, coloured silks, a small piece of knitting half done. He laughed as they rolled out at his feet, and tried to stoop to collect them, then tottered to a chair, and covered for a moment his face with his hands.

No need to ask what they were. No woman's work had been seen in the house since I could recollect it. I gathered them up reverently and put them back. I could see, ignorant as I was, that the bit of knitting was something for an infant. What could I do less than put it to my lips? It had been left in the doing – for me.

'Yes, I think this is the best place,' my father said a minute after, in his usual tone.

We placed it there that evening with our own hands. The picture was large, and in a heavy frame, but my father would let no one help me but himself. And then, with a superstition for which I never could give any reason even to myself, having removed the packings, we closed and locked the door, leaving the candles about the room, in their soft strange illumination lighting the first night of her return to her old place.

That night no more was said. My father went to his room early, which was not his habit. He had never, however, accustomed me to sit late with him in the library. I had a little study or smoking-room of my own, in which all my special treasures were, the collections of my travels and my favourite books – and where I always sat after prayers, a ceremonial which was regularly kept up in the house. I retired as usual this night to my room, and as usual read – but tonight somewhat vaguely, often pausing to think. When it was quite late, I went out by the glass door to the lawn, and walked round the house, with the intention of looking in at the drawing-room windows, as I had done when a child. But I had forgotten that these windows were all shuttered at night, and nothing but a faint penetration of the light within through the crevices bore witness to the instalment of the new dweller there.

In the morning my father was entirely himself again. He told me without emotion of the manner in which he had obtained the picture. It had belonged to my mother's family, and had fallen eventually into the hands of a cousin of hers, resident abroad – 'A man whom I did not like, and who did not like me,' my father said; 'there was, or had been, some rivalry, he thought: a mistake, but he was never aware of that. He refused all my requests to have a copy made. You may suppose, Phil, that I wished this very much. Had I succeeded, you would have been acquainted, at least, with your mother's appearance, and need not have sustained this shock. But he would not consent. It gave him, I think, a certain pleasure to think that he had the only picture. But now he is dead – and out of remorse, or with some other intention, has left it to me.'

'That looks like kindness,' said I.

'Yes; or something else. He might have thought that by so doing he was establishing a claim upon me,' my father said: but he did not seem disposed to add any more. On whose behalf he meant to establish a claim I did not know, nor who the man was who had laid us under so great an obligation on his deathbed. He *had* established a claim on me at least: though, as he was dead, I could not see on whose behalf it was. And my father said nothing more. He seemed to dislike the subject. When I attempted to return to it, he had recourse to his letters or his newspapers. Evidently he had made up his mind to say no more.

Afterwards I went into the drawing-room to look at the picture once more. It seemed to me that the anxiety in her eyes was not so evident as I had thought it last night. The light possibly was more favourable. She stood just above the place where, I make no doubt, she had sat in life, where her little work-basket was – not very much above it. The picture was full-length, and we had hung it low, so that she might have been stepping into the room, and was little above my own level as I stood and looked at her again. Once more I smiled at the strange thought that this young creature, so young, almost childish, could be my mother; and once more my eyes grew wet looking at her. He was a benefactor, indeed, who had given her back to us. I said to myself, that if I could ever do anything for him or his, I would certainly do, for my – for this lovely young creature's sake.

And with this in my mind, and all the thoughts that came with it, I am obliged to confess that the other matter, which I had been so full of on the previous night, went entirely out of my head.

It is rarely, however, that such matters are allowed to slip out of one's mind. When I went out in the afternoon for my usual stroll – or rather when I returned from that stroll – I saw once more before me the woman with her baby whose story had filled me with dismay on the previous evening. She was waiting at the gate as before, and – 'Oh, gentleman, but haven't you got some news to give me?' she said.

'My good woman – I – have been greatly occupied. I have had – no time to do anything.'

'Ah!' she said, with a little cry of disappointment, 'my man said not to make too sure, and that the ways of the gentlefolks is hard to know.'

'I cannot explain to you,' I said, as gently as I could, 'what it is that has made me forget you. It was an event that can only do you good in the end. Go home now, and see the man that took your things from you, and tell him to come to me. I promise you it shall all be put right.'

The woman looked at me in astonishment, then burst forth, as it seemed, involuntarily, – 'What! without asking no questions?' After this there came a storm of tears and blessings, from which I made haste to escape, but not without carrying that curious commentary on my rashness away with me – 'Without asking no questions?' It might be foolish, perhaps: but after all how slight a matter. To make the poor creature comfortable at the cost of what – a box or two of cigars, perhaps, or some other trifle. And if it should be her own fault, or her husband's – what then? Had I been punished for all my faults, where should I have been now. And if the advantage should be only temporary, what then? To be relieved and comforted even for a day or two, was not that something to count in life? Thus I quenched the fiery dart of criticism which my *protégée* herself had thrown into the transaction, not without a certain sense of the humour of it. Its effect, however, was to make me less anxious to see my father, to repeat my proposal to him, and to call his attention to the cruelty performed in his name. This one case I had taken out of the category of wrongs to be righted, by assuming arbitrarily the position of Providence in my own person – for, of course, I had bound myself to pay the poor creature's rent as well as redeem her goods – and, whatever might happen to her in the future, had taken the past into my own hands. The man came presently to see me who, it seems, had acted as my father's agent in the matter. 'I don't know, sir, how Mr Canning will take it,' he said. 'He don't want none of those irregular, bad-paying ones in his property. He always says as to look over it and let the rent run on is making things worse in the end. His rule is, "Never more than a month, Stevens": that's what Mr Canning says to me, sir. He says, "More than that they can't pay. It's no use trying." And it's a good rule; it's a very good rule. He won't hear none of their stories, sir. Bless you, you'd never get a penny of rent from them small houses if you listened to their tales. But if so be as you'll pay Mrs Jordan's rent, it's none of my business how it's paid, so long as it's paid, and I'll send her back her things. But they'll just have to be took next time,' he added, composedly. 'Over and over: it's always the same story with them sort of poor folks – they're too poor for anything, that's the truth,' the man said.

Morphew came back to my room after my visitor was gone. 'Mr Philip,' he said, 'you'll excuse me, sir, but if you're going to pay all the poor folk's rent as have distresses put in, you may just go into the court at once, for it's without end—'

'I am going to be the agent myself, Morphew, and manage for my father: and we'll soon put a stop to that,' I said, more cheerfully than I felt.

'Manage for – master,' he said, with a face of consternation. 'You, Mr Philip!'

'You seem to have a great contempt for me, Morphew.'

He did not deny the fact. He said with excitement, 'Master, sir – master don't let himself be put a stop to by any man. Master's – not one to be managed. Don't you quarrel with master, Mr Philip, for the love of God.' The old man was quite pale.

'Quarrel!' I said. 'I have never quarrelled with my father, and I don't mean to begin now.'

Morphew dispelled his own excitement by making up the fire, which was dying in the grate. It was a very mild spring evening, and he made up a great blaze which would have suited December. This is one of many ways in which an old servant will relieve his mind. He muttered all the time as he threw on the coals and wood. 'He'll not like it – we all know as he'll not like it. Master won't stand no meddling, Mr Philip,' – this last he discharged at me like a flying arrow as he closed the door.

I soon found there was truth in what he said. My father was not angry; he was even half amused. 'I don't think that plan of yours will hold water, Phil. I hear you have been paying rents and redeeming furniture – that's an expensive game, and a very profitless one. Of course, so long as you are a benevolent gentleman acting for your own pleasure, it makes no difference to me. I am quite content if I get my money, even out of your pockets – so long as it amuses you. But as my collector, you know, which you are good enough to propose to be—'

'Of course I should act under your orders,' I said; 'but at least you might be sure that I would not commit you to any – to any—' I paused for a word.

'Act of oppression,' he said with a smile – 'piece of cruelty, exaction – there are half-a-dozen words—'

'Sir—' I cried.

'Stop, Phil, and let us understand each other. I hope I have always been a just man. I do my duty on my side, and I expect it from others. It is your benevolence that is cruel. I have calculated anxiously how much credit it is safe to allow; but I will allow no man, or woman either, to go beyond what he or she can make up. My law is fixed. Now you understand. My agents, as you call them, originate nothing – they execute only what I decide—'

'But then no circumstances are taken into account – no bad luck, no evil chances, no loss unexpected.'

'There are no evil chances,' he said, 'there is no bad luck – they reap as they sow. No, I don't go among them to be cheated by their stories, and spend quite unnecessary emotion in sympathising with them. You will find it much better for you that I don't. I deal with them on a general rule, made, I assure you, not without a great deal of thought.'

'And must it always be so?' I said. 'Is there no way of ameliorating or bringing in a better state of things?'

'It seems not,' he said; 'we don't get "no forrarder" in that direction so far as I can see.' And then he turned the conversation to general matters.

I retired to my room greatly discouraged that night. In former ages – or so one is led to suppose – and in the lower primitive classes who still linger near the primeval type, action of any kind was, and is, easier than amid the complications of our higher civilisation. A bad man is a distinct entity, against whom you know more or less what steps to take. A tyrant, an oppressor, a bad landlord, a man who lets miserable tenements at a rack-rent (to come down to particulars), and exposes his wretched tenants to all those abominations of which we have heard so much – well! he is more or less a satisfactory opponent. There he is, and there is nothing to be said for him – down with him! and let there be an end of his wickedness. But when, on the contrary, you have before you a good man, a just man, who has considered deeply a question which you allow to be full of difficulty; who regrets, but cannot, being human, avert, the miseries which to some unhappy individuals follow from the very wisdom of his rule, – what can you do – what is to be done? Individual benevolence at haphazard may baulk him here and there, but what have you to put in the place of his well-considered scheme? Charity which makes paupers? or what else? I had not considered the question deeply, but it seemed to me that I now came to a blank wall, which my vague human sentiment of pity and scorn could find no way to breach. There must be wrong somewhere – but where? There must be some change for the better to be made – but how?

I was seated with a book before me on the table, with my head supported on my hands. My eyes were on the printed page, but I was not reading – my mind was full of these thoughts, my heart of great discouragement and despondency, a sense that I could do nothing, yet that there surely must and ought, if I but knew it, be something to do. The fire which Morphew had built up before dinner was dying out, the shaded lamp on my table left all the corners in a mysterious twilight. The house was perfectly still, no one moving: my father in the library, where, after the habit of many solitary years, he liked to be left alone, and I here in my retreat, preparing for the formation of similar habits. I thought all at once of the third member of the party, the newcomer, alone too in the room that had been hers; and there suddenly occurred to me a strong desire to take up my lamp and go to the drawing-room and visit her, to see whether her soft angelic face would give any inspiration. I restrained, however, this futile impulse – for what could the picture say? – and instead wondered what might have been had she lived, had she been there, warmly enthroned beside the warm domestic centre, the hearth which would have been a common sanctuary, the true home. In that case what might have been? Alas! the question was no more simple to answer than the other: she might have been there alone too, her husband's business, her son's thoughts, as far from her as now, when her silent representative held her old place in the silence and darkness. I had known it so, often enough. Love itself does not always give comprehension and sympathy. It might be that she was more to us there, in the sweet image of her undeveloped beauty, than she might have been had she lived and grown to maturity and fading, like the rest.

I cannot be certain whether my mind was still lingering on this not very cheerful reflection, or if it had been left behind, when the strange occurrence came of which I have now to tell: can I call it an occurrence? My eyes were on my book, when I thought I heard the sound of a door opening and shutting, but so far away and faint that if real at all it must have been in a far corner of the house. I did not move except to lift my eyes from the book, as one does instinctively the better to listen; when – But I cannot tell, nor have I ever been able to describe exactly what it was. My heart made all at once a sudden leap in my breast. I am aware that this language is figurative, and that the heart cannot leap: but it is a figure so entirely justified by sensation, that no one will have any difficulty in understanding what I mean. My heart leapt up and began beating wildly in my throat, in my ears, as if my whole being had received a sudden and intolerable shock. The sound went through my head like the dizzy sound of some strange mechanism, a thousand wheels and springs, circling, echoing, working in my brain. I felt the blood bound in my veins, my mouth became dry, my eyes hot, a sense of something insupportable took possession of me. I sprang to my feet, and then I sat down again. I cast a quick glance round me beyond the brief circle of the lamplight, but there was nothing there to account in any way for this sudden extraordinary rush of sensation – nor could I feel any meaning in it, any suggestion, any moral impression. I thought I must be going to be ill, and got out my watch and felt my pulse: it was beating furiously, about 125 throbs in a minute. I knew of no illness that could come on like this without warning, in a moment, and I tried to subdue myself, to say to myself that it was nothing, some flutter of the nerves, some physical disturbance. I laid myself down upon my sofa to try if rest would help me, and kept still – as long as the thumping and throbbing of this wild excited mechanism within, like a wild beast plunging and struggling, would let me. I am quite aware of the confusion of the metaphor – the reality was just so. It was like a mechanism deranged, going wildly with ever-increasing precipitation, like those horrible wheels that from time to time catch a helpless human being in them and tear him to pieces: but at the same time it was like a maddened living creature making the wildest efforts to get free.

When I could bear this no longer I got up and walked about my room; then having still a certain command of myself, though I could not master the commotion within me, I deliberately took down an exciting book from the shelf, a book of breathless adventure which had always interested me, and tried with that to break the spell. After a few minutes, however, I flung the book aside; I was gradually losing all power over myself. What I should be moved to do, – to shout aloud, to struggle with I know not what; or if I was going mad altogether, and next moment must be a raving lunatic, – I could not tell. I kept looking round, expecting I don't know what: several times, with the corner of my eye I seemed to see

a movement, as if some one was stealing out of sight; but
when I looked straight, there was never anything but the plain
outlines of the wall and carpet, the chairs standing in good
order. At last I snatched up the lamp in my hand and went out
of the room. To look at the picture? which had been faintly
showing in my imagination from time to time, the eyes, more
anxious than ever, looking at me from out the silent air. But
no; I passed the door of that room swiftly, moving, it seemed,
without any volition of my own, and before I knew where I
was going, went into my father's library with my lamp in my
hand.

He was still sitting there at his writing-table; he looked up
astonished to see me hurrying in with my light. 'Phil!' he said,
surprised. I remember that I shut the door behind me, and
came up to him, and set down the lamp on his table. My
sudden appearance alarmed him. 'What is the matter?' he
cried. 'Philip, what have you been doing with yourself?'

I sat down on the nearest chair and gasped, gazing at him.
The wild commotion ceased, the blood subsided into its
natural channels, my heart resumed its place. I use such
words as mortal weakness can to express the sensations I
felt. I came to myself thus, gazing at him, confounded, at once
by the extraordinary passion which I had gone through, and
its sudden cessation. 'The matter?' I cried; 'I don't know
what is the matter.'

My father had pushed his spectacles up from his eyes. He
appeared to me as faces appear in a fever, all glorified with
light which is not in them – his eyes glowing, his white hair
shining like silver; but his look was severe. 'You are not a boy,
that I should reprove you; but you ought to know better,' he
said.

Then I explained to him, so far as I was able, what had
happened. Had happened? nothing had happened. He did not
understand me – nor did I, now that it was over, understand
myself; but he saw enough to make him aware that the
disturbance in me was serious, and not caused by any folly
of my own. He was very kind as soon as he had assured
himself of this, and talked, taking pains to bring me back to
unexciting subjects. He had a letter in his hand with a very
deep border of black when I came in. I observed it, without
taking any notice or associating it with anything I knew. He
had many correspondents, and although we were excellent

friends, we had never been on those confidential terms which warrant one man in asking another from whom a special letter has come. We were not so near to each other as this, though we were father and son. After a while I went back to my own room, and finished the evening in my usual way, without any return of the excitement which, now that it was over, looked to me like some extraordinary dream. What had it meant? had it meant anything? I said to myself that it must be purely physical, something gone temporarily amiss, which had righted itself. It was physical; the excitement did not affect my mind. I was independent of it all the time, a spectator of my own agitation – a clear proof that, whatever it was, it had affected my bodily organisation alone.

Next day I returned to the problem which I had not been able to solve. I found out my petitioner in the back street, and that she was happy in the recovery of her possessions, which to my eyes indeed did not seem very worthy either of lamentation or delight. Nor was her house the tidy house which injured virtue should have when restored to its humble rights. She was not injured virtue, it was clear. She made me a great many curtseys, and poured forth a number of blessings. Her 'man' came in while I was there, and hoped in a gruff voice that God would reward me, and that the old gentleman 'd let 'em alone. I did not like the looks of the man. It seemed to me that in the dark lane behind the house of a winter's night he would not be a pleasant person to find in one's way. Nor was this all: when I went out into the little street which it appeared was all, or almost all, my father's property, a number of groups formed in my way, and at least half-a-dozen applicants sidled up. 'I've more claims nor Mary Jordan any day,' said one; 'I've lived on Squire Canning's property, one place and another, this twenty year.' 'And what do you say to me,' said another; 'I've six children to her two, bless you, sir, and ne'er a father to do for them.' I believed in my father's rule before I got out of the street, and approved his wisdom in keeping himself free from personal contact with his tenants. Yet when I looked back upon the swarming thoroughfare, the mean little houses, the women at their doors all so open-mouthed, and eager to contend for my favour, my heart sank within me at the thought that out of their misery some portion of our wealth came – I don't care how small a portion: that I, young and strong, should be kept idle and in luxury, in some part through the money screwed out of their necessities, obtained sometimes by the sacrifice of everything they prized! Of course I know all the ordinary commonplaces of life as well as any one – that if you build a house with your hands or your money, and let it, the rent of it is your just due, and must be paid. But yet—

'Don't you think, sir,' I said that evening at dinner, the subject being reintroduced by my father himself, 'that we have some duty towards them when we draw so much from them?'

'Certainly,' he said; 'I take as much trouble about their drains as I do about my own.'

'That is always something, I suppose.'

'Something! it is a great deal – it is more than they get anywhere else. I keep them clean, as far as that's possible. I give them at least the means of keeping clean, and thus check disease, and prolong life – which is more, I assure you, than they've any right to expect.'

I was not prepared with arguments as I ought to have been. That is all in the Gospel according to Adam Smith, which my father had been brought up in, but of which the tenets had begun to be less binding in my day. I wanted something more, or else something less; but my views were not so clear, nor my system so logical and well-built, as that upon which my father rested his conscience, and drew his percentage with a light heart.

Yet I thought there were signs in him of some perturbation. I met him one morning coming out of the room in which the portrait hung, as if he had gone to look at it stealthily. He was shaking his head, and saying 'No, no,' to himself, not perceiving me, and I stepped aside when I saw him so absorbed. For myself, I entered that room but little. I went outside, as I had so often done when I was a child, and looked through the windows into the still and now sacred place, which had always impressed me with a certain awe. Looked at so, the slight figure in its white dress seemed to be stepping down into the room from some slight visionary altitude, looking with that which had seemed to me at first anxiety, which I sometimes represented to myself now as a wistful curiosity, as if she were looking for the life which might have been hers. Where was the existence that had belonged to her, the sweet household place, the infant she had left? She would no more recognise the man who thus came to look at her as through a veil with a mystic reverence, than I could recognise her. I could never be her child to her, any more than she could be a mother to me.

Thus time passed on for several quiet days. There was nothing to make us give any special heed to the passage of time, life being very uneventful and its habits unvaried. My mind was very much preoccupied by my father's tenants. He had a great deal of property in the town which was so near us, – streets of small houses, the best-paying property (I was assured) of any. I was very anxious to come to some settled conclusion: on the one hand, not to let myself be carried away by sentiment; on the other, not to allow my strongly roused feelings to fall into the blank of routine, as his had done. I was seated one evening in my own sitting-room busy with this matter, – busy with calculations as to cost and profit, with an anxious desire to convince him, either that his profits were greater than justice allowed, or that they carried with them a more urgent duty than he had conceived.

It was night, but not late, not more than ten o'clock, the household still astir. Everything was quiet – not the solemnity of midnight silence, in which there is always something of mystery, but the soft-breathing quiet of the evening, full of the faint habitual sounds of a human dwelling, a conscious-ness of life about. And I was very busy with my figures, interested, feeling no room in my mind for any other thought. The singular experience which had startled me so much had passed over very quickly, and there had been no return. I had ceased to think of it: indeed I had never thought of it save for the moment, setting it down after it was over to a physical cause without much difficulty. At this time I was far too busy to have thoughts to spare for anything, or room for imagina-tion: and when suddenly in a moment, without any warning, the first symptom returned, I started with it into determined resistance, resolute not to be fooled by any mock influence which could resolve itself into the action of nerves or gang-lions. The first symptom, as before, was that my heart sprang up with a bound, as if a cannon had been fired at my ear. My whole being responded with a start. The pen fell out of my fingers, the figures went out of my head as if all faculty had departed: and yet I was conscious for a time at least of keeping my self-control. I was like the rider of a frightened horse, rendered almost wild by something which in the mystery of its voiceless being it has seen, something on the road which it will not pass, but wildly plunging, resisting every persuasion, turns from, with ever increasing passion. The rider himself after a time becomes infected with this inexplainable desperation of terror, and I suppose I must have done so: but for a time I kept the upper hand. I would not allow myself to spring up as I wished, as my impulse was, but sat there doggedly, clinging to my books, to my table, fixing myself on I did not mind what, to resist the flood of sensation, of emotion, which was sweeping through me, carrying me away. I tried to continue my calculations. I tried to stir myself up with recollections of the miserable sights I had seen, the poverty, the helplessness. I tried to work myself into indignation; but all through these efforts I felt the contagion growing upon me, my mind falling into sympathy with all those straining faculties of the body, startled, excited, driven wild by something I knew not what. It was not fear. I was like a ship at sea straining and plunging against wind and tide, but I was not afraid. I am obliged to use these metaphors, otherwise I could give no explanation of my condition, seized upon against my will, and torn from all those moorings of reason to which I clung with desperation – as long as I had the strength.

When I got up from my chair at last, the battle was lost, so far as my powers of self-control were concerned. I got up, or rather was dragged up, from my seat, clutching at these material things round me as with a last effort to hold my own. But that was no longer possible; I was overcome. I stood for a moment looking round me feebly, feeling myself begin to babble with stammering lips, which was the alternative of shrieking, and which I seemed to choose as a lesser evil. What I said was, 'What am I to do?' and after a while, 'What do you want me to do?' although throughout I saw no one, heard no voice, and had in reality not power enough in my dizzy and confused brain to know what I myself meant. I stood thus for a moment looking blankly round me for guidance, repeating the question, which seemed after a time to become almost mechanical. What do you want me to do? though I neither knew to whom I addressed it nor why I said it. Presently – whether in answer, whether in mere yielding of nature, I cannot tell – I became aware of a difference: not a lessening of the agitation, but a softening, as if my powers of resistance being exhausted, a gentler force, a more benignant influence, had room. I felt myself consent to whatever it was. My heart melted in the midst of the tumult; I seemed to give myself up, and move as if drawn by some one whose arm was in mine, as if softly swept along, not forcibly, but with an utter consent of all my faculties to do I knew not what, for love of I knew not whom. For love – that was how it seemed – not by force, as when I went before. But my steps took the same course: I went through the dim passages in an exaltation indescribable, and opened the door of my father's room.

He was seated there at his table as usual, the light of the lamp falling on his white hair: he looked up with some surprise at the sound of the opening door. 'Phil,' he said, and, with a look of wondering apprehension on his face, watched my approach. I went straight up to him, and put my hand on his shoulder. 'Phil, what is the matter? What do you want with me? What is it?' he said.

'Father, I can't tell you. I come not of myself. There must be something in it, though I don't know what it is. This is the second time I have been brought to you here.'

'Are you going—?' he stopped himself. The exclamation had been begun with an angry intention. He stopped, looking at me with a scared look, as if perhaps it might be true.

'Do you mean mad? I don't think so. I have no delusions that I know of. Father, think – do you know any reason why I am brought here? for some cause there must be.'

I stood with my hand upon the back of his chair. His table was covered with papers, among which were several letters with the broad black border which I had before observed. I noticed this now in my excitement without any distinct associations of thoughts, for that I was not capable of; but the black border caught my eye. And I was conscious that he, too, gave a hurried glance at them, and with one hand swept them away.

'Philip,' he said, pushing back his chair, 'you must be ill, my poor boy. Evidently we have not been treating you rightly: you have been more ill all through than I supposed. Let me persuade you to go to bed.'

'I am perfectly well,' I said. 'Father, don't let us deceive one another. I am neither a man to go mad nor to see ghosts. What it is that has got the command over me I can't tell: but there is some cause for it. You are doing something or planning something with which I have a right to interfere.'

He turned round squarely in his chair with a spark in his blue eyes. He was not a man to be meddled with. 'I have yet to learn what can give my son a right to interfere. I am in possession of all my faculties, I hope.'

'Father,' I cried, 'won't you listen to me? no one can say I have been undutiful or disrespectful. I am a man, with a right to speak my mind, and I have done so; but this is different. I am not here by my own will. Something that is stronger than I has brought me. There is something in your mind which disturbs – others. I don't know what I am saying. This is not what I meant to say: but you know the meaning better than I. Some one – who can speak to you only by me – speaks to you by me; and I know that you understand.'

He gazed up at me, growing pale, and his under lip fell. I, for my part, felt that my message was delivered. My heart sank into a stillness so sudden that it made me faint. The light swam in my eyes: everything went round with me. I kept upright only by my hold upon the chair; and in the sense of utter weakness that followed, I dropped on my knees I think first, then on the nearest seat that presented itself, and covering my face with my hands, had hard ado not to sob, in the sudden removal of that strange influence, the relaxation of the strain.

There was silence between us for some time; then he said, but with a voice slightly broken, 'I don't understand you, Phil. You must have taken some fancy into your mind which my slower intelligence – Speak out what you want to say. What do you find fault with? Is it all – all that woman Jordan?'

He gave a short forced laugh as he broke off, and shook me almost roughly by the shoulder, saying, 'Speak out! what – what do you want to say?'

'It seems, sir, that I have said everything.' My voice trembled more than his, but not in the same way. 'I have told you that I did not come by my own will – quite otherwise. I resisted as long as I could: now all is said. It is for you to judge whether it was worth the trouble or not.'

He got up from his seat in a hurried way. 'You would have me as – mad as yourself,' he said, then sat down again as quickly. 'Come, Phil: if it will please you, not to make a breach, the first breach, between us, you shall have your way.

I consent to your looking into that matter about the poor tenants. Your mind shall not be upset about that, even though I don't enter into all your views.'

'Thank you,' I said; 'but, father, that is not what it is.'

'Then it is a piece of folly,' he said, angrily. 'I suppose you mean – but this is a matter in which I choose to judge for myself.'

'You know what I mean,' I said, as quietly as I could, 'though I don't myself know; that proves there is good reason for it. Will you do one thing for me before I leave you? Come with me into the drawing-room—'

'What end,' he said, with again the tremble in his voice, 'is to be served by that?'

'I don't very well know; but to look at her, you and I together, will always do something for us, sir. As for breach, there can be no breach when we stand there.'

He got up, trembling like an old man, which he was, but which he never looked like save at moments of emotion like this, and told me to take the light; then stopped when he had got half-way across the room. 'This is a piece of theatrical sentimentality,' he said.

'No, Phil, I will not go. I will not bring her into any such – Put down the lamp, and if you will take my advice, go to bed.'

'At least,' I said, 'I will trouble you no more, father, to-night. So long as you understand, there need be no more to say.'

He gave me a very curt 'good-night', and turned back to his papers – the letters with the black edge, either by my imagination or in reality, always keeping uppermost. I went to my own room for my lamp, and then alone proceeded to the silent shrine in which the portrait hung. I at least would look at her tonight. I don't know whether I asked myself, in so many words, if it were she who – or if it was any one – I knew nothing; but my heart was drawn with a softness – born, perhaps, of the great weakness in which I was left after that visitation – to her, to look at her, to see perhaps if there was any sympathy, any approval in her face. I set down my lamp on the table where her little work-basket still was: the light threw a gleam upward upon her, – she seemed more than ever to be stepping into the room, coming down towards me, coming back to her life. Ah no! her life was lost and vanished: all mine stood between her and the days she knew. She looked at me with eyes that did not change. The anxiety I had seen at first seemed now a wistful subdued question; but that difference was not in her look but in mine.

I need not linger on the intervening time. The doctor who attended us usually, came in next day 'by accident', and we had a long conversation. On the following day a very impressive yet genial gentleman from town lunched with us – a friend of my father's, Dr Something; but the introduction was hurried, and I did not catch his name. He, too, had a long talk with me afterwards – my father being called away to speak to some one on business. Dr—drew me out on the subject of the dwellings of the poor. He said he heard I took great interest in this question, which had come so much to the front at the present moment. He was interested in it too, and wanted to know the view I took. I explained at considerable length that my view did not concern the general subject, on which I had scarcely thought, so much as the individual mode of management of my father's estate. He was a most patient and intelligent listener, agreeing with me on some points, differing in others; and his visit was very pleasant. I had no idea until after of its special object: though a certain puzzled look and slight shake of the head when my father returned, might have thrown some light upon it. The report of the medical experts in my case must, however, have been quite satisfactory, for I heard nothing more of them. It was, I think, a fortnight later when the next and last of these strange experiences came.

This time it was morning, about noon, – a wet and rather dismal spring day. The half-spread leaves seemed to tap at the window, with an appeal to be taken in; the primroses, that showed golden upon the grass at the roots of the trees, just beyond the smooth-shorn grass of the lawn, were all drooped and sodden among their sheltering leaves. The very growth seemed dreary – the sense of spring in the air making the feeling of winter a grievance, instead of the natural effect which it had conveyed a few months before. I had been writing letters, and was cheerful enough, going back among the associates of my old life, with, perhaps, a little longing for its freedom and independence, but at the same time a not ungrateful consciousness that for the moment my present tranquillity might be best.

This was my condition – a not unpleasant one – when suddenly the now well-known symptoms of the visitation to which I had become subject suddenly seized upon me, – the leap of the heart; the sudden, causeless, overwhelming physical excitement, which I could neither ignore nor allay. I was terrified beyond description, beyond reason, when I became conscious that this was about to begin over again: what purpose did it answer, what good was in it? My father indeed understood the meaning of it, though I did not understand: but it was little agreeable to be thus made a helpless instrument without any will of mine, in an operation of which I knew nothing; and to enact the part of the oracle unwillingly, with suffering and such a strain as it took me days to get over. I resisted, not as before, but yet desperately, trying with better knowledge to keep down the growing passion. I hurried to my room and swallowed a dose of a sedative which had been given me to procure sleep on my first return from India. I saw Morphew in the hall, and called him to talk to him, and cheat myself, if possible, by that means. Morphew lingered, however, and, before he came, I was beyond conversation. I heard him speak, his voice coming vaguely through the turmoil which was already in my ears, but what he said I have never known. I stood staring, trying to recover my power of attention, with an aspect which ended by completely frightening the man. He cried out at last that he was sure I was ill, that he must bring me something; which words penetrated more or less into my maddened brain. It became impressed upon me that he was going to get some one – one of my father's doctors, perhaps – to prevent me from acting, to stop my interference, – and that if I waited a moment longer I might be too late. A vague idea seized me at the same time, of taking refuge with the portrait – going to its feet, throwing myself there, perhaps, till the paroxysm should be over. But it was not there that my footsteps were directed. I can remember making an effort to open the door of the drawing-room, and feeling myself swept past it, as if by a gale of wind. It was not there that I had to go. I knew very well where I had to go, – once more on my confused and voiceless mission to my father, who understood, although I could not understand.

Yet as it was daylight, and all was clear, I could not help noting one or two circumstances on my way. I saw some one sitting in the hall as if waiting – a woman, a girl, a black-shrouded figure, with a thick veil over her face: and asked myself who she was, and what she wanted there? This question, which had nothing to do with my present condition, somehow got into my mind, and was tossed up and down upon the tumultuous tide like a stray log on the breast of a fiercely rolling stream, now submerged, now coming uppermost, at the mercy of the waters. It did not stop me for a moment, as I hurried towards my father's room, but it got upon the current of my mind. I flung open my father's door, and closed it again after me, without seeing who was there or how he was engaged. The full clearness of the daylight did not identify him as the lamp did at night. He looked up at the sound of the door, with a glance of apprehension; and rising suddenly, interrupting some one who was standing speaking to him with much earnestness and even vehemence, came forward to meet me. 'I cannot be disturbed at present,' he said quickly; 'I am busy.' Then seeing the look in my face, which by this time he knew, he too changed colour. 'Phil,' he said, in a low, imperative voice, 'wretched boy, go away – go away; don't let a stranger see you—'

'I can't go away,' I said. 'It is impossible. You know why I have come. I cannot, if I would. It is more powerful than I—'

'Go, sir,' he said; 'go at once – no more of this folly. I will not have you in this room. Go – go!'

I made no answer. I don't know that I could have done so. There had never been any struggle between us before; but I had no power to do one thing or another. The tumult within me was in full career. I heard indeed what he said, and was able to reply; but his words, too, were like straws tossed upon the tremendous stream. I saw now with my feverish eyes who the other person present was. It was a woman, dressed also in mourning similar to the one in the hall; but this a middle-aged woman, like a respectable servant. She had been crying, and in the pause caused by this encounter between my father and myself, dried her eyes with a handkerchief, which she rolled like a ball in her hand, evidently in strong emotion. She turned and looked at me as my father spoke to me, for a moment with a gleam of hope, then falling back into her former attitude.

My father returned to his seat. He was much agitated too, though doing all that was possible to conceal it. My inopportune arrival was evidently a great and unlooked-for vexation to him. He gave me the only look of passionate displeasure I have ever had from him, as he sat down again: but he said nothing more.

'You must understand,' he said, addressing the woman, 'that I have said my last words on this subject. I don't choose to enter into it again in the presence of my son, who is not well enough to be made a party to any discussion. I am sorry that you should have had so much trouble in vain; but you were warned beforehand, and you have only yourself to blame. I acknowledge no claim, and nothing you can say will change my resolution. I must beg you to go away. All this is very painful and quite useless. I acknowledge no claim.'

'Oh, sir,' she cried, her eyes beginning once more to flow, her speech interrupted by little sobs. 'Maybe I did wrong to speak of a claim. I'm not educated to argue with a gentleman. Maybe we have no claim. But if it's not by right, oh, Mr Canning, won't you let your heart be touched by pity? She don't know what I'm saying, poor dear. She's not one to beg and pray for herself, as I'm doing for her. Oh sir, she's so young! She's so lone in this world – not a friend to stand by her, nor a house to take her in! You are the nearest to her of any one that's left in this world. She hasn't a relation – not one so near as you – oh!' she cried, with a sudden thought, turning quickly round upon me, 'this gentleman's your son! Now I think of it, it's not your relation she is, but his, through his mother! That's nearer, nearer! Oh, sir! you're young; your heart should be more tender. Here is my young lady that has no one in the world to look to her. Your own flesh and blood: your mother's cousin – your mother's—'

My father called to her to stop, with a voice of thunder. 'Philip, leave us at once. It is not a matter to be discussed with you.'

And then in a moment it became clear to me what it was. It had been with difficulty that I had kept myself still. My breast was labouring with the fever of an impulse poured into me, more than I could contain. And now for the first time I knew why. I hurried towards him, and took his hand, though he resisted, into mine. Mine were burning, but his like ice: their touch burnt me with its chill, like fire. 'This is what it is?' I cried. 'I had no knowledge before. I don't know now what is being asked of you. But, father – understand! You know, and I know now, that some one sends me – some one – who has a right to interfere.'

He pushed me away with all his might. 'You are mad,' he cried. 'What right have you to think——? Oh, you are mad – mad! I have seen it coming on—'

The woman, the petitioner, had grown silent, watching this brief conflict with the terror and interest with which women watch a struggle between men. She started and fell back when she heard what he said, but did not take her eyes off me, following every movement I made. When I turned to go away, a cry of indescribable disappointment and remonstrance burst from her, and even my father raised himself up and stared at my withdrawal, astonished to find that he had overcome me so soon and easily. I paused for a moment, and looked back on them, seeing them large and vague through the mist of fever. 'I am not going away,' I said. 'I am going for another messenger – one you can't gainsay.'

My father rose. He called out to me threateningly, 'I will have nothing touched that is hers. Nothing that is hers shall be profaned—'

I waited to hear no more: I knew what I had to do. By what means it was conveyed to me I cannot tell; but the certainty of an influence which no one thought of calmed me in the midst of my fever. I went out into the hall, where I had seen the young stranger waiting. I went up to her and touched her on the shoulder. She rose at once, with a little movement of alarm, yet with docile and instant obedience, as if she had expected the summons. I made her take off her veil and her bonnet, scarcely looking at her, scarcely seeing her, knowing how it was: I took her soft, small, cool, yet trembling hand into mine; it was so soft and cool, not cold, it refreshed me with its tremulous touch. All through I moved and spoke like a man in a dream, swiftly, noiselessly, all the complications of waking life removed, without embarrassment, without reflection, without the loss of a moment. My father was still standing up, leaning a little forward as he had done when I withdrew, threatening, yet terror-stricken, not knowing what I might be about to do, when I returned with my companion. That was the one thing he had not thought of. He was entirely undefended, unprepared. He gave her one look, flung up his arms above his head, and uttered a distracted cry, so wild that it seemed the last outcry of nature – 'Agnes!' then fell back like a sudden ruin, upon himself, into his chair.

I had no leisure to think how he was, or whether he could hear what I said. I had my message to deliver. 'Father,' I said, labouring with my panting breath, 'it is for this that heaven has opened, and one whom I never saw, one whom I know not, has taken possession of me. Had we been less earthly we should have seen her – herself, and not merely her image. I have not even known what she meant. I have been as a fool without understanding. This is the third time I have come to you with her message, without knowing what to say. But now I have found it out. This is her message. I have found it out at last.'

There was an awful pause – a pause in which no one moved or breathed. Then there came a broken voice out of my father's chair. He had not understood, though I think he heard what I said. He put out two feeble hands. 'Phil – I think I am dying – has she – has she come for me?' he said.

We had to carry him to his bed. What struggles he had gone through before I cannot tell. He had stood fast, and had refused to be moved, and now he fell – like an old tower, like an old tree. The necessity there was for thinking of him saved me from the physical consequences which had prostrated me on a former occasion. I had no leisure now for any consciousness of how matters went with myself.

His delusion was not wonderful, but most natural. She was clothed in black from head to foot, instead of the white dress of the portrait. She had no knowledge of the conflict, of nothing but that she was called for, that her fate might depend on the next few minutes. In her eyes there was a pathetic question, a line of anxiety in the lids, an innocent appeal in the looks. And the face the same: the same lips, sensitive, ready to quiver; the same innocent, candid brow; the look of a common race, which is more subtle than mere resemblance. How I knew that it was so, I cannot tell, nor any man. It was the other – the elder – ah no! not elder; the ever young, the Agnes to whom age can never come – she who they say was the mother of a man who never saw her – it was she who led her kinswoman, her representative, into our hearts.

My father recovered after a few days: he had taken cold, it was said, the day before – and naturally, at seventy, a small matter is enough to upset the balance even of a strong man. He got quite well; but he was willing enough afterwards to leave the management of that ticklish kind of property which involves human well-being in my hands, who could move about more freely, and see with my own eyes how things were going on. He liked home better, and had more pleasure in his personal existence in the end of his life. Agnes is now my wife, as he had, of course, foreseen. It was not merely the disinclination to receive her father's daughter, or to take upon him a new responsibility, that had moved him, to do him justice. But both these motives had told strongly. I have never been told, and now will never be told, what his griefs against my mother's family, and specially against that cousin, had been; but that he had been very determined, deeply prejudiced, there can be no doubt. It turned out after, that the first occasion on which I had been mysteriously commissioned to him with a message which I did not understand, and which for that time he did not understand, was the evening of the day on which he had received the dead man's letter, appealing to him – to him, a man whom he had wronged – on behalf of the child who was about to be left friendless in the world. The second time, further letters, from the nurse who was the only guardian of the orphan, and the chaplain of the place where her father had died, taking it for granted that my father's house was her natural refuge – had been received. The third I have already described, and its results.

For a long time after, my mind was never without a lurking fear that the influence which had once taken possession of me might return again. Why should I have feared to be influenced – to be the messenger of a blessed creature, whose wishes could be nothing but heavenly? Who can say? Flesh and blood is not made for such encounters: they were more than I could bear. But nothing of the kind has ever occurred again.

Agnes had her peaceful domestic throne established under the picture. My father wished it to be so, and spent his evenings there in the warmth and light, instead of in the old library, in the narrow circle cleared by our lamp out of the darkness, as long as he lived. It is supposed by strangers that the picture on the wall is that of my wife; and I have always been glad that it should be so supposed. She who was my mother, who came back to me and became as my soul for three strange moments and no more, but with whom I can feel no credible relationship as she stands there, has retired for me into the tender regions of the unseen. She has passed once more into the secret company of those shadows, who can only become real in an atmosphere fitted to modify and harmonise all differences, and make all wonders possible – the light of the perfect day.

The Land of Darkness

[The following narrative forms a necessary part of the Little Pilgrim's experiences in the spiritual world, though it is not her personal story, but is drawn from the Archives of which, in their bearing upon the universal history of mankind, she was informed.]

I FOUND MYSELF standing on my feet, with the tingling sensation of having come down rapidly upon the ground from a height. There was a similar feeling in my head, as of the whirling and sickening sensation of passing downward through the air, like the description Dante gives of his descent upon Geryon. My mind, curiously enough, was sufficiently disengaged to think of that, or at least to allow swift passage for the recollection through my thoughts. All the aching of wonder, doubt, and fear which I had been conscious of a little while before was gone. There was no distinct interval between the one condition and the other, nor in my fall (as I supposed it must have been) had I any consciousness of change. There was the whirling of the air, resisting my passage, yet giving way under me in giddy circles, and then the sharp shock of once more feeling under my feet something solid, which struck yet sustained. After a little while the giddiness above and the tingling below passed away, and I felt able to look about me and discern where I was. But not all at once: the things immediately about me impressed me first – then the general aspect of the new place.

First of all the light, which was lurid, as if a thunderstorm were coming on. I looked up involuntarily to see if it had begun to rain; but there was nothing of the kind, though what I saw above me was a lowering canopy of cloud, dark, threatening, with a faint reddish tint diffused upon the vaporous darkness. It was, however, quite sufficiently clear to see everything, and there was a good deal to see. I was in a street of what seemed a great and very populous place. There were shops on either side, full apparently of all sorts of costly wares. There was a continual current of passengers up and down on both sides of the way, and in the middle of the street carriages of every description, humble and splendid. The noise was great and ceaseless, the traffic continual. Some of the shops were most brilliantly lighted, attracting one's eyes in the sombre light outside, which, however, had just enough of day in it to make these spots of illumination look sickly; most of the places thus distinguished were apparently bright with the electric or some other scientific light; and delicate machines of every description, brought to the greatest perfection, were in some windows, as were also many fine productions of art, but mingled with the gaudiest and coarsest in a way which struck me with astonishment. I was also much surprised by the fact that the traffic, which was never stilled for a moment, seemed to have no sort of regulation. Some carriages dashed along, upsetting the smaller vehicles in their way, without the least restraint or order, either, as it seemed, from their own good sense, or from the laws and customs of the place. When an accident happened, there was a great shouting, and sometimes a furious encounter – but nobody seemed to interfere. This was the first impression made upon me. The passengers on the pavement were equally regardless. I was myself pushed out of the way, first to one side, then to another, hustled when I paused for a moment, trodden upon and driven about. I retreated soon to the doorway of a shop, from whence with a little more safety I could see what was going on. The noise made my head ring. It seemed to me that I could not hear myself think. If this were to go on for ever, I said to myself, I should soon go mad.

'Oh no,' said some one behind me, 'not at all; you will get used to it; you will be glad of it. One does not want to hear one's thoughts; most of them are not worth hearing.'

I turned round and saw it was the master of the shop, who had come to the door on seeing me. He had the usual smile of a man who hoped to sell his wares; but to my horror and astonishment, by some process which I could not understand, I saw that he was saying to himself, 'What a d——d fool! here's another of those cursed wretches, d——him!' all with the same smile. I started back, and answered him as hotly, 'What do you mean by calling me a d——d fool? –

fool yourself, and all the rest of it. Is this the way you receive strangers here?'

'Yes,' he said, with the same smile, 'this is the way; and I only describe you as you are, as you will soon see. Will you walk in and look over my shop? Perhaps you will find something to suit you if you are just setting up, as I suppose.'

I looked at him closely, but this time I could not see that he was saying anything beyond what was expressed by his lips, and I followed him into the shop, principally because it was quieter than the street, and without any intention of buying – for what should I buy in a strange place where I had no settled habitation, and which probably I was only passing through?

'I will look at your things,' I said, in a way which I believe I had, of perhaps undue pretension. I had never been over-rich, or of very elevated station; but I was believed by my friends (or enemies) to have an inclination to make myself out something more important than I was. 'I will look at your things, and possibly I may find something that may suit me; but with all the *ateliers* of Paris and London to draw from, it is scarcely to be expected that in a place like this—'

Here I stopped to draw my breath, with a good deal of confusion; for I was unwilling to let him see that I did not know where I was.

'A place like this,' said the shopkeper, with a little laugh which seemed to me full of mockery, 'will supply you better, you will find, than – any other place. At least you will find it the only place practicable,' he added. 'I perceive you are a stranger here.'

'Well – I may allow myself to be so – more or less. I have not had time to form much acquaintance with – the place: what – do you call the place? – its formal name, I mean,' I said, with a great desire to keep up the air of superior information. Except for the first moment I had not experienced that strange power of looking into the man below the surface which had frightened me. Now there occurred another gleam of insight, which gave me once more a sensation of alarm. I seemed to see a light of hatred and contempt below his smile, and I felt that he was not in the least taken in by the air which I assumed.

'The name of the place,' he said, 'is not a pretty one. I hear the gentlemen who come to my shop say that it is not to be named to ears polite; and I am sure your ears are very polite.'

He said this with the most offensive laugh, and I turned upon him and answered him, without mincing matters, with a plainness of speech which startled myself, but did not seem to move him, for he only laughed again. 'Are you not afraid,' I said, 'that I will leave your shop and never enter it more?'

'Oh, it helps to pass the time,' he said; and without any further comment began to show me very elaborate and fine articles of furniture. I had always been attracted to this sort of thing, and had longed to buy such articles for my house when I had one, but never had it in my power. Now I had no house, nor any means of paying so far as I knew, but I felt quite at my ease about buying, and inquired into the prices with the greatest composure.

'They are just the sort of thing I want. I will take these, I think; but you must set them aside for me, for I do not at the present moment exactly know—'

'You mean you have got no rooms to put them in,' said the master of the shop. 'You must get a house directly, that's all. If you're only up to it, it is easy enough. Look about until you find something you like, and then – take possession.'

'Take possession' – I was so much surprised that I stared at him with mingled indignation and surprise – 'of what belongs to another man?' I said.

I was not conscious of anything ridiculous in my look. I was indignant, which is not a state of mind in which there is any absurdity; but the shopkeeper suddenly burst into a storm of laughter. He laughed till he seemed almost to fall into convulsions, with a harsh mirth which reminded me of the old image of the crackling of thorns, and had neither amusement nor warmth in it; and presently this was echoed all around, and looking up, I saw grinning faces full of derision, bent upon me from every side, from the stairs which led to the upper part of the house and from the depths of the shop behind – faces with pens behind their ears, faces in workmen's caps, all distended from ear to ear, with a sneer and a mock and a rage of laughter which nearly sent me mad. I hurled I don't know what imprecations at them as I rushed out, stopping my ears in a paroxysm of fury and mortification. My mind was so distracted by this occurrence that I rushed without knowing it upon some one who was passing, and threw him down with the violence of my exit; upon which I was set on by a party of half-a-dozen ruffians, apparently his companions, who would, I thought, kill me, but who only flung me, wounded, bleeding, and feeling as if every bone in my body had been broken, down on the pavement – when they went away, laughing too.

I picked myself up from the edge of the causeway, aching and sore from head to foot, scarcely able to move, yet conscious that if I did not get myself out of the way one or other of the vehicles which were dashing along would run over me. It would be impossible to describe the miserable sensations, both of body and mind, with which I dragged myself across the crowded pavement, not without curses and even kicks from the passers-by; and, avoiding the shop from which I still heard those shrieks of devilish laughter, gathered myself up in the shelter of a little projection of a wall, where I was for the moment safe. The pain which I felt was as nothing to the sense of humiliation, the mortification, the rage with which I was possessed. There is nothing in existence more dreadful than rage which is impotent, which cannot punish or avenge, which has to restrain itself and put up with insults showered upon it. I had never known before what that helpless, hideous exasperation was; and I was humiliated beyond description, brought down – I, whose inclination it was to make more of myself than was justifiable – to the aspect of a miserable ruffian beaten in a brawl, soiled, covered with mud and dust, my clothes torn, my face bruised and disfigured: all this within half an hour or thereabout of my arrival in a strange place where nobody knew me or could do me justice! I kept looking out feverishly for some one with an air of authority to whom I could appeal. Sooner or later somebody must go by, who, seeing me in such a plight, must inquire how it came about, must help me and vindicate me. I sat there for I cannot tell how long, expecting every moment that, were it but a policeman, somebody would notice and help me. But no one came. Crowds seemed to sweep by without a pause – all hurrying, restless: some with anxious faces, as if any delay would be mortal; some in noisy groups intercepting the passage of the others. Sometimes one would pause to point me out to his comrades, with a shout of derision at my miserable plight; or if by a change of posture I got outside the protection of my wall, would kick me back with a coarse injunction to keep out of the way. No one was sorry for me – not a look of compassion, not a word of inquiry was wasted upon me; no representative of authority appeared. I saw a dozen quarrels while I lay there, cries of the weak, and triumphant shouts of the strong; but that was all.

I was drawn after a while from the fierce and burning sense of my own grievances by a querulous voice quite close to me. 'This is my corner,' it said. 'I've sat here for years, and I have a right to it. And here you come, you big ruffian, because you know I haven't got the strength to push you away.'

'Who are you?' I said, turning round horror-stricken; for close beside me was a miserable man, apparently in the last stage of disease. He was pale as death, yet eaten up with sores. His body was agitated by a nervous trembling. He seemed to shuffle along on hands and feet, as though the ordinary mode of locomotion was impossible to him, and yet was in possession of all his limbs. Pain was written in his face. I drew away to leave him room, with mingled pity and horror that this poor wretch should be the partner of the only shelter I could find within so short a time of my arrival. I who – It was horrible, shameful, humiliating; and yet the suffering in his wretched face was so evident that I could not but feel a pang of pity too. 'I have nowhere to go,' I said. 'I am – a stranger. I have been badly used, and nobody seems to care.'

'No,' he said; 'nobody cares – don't you look for that. Why should they? Why, you look as if you were sorry for *me!* What a joke!' he murmured to himself – 'what a joke! Sorry for some one else! What a fool the fellow must be!'

'You look,' I said, 'as if you were suffering horribly; and you say you have come here for years.'

'Suffering! I should think I was,' said the sick man; 'but what is that to you? Yes; I've been here for years – oh, years! – that means nothing, – for longer than can be counted. Suffering is not the word – it's torture – it's agony. But who cares? Take your leg out of my way.'

I drew myself out of his way from a sort of habit, though against my will, and asked, from habit too, 'Are you never any better than now?'

He looked at me more closely, and an air of astonishment came over his face. 'What d'ye want here,' he said, 'pitying a man! That's something new here. No; I'm not always so bad, if you want to know. I get better, and then I go and do what makes me bad again, and that's how it will go on; and I choose it to be so, and you needn't bring any of your d——d pity here.'

'I may ask, at least, why aren't you looked after? Why don't you get into some hospital?' I said.

'Hospital!' cried the sick man, and then he too burst out into that furious laugh, the most awful sound I ever had heard. Some of the passers-by stopped to hear what the joke was, and surrounded me with once more a circle of mockers. 'Hospitals! perhaps you would like a whole Red Cross Society, with ambulances and all arranged?' cried one. 'Or the *Misericordia!*' shouted another. I sprang up to my feet, crying, 'Why not?' with an impulse of rage which gave me strength. Was I never to meet with anything but this fiendish laughter? 'There's some authority, I suppose,' I cried in my fury. 'It is not the rabble that is the only master here, I hope.' But nobody took the least trouble to hear what I had to say for myself. The last speaker struck me on the mouth, and called me an accursed fool for talking of what I did not understand; and finally they all swept on and passed away.

I had been, as I thought, severely injured when I dragged myself into that corner to save myself from the crowd; but I sprang up now as if nothing had happened to me. My wounds had disappeared, my bruises were gone. I was, as I had been when I dropped, giddy and amazed, upon the same pavement, how long – an hour? – before? It might have been an hour, it might have been a year, I cannot tell. The light was the same as ever, the thunderous atmosphere unchanged. Day, if it was day, had made no progress; night, if it was evening, had come no nearer: all was the same.

As I went on again presently, with a vexed and angry spirit, regarding on every side around me the endless surging of the crowd, and feeling a loneliness, a sense of total abandonment and solitude, which I cannot describe, there came up to me a man of remarkable appearance. That he was a person of importance, of great knowledge and information, could not be doubted. He was very pale, and of a worn but commanding aspect. The lines of his face were deeply drawn, his eyes were sunk under high arched brows, from which they looked out as from caves, full of a fiery impatient light. His thin lips were never quite without a smile; but it was not a smile in which any pleasure was. He walked slowly, not hurrying, like most of the passengers. He had a reflective look, as if pondering many things. He came up to me suddenly, without introduction or preliminary, and took me by the arm. 'What object had you in talking of these antiquated institutions?' he said.

And I saw in his mind the gleam of the thought, which seemed to be the first with all, that I was a fool, and that it was the natural thing to wish me harm, – just as in the earth above it was the natural thing, professed at least, to wish well – to say, Good morning, good day, by habit and without thought. In this strange country the stranger was received with a curse, and it woke an answer not unlike the hasty 'Curse you, then, also!' which seemed to come without any will of mine through my mind. But this provoked only a smile from my new friend. He took no notice. He was disposed to examine me – to find some amusement perhaps – how could I tell? – in what I might say.

'What antiquated things?'

'Are you still so slow of understanding? What were they? hospitals: the pretences of a world that can still deceive itself. Did you expect to find them here?'

'I expected to find – how should I know?' I said, bewildered – 'some shelter for a poor wretch where he could be cared for – not to be left there to die in the street. Expected! I never thought. I took it for granted—'

'To die in the street!' he cried, with a smile, and a shrug of his shoulders. 'You'll learn better by-and-by. And if he did die in the street, what then? What is that to you?'

'To me!' I turned and looked at him amazed; but he had somehow shut his soul, so that I could see nothing but the deep eyes in their caves, and the smile upon the close-shut mouth. 'No more to me than to any one. I only spoke for humanity's sake, as – a fellow-creature.'

My new acquaintance gave way to a silent laugh within himself, which was not so offensive as the loud laugh of the crowd, but yet was more exasperating than words can say. 'You think that matters? But it does not hurt you that he should be in pain. It would do you no good if he were to get well. Why should you trouble yourself one way or the other? Let him die – if he can – That makes no difference to you or me.'

'I must be dull indeed,' I cried, – 'slow of understanding, as you say. This is going back to the ideas of times beyond knowledge – before Christianity—.' As soon as I had said this I felt somehow – I could not tell how – as if my voice jarred, as

if something false and unnatural was in what I said. My
companion gave my arm a twist as if with a shock of surprise,
then laughed in his inward way again.

'We don't think much of that here; nor of your modern
pretences in general. The only thing that touches you and me
is what hurts or helps ourselves. To be sure, it all comes to the
same thing – for I suppose it annoys you to see that wretch
writhing: it hurts your more delicate, highly cultivated consciousness.'

'It has nothing to do with my consciousness,' I cried,
angrily; 'it is a shame to let a fellow-creature suffer if we
can prevent it.'

'Why shouldn't he suffer?' said my companion. We passed
as he spoke some other squalid wretched creatures shuffling
among the crowd, whom he kicked with his foot, calling forth
a yell of pain and curses. This he regarded with a supreme
contemptuous calm which stupefied me. Nor did any of the
passers-by show the slightest inclination to take the part of
the sufferers. They laughed, or shouted out a gibe, or, what
was still more wonderful, went on with a complete unaffected
indifference, as if all this was natural. I tried to disengage my
arm in horror and dismay, but he held me fast, with a pressure
that hurt me. 'That's the question,' he said. 'What have we to
do with it? Your fictitious consciousness makes it painful to
you. To me, on the contrary, who take the view of nature, it is
a pleasurable feeling. It enhances the amount of ease, whatever that may be, which I enjoy. I am in no pain. That brute
who is' – and he flicked with a stick he carried the uncovered
wound of a wretch upon the road-side – 'makes me more
satisfied with my condition. Ah! you think it is I who am the
brute? You will change your mind by-and-by.'

'Never!' I cried, wrenching my arm from his with an effort,
'if I should live a hundred years.'

'A hundred years – a drop in the bucket!' he said, with his
silent laugh. 'You will live for ever, and you will come to my
view; and we shall meet in the course of ages, from time to
time, to compare notes. I would say good-bye after the old
fashion, but you are but newly arrived, and I will not treat you
so badly as that.' With which he parted from me, waving his
hand, with his everlasting horrible smile.

'Good-bye!' I said to myself, 'good-bye – why should it be
treating me badly to say good-bye—'

I was startled by a buffet on the mouth. 'Take that!' cried some one, 'to teach you how to wish the worst of tortures to people who have done you no harm.'

'What have I said? I meant no harm. I repeated only what is the commonest civility, the merest good manners.'

'You wished,' said the man who had struck me, – 'I won't repeat the words: to me, for it was I only that heard them, the awful company that hurts most – that sets everything before us, both past and to come, and cuts like a sword and burns like fire. I'll say it to yourself, and see how it feels. God be with you! There! it is said, and we all must bear it, thanks, you fool and accursed, to you.'

And then there came a pause over all the place – an awful stillness – hundreds of men and women standing clutching with desperate movements at their hearts as if to tear them out, moving their heads as if to dash them against the wall, wringing their hands, with a look upon all their convulsed faces which I can never forget. They all turned to me, cursing me, with those horrible eyes of anguish. And everything was still – the noise all stopped for a moment – the air all silent, with a silence that could be felt. And then suddenly out of the crowd there came a great piercing cry; and everything began again exactly as before.

While this pause occurred, and while I stood wondering, bewildered, understanding nothing, there came over me a darkness, a blackness, a sense of misery such as never in all my life, though I have known troubles enough, I had felt before. All that had happened to me throughout my existence seemed to rise pale and terrible in a hundred scenes before me, all momentary, intense, as if each was the present moment. And in each of these scenes I saw what I had never seen before. I saw where I had taken the wrong instead of the right step – in what wantonness, with what self-will it had been done; how God (I shuddered at the name) had spoken and called me, and even entreated, and I had withstood and refused. All the evil I had done came back, and spread itself out before my eyes; and I loathed it, yet knew that I had chosen it, and that it would be with me for ever. I saw it all in the twinkling of an eye, in a moment, while I stood there, and all men with me, in the horror of awful thought. Then it ceased as it had come, instantaneously, and the noise and the laughter, and the quarrels and cries, and all the commotion of this new bewildering place, in a moment began again. I had seen no one while this strange paroxysm lasted. When it disappeared, I came to myself emerging as from a dream, and looked into the face of the man whose words, not careless like mine, had brought it upon us. Our eyes met, and his were surounded by curves and lines of anguish which were terrible to see.

'Well,' he said, with a short laugh, which was forced and harsh, 'how do you like it? that is what happens when – If it came often, who could endure it?' He was not like the rest. There was no sneer upon his face, no gibe at my simplicity. Even now, when all had recovered, he was still quivering with something that looked like a nobler pain. His face was very grave, the lines deeply drawn in it, and he seemed to be seeking no amusement or distraction, nor to take any part in the noise and tumult which was going on around.

'Do you know what that cry meant?' he said. 'Did you hear that cry? It was some one who saw – even here once in a long time, they say, it can be seen—'

'What can be seen?'

He shook his head, looking at me with a meaning which I could not interpret. It was beyond the range of my thoughts. I came to know after, or I never could have made this record. But on that subject he said no more. He turned the way I was going, though it mattered nothing what way I went, for all were the same to me. 'You are one of the newcomers?' he said; 'you have not been long here—'

'Tell me,' I cried, 'what you mean by *here*. Where are we? How can one tell who has fallen – he knows not whence or where? What is this place? I have never seen anything like it. It seems to me that I hate it already, though I know not what it is.'

He shook his head once more. 'You will hate it more and more,' he said; 'but of these dreadful streets you will never be free, unless—' And here he stopped again.

'Unless – what? If it is possible, I will be free of them, and that before long.'

He smiled at me faintly, as we smile at children, but not with derision.

'How shall you do that? Between this miserable world and all others there is a great gulf fixed. It is full of all the bitterness and tears that come from all the universe. These drop from them, but stagnate here. We, you perceive, have no tears, not even at moments—' Then, 'You will soon be accustomed to all this,' he said. 'You will fall into the way. Perhaps you will be able to amuse yourself, to make it passable. Many do. There are a number of fine things to be seen here. If you are curious, come with me and I will show you. Or work – there is even work. There is only one thing that is impossible – or if not impossible—' And here he paused again, and raised his eyes to the dark clouds and lurid sky overhead. 'The man who gave that cry! if I could but find him – he must have seen—'

'What could he see?' I asked. But there rose in my mind something like contempt. A visionary! who could not speak plainly, who broke off into mysterious inferences, and appeared to know more than he would say. It seemed foolish to waste time when evidently there was still so much to see, in the company of such a man. And I began already to feel more at home. There was something in that moment of anguish which had wrought a strange familiarity in me with my surroundings. It was so great a relief to return out of the misery of that sharp and horrible self-realisation, to what had come to be, in comparison, easy and well known. I had no desire to go back and grope among the mysteries and anguish so suddenly revealed. I was glad to be free from them, to be left to myself, to get a little pleasure perhaps like the others. While these thoughts passed through my mind, I had gone on without any active impulse of my own, as everybody else did; and my latest companion had disappeared. He saw, no doubt, without any need for words, what my feelings were. And I proceeded on my way. I felt better as I got more accustomed to the place, or perhaps it was the sensation or relief after that moment of indescribable pain. As for the sights in the streets, I began to grow used to them. The wretched creatures who strolled or sat about with signs of sickness or wounds upon them disgusted me only, they no longer called forth my pity. I began to feel ashamed of my silly questions about the hospital. All the same, it would have been a good thing to have had some receptacle for them, into which they might have been driven out of the way. I felt an inclination to push them aside as I saw other people do, but was a little ashamed of that impulse too; and so I went on. There seemed no quiet streets, so far as I could make out, in the place. Some were smaller, meaner, with a different kind of passengers, but the same hubbub and unresting movement everywhere. I saw no signs of melancholy or seriousness; active pain, violence, brutality, the continual shock of quarrels and blows: but no pensive faces about, no sorrowfulness, nor the kind of trouble which brings thought. Everybody was fully occupied, pushing on as if in a race, pausing for nothing.

The glitter of the lights, the shouts, and sounds of continual going, the endless whirl of passers-by, confused and tired me after a while. I went as far out as I could go to what seemed the outskirts of the place, where I could by glimpses perceive a low horizon all lurid and glowing, which seemed to sweep round and round. Against it in the distance stood up the outline, black against that red glow, of other towers and house-tops, so many and great that there was evidently another town between us and the sunset, if sunset it was. I have seen a western sky like it when there were storms about, and all the colours of the sky were heightened and darkened by angry influences. The distant town rose against it, cutting the firmament so that it might have been tongues of flame flickering between the dark solid outlines; and across the waste open country which lay between the two cities, there came a distant hum like the sound of the sea, which was in reality the roar of that other multitude. The country between showed no greenness or beauty; it lay dark under the dark overhanging sky. Here and there seemed a cluster of giant trees scathed as if by lightning, their bare boughs standing up as high as the distant towers, their trunks like black columns without foliage; openings here and there, with glimmering lights, looked like the mouths of mines: but of passengers there were scarcely any. A figure here and there flew along as if pursued, imperfectly seen, a shadow only a little darker than the space about. And in contrast with the sound of the city, here was no sound at all, except the low roar on either side, and a vague cry or two from the openings of the mine – a scene all drawn in darkness, in variations of gloom, deriving scarcely any light at all from the red and gloomy burning of that distant evening sky.

A faint curiosity to go forward, to see what the mines were, perhaps to get a share in what was brought up from them, crossed my mind. But I was afraid of the dark, of the wild uninhabited savage look of the landscape: though when I thought of it, there seemed no reason why a narrow stretch of country between two great towns should be alarming. But the impression was strong and above reason. I turned back to the street in which I had first alighted, and which seemed to end in a great square full of people. In the middle there was a stage erected, from which some one was delivering an oration or address of some sort. He stood beside a long table, upon which lay something which I could not clearly distinguish, except that it seemed alive and moved, or rather writhed with convulsive twitchings, as if trying to get free of the bonds which confined it. Round the stage in front were a number of seats occupied by listeners, many of whom were women, whose interest seemed to be very great, some of them being furnished with notebooks; while a great unsettled crowd coming and going, drifted round – many, arrested for a time as they passed, proceeding on their way when the interest flagged, as is usual to such open-air assemblies. I followed two of those who pushed their way to within a short distance of the stage, and who were strong, big men, more fitted to elbow the crowd aside than I, after my rough treatment in the first place, and the agitation I had passed through, could be. I was glad, besides, to take advantage of the explanation which one was giving to the other. 'It's always fun to see this fellow demonstrate,' he said, 'and the subject today's a capital one. Let's get well forward, and see all that's going on.'

'Which subject do you mean?' said the other; 'the theme or the example?' And they both laughed, though I did not seize the point of the wit.

'Well, both,' said the first speaker; 'the theme is nerves: and as a lesson in construction and the calculation of possibilities, it's fine. He's very clever at that. He shows how they are all strung to give as much pain and do as much harm as can be; and yet how well it's all managed, don't you know, to look the reverse. As for the example, he's a capital one – all nerves together, lying, if you like, just on the surface, ready for the knife.'

'If they're on the surface I can't see where the fun is,' said the other.

'Metaphorically speaking: of course they are just where other people's nerves are; but he's what you call a highly organised nervous specimen. There will be plenty of fun. Hush! he is just going to begin.'

'The arrangement of these threads of being,' said the

lecturer, evidently resuming after a pause, 'so as to convey to the brain the most instantaneous messages of pain or pleasure, is wonderfully skilful and clever. I need not say to the audience before me, enlightened as it is by experiences of the most striking kind, that the messages are less of pleasure than of pain. They report to the brain the stroke of injury far more often than the thrill of pleasure: though sometimes that too, no doubt, or life could scarcely be maintained. The powers that be have found it necessary to mingle a little sweet of pleasurable sensation, else our miserable race would certainly have found some means of procuring annihilation. I do not for a moment pretend to say that the pleasure is sufficient to offer a just counterbalance to the other. None of my hearers will, I hope, accuse me of inconsistency. I am ready to allow that in a previous condition I asserted somewhat strongly that this was the case. But experience has enlightened us on that point. Our circumstances are now understood by us all, in a manner impossible while we were still in a condition of incompleteness. We are all convinced that there is no compensation. The pride of the position, of bearing everything rather than give in, or making a submission we do not feel, of preserving our own will and individuality to all eternity, is the only compensation. I am satisfied with it, for my part.'

The orator made a pause, holding his head high, and there was a certain amount of applause. The two men before me cheered vociferously. 'That is the right way to look at it,' one of them said. My eyes were upon them, with no particular motive, and I could not help starting, as I saw suddenly underneath their applause and laughter a snarl of cursing, which was the real expression of their thoughts. I felt disposed in the same way to curse the speaker, though I knew no reason why.

He went on a little further, explaining what he meant to do; and then turning round, approached the table. An assistant, who was waiting, uncovered it quickly. The audience stirred with quickened interest, and I with consternation made a step forward, crying out with horror. The object on the table, writhing, twitching, to get free, but bound down by every limb, was a living man. The lecturer went forward calmly, taking his instruments from their case with perfect composure and coolness. 'Now, ladies and gentlemen,' he said: and inserted the knife in the flesh, making a long clear cut in the bound arm. I shrieked out, unable to restrain myself. The sight of the deliberate wound, the blood, the cry of agony that came from the victim, the calmness of all the lookers-on, filled me with horror and rage indescribable. I felt myself clear the crowd away with a rush, and spring on the platform, I could not tell how. 'You devil!' I cried, 'let the man go. Where is the police? – where is a magistrate? – let the man go this moment! fiends in human shape! I'll have you brought to justice!' I heard myself shouting wildly, as I flung myself upon the wretched sufferer, interposing between him and the knife. It was something like this that I said. My horror and rage were delirious, and carried me beyond all attempt at control.

Through it all I heard a shout of laughter rising from everybody round. The lecturer laughed, the audience roared with that sound of horrible mockery which had driven me out of myself in my first experience. All kinds of mocking cries sounded around me. 'Let him a little blood to calm him down.' 'Let the fool have a taste of it himself, doctor.' Last of all came a voice mingled with the cries of the sufferer whom I was trying to shield – 'Take him instead; curse him! take him instead.' I was bending over the man with my arms out-stretched, protecting him, when he gave vent to this cry. And I heard immediately behind me a shout of assent, which seemed to come from the two strong young men with whom I had been standing, and the sound of a rush to seize me. I looked round, half mad with terror and rage; a second more and I should have been strapped on the table too. I made one wild bound into the midst of the crowd, and struggling among the arms stretched out to catch me, amid the roar of the laughter and cries – fled – fled wildly, I knew not whither, in panic and rage and horror, which no words could describe. Terror winged my feet. I flew, thinking as little of whom I met, or knocked down, or trod upon in my way, as the others did at whom I had wondered a little while ago.

No distinct impression of this headlong course remains in my mind, save the sensation of mad fear such as I had never felt before. I came to myself on the edge of the dark valley which surrounded the town. All my pursuers had dropped off before that time, and I have the recollection of flinging myself upon the ground on my face in the extremity of fatigue and exhaustion. I must have lain there undisturbed for some time.

A few steps came and went, passing me; but no one took any notice, and the absence of the noise and crowding gave me a momentary respite. But in my heat and fever I got no relief of coolness from the contact of the soil. I might have flung myself upon a bed of hot ashes, so much was it unlike the dewy cool earth which I expected, upon which one can always throw one's self with a sensation of repose. Presently the uneasiness of it made me struggle up again and look around me. I was safe: at least the cries of the pursuers had died away, the laughter which made my blood boil offended my ears no more. The noise of the city was behind me, softened into an indefinite roar by distance, and before me stretched out the dreary landscape in which there seemed no features of attraction. Now that I was nearer to it, I found it not so unpeopled as I thought. At no great distance from me was the mouth of one of the mines, from which came an indication of subterranean lights: and I perceived that the flying figures which I had taken for travellers between one city and another, were in reality wayfarers endeavouring to keep clear of what seemed a sort of press-gang at the openings. One of them, unable to stop himself in his flight, adopted the same expedient as myself, and threw himself on the ground close to me when he had got beyond the range of pursuit. It was curious that we should meet there, he flying from danger which I was about to face, and ready to encounter that from which I had fled. I waited for a few minutes till he had recovered his breath, and then: 'What are you running from?' I said; 'is there any danger there?' The man looked up at me with the same continual question in his eyes – Who is this fool?

'Danger!' he said. 'Are you so new here, or such a cursed idiot, as not to know the danger of the mines? You are going across yourself, I suppose, and then you'll see.'

'But tell me,' I said; 'my experience may be of use to you afterwards, if you will tell me yours now.'

'Of use!' he cried, staring; 'who cares? Find out for yourself. If they got hold of you, you will soon understand.'

I no longer took this for rudeness, but answered in his own way, cursing him too for a fool. 'If I ask a warning I can give one; as for kindness,' I said, 'I was not looking for that.'

At this he laughed, indeed we laughed together – there seemed something ridiculous in the thought: and presently he told me, for the mere relief of talking, that round each of these pit-mouths there was a band to entrap every passer-by who allowed himself to be caught, and send him down below to work in the mine. 'Once there, there is no telling when you may get free,' he said; 'one time or other most people have a taste of it. You don't know what hard labour is if you have never been there. I had a spell once. There is neither air nor light, your blood boils in your veins from the fervent heat, you are never allowed to rest. You are put in every kind of contortion to get at it, your limbs twisted, and your muscles strained.'

'For what?' I said.

'For gold!' he cried with a flash in his eyes – 'gold! there it is inexhaustible; however hard you may work there is always more, and more!'

'And to whom does all that belong?' I said.

'To whoever is strong enough to get hold and keep possession – sometimes one, sometimes another. The only thing you are sure of is that it will never be you.'

Why not I as well as another? was the thought that went through my mind, and my new companion spied it with a shriek of derision.

'It is not for you nor your kind,' he cried. 'How do you think you could force other people to serve *you*? Can you terrify them or hurt them, or give them anything? You have not learnt yet who are the masters here.'

This troubled me, for it was true. 'I had begun to think,' I said, 'that there was no authority at all – for every man seems to do as he pleases: you ride over one, and knock another down; or you seize a living man and cut him to pieces' – I shuddered as I thought of it – 'and there is nobody to interfere.'

'Who should interfere?' he said. 'Why shouldn't every man amuse himself as he can? But yet for all that we've got our masters,' he cried, with a scowl, waving his clenched fist in the direction of the mines; 'you'll find it out when you get there.'

It was a long time after this before I ventured to move – for here it seemed to me that for the moment I was safe – outside the city, yet not within reach of the dangers of that intermediate space which grew clearer before me as my eyes became accustomed to the lurid threatening afternoon light.

One after another the fugitives came flying past me, – people who had escaped from the armed bands whom I could now see on the watch near the pit's mouth. I could see, too, the tactics of these bands – how they retired, veiling the lights and the opening, when a greater number than usual of travellers appeared on the way, and then suddenly widening out, throwing out flanking lines, surrounded and drew in the unwary. I could even hear the cries with which their victims disappeared over the opening which seemed to go down into the bowels of the earth. By-and-by there came flying towards me a wretch more dreadful in aspect than any I had seen. His scanty clothes seemed singed and burnt into rags; his hair, which hung about his face unkempt and uncared for, had the same singed aspect; his skin was brown and baked. I got up as he approached, and caught him and threw him to the ground, without heeding his struggles to get on. 'Don't you see,' he cried with a gasp, 'they may get me again.' He was one of those who had escaped out of the mines; but what was it to me whether they caught him again or not? I wanted to know how he had been caught, and what he had been set to do, and how he had escaped. Why should I hesitate to use my superior strength when no one else did? I kept watch over him that he should not get away.

'You have been in the mines?' I said.

'Let me go!' he cried; 'do you need to ask?' and he cursed me as he struggled, with the most terrible imprecations. 'They may get me yet. Let me go!'

'Not till you tell me,' I cried. 'Tell me and I'll protect you. If they come near I'll let you go. Who are they, man? I must know.'

He struggled up from the ground, clearing his hot eyes from the ashes that were in them, and putting aside his singed hair. He gave me a glance of hatred and impotent resistance (for I was stronger than he), and then cast a wild terrified look back. The skirmishers did not seem to remark that anybody had escaped, and he became gradually a little more composed. 'Who are they!' he said hoarsely; 'they're cursed wretches like you and me: and there are as many bands of them as there are mines on the road: and you'd better turn back and stay where you are. You are safe here.'

'I will not turn back,' I said.

'I know well enough: you can't. You've got to go the round

like the rest,' he said, with a laugh which was like a sound uttered by a wild animal rather than a human voice. The man was in my power, and I struck him, miserable as he was. It seemed a relief thus to get rid of some of the fury in my mind. 'It's a lie,' I said; 'I go because I please. Why shouldn't I gather a band of my own if I please, and fight those brutes, not fly from them like you?'

He chuckled and laughed below his breath, struggling and cursing and crying out, as I struck him again, '*You* gather a band! What could you offer them? – where would you find them? Are you better than the rest of us? Are you not a man like the rest? Strike me you can, for I'm down. But make yourself a master and a chief – you!'

'Why not I?' I shouted again, wild with rage and the sense that I had no power over him, save to hurt him. That passion made my hands tremble: he slipped from me in a moment, bounded from the ground like a ball, and with a yell of derision escaped, and plunged into the streets and the clamour of the city from which I had just flown. I felt myself rage after him, shaking my fists with a consciousness of the ridiculous passion of impotence that was in me, but no power of restraining it; and there was not one of the fugitives who passed, however desperate he might be, who did not make a mock at me as he darted by. The laughing-stock of all those miserable objects, the sport of fate, afraid to go forward, unable to go back, with a fire in my veins urging me on! But presently I grew a little calmer out of mere exhaustion, which was all the relief that was possible to me. And by-and-by, collecting all my faculties, and impelled by this impulse, which I seemed unable to resist, I got up and went cautiously on.

Fear can act in two ways: it paralyses and it renders cunning. At this moment I found it inspire me. I made my plans before I started, how to steal along under the cover of the blighted brushwood which broke the line of the valley here and there. I set out only after long thought, seizing the moment when the vaguely perceived band were scouring in the other direction intercepting the travellers. Thus, with many pauses, I got near to the pit's mouth in safety. But my curiosity was as great as, almost greater than, my terror. I had kept far from the road, dragging myself sometimes on hands and feet over broken ground, tearing my clothes and my flesh upon the thorns; and on that further side all seemed so silent and so dark in the shadow cast by some disused machinery, behind which the glare of the fire from below blazed upon the other side of the opening, that I could not crawl along in the darkness, and pass, which would have been the safe way; but with a breathless hot desire to see and know, dragged myself to the very edge to look down. Though I was in the shadow, my eyes were nearly put out by the glare on which I gazed. It was not fire; it was the lurid glow of the gold, glowing like flame, at which countless miners were working. They were all about like flies, some on their knees, some bent double as they stooped over their work, some lying cramped upon shelves and ledges. The sight was wonderful, and terrible beyond description. The workmen seemed to consume away with the heat and the glow, even in the few minutes I gazed. Their eyes shrank into their heads, their faces blackened. I could see some trying to secrete morsels of the glowing metal, which burned whatever it touched, and some who were being searched by the superiors of the mines, and some who were punishing the offenders, fixing them up against the blazing wall of gold. The fear went out of my mind, so much absorbed was I in this sight. I gazed, seeing further and further every moment, into crevices and seams of the glowing metal, always with more and more slaves at work, and the entire pantomime of labour and theft, and search and punishment, going on and on – the baked faces dark against the golden glare, the hot eyes taking a yellow reflection, the monotonous clamour of pick and shovel, and cries and curses, and all the indistinguishable sound of a multitude of human creatures. And the floor below, and the low roof which overhung whole myriads within a few inches of their faces, and the irregular walls all breached and shelved, were every one the same, a pandemonium of gold, – gold everywhere. I had loved many foolish things in my life, but never this: which was perhaps why I gazed and kept my sight, though there rose out of it a blast of heat which scorched the brain.

While I stooped over, intent on the sight, some one who had come up by my side to gaze too was caught by the fumes (as I suppose); for suddenly I was aware of a dark object falling prone into the glowing interior with a cry and crash which brought back my first wild panic. He fell in a heap, from which his arms shot forth wildly as he reached the bottom, and his cry was half anguish yet half desire. I saw him seized by half-a-dozen eager watchers, and pitched upon a ledge just under the roof, and tools thrust into his hands. I held on by an old shaft, trembling, unable to move. Perhaps I cried too in my horror – for one of the overseers who stood in the centre of the glare looked up. He had the air of ordering all that was going on, and stood unaffected by the blaze, commanding the other wretched officials, who obeyed him like dogs. He seemed to me, in my terror, like a figure of gold, the image, perhaps, of wealth or Pluto, or I know not what: for I suppose my brain began to grow confused, and my hold on the shaft to relax. I had strength enough, however, for I cared not for the gold, to fling myself back the other way upon the ground, where I rolled backward, downward, I knew not how, turning over and over, upon sharp ashes and metallic edges, which tore my hair and beard, – and for a moment I knew no more.

This fall saved me. I came to myself after a time, and heard the press-gang searching about. I had sense to lie still among the ashes thrown up out of the pit, while I heard their voices. Once I gave myself up for lost. The glitter of a lantern flashed in my eyes, a foot passed, crashing among the ashes so close to my cheek that the shoe grazed it. I found the mark after, burned upon my flesh: but I escaped notice by a miracle. And presently I was able to drag myself up and crawl away. But how I reached the end of the valley I cannot tell. I pushed my way along mechanically on the dark side. I had no further desire to see what was going on in the openings of the mines. I went on, stumbling and stupid, scarcely capable even of fear, conscious only of wretchedness and weariness, till at last I felt myself drop across the road within the gateway of the other town – and lay there, with no thought of anything but the relief of being at rest.

When I came to myself, it seemed to me that there was a change in the atmosphere and the light. It was less lurid, paler, grey, more like twilight than the stormy afternoon of the other city. A certain dead serenity was in the sky – a black paleness, whiteness, everything faint in it. This town was walled, but the gates stood open, and I saw no defences of troops or other guardians. I found myself lying across the threshold, but pushed to one side, so that the carriages which went and came should not be stopped or I injured by their passage. It seemed to me that there was some thoughtfulness and kindness in this action, and my heart sprang up in a reaction of hope. I looked back as if upon a nightmare on the dreadful city which I had left, on its tumults and noise, the wild racket of the streets, the wounded wretches who sought refuge in the corners, the strife and misery that were abroad, and, climax of all, the horrible entertainment which had been going on in the square, the unhappy being strapped upon the table. How, I said to myself, could such things be? Was it a dream? was it a nightmare? was it something presented to me in a vision – a strong delusion to make me think that the old fables which had been told concerning the end of mortal life were true? When I looked back it appeared like an allegory, so that I might have seen it in a dream; and still more like an allegory were the gold-mines in the valley, and the myriads who laboured there. Was it all true? or only a reflection from the old life, mingling with the strange novelties which would most likely elude understanding, on the entrance into this new? I sat within the shelter of the gateway, on my awakening, and thought over all this. My heart was quite calm – almost, in the revulsion from the terrors I had been through, happy. I persuaded myself that I was but now beginning; that there had been no reality in these latter experiences, only a curious succession of nightmares, such as might so well be supposed to follow a wonderful transformation like that which must take place between our mortal life and – the world to come. The world to come! I paused and thought of it all, until the heart began to beat loud in my breast. What was this, where I lay? Another world; a world which was not happiness, not bliss? Oh no – perhaps there was no world of bliss save in dreams. This, on the other hand, I said to myself, was not misery: for was not I seated here, with a certain tremulousness about me it was true, after all the experiences which, supposing them even to have been but dreams, I had come through, – a tremulousness very comprehensible, and not at all without hope?

I will not say that I believed even what I tried to think. Something in me lay like a dark shadow in the midst of all my theories; but yet I succeeded to a great degree in convincing myself that the hope in me was real, and that I was but now beginning – beginning with at least a possibility that all might be well. In this half conviction, and after all the troubles that

were over (even though they might only have been imaginary
troubles), I felt a certain sweetness in resting there, within the
gateway, with my back against it. I was unwilling to get up
again, and bring myself in contact with reality. I felt that there
was pleasure in being left alone. Carriages rolled past me
occasionally, and now and then some people on foot; but they
did not kick me out of the way or interfere with my repose.

Presently as I sat trying to persuade myself to rise and
pursue my way, two men came up to me in a sort of uniform. I
recognised with another distinct sensation of pleasure that
here were people who had authority, representatives of some
kind of government. They came up to me and bade me come
with them in tones which were peremptory enough: but what
of that? – better the most peremptory supervision than the
lawlessness from which I had come. They raised me from the
ground with a touch, for I could not resist them, and led me
quickly along the street, into which that gateway gave access,
which was a handsome street with tall houses on either side.
Groups of people were moving about along the pavement,
talking now and then with considerable animation; but when
my companions were seen, there was an immediate modera-
tion of tone, a sort of respect which looked like fear. There
was no brawling nor tumult of any kind in the street. The only
incident that occurred was this: when we had gone some way,
I saw a lame man dragging himself along with difficulty on
the other side of the street. My conductors had no sooner
perceived him than they gave each other a look and darted
across, conveying me with them, by a sweep of magnetic
influence I thought, that prevented me from staying behind.
He made an attempt with his crutches to get out of the way,
hurrying on – and I will allow that this attempt of his seemed
to me very grotesque, so that I could scarcely help laughing:
the other lookers-on in the street laughed too, though some
put on an aspect of disgust. 'Look, the tortoise!' some one
said; 'does he think he can go quicker than the orderlies?' My
companions came up to the man while this commentary was
going on, and seized him by each arm. 'Where were you
going? Where have you come from? How dare you make an
exhibition of yourself?' they cried. They took the crutches
from him as they spoke and threw them away, and dragged
him on until we reached a great grated door which one of
them opened with a key, while the other held the offender, for

he seemed an offender, roughly up by one shoulder, causing him great pain. When the door was opened, I saw a number of people within, who seemed to crowd to the door as if seeking to get out. But this was not at all what was intended. My second companion dragged the lame man forward, and pushed him in with so much violence that I could see him fall forward on his face on the floor. Then the other locked the door, and we proceeded on our way. It was not till some time later that I understood why.

In the meantime I was hurried on, meeting a great many people who took no notice of me, to a central building in the middle of the town, where I was brought before an official attended by clerks, with great books spread out before him. Here I was questioned as to my name and my antecedents, and the time of my arrival, then dismissed with a nod to one of my conductors. He led me back again down the street, took me into one of the tall great houses, opened the door of a room which was numbered, and left me there without a word. I cannot convey to any one the bewildered consternation with which I felt myself deposited here; and as the steps of my conductor died away in the long corridor, I sat down, and looking myself in the face as it were, tried to make out what it was that had happened to me. The room was small and bare. There was but one thing hung upon the undecorated walls, and that was a long list of printed regulations which I had not the courage for the moment to look at. The light was indifferent, though the room was high up, and the street from the window looked far away below. I cannot tell how long I sat there thinking, and yet it could scarcely be called thought. I asked myself over and over again, Where am I? is it a prison? am I shut in, to leave this enclosure no more? what am I to do? how is the time to pass? I shut my eyes for a moment and tried to realise all that had happened to me; but nothing save a whirl through my head of disconnected thoughts seemed possible, and some force was upon me to open my eyes again, to see the blank room, the dull light, the vacancy round me in which there was nothing to interest the mind, nothing to please the eye, a blank wherever I turned. Presently there came upon me a burning regret for everything I had left, for the noisy town with all its tumults and cruelties, for the dark valley with all its dangers. Everything seemed bearable, almost agreeable, in comparison with this. I seemed to have been brought here to make acquaintance once more with myself, to learn over again what manner of man I was. Needless knowledge, acquaintance unnecessary, unhappy! for what was there in me to make me to myself a good companion? Never, I knew, could I separate myself from that eternal consciousness; but it was cruelty to force the contemplation upon me. All blank, blank, around me, a prison! And was this to last for ever?

I do not know how long I sat, rapt in this gloomy vision; but at last it occurred to me to rise and try the door, which to my astonishment was open. I went out with a throb of new hope. After all, it might not be necessary to come back; there might be other expedients: I might fall among friends. I turned down the long echoing stairs, on which I met various people, who took no notice of me, and in whom I felt no interest save a desire to avoid them, and at last reached the street. To be out of doors in the air was something, though there was no wind, but a motionless still atmosphere which nothing disturbed. The streets, indeed, were full of movement, but not of life – though this seems a paradox. The passengers passed on their way in long regulated lines – those who went towards the gates keeping rigorously to one side of the pavement, those who came, to the other. They talked to each other here and there; but whenever two men in uniform, such as those who had been my conductors, appeared, silence ensued, and the wayfarers shrank even from the looks of these persons in authority. I walked all about the spacious town. Everywhere there were tall houses, everywhere streams of people coming and going, but no one spoke to me, or remarked me at all. I was as lonely as if I had been in a wilderness. I was indeed in a wilderness of men, who were as though they did not see me, passing without even a look of human fellowship, each absorbed in his own concerns. I walked and walked till my limbs trembled under me, from one end to another of the great streets, up and down, and round and round. But no one said, How are you? Whence come you? What are you doing? At length in despair I turned again to the blank and miserable room, which had looked to me like a cell in a prison. I had wilfully made no note of its situation, trying to avoid rather than to find it, but my steps were drawn thither against my will. I found myself retracing my steps, mounting the long stairs, passing the same people, who streamed along with no recognition of me, as I desired nothing to do with them; and at last found myself within the same four blank walls as before.

Soon after I returned I became conscious of measured steps passing the door, and of an eye upon me. I can say no more than this. From what point it was that I was inspected I cannot tell; but that I was inspected, closely scrutinised by some one, and that not only externally, but by a cold observation that went through and through me, I knew and felt beyond any possibility of mistake. This recurred from time to time, horribly, at uncertain moments, so that I never felt myself secure from it. I knew when the watcher was coming by tremors and shiverings through all my being: and no sensation so unsupportable has it ever been mine to bear. How much that is to say, no one can tell who has not gone through those regions of darkness, and learned what is in all their abysses. I tried at first to hide, to fling myself on the floor, to cover my face, to burrow in a dark corner. Useless attempts! The eyes that looked in upon me had powers beyond my powers. I felt sometimes conscious of the derisive smile with which my miserable subterfuges were regarded. They were all in vain.

And what was still more strange was that I had not energy to think of attempting any escape. My steps, though watched, were not restrained in any way, so far as I was aware. The gates of the city stood open on all sides, free to those who went as well as to those who came; but I did not think of flight. Of flight! Whence should I go from myself? Though that horrible inspection was from the eyes of some unseen being, it was in some mysterious way connected with my own thinking and reflections, so that the thought came ever more and more strongly upon me, that from myself I could never escape. And that reflection took all energy, all impulse from me. I might have gone away when I pleased, beyond reach of the authority which regulated everything, – how one should walk, where one should live, – but never from my own consciousness. On the other side of the town lay a great plain, traversed by roads on every side. There was no reason why I should not continue my journey there. But I did not. I had no wish nor any power in me to go away.

In one of my long, dreary, companionless walks, unshared by any human fellowship, I saw at last a face which I remembered; it was that of the cynical spectator who had spoken to me in the noisy street in the midst of my early experiences. He gave a glance round him to see that there were no officials in sight, then left the file in which he was walking, and joined me. 'Ah!' he said, 'you are here already,' with the same derisive smile with which he had before regarded me. I hated the man and his sneer, yet that he should speak to me was something, almost a pleasure.

'Yes,' said I, 'I am here.' Then, after a pause, in which I did not know what to say – 'It is quiet here,' I said.

'Quiet enough. Do you like it better for that? To do whatever you please with no one to interfere; or to do nothing you please, but as you are forced to do it, – which do you think is best?'

I felt myself instinctively glance round, as he had done, to make sure that no one was in sight. Then I answered, faltering, 'I have always held that law and order were necessary things; and the lawlessness of that – that place – I don't know its name – if there is such a place,' I cried, 'I thought it was a dream.'

He laughed in his mocking way. 'Perhaps it is all a dream – who knows?' he said.

'Sir,' said I, 'you have been longer here than I—'

'Oh,' cried he, with a laugh that was dry and jarred upon the air almost like a shriek, 'since before your forefathers were born!' It seemed to me that he spoke like one who, out of bitterness and despite, made every darkness blacker still. A kind of madman in his way; for what was this claim of age? – a piece of bravado, no doubt, like the rest.

'That is strange,' I said, assenting, as when there is such a hallucination it is best to do. 'You can tell me, then, whence all this authority comes, and why we are obliged to obey.'

He looked at me as if he were thinking in his mind how to hurt me most. Then, with that dry laugh, 'We have trial of all things in this world,' he said, 'to see if perhaps we can find something we shall like – discipline here, freedom in the other place. When you have gone all the round like me, then, perhaps, you will be able to choose.'

'Have you chosen?' I asked.

He only answered with a laugh. 'Come,' he said, 'there is amusement to be had too, and that of the most elevated kind. We make researches here into the moral nature of man. Will you come? But you must take the risk,' he added, with a smile which afterwards I understood.

We went on together after this till we reached the centre of the place, in which stood an immense building with a dome, which dominated the city, and into a great hall in the centre of that, where a crowd of people were assembled. The sound of human speech, which murmured all around, brought new life to my heart. And as I gazed at a curious apparatus erected on a platform, several people spoke to me.

'We have again,' said one, 'the old subject today.'

'Is it something about the constitution of the place?' I asked, in the bewilderment of my mind.

My neighbours looked at me with alarm, glancing behind them to see what officials might be near.

'The constitution of the place is the result of the sense of the inhabitants that order must be preserved,' said the one who had spoken to me first. 'The lawless can find refuge in other places. Here we have chosen to have supervision, nuisances removed, and order kept. That is enough. The constitution is not under discussion.'

'But man is,' said a second speaker. 'Let us keep to that in which we can mend nothing. Sir, you may have to contribute your quota to our enlightenment. We are investigating the rise of thought. You are a stranger; you may be able to help us.'

'I am no philosopher,' I said, with a panic which I could not explain to myself.

'That does not matter. You are a fresh subject.' The speaker made a slight movement with his hand, and I turned round to escape in wild, sudden fright, though I had no conception what could be done to me. But the crowd had pressed close round me, hemming me in on every side. I was so wildly alarmed that I struggled among them, pushing backwards with all my force, and clearing a space round me with my arms. But my efforts were vain. Two of the officers suddenly appeared out of the crowd, and seizing me by the arms, forced me forward. The throng dispersed before them on either side, and I was half dragged, half lifted up upon the platform which I had contemplated with a dull wonder when I came into the hall. My wonder did not last long. I felt myself fixed in it, standing supported in that position by bands and springs, so that no effort of mine was necessary to hold myself up, and none possible to release myself. I was caught by every joint, sustained, supported, exposed to the gaze of what seemed a world of upturned faces: among which I saw, with a sneer upon it, keeping a little behind the crowd, the face of the man who had led me here. Above my head was a strong light, more brilliant than anything I had ever seen, and which blazed upon my brain till the hair seemed to singe and the skin shrink. I hope I may never feel such a sensation again. The pitiless light went into me like a knife; but even my cries were stopped by the framework in which I was bound. I could breathe and suffer, but that was all.

Then some one got up on the platform above me and began to speak. He said, so far as I could comprehend in the anguish and torture in which I was held, that the origin of thought was the question he was investigating, but that in every previous subject the confusion of ideas had bewildered them, and the rapidity with which one followed another. 'The present example has been found to exhibit great persistency of idea,' he said. 'We hope that by his means some clearer theory may be arrived at.' Then he pulled over me a great movable lens as of a microscope, which concentrated the insupportable light. The wild, hopeless passion that raged within my soul had no outlet in the immovable apparatus that held me. I was let down among the crowd, and exhibited to them, every secret movement of my being, by some awful process which I have never fathomed. A burning fire was in my brain, flame seemed to run along all my nerves, speechless, horrible, incommunicable fury raged in my soul. But I was like a child – nay, like an image of wood or wax in the pitiless hands that held me. What was the cut of a surgeon's knife to this? And I had thought *that* cruel! And I was powerless, and could do nothing – to blast, to destroy, to burn with this same horrible flame the fiends that surrounded me, as I desired to do.

Suddenly, in the raging fever of my thoughts, there surged up the recollection of that word which had paralysed all around, and myself with them. The thought that I must share the anguish, did not restrain me from my revenge. With a tremendous effort I got my voice, though the instrument pressed upon my lips. I know not what I articulated save 'God', whether it was a curse or a blessing. I had been swung out into the middle of the hall, and hung amid the crowd,

exposed to all their observations, when I succeeded in gaining
utterance. My God! my God! Another moment and I had
forgotten them and all my fury in the tortures that arose
within myself. What, then, was the light that racked my
brain? Once more my life from its beginning to its end rose
up before me – each scene like a spectre, like the harpies of the
old fables rending me with tooth and claw. Once more I saw
what might have been, the noble things I might have done,
the happiness I had lost, the turnings of the fated road which
I might have taken, – everything that was once so possible, so
possible, so easy! but now possible no more. My anguish was
immeasurable; I turned and wrenched myself, in the strength
of pain, out of the machinery that held me, and fell down,
down among all the curses that were being hurled at me –
among the horrible and miserable crowd. I had brought upon
them the evil which I shared, and they fell upon me with a
fury which was like that which had prompted myself a few
minutes before. But they could do nothing to me so tremendous as the vengeance I had taken upon them. I was too
miserable to feel the blows that rained upon me, but presently
I suppose I lost consciousness altogether, being almost torn to
pieces by the multitude.

While this lasted, it seemed to me that I had a dream. I felt
the blows raining down upon me, and my body struggling
upon the ground; and yet it seemed to me that I was lying
outside upon the ground, and above me the pale sky which
never brightened at the touch of the sun. And I thought that
dull, persistent cloud wavered and broke for an instant, and
that I saw behind a glimpse of that blue which is heaven when
we are on the earth – the blue sky – which is nowhere to be
seen but in the mortal life; which is heaven enough, which is
delight enough, for those who can look up to it, and feel
themselves in the land of hope. It might be but a dream: in
this strange world who could tell what was vision and what
was true?

The next thing I remember was, that I found myself lying
on the floor of a great room full of people, with every kind of
disease and deformity, some pale with sickness, some with
fresh wounds, the lame, and the maimed, and the miserable.
They lay round me in every attitude of pain, many with sores,
some bleeding, with broken limbs, but all struggling, some on
hands and knees, dragging themselves up from the ground to

stare at me. They roused in my mind a loathing and sense of disgust which it is impossible to express. I could scarcely tolerate the thought that I – I! should be forced to remain a moment in this lazar-house. The feeling with which I had regarded the miserable creature who shared the corner of the wall with me, and who had cursed me for being sorry for him, had altogether gone out of my mind. I called out, to whom I know not, adjuring some one to open the door and set me free; but my cry was answered only by a shout from my companions in trouble. 'Who do you think will let you out?' 'Who is going to help you more than the rest?' My whole body was racked with pain; I could not move from the floor, on which I lay. I had to put up with the stares of the curious, and the mockeries, and remarks on me of whoever chose to criticise. Among them was the lame man whom I had seen thrust in by the two officers who had taken me from the gate. He was the first to gibe. 'But for him they would never have seen me,' he said. 'I should have been well by this time in the fresh air.' 'It is his turn now,' said another. I turned my head as well as I could and spoke to them all.

'I am a stranger here,' I cried. 'They have made my brain burn with their experiments. Will nobody help me? It is no fault of mine, it is their fault. If I am to be left here uncared for, I shall die.'

At this a sort of dreadful chuckle ran round the place. 'If that is what you are afraid of, you will not die,' somebody said, touching me on my head in a way which gave me intolerable pain, 'Don't touch me,' I cried. 'Why shouldn't I?' said the other, and pushed me again upon the throbbing brain. So far as my sensations went, there were no coverings at all, neither skull nor skin upon the intolerable throbbing of my head, which had been exposed to the curiosity of the crowd, and every touch was agony; but my cry brought no guardian, nor any defence or soothing. I dragged myself into a corner after a time, from which some other wretch had been rolled out in the course of a quarrel; and as I found that silence was the only policy, I kept silent, with rage consuming my heart.

Presently I discovered by means of the new arrivals which kept coming in, hurled into the midst of us without thought or question, that this was the common fate of all who were repulsive to the sight, or who had any weakness or imperfection which offended the eyes of the population. They were tossed in among us, not to be healed, or for repose or safety, but to be out of sight, that they might not disgust or annoy those who were more fortunate to whom no injury had happened; and because in their sickness and imperfection they were of no use in the studies of the place and disturbed the good order of the streets. And there they lay one above another, a mass of bruised and broken creatures, most of them suffering from injuries which they had sustained in what would have been called in other regions the service of the State. They had served like myself as objects of experiments. They had fallen from heights where they had been placed, in illustration of some theory. They had been tortured or twisted to give satisfaction to some question. And then, that the consequences of these proceedings might offend no one's eyes, they were flung into this receptacle, to be released if chance or strength enabled them to push their way out when others were brought in, or when their importunate knocking wearied some watchman, and brought him angry and threatening to hear what was wanted. The sound of this knocking against the door, and of the cries that accompanied it, and the rush towards the opening when any one was brought in, caused a hideous continuous noise and scuffle which was agony to my brain. Every one pushed before the other; there was an endless rising and falling as in the changes of a feverish dream, each man as he got strength to struggle forward himself, thrusting back his neighbours, and those who were nearest to the door beating upon it without cease, like the beating of a drum without cadence or measure, sometimes a dozen passionate hands together, making a horrible din and riot. As I lay unable to join in that struggle, and moved by rage unspeakable towards all who could, I reflected strangely that I had never heard when outside this horrible continual appeal of the suffering. In the streets of the city, as I now reflected, quiet reigned. I had even made comparisons on my first entrance, in the moment of pleasant anticipation which came over me, of the happy stillness here, with the horror and tumult of that place of unrule which I had left.

When my thoughts reached this point I was answered by the voice of some one on a level with myself, lying helpless like me on the floor of the lazar-house. 'They have taken their precautions,' he said; 'if they will not endure the sight of suffering, how should they hear the sound of it? Every cry is silenced there.'

'I wish they could be silenced within too,' I cried savagely; 'I would make them dumb had I the power.'

'The spirit of the place is in you,' said the other voice.

'And not in you?' I said, raising my head, though every movement was agony; but this pretence of superiority was more than I could bear.

The other made no answer for a moment: then he said, faintly, 'If it is so, it is but for greater misery.'

And then his voice died away, and the hubbub of beating, and crying, and cursing, and groaning filled all the echoes. They cried, but no one listened to them. They thundered on the door, but in vain. They aggravated all their pangs in that mad struggle to get free. After a while my companion, whoever he was, spoke again.

'They would rather,' he said, 'lie on the roadside to be kicked and trodden on, as we have seen; though to see that made you miserable.'

'Made me miserable! You mock me,' I said. 'Why should a man be miserable save for suffering of his own?'

'You thought otherwise once,' my neighbour said.

And then I remembered the wretch in the corner of the wall in the other town, who had cursed me for pitying him. I cursed myself now for that folly. Pity him! was he not better off than I? 'I wish,' I cried, 'that I could crush them into nothing, and be rid of this infernal noise they make!'

'The spirit of the place has entered into you,' said that voice.

I raised my arm to strike him; but my hand fell on the stone floor instead, and sent a jar of new pain all through my battered frame. And then I mastered my rage, and lay still, for I knew there was no way but this of recovering my strength, – the strength with which, when I got it back, I would annihilate that reproachful voice, and crush the life out of those groaning fools, whose cries and impotent struggles I could not endure. And we lay a long time without moving, with always that tumult raging in our ears. At last there came into my mind a longing to hear spoken words again. I said, 'Are you still there?'

'I shall be here,' he said, 'till I am able to begin again.'

'To begin! Is there here, then, either beginning or

ending? Go on: speak to me: it makes me a little forget my pain.'

'I have a fire in my heart,' he said; 'I must begin and begin – till perhaps I find the way.'

'What way?' I cried, feverish and eager; for though I despised him, yet it made me wonder to think that he should speak riddles which I could not understand.

He answered very faintly, 'I do not know.' The fool! then it was only folly, as from the first I knew it was. I felt then that I could treat him roughly, after the fashion of the place – which he said had got into me. 'Poor wretch!' I said, 'you have hopes, have you? Where have you come from? You might have learned better before now.'

'I have come,' he said, 'from where we met before. I have come by the valley of gold. I have worked in the mines. I have served in the troops of those who are masters there. I have lived in this town of tyrants, and lain in this lazar-house before. Everything has happened to me, more and worse than you dream of.'

'And still you go on? I would dash my head against the wall and die.'

'When will you learn,' he said, with a strange tone in his voice, which, though no one had been listening to us, made a sudden silence for a moment – it was so strange: it moved me like that glimmer of the blue sky in my dream, and roused all the sufferers round with an expectation – though I know not what. The cries stopped, the hands beat no longer. I think all the miserable crowd were still, and turned to where he lay. 'When will you learn – that you have died, and can die no more?'

There was a shout of fury all round me. 'Is that all you have to say?' the crowd burst forth: and I think they rushed upon him and killed him: for I heard no more: until the hubbub began again more wild than ever, with furious hands beating, beating, against the locked door.

After a while I began to feel my strength come back. I raised my head. I sat up. I began to see the faces of those around me, and the groups into which they gathered; the noise was no longer so insupportable – my racked nerves were regaining health. It was with a mixture of pleasure and despair that I became conscious of this. I had been through many deaths; but I did not die, perhaps could not, as that man

had said. I looked about for him, to see if he had contradicted
his own theory. But he was not dead. He was lying close to
me, covered with wounds; but he opened his eyes, and
something like a smile came upon his lips. A smile – I had
heard laughter, and seen ridicule and derision, but this I had
not seen. I could not bear it. To seize him and shake the little
remaining life out of him was my impulse. But neither did I
obey that. Again he reminded me of my dream – was it a
dream? – of the opening in the clouds. From that moment I
tried to shelter him, and as I grew stronger and stronger, and
pushed my way to the door, I dragged him along with me.
How long the struggle was I cannot tell, or how often I was
balked – or how many darted through before me when the
door was opened. But I did not let him go; and at the last, for
now I was as strong as before – stronger than most about me –
I got out into the air and brought him with me. Into the air! it
was an atmosphere so still and motionless that there was no
feeling of life in it, as I have said; but the change seemed to me
happiness for the moment. It was freedom. The noise of the
struggle was over, the horrible sights were left behind. My
spirit sprang up as if I had been born into new life. It had the
same effect, I suppose, upon my companion, though he was
much weaker than I, for he rose to his feet at once with almost
a leap of eagerness, and turned instantaneously towards the
other side of the city.

'Not that way,' I said; 'come with me and rest.'

'No rest – no rest – my rest is to go on;' and then he turned
towards me and smiled and said 'Thanks' – looking into my
face. What a word to hear! I had not heard it since – A rush of
strange and sweet and dreadful thoughts came into my mind.
I shrank and trembled, and let go his arm, which I had been
holding. But when I left that hold I seemed to fall back into
depths of blank pain and longing. I put out my hand again and
caught him. 'I will go,' I said, 'where you go.'

A pair of the officials of the place passed as I spoke. They
looked at me with a threatening glance, and half paused, but
then passed on. It was I now who hurried my companion
along. I recollected him now. He was a man who had met me
in the streets of the other city when I was still ignorant, who
had convulsed me with the utterance of that name which, in
all this world where we were, is never named but for punishment, – the name which I had named once more in the great

hall in the midst of my torture, so that all who heard me were transfixed with that suffering too. He had been haggard then, but he was more haggard now. His features were sharp with continual pain, his eyes were wild with weakness and trouble, though there was a meaning in them which went to my heart. It seemed to me that in his touch there was a certain help, though he was weak and tottered, and every moment seemed full of suffering. Hope sprang up in my mind – the hope that where he was so eager to go there would be something better, a life more liveable than in this place. In every new place there is new hope. I was not worn out of that human impulse. I forgot the nightmare which had crushed me before – the horrible sense that from myself there was no escape – and holding fast to his arm, I hurried on with him, not heeding where. We went aside into less frequented streets, that we might escape observation. I seemed to myself the guide, though I was the follower. A great faith in this man sprang up in my breast. I was ready to go with him wherever he went, anywhere – anywhere must be better than this. Thus I pushed him on, holding by his arm, till we reached the very outmost limits of the city. Here he stood still for a moment, turning upon me, and took me by the hands.

'Friend,' he said, 'before you were born into the pleasant earth I had come here. I have gone all the weary round. Listen to one who knows: all is harder, harder, as you go on. You are stirred to go on by the restlessness in your heart, and each new place you come to the spirit of that place enters into you. You are better here than you will be further on. You were better where you were at first, or even in the mines than here. Come on further. Stay – unless—' but here his voice gave way. He looked at me with anxiety in his eyes, and said no more.

'Then why,' I cried, 'do you go on? Why do you not stay?'

He shook his head, and his eyes grew more and more soft. 'I am going,' he said, and his voice shook again. 'I am going – to try – the most awful and the most dangerous journey—' His voice died away altogether, and he only looked at me to say the rest.

'A journey? Where?'

I can tell no man what his eyes said. I understood, I cannot tell how; and with trembling all my limbs seemed to drop out of joint and my face grow moist with terror. I could not speak any more than he, but with my lips shaped, How? The awful thought made a tremor in the very air around. He shook his head slowly as he looked at me – his eyes, all circled with deep lines, looking out of caves of anguish and anxiety; and then I remembered how he had said, and I had scoffed at him, that the way he sought was one he did not know. I had dropped his hands in my fear; and yet to leave him seemed dragging the heart out of my breast, for none but he had spoken to me like a brother – had taken my hand and thanked me. I looked out across the plain, and the roads seemed tranquil and still. There was a coolness in the air. It looked like evening, as if somewhere in those far distances there might be a place where a weary soul might rest. Then I looked behind me, and thought what I had suffered, and remembered the lazar-house and the voices that cried and the hands that beat against the door; and also the horrible quiet of the room in which I lived, and the eyes which looked in at me and turned my gaze upon myself. Then I rushed after him, for he had turned to go on upon his way; and caught at his clothes, crying – 'Behold me, behold me! I will go too!'

He reached me his hand and went on without a word; and I with terror crept after him, treading in his step, following like his shadow. What it was to walk with another, and follow, and be at one, is more than I can tell; but likewise my heart failed me for fear, for dread of what we might encounter, and of hearing that name, or entering that presence, which was more terrible than all torture. I wondered how it could be that one should willingly face *that* which racked the soul, and how he had learned that it was possible, and where he had heard of the way. And as we went on I said no word – for he began to seem to me a being of another kind, a figure full of awe; and I followed as one might follow a ghost. Where would he go? Were we not fixed here for ever, where our lot had been cast? and there were still many other great cities where there might be much to see, and something to distract the mind, and where it might be more possible to live than it had proved in the other places. There might be no tyrants there, nor cruelty, nor horrible noises, nor dreadful silence. Towards the right hand, across the plain, there seemed to rise out of the grey distance a cluster of towers and roofs like another habitable place – and who could tell that something better might not be there? Surely everything could not turn to torture and misery. I dragged on behind him, with all these thoughts hurrying through my mind. He was going – I dare to say it now, though I did not dare then – to seek out a way to God; to try, if it was possible, to find the road that led back – that road which had been open once to all. But for me, I trembled at the thought of that road. I feared the name, which was as the plunging of a sword into my inmost parts. All things could be borne but that. I dared not even think upon that name. To feel my hand in another man's hand was much, but to be led into that awful presence, by awful ways, which none knew – how could I bear it? My spirits failed me, and my strength. My hand became loose in his hand: he grasped me still, but my hold failed, and ever with slower and slower steps I followed, while he seemed to acquire strength with every winding of the way. At length he said to me, looking back upon me, 'I cannot stop: but your heart fails you. Shall I loose my hand and let you go?'

'I am afraid; I am afraid!' I cried.

'And I too am afraid; but it is better to suffer more and to escape than to suffer less and to remain.'

'Has it ever been known that one escaped? No one has ever escaped. This is our place,' I said, 'there is no other world.'

'There are other worlds – there is a world where every way leads to One who loves us still.'

I cried out with a great cry of misery and scorn. 'There is no love!' I said.

He stood still for a moment and turned and looked at me. His eyes seemed to melt my soul. A great cloud passed over them, as in the pleasant earth a cloud will sweep across the moon; and then the light came out and looked at me again. For neither did he know. Where he was going all might end in despair and double pain. But if it were possible that at the end there should be found that for which he longed, upon which his heart was set! He said with a faltering voice – 'Among all whom I have questioned and seen there was but one who found the way. But if one has found it, so may I. If you will not come, yet let me go.'

'They will tear you limb from limb – they will burn you in the endless fires,' I said. But what is it to be torn limb from limb, or burned with fire? There came upon his face a smile, and in my heart even I laughed to scorn what I had said.

'If I were dragged every nerve apart, and every thought turned into a fiery dart – and that is so,' he said; 'yet will I go, if but, perhaps, I may see Love at the end.'

'There is no love!' I cried again, with a sharp and bitter cry; and the echo seemed to come back and back from every side, No love! no love! till the man who was my friend faltered and stumbled like a drunken man; but afterwards he recovered strength and resumed his way.

And thus once more we went on. On the right hand was that city, growing ever clearer, with noble towers rising up to the sky, and battlements and lofty roofs, and behind a yellow clearness, as of a golden sunset. My heart drew me there; it sprang up in my breast and sang in my ears, Come, and Come. Myself invited me to this new place as to a home. The others were wretched, but this will be happy: delights and pleasures will be there. And before us the way grew dark with storms, and there grew visible among the mists a black line of mountains, perpendicular cliffs, and awful precipices, which seemed to bar the way. I turned from that line of gloomy heights, and gazed along the path to where the towers stood up against the sky. And presently my hand dropped by my side, that had been held in my companion's hand; and I saw him no more.

I went on to the city of the evening light. Ever and ever, as I proceeded on my way, the sense of haste and restless impatience grew upon me, so that I felt myself incapable of remaining long in a place, and my desire grew stronger to hasten on and on; but when I entered the gates of the city this longing vanished from my mind. There seemed some great festival or public holiday going on there. The streets were full of pleasure-parties, and in every open place (of which there were many) were bands of dancers, and music playing; and the houses about were hung with tapestries and embroideries and garlands of flowers. A load seemed to be taken from my spirit when I saw all this – for a whole population does not rejoice in such a way without some cause. And to think that, after all, I had found a place in which I might live and forget the misery and pain which I had known, and all that was behind me, was delightful to my soul. It seemed to me that all the dancers were beautiful and young, their steps went gaily to the music, their faces were bright with smiles. Here and there was a master of the feast, who arranged the dances and guided the musicians, yet seemed to have a look and smile for newcomers too. One of these came forward to meet me, and received me with a welcome, and showed me a vacant place at a table, on which were beautiful fruits piled up in baskets, and all the provisions for a meal. 'You were expected, you perceive,' he said. A delightful sense of well-being came into my mind. I sat down in the sweetness of ease after fatigue, of refreshment after weariness, of pleasant sounds and sights after the arid way. I said to myself that my past experiences had been a mistake, that this was where I ought to have come from the first, that life here would be happy, and that all intruding thoughts must soon vanish and die away.

After I had rested, I strolled about, and entered fully into the pleasures of the place. Wherever I went, through all the city, there was nothing but brightness and pleasure, music playing, and flags waving, and flowers and dancers and everything that was most gay. I asked several people whom I met what was the cause of the rejoicing; but either they were too much occupied with their own pleasures, or my question was lost in the hum of merriment, the sound of the instruments and of the dancers' feet. When I had seen as much as I desired of the pleasure out of doors, I was taken by some to see the interiors of houses, which were all decorated for this festival, whatever it was – lighted up with curious varieties of lighting, in tints of different colours. The doors and windows were all open, and whosoever would could come in from the dance or from the laden tables, and sit down where they pleased and rest, always with a pleasant view out upon the streets, so that they should lose nothing of the spectacle. And the dresses, both of women and men, were beautiful in form and colour, made in the finest fabrics, and affording delightful combinations to the eye. The pleasure which I took in all I saw and heard was enhanced by the surprise of it, and by the aspect of the places from which I had come, where there was no regard to beauty nor anything lovely or bright. Before my arrival here I had come in my thoughts to the conclusion that life had no brightness in these regions, and that whatever occupation or study there might be, pleasure had ended and was over, and everything that had been sweet in the former life. I changed that opinion with a sense of relief, which was more warm even than the pleasure of the present moment; for having made one such mistake, how could I tell that there were not more discoveries awaiting me, that life might not prove more endurable, might not rise to something grander and more powerful? The old prejudices, the old foregone conclusion of earth that this was a world of punishment, had warped my vision and my thoughts. With so many added faculties of being, incapable of fatigue as we were, incapable of death, recovering from every wound or accident as I had myself done, and with no foolish restraint as to what we should or should not do, why might not we rise in this land to strength unexampled, to the highest powers? I rejoiced that I had dropped my companion's hand, that I had not followed him in his mad quest. Some time, I said to myself, I would make a pilgrimage to the foot of those gloomy mountains, and bring him back, all racked and tortured as he was, and show him the pleasant place which he had missed.

In the meantime the music and dance went on. But it began to surprise me a little that there was no pause, that the festival continued without intermission. I went up to one of those who seemed the masters of ceremony, directing what was going on. He was an old man, with a flowing robe of brocade, and a chain and badge which denoted his office. He stood with a smile upon his lips, beating time with his hand to the music, watching the figure of the dance.

'I can get no one to tell me,' I said, 'what the occasion of all this rejoicing is.'

'It is for your coming,' he replied, without hesitation, with a smile and a bow.

For a moment a wonderful elation came over me. 'For my coming!' But then I paused and shook my head. 'There are others coming besides me. See! they arrive every moment.'

'It is for their coming too,' he said, with another smile and a still deeper bow; 'but you are the first as you are the chief.'

This was what I could not understand; but it was pleasant to hear, and I made no further objection. 'And how long will it go on?' I said.

'So long as it pleases you,' said the old courtier.

How he smiled! His smile did not please me. He saw this, and distracted my attention. 'Look at this dance,' he said; 'how beautiful are those round young limbs! Look how the dress conceals yet shows the form and beautiful movements! It was invented in your honour. All that is lovely is for you. Choose where you will, all yours. We live only for this: all is for you.' While he spoke, the dancers came nearer and nearer till they circled us round, and danced and made their pretty obeisances, and sang: 'All is yours; all is for you:'

then breaking their lines floated away in other circles and processions and endless groups, singing and laughing till it seemed to ring from every side, 'Everything is yours; all is for you.'

I accepted this flattery I know not why: for I soon became aware that I was no more than others, and that the same words were said to every newcomer. Yet my heart was elated, and I threw myself into all that was set before me. But there was always in my mind an expectation that presently the music and the dancing would cease, and the tables be withdrawn, and a pause come. At one of the feasts I was placed by the side of a lady very fair and richly dressed, but with a look of great weariness in her eyes. She turned her beautiful face to me, not with any show of pleasure, and there was something like compassion in her look. She said, 'You are very tired,' as she made room for me by her side.

'Yes,' I said, though with surprise, for I had not yet acknowledged that even to myself. 'There is so much to enjoy. We have need of a little rest.'

'Of rest,' said she, shaking her head, 'this is not the place for rest.'

'Yet pleasure requires it,' I said, 'as much as—' I was about to say pain; but why should one speak of pain in a place given up to pleasure? She smiled faintly and shook her head again. All her movements were languid and faint; her eyelids drooped over her eyes. Yet, when I turned to her, she made an effort to smile. 'I think you are also tired,' I said.

At this she roused herself a little. 'We must not say so: nor do I say so. Pleasure is very exacting. It demands more of you than anything else. One must be always ready—'

'For what?'

'To give enjoyment, and to receive it.' There was an effort in her voice to rise to this sentiment, but it fell back into weariness again.

'I hope you receive as well as give,' I said.

The lady turned her eyes to me with a look which I cannot forget, and life seemed once more to be roused within her. But not the life of pleasure: her eyes were full of loathing, and fatigue, and disgust, and despair. 'Are you so new to this place,' she said, 'and have not learned even yet what is the height of all misery and all weariness: what is worse than pain and trouble, more dreadful than the lawless streets and the burning mines, and the torture of the great hall and the misery of the lazar-house—'

'Oh, lady!' I said, 'have you been there?'

She answered me with her eyes alone; there was no need of more. 'But pleasure is more terrible than all,' she said; and I knew in my heart that what she said was true.

There is no record of time in that place. I could not count it by days or nights: but soon after this it happened to me that the dances and the music became no more than a dizzy maze of sound and sight, which made my brain whirl round and round; and I too loathed what was spread on the table, and the soft couches, and the garlands, and the fluttering flags and ornaments. To sit for ever at a feast, to see for ever the merry-makers turn round and round, to hear in your ears for ever the whirl of the music, the laughter, the cries of pleasure! There were some who went on and on, and never seemed to tire; but to me the endless round came at last to be a torture from which I could not escape. Finally, I could distinguish nothing – neither what I heard nor what I saw: and only a conscious-ness of something intolerable buzzed and echoed in my brain. I longed for the quiet of the place I had left; I longed for the noise in the streets, and the hubbub and tumult of my first experiences. Anything, anything rather than this! I said to myself; and still the dancers turned, the music sounded, the bystanders smiled, and everything went on and on. My eyes grew weary with seeing, and my ears with hearing. To watch the newcomers rush in, all pleased and eager, to see the eyes of the others glaze with weariness, wrought upon my strained nerves. I could not think, I could not rest, I could not endure. Music for ever and ever – a whirl, a rush of music, always going on and on; and ever that maze of movement, till the eyes were feverish and the mouth parched; ever that mist of faces, now one gleaming out of the chaos, now another, some like the faces of angels, some miserable, weary, strained with smiling, with the monotony, and the endless, aimless, never-changing round. I heard myself calling to them to be still – to be still! to pause a moment. I felt myself stumble and turn round in the giddiness and horror of that movement without repose. And finally, I fell under the feet of the crowd, and felt the whirl go over and over me, and beat upon my brain, until I was pushed and thrust out of the way lest I should stop the measure. There I lay, sick, satiate, for I know not how long; loathing everything around me, ready to give all I had (but what had I to give?) for one moment of silence. But always the music went on, and the dancers danced, and the people feasted, and the songs and the voices echoed up to the skies.

How at last I stumbled forth I cannot tell. Desperation must have moved me, and that impatience which, after every hope and disappointment, comes back and back, the one sensation that never fails. I dragged myself at last by intervals, like a sick dog, outside the revels, still hearing them, which was torture to me, even when at last I got beyond the crowd. It was something to lie still upon the ground, though without power to move, and sick beyond all thought, loathing myself and all that I had been and seen. For I had not even the sense that I had been wronged to keep me up, but only a nausea and horror of movement, a giddiness and whirl of every sense. I lay like a log upon the ground.

When I recovered my faculties a little, it was to find myself once more in the great vacant plain which surrounded that accursed home of pleasure – a great and desolate waste upon which I could see no track, which my heart fainted to look at, which no longer roused any hope in me, as if it might lead to another beginning, or any place in which yet at the last it might be possible to live. As I lay in that horrible giddiness and faintness, I loathed life and this continuance which brought me through one misery after another, and forbade me to die. Oh that death would come – death which is silent and still, which makes no movement and hears no sound! that I might end and be no more! Oh that I could go back even to the stillness of that chamber which I had not been able to endure! Oh that I could return – return! to what? to other miseries and other pain, which looked less because they were past. But I knew now that return was impossible until I had circled all the dreadful round; and already I felt again the burning of that desire that pricked and drove me on – not back, for that was impossible. Little by little I had learned to understand, each step printed upon my brain as with red-hot irons: not back, but on, and on. To greater anguish, yes; but on: to fuller despair, to experiences more terrible: but on, and on, and on. I arose again, for this was my fate. I could not pause even for all the teachings of despair.

The waste stretched far as eyes could see. It was wild and

terrible, with neither vegetation nor sign of life. Here and there were heaps of ruin, which had been villages and cities; but nothing was in them save reptiles and crawling poisonous life, and traps for the unwary wanderer. How often I stumbled and fell among these ashes and dust-heaps of the past – through what dread moments I lay, with cold and slimy things leaving their trace upon my flesh – the horrors which seized me, so that I beat my head against a stone, – why should I tell? These were nought; they touched not the soul. They were but accidents of the way.

At length, when body and soul were low and worn out with misery and weariness, I came to another place, where all was so different from the last, that the sight gave me a momentary solace. It was full of furnaces and clanking machinery and endless work. The whole air round was aglow with the fury of the fires, and men went and came like demons in the flames, with red-hot melting metal, pouring it into moulds and beating it on anvils. In the huge workshops in the background there was a perpetual whir of machinery – of wheels turning and turning, and pistons beating, and all the din of labour, which for a time renewed the anguish of my brain, yet also soothed it; for there was meaning in the beatings and the whirlings. And a hope rose within me that with all the forces that were here, some revolution might be possible – something that would change the features of this place and overturn the worlds. I went from workshop to workshop, and examined all that was being done and understood – for I had known a little upon the earth, and my old knowledge came back, and to learn so much more filled me with new life. The master of all was one who never rested, nor seemed to feel weariness, nor pain, nor pleasure. He had everything in his hand. All who were there were his workmen, or his assistants, or his servants. No one shared with him in his councils. He was more than a prince among them – he was as a god. And the things he planned and made, and at which in armies and legions his workmen toiled and laboured, were like living things. They were made of steel and iron, but they moved like the brains and nerves of men. They went where he directed them, and did what he commanded, and moved at a touch. And though he talked little, when he saw how I followed all that he did, he was a little moved towards me, and spoke and explained to me the conceptions that were in his mind, one rising out of another, like the leaf out of the stem and the flower out of the bud. For nothing pleased him that he did, and necessity was upon him to go on and on.

'They are like living things,' I said – 'they do your bidding whatever you command them. They are like another and a stronger race of men.'

'Men!' he said, 'what are men? the most contemptible of all things that are made – creatures who will undo in a moment what it has taken millions of years, and all the skill and all the strength of generations to do. These are better than men. They cannot think or feel. They cannot stop but at my bidding, or begin unless I will. Had men been made so, we should be masters of the world.'

'Had men been made so, you would never have been – for what could genius have done or thought? – you would have been a machine like all the rest.'

'And better so!' he said, and turned away; for at that moment, watching keenly as he spoke the action of a delicate combination of movements, all made and balanced to a hair's breadth, there had come to him suddenly the idea of something which made it a hundredfold more strong and terrible. For they were terrible these things that lived yet did not live, which were his slaves, and moved at his will. When he had done this, he looked at me, and a smile came upon his mouth: but his eyes smiled not, nor ever changed from the set look they wore. And the words he spoke were familiar words, not his, but out of the old life. 'What a piece of work is a man!' he said; 'how noble in reason, how infinite in faculty! in form and moving how express and admirable! And yet to me what is this quintessence of dust?' His mind had followed another strain of thought, which to me was bewildering, so that I did not know how to reply. I answered like a child, upon his last word.

'We are dust no more,' I cried, for pride was in my heart – pride of him and his wonderful strength, and his thoughts which created strength, and all the marvels he did – 'those things which hindered are removed. Go on, go on – you want but another step. What is to prevent that you should not shake the universe, and overturn this doom, and break all our bonds? There is enough here to explode this grey fiction of a firmament, and to rend those precipices and to dissolve that waste – as at the time when the primeval seas dried up, and those infernal mountains rose.'

He laughed, and the echoes caught the sound and gave it back as if they mocked it. 'There is enough to rend us all into shreds,' he said, 'and shake, as you say, both heaven and earth, and these plains and those hills.'

'Then why,' I cried in my haste, with a dreadful hope piercing through my soul – 'why do you create and perfect, but never employ? When we had armies on the earth we used them. You have more than armies. You have force beyond the thoughts of man: but all without use as yet.'

'All,' he cried, 'for no use! All in vain! – in vain!'

'O master!' I said, 'great, and more great, in time to come. Why? – why?'

He took me by the arm and drew me close.

'Have you strength,' he said, 'to bear it if I tell you why?'

I knew what he was about to say. I felt it in the quivering of my veins, and my heart that bounded as if it would escape from my breast. But I would not quail from what he did not shrink to utter. I could speak no word, but I looked him in the face and waited – for that which was more terrible than all.

He held me by the arm, as if he would hold me up when the shock of anguish came. 'They are in vain,' he said, 'in vain – because God rules over all.'

His arm was strong; but I fell at his feet like a dead man.

How miserable is that image, and how unfit to use! Death is still and cool and sweet. There is nothing in it that pierces like a sword, that burns like fire, that rends and tears like the turning wheels. O life, O pain, O terrible name of God, in which is all succour and all torment! What are pangs and tortures to that, which ever increases in its awful power, and has no limit, nor any alleviation, but whenever it is spoken penetrates through and through the miserable soul? O God, whom once I called my Father! O Thou who gavest me being, against whom I have fought, whom I fight to the end, shall there never be anything but anguish in the sound of Thy great name?

When I returned to such command of myself as one can have who has been transfixed by that sword of fire, the master stood by me still. He had not fallen like me, but his face was drawn with anguish and sorrow like the face of my friend who had been with me in the lazar-house, who had disappeared on the dark mountains. And as I looked at him, terror seized hold upon me, and a desire to flee and save myself, that I might not be drawn after him by the longing that was in his eyes.

The Master gave me his hand to help me to rise, and it trembled, but not like mine.

'Sir,' I cried, 'have not we enough to bear? Is it for hatred, is it for vengeance, that you speak that name?'

'O friend,' he said, 'neither for hatred nor revenge. It is like a fire in my veins: if one could find Him again—!'

'You, who are as a god – who can make and destroy – you, who could shake His throne!'

He put up his hand. 'I who am His creature, even here – and still His child, though I am so far, so far—' He caught my hand in his, and pointed with the other trembling. 'Look! your eyes are more clear than mine, for they are not anxious like mine. Can you see anything upon the way?'

The waste lay wild before us, dark with a faintly rising cloud, for darkness and cloud and the gloom of death attended upon that name. I thought, in his great genius and splendour of intellect, he had gone mad, as sometimes may be. 'There is nothing,' I said, and scorn came into my soul; but even as I spoke I saw – I cannot tell what I saw – a moving spot of milky whiteness in that dark and miserable wilderness, – no bigger than a man's hand, no bigger than a flower. 'There is something,' I said unwillingly; 'it has no shape nor form. It is a gossamer-web upon some bush, or a butterfly blown on the wind.'

'There are neither butterflies nor gossamers here.'

'Look for yourself then!' I cried, flinging his hand from me. I was angry with a rage which had no cause. I turned from him, though I loved him, with a desire to kill him in my heart; and hurriedly took the other way. The waste was wild: but rather that than to see the man who might have shaken earth and hell thus turning, turning to madness and the awful journey. For I knew what in his heart he thought, and I knew that it was so. It was something from that other sphere – can I tell you what? a child perhaps – oh, thought that wrings the heart! for do you know what manner of thing a child is? There are none in the land of darkness. I turned my back upon the place where that whiteness was. On, on, across the waste! On to the cities of the night! On, far away from maddening thought, from hope that is torment, and from the awful Name!

The Library Window

I

I WAS NOT aware at first of the many discussions which had gone on about that window. It was almost opposite one of the windows of the large old-fashioned drawing-room of the house in which I spent that summer, which was of so much importance in my life. Our house and the library were on opposite sides of the broad High Street of St Rule's, which is a fine street, wide and ample, and very quiet, as strangers think who come from noisier places; but in a summer evening there is much coming and going, and the stillness is full of sound – the sound of footsteps and pleasant voices, softened by the summer air. There are even exceptional moments when it is noisy: the time of the fair, and on Saturday nights sometimes, and when there are excursion trains. Then even the softest sunny air of the evening will not smooth the harsh tones and the stumbling steps; but at these unlovely moments we shut the windows, and even I, who am so fond of that deep recess where I can take refuge from all that is going on inside, and make myself a spectator of all the varied story out of doors, withdraw from my watch-tower. To tell the truth, there never was very much going on inside. The house belonged to my aunt, to whom (she says, Thank God!) nothing ever happens. I believe that many things have happened to her in her time; but that was all over at the period of which I am speaking, and she was old, and very quiet. Her life went on in a routine never broken. She got up at the same hour every day, and did the same things in the same rotation, day by day the same. She said that this was the greatest support in the world, and that routine is a kind of salvation. It may be so; but it is a very dull salvation, and I used to feel that I would rather have incident, whatever kind of incident it might be. But then at that time I was not old, which makes all the difference.

At the time of which I speak the deep recess of the drawing-room window was a great comfort to me. Though she was an old lady (perhaps because she was so old) she was very tolerant, and had a kind of feeling for me. She never said a word, but often gave me a smile when she saw how I had built myself up, with my books and my basket of work. I did very little work, I fear – now and then a few stitches when the spirit moved me, or when I had got well afloat in a dream, and was more tempted to follow it out than to read my book, as sometimes happened. At other times, and if the book were interesting, I used to get through volume after volume sitting there, paying no attention to anybody. And yet I did pay a kind of attention. Aunt Mary's old ladies came in to call, and I heard them talk, though I very seldom listened; but for all that, if they had anything to say that was interesting, it is curious how I found it in my mind afterwards, as if the air had blown it to me. They came and went, and I had the sensation of their old bonnets gliding out and in, and their dresses rustling; and now and then had to jump up and shake hands with some one who knew me, and asked after my papa and mamma. Then Aunt Mary would give me a little smile again, and I slipped back to my window. She never seemed to mind. My mother would not have let me do it, I know. She would have remembered dozens of things there were to do. She would have sent me upstairs to fetch something which I was quite sure she did not want, or downstairs to carry some quite unnecessary message to the housemaid. She liked to keep me running about. Perhaps that was one reason why I was so fond of Aunt Mary's drawing-room, and the deep recess of the window, and the curtain that fell half over it, and the broad window-seat, where one could collect so many things without being found fault with for untidiness. Whenever we had anything the matter with us in these days, we were sent to St Rule's to get up our strength. And this was my case at the time of which I am going to speak.

Everybody had said, since ever I learned to speak, that I was fantastic and fanciful and dreamy, and all the other words with which a girl who may happen to like poetry, and to be fond of thinking, is so often made uncomfortable. People don't know what they mean when they say fantastic. It sounds like Madge Wildfire or something of that sort. My mother thought I should always be busy, to keep nonsense out of my head. But really I was not at all fond of nonsense. I was rather serious than otherwise. I would have been no trouble to anybody if I had been left to myself. It was only that I had a sort of second-sight, and was conscious of things to which I paid no attention. Even when reading the most interesting book, the things that were being talked about blew in to me; and I heard what the people were saying in the streets as they passed under the window. Aunt Mary always said I could do two or indeed three things at once – both read and listen, and see. I am sure that I did not listen much, and seldom looked out, of set purpose – as some people do who notice what bonnets the ladies in the street have on; but I did hear what I couldn't help hearing, even when I was reading my book, and I did see all sorts of things, though often for a whole half-hour I might never lift my eyes.

This does not explain what I said at the beginning, that there were many discussions about that window. It was, and still is, the last window in the row, of the College Library, which is opposite my aunt's house in the High Street. Yet it is not exactly opposite, but a little to the west, so that I could see it best from the left side of my recess. I took it calmly for granted that it was a window like any other till I first heard the talk about it which was going on in the drawing-room. 'Have you never made up your mind, Mrs Balcarres,' said old Mr Pitmilly, 'whether that window opposite is a window or no?' He said Mistress Balcarres – and he was always called Mr Pitmilly, Morton: which was the name of his place.

'I am never sure of it, to tell the truth,' said Aunt Mary, 'all these years.'

'Bless me!' said one of the old ladies, 'and what window may that be?'

Mr Pitmilly had a way of laughing as he spoke, which did not please me; but it was true that he was not perhaps desirous of pleasing me. He said, 'Oh, just the window opposite,' with his laugh running through his words; 'our friend can never make up her mind about it, though she has been living opposite it since—'

'You need never mind the date,' said another; 'the Lee-brary window! Dear me, what should it be but a window? up at that height it could not be a door.'

'The question is,' said my aunt, 'if it is a real window with glass in it, or if it is merely painted, or if it once was a window, and has been built up. And the oftener people look at it, the less they are able to say.'

'Let me see this window,' said old Lady Carnbee, who was very active and strong-minded; and then they all came crowding upon me – three or four old ladies, very eager, and Mr Pitmilly's white hair appearing over their heads, and my aunt sitting quiet and smiling behind.

'I mind the window very well,' said Lady Carnbee; 'ay: and so do more than me. But in its present appearance it is just like any other window; but has not been cleaned, I should say, in the memory of man.'

'I see what ye mean,' said one of the others. 'It is just a very dead thing without any reflection in it; but I've seen as bad before.'

'Ay, it's dead enough,' said another, 'but that's no rule; for these hizzies of women-servants in this ill age—'

'Nay, the women are well enough,' said the softest voice of all, which was Aunt Mary's. 'I will never let them risk their lives cleaning the outside of mine. And there are no women-servants in the Old Library: there is maybe something more in it than that.'

They were all pressing into my recess, pressing upon me, a row of old faces, peering into something they could not understand. I had a sense in my mind how curious it was, the wall of old ladies in their old satin gowns all glazed with age, Lady Carnbee with her lace about her head. Nobody was looking at me or thinking of me; but I felt unconsciously the contrast of my youngness to their oldness, and stared at them as they stared over my head at the Library window. I had given it no attention up to this time. I was more taken up with the old ladies than with the thing they were looking at.

'The framework is all right at least, I can see that, and pented black—'

'And the panes are pented black too. It's no window, Mrs Balcarres. It has been filled in, in the days of the window duties: you will mind, Leddy Carnbee.'

'Mind!' said that oldest lady. 'I mind when your mother was marriet, Jeanie: and that's neither the day nor yesterday. But as for the window, it's just a delusion: and that is my opinion of the matter, if you ask me.'

'There's a great want of light in that muckle room at the

college,' said another. 'If it was a window, the Leebrary would have more light.'

'One thing is clear,' said one of the younger ones, 'it cannot be a window to see through. It may be filled in or it may be built up, but it is not a window to give light.'

'And who ever heard of a window that was no to see through?' Lady Carnbee said. I was fascinated by the look on her face, which was a curious scornful look as of one who knew more than she chose to say: and then my wandering fancy was caught by her hand as she held it up, throwing back the lace that dropped over it. Lady Carnbee's lace was the chief thing about her – heavy black Spanish lace with large flowers. Everything she wore was trimmed with it. A large veil of it hung over her old bonnet. But her hand coming out of this heavy lace was a curious thing to see. She had very long fingers, very taper, which had been much admired in her youth; and her hand was very white, or rather more than white, pale, bleached, and bloodless, with large blue veins standing up upon the back; and she wore some fine rings, among others a big diamond in an ugly old claw setting. They were too big for her, and were wound round and round with yellow silk to make them keep on: and this little cushion of silk, turned brown with long wearing, had twisted round so that it was more conspicuous than the jewels; while the big diamond blazed underneath in the hollow of her hand, like some dangerous thing hiding and sending out darts of light. The hand, which seemed to come almost to a point, with this strange ornament underneath, clutched at my half-terrified imagination. It too seemed to mean far more than was said. I felt as if it might clutch me with sharp claws, and the lurking, dazzling creature bite – with a sting that would go to the heart.

Presently, however, the circle of the old faces broke up, the old ladies returned to their seats, and Mr Pitmilly, small but very erect, stood up in the midst of them, talking with mild authority like a little oracle among the ladies. Only Lady Carnbee always contradicted the neat, little, old gentleman. She gesticulated, when she talked, like a Frenchwoman, and darted forth that hand of hers with the lace hanging over it, so that I always caught a glimpse of the lurking diamond. I thought she looked like a witch among the comfortable little group which gave such attention to everything Mr Pitmilly said.

'For my part, it is my opinion there is no window there at all,' he said. 'It's very like the thing that's called in scientific language an optical illusion. It arises generally, if I may use such a word in the presence of ladies, from a liver that is not just in the perfitt order and balance that organ demands – and then you will see things – a blue dog, I remember, was the thing in one case, and in another—'

'The man has gane gyte,' said Lady Carnbee; 'I mind the windows in the Auld Leebrary as long as I mind anything. Is the Leebrary itself an optical illusion too?'

'Na, na,' and 'No, no,' said the old ladies; 'a blue dogue would be a strange vagary: but the Library we have all kent from our youth,' said one. 'And I mind when the Assemblies were held there one year when the Town Hall was building,' another said.

'It is just a great divert to me,' said Aunt Mary: but what was strange was that she paused there, and said in a low tone, 'now': and then went on again, 'for whoever comes to my house, there are aye discussions about that window. I have never just made up my mind about it myself. Sometimes I think it's a case of these wicked window duties, as you said, Miss Jeanie, when half the windows in our houses were blocked up to save the tax. And then, I think, it may be due to that blank kind of building like the great new buildings on the Earthen Mound in Edinburgh, where the windows are just ornaments. And then whiles I am sure I can see the glass shining when the sun catches it in the afternoon.'

'You could so easily satisfy yourself, Mrs Balcarres, if you were to—'

'Give a laddie a penny to cast a stone, and see what happens,' said Lady Carnbee.

'But I am not sure that I have any desire to satisfy myself,' Aunt Mary said. And then there was a stir in the room, and I had to come out from my recess and open the door for the old ladies and see them downstairs, as they all went away following one another. Mr Pitmilly gave his arm to Lady Carnbee, though she was always contradicting him; and so the tea-party dispersed. Aunt Mary came to the head of the stairs with her guests in an old-fashioned gracious way, while I went down with them to see that the maid was ready at the door. When I came back Aunt Mary was still standing in the recess looking out. Returning to my seat she said, with a kind of wistful look, 'Well, honey: and what is your opinion?'

'I have no opinion. I was reading my book all the time,' I said.

'And so you were, honey, and no' very civil; but all the same I ken well you heard every word we said.'

II

It was a night in June; dinner was long over, and had it been winter the maids would have been shutting up the house, and my Aunt Mary preparing to go upstairs to her room. But it was still clear daylight, that daylight out of which the sun has been long gone, and which has no longer any rose reflections, but all has sunk into a pearly neutral tint – a light which is daylight yet is not day. We had taken a turn in the garden after dinner, and now we had returned to what we called our usual occupations. My aunt was reading. The English post had come in, and she had got her 'Times', which was her great diversion. The 'Scotsman' was her morning reading, but she liked her 'Times' at night.

As for me, I too was at my usual occupation, which at that time was doing nothing. I had a book as usual, and was absorbed in it: but I was conscious of all that was going on all the same. The people strolled along the broad pavement, making remarks as they passed under the open window which came up into my story or my dream, and sometimes made me laugh. The tone and the faint sing-song, or rather chant, of the accent, which was 'a wee Fifish', was novel to me, and associated with holiday, and pleasant; and sometimes they said to each other something that was amusing, and often something that suggested a whole story; but presently they began to drop off, the footsteps slackened, the voices died away. It was getting late, though the clear soft daylight went on and on. All through the lingering evening, which seemed to consist of interminable hours, long but not weary, drawn out as if the spell of the light and the outdoor life might never end, I had now and then, quite unawares, cast a glance at the mysterious window which my aunt and her friends had discussed, as I felt, though I dared not say it even to myself, rather foolishly. It caught my eye without any intention on my part, as I paused, as it were, to take breath, in the flowing and current of undistinguishable thoughts and things from without and within which carried me along. First it occurred to me, with a little sensation of discovery, how absurd to say it was not a window, a living window, one to see through! Why, then, had they never *seen* it, these old folk? I saw as I looked up suddenly the faint greyness as of visible space within – a room behind, certainly – dim, as it was natural a room should be on the other side of the street – quite indefinite: yet so clear that if some one were to come to the window there would be nothing surprising in it. For certainly there was a feeling of space behind the panes which these old half-blind ladies had disputed about whether they were glass or only fictitious panes marked on the wall. How silly! when eyes that could see could make it out in a minute. It was only a greyness at present, but it was unmistakable, a space that went back into gloom, as every room does when you look into it across a street. There were no curtains to show whether it was inhabited or not; but a room – oh, as distinctly as ever room was! I was pleased with myself, but said nothing, while Aunt Mary rustled her paper, waiting for a favourable moment to announce a discovery which settled her problem at once. Then I was carried away upon the stream again, and forgot the window, till somebody threw unawares a word from the outer world, 'I'm goin' hame; it'll soon be dark.' Dark! what was the fool thinking of? it never would be dark if one waited out, wandering in the soft air for hours longer; and then my eyes, acquiring easily that new habit, looked across the way again.

Ah, now! nobody indeed had come to the window; and no light had been lighted, seeing it was still beautiful to read by – a still, clear, colourless light; but the room inside had certainly widened. I could see the grey space and air a little deeper, and a sort of vision, very dim, of a wall, and something against it; something dark, with the blackness that a solid article, however indistinctly seen, takes in the lighter darkness that is only space – a large, black, dark thing coming out into the grey. I looked more intently, and made sure it was a piece of furniture, either a writing-table or perhaps a large book-case. No doubt it must be the last, since this was part of the old library. I never visited the old College Library, but I had seen such places before, and I could well imagine it to myself. How curious that for all the time these old people had looked at it, they had never seen this before!

It was more silent now, and my eyes, I suppose, had grown dim with gazing, doing my best to make it out, when suddenly Aunt Mary said, 'Will you ring the bell, my dear? I must have my lamp.'

'Your lamp?' I cried, 'when it is still daylight.' But then I gave another look at my window, and perceived with a start that the light had indeed changed: for now I saw nothing. It was still light, but there was so much change in the light that my room, with the grey space and the large shadowy book-case, had gone out, and I saw them no more: for even a Scotch night in June, though it looks as if it would never end, does darken at the last. I had almost cried out, but checked myself, and rang the bell for Aunt Mary, and made up my mind I would say nothing till next morning, when to be sure natu-rally it would be more clear.

Next morning I rather think I forgot all about it – or was busy: or was more idle than usual: the two things meant nearly the same. At all events I thought no more of the window, though I still sat in my own, opposite to it, but occupied with some other fancy. Aunt Mary's visitors came as usual in the afternoon; but their talk was of other things, and for a day or two nothing at all happened to bring back my thoughts into this channel. It might be nearly a week before the subject came back, and once more it was old Lady Carnbee who set me thinking; not that she said anything upon that particular theme. But she was the last of my aunt's afternoon guests to go away, and when she rose to leave she threw up her hands, with those lively gesticulations which so many old Scotch ladies have. 'My faith!' said she, 'there is that bairn there still like a dream. Is the creature bewitched, Mary Balcarres? and is she bound to sit there by night and by day for the rest of her days? You should mind that there's things about, uncanny for women of our blood.'

I was too much startled at first to recognise that it was of me she was speaking. She was like a figure in a picture, with her pale face the colour of ashes, and the big pattern of the Spanish lace hanging half over it, and her hand held up, with the big diamond blazing at me from the inside of her uplifted palm. It was held up in surprise, but it looked as if it were raised in malediction; and the diamond threw out darts of light and glared and twinkled at me. If it had been in its right place it would not have mattered; but there, in the open of the hand! I started up, half in terror, half in wrath. And then the old lady laughed, and her hand dropped. 'I've wakened you to life, and broke the spell,' she said, nodding her old head at me, while the large black silk flowers of the lace waved and threatened. And she took my arm to go downstairs, laughing and bidding me be steady, and no' tremble and shake like a broken reed. 'You should be as steady as a rock at your age. I was like a young tree,' she said, leaning so heavily that my willowy girlish frame quivered – 'I was a support to virtue, like Pamela, in my time.'

'Aunt Mary, Lady Carnbee is a witch!' I cried, when I came back.

'Is that what you think, honey? well: maybe she once was,' said Aunt Mary, whom nothing surprised.

And it was that night once more after dinner, and after the post came in, and the 'Times', that I suddenly saw the library window again. I had seen it every day – and noticed nothing; but tonight, still in a little tumult of mind over Lady Carnbee and her wicked diamond which wished me harm, and her lace which waved threats and warnings at me, I looked across the street, and there I saw quite plainly the room opposite, far more clear than before. I saw dimly that it must be a large room, and that the big piece of furniture against the wall was a writing-desk. That in a moment, when first my eyes rested upon it, was quite clear: a large old-fashioned escritoire, standing out into the room: and I knew by the shape of it that it had a great many pigeon-holes and little drawers in the back, and a large table for writing. There was one just like it in my father's library at home. It was such a surprise to see it all so clearly that I closed my eyes, for the moment almost giddy, wondering how papa's desk could have come here – and then when I reminded myself that this was nonsense, and that there were many such writing-tables besides papa's, and looked again – lo! it had all become quite vague and indistinct as it was at first; and I saw nothing but the blank window, of which the old ladies could never be certain whether it was filled up to avoid the window-tax, or whether it had ever been a window at all.

This occupied my mind very much, and yet I did not say anything to Aunt Mary. For one thing, I rarely saw anything at all in the early part of the day; but then that is natural: you can never see into a place from outside, whether it is an empty room or a looking-glass, or people's eyes, or anything else that is mysterious, in the day. It has, I suppose, something to do with the light. But in the evening in June in Scotland – then is the time to see. For it is daylight, yet it is not day, and there is a quality in it which I cannot describe, it is so clear, as if every object was a reflection of itself.

I used to see more and more of the room as the days went on. The large escritoire stood out more and more into the space: with sometimes white glimmering things, which looked like papers, lying on it: and once or twice I was sure I saw a pile of books on the floor close to the writing-table, as if they had gilding upon them in broken specks, like old books. It was always about the time when the lads in the street began to call to each other that they were going home, and sometimes a shriller voice would come from one of the doors, bidding somebody to 'cry upon the laddies' to come back to their suppers. That was always the time I saw best, though it was close upon the moment when the veil seemed to fall and the clear radiance became less living, and all the sounds died out of the street, and Aunt Mary said in her soft voice, 'Honey! will you ring for the lamp?' She said honey as people say darling: and I think it is a prettier word.

Then finally, while I sat one evening with my book in my hand, looking straight across the street, not distracted by anything, I saw a little movement within. It was not any one visible – but everybody must know what it is to see the stir in the air, the little disturbance – you cannot tell what it is, but that it indicates some one there, even though you can see no one. Perhaps it is a shadow making just one flicker in the still place. You may look at an empty room and the furniture in it for hours, and then suddenly there will be the flicker, and you know that something has come into it. It might only be a dog or a cat; it might be, if that were possible, a bird flying across; but it is some one, something living, which is so different, so completely different, in a moment from the things that are not living. It seemed to strike quite through me, and I gave a little cry. Then Aunt Mary stirred a little, and put down the huge newspaper that almost covered her from sight, and said, 'What is it, honey?' I cried 'Nothing,' with a little gasp, quickly, for I did not want to be disturbed just at this moment when somebody was coming! But I suppose she was not satisfied, for she got up and stood behind to see what it was, putting her hand on my shoulder. It was the softest touch in the world, but I could have flung it off angrily: for that moment everything was still again, and the place grew grey and I saw no more.

'Nothing,' I repeated, but I was so vexed I could have cried. 'I told you it was nothing, Aunt Mary. Don't you believe me, that you come to look – and spoil it all!'

I did not mean of course to say these last words; they were forced out of me. I was so much annoyed to see it all melt away like a dream: for it was no dream, but as real as – as real as – myself or anything I ever saw.

She gave my shoulder a little pat with her hand. 'Honey,' she said, 'were you looking at something? Is't that? is't that?' 'Is it what?' I wanted to say, shaking off her hand, but something in me stopped me: for I said nothing at all, and she went quietly back to her place. I suppose she must have rung the bell herself, for immediately I felt the soft flood of the light behind me, and the evening outside dimmed down, as it did every night, and I saw nothing more.

It was next day, I think, in the afternoon that I spoke. It was brought on by something she said about her fine work. 'I get a mist before my eyes,' she said; 'you will have to learn my old lace stitches, honey – for I soon will not see to draw the threads.'

'Oh, I hope you will keep your sight,' I cried, without thinking what I was saying. I was then young and very matter-of-fact. I had not found out that one may mean something, yet not half or a hundredth part of what one seems to mean: and even then probably hoping to be contradicted if it is anyhow against one's self.

'My sight!' she said, looking up at me with a look that was almost angry; 'there is no question of losing my sight – on the contrary, my eyes are very strong. I may not see to draw fine threads, but I see at a distance as well as ever I did – as well as you do.'

'I did not mean any harm, Aunt Mary,' I said. 'I thought you said – But how can your sight be as good as ever when you are in doubt about that window? I can see into the room as clear as—' My voice wavered, for I had just looked up and across the street, and I could have sworn that there was no window at all, but only a false image of one painted on the wall.

'Ah!' she said, with a little tone of keenness and of surprise: and she half rose up, throwing down her work hastily, as if she meant to come to me: then, perhaps seeing the bewildered look on my face, she paused and hesitated – 'Ay, honey!' she said, 'have you got so far ben as that?'

What did she mean? Of course I knew all the old Scotch phrases as well as I knew myself; but it is a comfort to take refuge in a little ignorance, and I know I pretended not to understand whenever I was put out. 'I don't know what you mean by "far ben",' I cried out, very impatient. I don't know what might have followed, but some one just then came to call, and she could only give me a look before she went forward, putting out her hand to her visitor. It was a very soft look, but anxious, and as if she did not know what to do: and she shook her head a very little, and I thought, though there was a smile on her face, there was something wet about her eyes. I retired into my recess, and nothing more was said.

But it was very tantalising that it should fluctuate so; for sometimes I saw that room quite plain and clear – quite as clear as I could see papa's library, for example, when I shut my eyes. I compared it naturally to my father's study, because of the shape of the writing-table, which, as I tell you, was the same as his. At times I saw the papers on the table quite plain, just as I had seen his papers many a day. And the little pile of books on the floor at the foot – not ranged regularly in order, but put down one above the other, with all their angles going different ways, and a speck of the old gilding shining here and there. And then again at other times I saw nothing, absolutely nothing, and was no better than the old ladies who had peered over my head, drawing their eyelids together, and arguing that the window had been shut up because of the old long-abolished window tax, or else that it had never been a window at all. It annoyed me very much at those dull moments to feel that I too puckered up my eyelids and saw no better than they.

Aunt Mary's old ladies came and went day after day while June went on. I was to go back in July, and I felt that I should be very unwilling indeed to leave until I had quite cleared up – as I was indeed in the way of doing – the mystery of that window which changed so strangely and appeared quite a different thing, not only to different people, but to the same eyes at different times. Of course I said to myself it must simply be an effect of the light. And yet I did not quite like that explanation either, but would have been better pleased to make out to myself that it was some superiority in me which made it so clear to me, if it were only the great superiority of young eyes over old – though that was not quite enough to satisfy me, seeing it was a superiority which I shared with every little lass and lad in the street. I rather wanted, I believe, to think that there was some particular insight in me which gave clearness to my sight – which was a most impertinent assumption, but really did not mean half the harm it seems to mean when it is put down here in black and white. I had several times again, however, seen the room quite plain, and made out that it was a large room, with a great picture in a dim gilded frame hanging on the farther wall, and many other pieces of solid furniture making a blackness here and there, besides the great escritoire against the wall, which had evidently been placed near the window for the sake of the light. One thing became visible to me after another, till I almost thought I should end by being able to read the old lettering on one of the big volumes which projected from the others and caught the light; but this was all preliminary to the great event which happened about Midsummer Day – the day of St John, which was once so much thought of as a festival, but now means nothing at all in Scotland any more than any other of the saints' days: which I shall always think a great pity and loss to Scotland, whatever Aunt Mary may say.

III

It was about midsummer, I cannot say exactly to a day when, but near that time, when the great event happened. I had grown very well acquainted by this time with that large dim room. Not only the escritoire, which was very plain to me now, with the papers upon it, and the books at its foot, but the great picture that hung against the farther wall, and various other shadowy pieces of furniture, especially a chair which one evening I saw had been moved into the space before the escritoire, – a little change which made my heart beat, for it spoke so distinctly of some one who must have been there, the some one who had already made me start, two or three times before, by some vague shadow of him or thrill of him which made a sort of movement in the silent space: a movement which made me sure that next minute I must see something or hear something which would explain the whole – if it were not that something always happened outside to stop it, at the very moment of its accomplishment. I had no warning this time of movement or shadow. I had been looking into the room very attentively a little while before, and had made out everything almost clearer than ever; and then had bent my attention again on my book, and read a chapter or two at a most exciting period of the story: and consequently had quite left St Rule's, and the High Street, and the College Library, and was really in a South American forest, almost throttled by the flowery creepers, and treading softly lest I should put my foot on a scorpion or a dangerous snake. At this moment something suddenly calling my attention to the outside, I looked across, and then, with a start, sprang up, for I could not contain myself. I don't know what I said, but enough to startle the people in the room, one of whom was old Mr Pitmilly. They all looked round upon me to ask what was the matter. And when I gave my usual answer of 'Nothing', sitting down again shamefaced but very much excited, Mr Pitmilly got up and came forward, and looked out, apparently to see what was the cause. He saw nothing, for he went back again, and I could hear him telling Aunt Mary not to be alarmed, for Missy had fallen into a doze with the heat, and had startled herself waking up, at which they all laughed: another time I could have killed him for his impertinence, but my mind was too much taken up now to pay any attention. My head was throbbing and my heart beating. I was in such high excitement, however, that to restrain myself completely, to be perfectly silent, was more easy to me then than at any other time of my life. I waited until the old gentleman had taken his seat again, and then I looked back. Yes, there he was! I had not been deceived. I knew then, when I looked across, that this was what I had been looking for all the time – that I had known he was there, and had been waiting for him, every time there was that flicker of movement in the room – him and no one else. And there at last, just as I had expected, he was. I don't know that in reality I ever had expected him, or any one: but this was what I felt when, suddenly looking into that curious dim room, I saw him there.

He was sitting in the chair, which he must have placed for himself, or which some one else in the dead of night when nobody was looking must have set for him, in front of the escritoire – with the back of his head towards me, writing. The light fell upon him from the left hand, and therefore upon his shoulders and the side of his head, which, however, was too much turned away to show anything of his face. Oh, how strange that there should be some one staring at him as I was doing, and he never to turn his head, to make a movement! If any one stood and looked at me, were I in the soundest sleep that ever was, I would wake, I would jump up, I would feel it through everything. But there he sat and never moved. You are not to suppose, though I said the light fell upon him from the left hand, that there was very much light. There never is in a room you are looking into like that across the street; but there was enough to see him by – the outline of his figure dark and solid, seated in the chair, and the fairness of his head visible faintly, a clear spot against the dimness. I saw this outline against the dim gilding of the frame of the large picture which hung on the farther wall.

I sat all the time the visitors were there, in a sort of rapture, gazing at this figure. I knew no reason why I should be so much moved. In an ordinary way, to see a student at an opposite window quietly doing his work might have interested me a little, but certainly it would not have moved me in any such way. It is always interesting to have a glimpse like this of an unknown life – to see so much and yet know so little, and to wonder, perhaps, what the man is doing, and why he never turns his head. One would go to the window – but not too close, lest he should see you and think you were spying upon him – and one would ask, Is he still there? is he writing, writing always? I wonder what he is writing! And it would be a great amusement: but no more. This was not my feeling at all in the present case. It was a sort of breathless watch, an absorption. I did not feel that I had eyes for anything else, or any room in my mind for another thought. I no longer heard, as I generally did, the stories and the wise remarks (or foolish) of Aunt Mary's old ladies or Mr Pitmilly. I heard only a murmur behind me, the interchange of voices, one softer, one sharper; but it was not as in the time when I sat reading and heard every word, till the story in my book, and the stories they were telling (what they said almost always shaped into stories), were all mingled into each other, and the hero in the novel became somehow the hero (or more likely heroine) of them all. But I took no notice of what they were saying now. And it was not that there was anything very interesting to look at, except the fact that he was there. He did nothing to keep up the absorption of my thoughts. He moved just so much as a man will do when he is very busily writing, thinking of nothing else. There was a faint turn of his head as he went from one side to another of the page he was writing; but it appeared to be a long page which never wanted turning. Just a little inclination when he was at the end of the line, outward, and then a little inclination inward when he began the next. That was little enough to keep one gazing. But I suppose it was the gradual course of events leading up to this, the finding out of one thing after another as the eyes got accustomed to the vague light: first the room itself, and then the writing-table, and then the other furniture, and last of all the human inhabitant who gave it all meaning. This was all so interesting that it was like a country which one had discovered. And then the extraordinary blindness of the other people who disputed among themselves whether it was a window at all! I did not, I am sure, wish to be disrespectful, and I was very fond of my Aunt Mary, and I liked Mr Pitmilly well enough, and I was afraid of Lady Carnbee. But yet to think of the – I know I ought not to say stupidity – the blindness of them, the foolishness, the insensibility! discussing it as if a thing that your eyes could see was a thing to discuss! It would have been unkind to think it was because they were old and their faculties dimmed. It is so sad to think that the faculties grow dim, that such a woman as my Aunt Mary should fail in seeing, or hearing, or feeling, that I would not have dwelt on it for a moment, it would have seemed so cruel! And then such a clever old lady as Lady Carnbee, who could see through a millstone, people said – and Mr Pitmilly, such an old man of the world. It did indeed bring tears to my eyes to think that all those clever people, solely by reason of being no longer young as I was, should have the simplest things shut out from them; and for all their wisdom and their knowledge be unable to see what a girl like me could see so easily. I was too much grieved for them to dwell upon that thought, and half ashamed, though perhaps half proud too, to be so much better off than they.

All those thoughts flitted through my mind as I sat and gazed across the street. And I felt there was so much going on in that room across the street! He was so absorbed in his writing, never looked up, never paused for a word, never turned round in his chair, or got up and walked about the room as my father did. Papa is a great writer, everybody says: but he would have come to the window and looked out, he would have drummed with his fingers on the pane, he would have watched a fly and helped it over a difficulty, and played with the fringe of the curtain, and done a dozen other nice, pleasant, foolish things, till the next sentence took shape. 'My dear, I am waiting for a word,' he would say to my mother when she looked at him, with a question why he was so idle, in her eyes; and then he would laugh, and go back again to his writing-table. But He over there never stopped at all. It was like a fascination. I could not take my eyes from him and that little scarcely perceptible movement he made, turning his head. I trembled with impatience to see him turn the page, or perhaps throw down his finished sheet on the floor, as somebody looking into a window like me once saw Sir Walter do, sheet after sheet. I should have cried out if this Unknown had done that. I should not have been able to help myself, whoever had been present; and gradually I got into such a state of suspense waiting for it to be done that my head grew hot and my hands cold. And then, just when there was a little movement of his elbow, as if he were about to do this, to be called away by Aunt Mary to see Lady Carnbee to the door! I believe I did not hear her till she had called me three times, and then I stumbled up, all flushed and hot, and nearly crying. When I came out from the recess to give the old lady my arm (Mr Pitmilly had gone away some time before), she put up her hand and stroked my cheek. 'What ails the bairn?' she said; 'she's fevered. You must not let her sit her lane in the window, Mary Balcarres. You and me know what comes of that.' Her old fingers had a strange touch, cold like something not living, and I felt that dreadful diamond sting me on the cheek.

I do not say that this was not just a part of my excitement and suspense; and I know it is enough to make any one laugh

when the excitement was all about an unknown man writing
in a room on the other side of the way, and my impatience
because he never came to an end of the page. If you think I
was not quite as well aware of this as any one could be! but the
worst was that this dreadful old lady felt my heart beating
against her arm that was within mine. 'You are just in a
dream,' she said to me, with her old voice close at my ear as we
went downstairs. 'I don't know who it is about, but it's bound
to be some man that is not worth it. If you were wise you
would think of him no more.'

'I am thinking of no man!' I said, half crying. 'It is very
unkind and dreadful of you to say so, Lady Carnbee. I never
thought of – any man, in all my life!' I cried in a passion of
indignation. The old lady clung tighter to my arm, and
pressed it to her, not unkindly.

'Poor little bird,' she said, 'how it's strugglin' and flutter-
in'! I'm not saying but what it's more dangerous when it's all
for a dream.'

She was not at all unkind; but I was very angry and excited,
and would scarcely shake that old pale hand which she put out
to me from her carriage window when I had helped her in. I
was angry with her, and I was afraid of the diamond, which
looked up from under her finger as if it saw through and
through me; and whether you believe me or not, I am certain
that it stung me again – a sharp malignant prick, oh full of
meaning! She never wore gloves, but only black lace mittens,
through which that horrible diamond gleamed.

I ran upstairs – she had been the last to go – and Aunt Mary
too had gone to get ready for dinner, for it was late. I hurried
to my place, and looked across, with my heart beating more
than ever. I made quite sure I should see the finished sheet
lying white upon the floor. But what I gazed at was only the
dim blank of that window which they said was no window.
The light had changed in some wonderful way during that
five minutes I had been gone, and there was nothing, nothing,
not a reflection, not a glimmer. It looked exactly as they all
said, the blank form of a window painted on the wall. It was
too much: I sat down in my excitement and cried as if my
heart would break. I felt that they had done something to it,
that it was not natural, that I could not bear their unkindness
– even Aunt Mary. They thought it not good for me! not good
for me! and they had done something – even Aunt Mary

herself – and that wicked diamond that hid itself in Lady Carnbee's hand. Of course I knew all this was ridiculous as well as you could tell me; but I was exasperated by the disappointment and the sudden stop to all my excited feelings, and I could not bear it. It was more strong than I.

I was late for dinner, and naturally there were some traces in my eyes that I had been crying when I came into the full light in the dining-room, where Aunt Mary could look at me at her pleasure, and I could not run away. She said, 'Honey, you have been shedding tears. I'm loth, loth that a bairn of your mother's should be made to shed tears in my house.'

'I have not been made to shed tears,' cried I; and then, to save myself another fit of crying, I burst out laughing and said, 'I am afraid of that dreadful diamond on old Lady Carnbee's hand. It bites – I am sure it bites! Aunt Mary, look here.'

'You foolish lassie,' Aunt Mary said; but she looked at my cheek under the light of the lamp, and then she gave it a little pat with her soft hand. 'Go away with you, you silly bairn. There is no bite; but a flushed cheek, my honey, and a wet eye. You must just read out my paper to me after dinner when the post is in: and we'll have no more thinking and no more dreaming for tonight.'

'Yes, Aunt Mary,' said I. But I knew what would happen; for when she opens up her 'Times', all full of the news of the world, and the speeches and things which she takes an interest in, though I cannot tell why – she forgets. And as I kept very quiet and made not a sound, she forgot tonight what she had said, and the curtain hung a little more over me than usual, and I sat down in my recess as if I had been a hundred miles away. And my heart gave a great jump, as if it would have come out of my breast; for he was there. But not as he had been in the morning – I suppose the light, perhaps, was not good enough to go on with his work without a lamp or candles – for he had turned away from the table and was fronting the window, sitting leaning back in his chair, and turning his head to me. Not to me – he knew nothing about me. I thought he was not looking at anything; but with his face turned my way. My heart was in my mouth: it was so unexpected, so strange! though why it should have seemed strange I know not, for there was no communication between him and me that it should have moved me; and what could be more natural than

that a man, wearied of his work, and feeling the want perhaps
of more light, and yet that it was not dark enough to light a
lamp, should turn round in his own chair, and rest a little, and
think – perhaps of nothing at all? Papa always says he is
thinking of nothing at all. He says things blow through his
mind as if the doors were open, and he has no responsibility.
What sort of things were blowing through this man's mind?
or was he thinking, still thinking, of what he had been writing
and going on with it still? The thing that troubled me most
was that I could not make out his face. It is very difficult to do
so when you see a person only through two windows, your
own and his. I wanted very much to recognise him afterwards
if I should chance to meet him in the street. If he had only
stood up and moved about the room, I should have made out
the rest of his figure, and then I should have known him
again; or if he had only come to the window (as papa always
did), then I should have seen his face clearly enough to have
recognised him. But, to be sure, he did not see any need to do
anything in order that I might recognise him, for he did not
know I existed; and probably if he had known I was watching
him, he would have been annoyed and gone away.

But he was as immovable there facing the window as he had
been seated at the desk. Sometimes he made a little faint stir
with a hand or a foot, and I held my breath, hoping he was
about to rise from his chair – but he never did it. And with all
the efforts I made I could not be sure of his face. I puckered
my eyelids together as old Miss Jeanie did who was short-
sighted, and I put my hands on each side of my face to
concentrate the light on him: but it was all in vain. Either the
face changed as I sat staring, or else it was the light that was
not good enough, or I don't know what it was. His hair
seemed to me light – certainly there was no dark line about his
head, as there would have been had it been very dark – and I
saw, where it came across the old gilt frame on the wall
behind, that it must be fair: and I am almost sure he had no
beard. Indeed I am sure that he had no beard, for the outline
of his face was distinct enough; and the daylight was still quite
clear out of doors, so that I recognised perfectly a baker's boy
who was on the pavement opposite, and whom I should have
known again whenever I had met him: as if it was of the least
importance to recognise a baker's boy! There was one thing,
however, rather curious about this boy. He had been

throwing stones at something or somebody. In St Rule's they have a great way of throwing stones at each other, and I suppose there had been a battle. I suppose also that he had one stone in his hand left over from the battle, and his roving eye took in all the incidents of the street to judge where he could throw it with most effect and mischief. But apparently he found nothing worthy of it in the street, for he suddenly turned round with a flick under his leg to show his cleverness, and aimed it straight at the window. I remarked without remarking that it struck with a hard sound and without any breaking of glass, and fell straight down on the pavement. But I took no notice of this even in my mind, so intently was I watching the figure within, which moved not nor took the slightest notice, and remained just as dimly clear, as perfectly seen, yet as indistinguishable, as before. And then the light began to fail a little, not diminishing the prospect within, but making it still less distinct than it had been.

Then I jumped up, feeling Aunt Mary's hand upon my shoulder. 'Honey,' she said, 'I asked you twice to ring the bell; but you did not hear me.'

'Oh, Aunt Mary!' I cried in great penitence, but turning again to the window in spite of myself.

'You must come away from there: you must come away from there,' she said, almost as if she were angry: and then her soft voice grew softer, and she gave me a kiss: 'never mind about the lamp, honey; I have rung myself, and it is coming; but, silly bairn, you must not aye be dreaming – your little head will turn.'

All the answer I made, for I could scarcely speak, was to give a little wave with my hand to the window on the other side of the street.

She stood there patting me softly on the shoulder for a whole minute or more, murmuring something that sounded like, 'She must go away, she must go away.' Then she said, always with her hand soft on my shoulder, 'Like a dream when one awaketh.' And when I looked again, I saw the blank of an opaque surface and nothing more.

Aunt Mary asked me no more questions. She made me come into the room and sit in the light and read something to her. But I did not know what I was reading, for there suddenly came into my mind and took possession of it, the thud of the stone upon the window, and its descent straight down, as if from some hard substance that threw it off: though I had myself seen it strike upon the glass of the panes across the way.

IV

I am afraid I continued in a state of great exaltation and commotion of mind for some time. I used to hurry through the day till the evening came, when I could watch my neighbour through the window opposite. I did not talk much to any one, and I never said a word about my own questions and wonderings. I wondered who he was, what he was doing, and why he never came till the evening (or very rarely); and I also wondered much to what house the room belonged in which he sat. It seemed to form a portion of the old College Library, as I have often said. The window was one of the line of windows which I understood lighted the large hall; but whether this room belonged to the library itself, or how its occupant gained access to it, I could not tell. I made up my mind that it must open out of the hall, and that the gentleman must be the Librarian or one of his assistants, perhaps kept busy all the day in his official duties, and only able to get to his desk and do his own private work in the evening. One has heard of so many things like that – a man who had to take up some other kind of work for his living, and then when his leisure-time came, gave it all up to something he really loved – some study or some book he was writing. My father himself at one time had been like that. He had been in the Treasury all day, and then in the evening wrote his books, which made him famous. His daughter, however little she might know of other things, could not but know that! But it discouraged me very much when somebody pointed out to me one day in the street an old gentleman who wore a wig and took a great deal of snuff, and said, That's the Librarian of the old College. It gave me a great shock for a moment; but then I remembered that an old gentleman has generally assistants, and that it must be one of them.

Gradually I became quite sure of this. There was another small window above, which twinkled very much when the sun shone, and looked a very kindly bright little window, above that dullness of the other which hid so much. I made up my mind this was the window of his other room, and that these two chambers at the end of the beautiful hall were really beautiful for him to live in, so near all the books, and so retired and quiet, that nobody knew of them. What a fine thing for him! and you could see what use he made of his good fortune as he sat there, so constant at his writing for hours together. Was it a book he was writing, or could it be perhaps Poems? This was a thought which made my heart beat; but I concluded with much regret that it could not be Poems, because no one could possibly write Poems like that, straight off, without pausing for a word or a rhyme. Had they been Poems he must have risen up, he must have paced about the room or come to the window as papa did – not that papa wrote Poems: he always said, 'I am not worthy even to speak of such prevailing mysteries,' shaking his head – which gave me a wonderful admiration and almost awe of a Poet, who was thus much greater even than papa. But I could not believe that a poet could have kept still for hours and hours like that. What could it be then? perhaps it was history; that is a great thing to work at, but you would not perhaps need to move nor to stride up and down, or look out upon the sky and the wonderful light.

He did move now and then, however, though he never came to the window. Sometimes, as I have said, he would turn round in his chair and turn his face towards it, and sit there for a long time musing when the light had begun to fail, and the world was full of that strange day which was night, that light without colour, in which everything was so clearly visible, and there were no shadows. 'It was between the night and the day, when the fairy folk have power.' This was the after-light of the wonderful, long, long summer evening, the light without shadows. It had a spell in it, and sometimes it made me afraid: and all manner of strange thoughts seemed to come in, and I always felt that if only we had a little more vision in our eyes we might see beautiful folk walking about in it, who were not of our world. I thought most likely he saw them, from the way he sat there looking out: and this made my heart expand with the most curious sensation, as if of pride that, though I could not see, he did, and did not even require to come to the window, as I did, sitting close in the depth of the recess, with my eyes upon him, and almost seeing things through his eyes.

I was so much absorbed in these thoughts and in watching him every evening – for now he never missed an evening, but was always there – that people began to remark that I was looking pale and that I could not be well, for I paid no attention when they talked to me, and did not care to go out, nor to join the other girls for their tennis, nor to do anything that others did; and some said to Aunt Mary that I was quickly losing all the ground I had gained, and that she could never send me back to my mother with a white face like that. Aunt Mary had begun to look at me anxiously for some time before that, and, I am sure, held secret consultations over me, sometimes with the doctor, and sometimes with her old ladies, who thought they knew more about young girls than even the doctors. And I could hear them saying to her that I wanted diversion, that I must be diverted, and that she must take me out more, and give a party, and that when the summer visitors began to come there would perhaps be a ball or two, or Lady Carnbee would get up a picnic. 'And there's my young lord coming home,' said the old lady whom they called Miss Jeanie, 'and I never knew the young lassie yet that would not cock up her bonnet at the sight of a young lord.'

But Aunt Mary shook her head. 'I would not lippen much to the young lord,' she said. 'His mother is sore set upon siller for him; and my poor bit honey has no fortune to speak of. No, we must not fly so high as the young lord; but I will gladly take her about the country to see the old castles and towers. It will perhaps rouse her up a little.'

'And if that does not answer we must think of something else,' the old lady said.

I heard them perhaps that day because they were talking of me, which is always so effective a way of making you hear – for latterly I had not been paying any attention to what they were saying; and I thought to myself how little they knew, and how little I cared about even the old castles and curious houses, having something else in my mind. But just about that time Mr Pitmilly came in, who was always a friend to me, and, when he heard them talking, he managed to stop them and turn the conversation into another channel. And after a while, when the ladies were gone away, he came up to my recess, and gave a glance right over my head. And then he asked my Aunt Mary if ever she had settled her question about the window opposite, 'that you thought was a window sometimes, and then not a window, and many curious things,' the old gentleman said.

My Aunt Mary gave me another very wistful look; and then she said, 'Indeed, Mr Pitmilly, we are just where we were, and I am quite as unsettled as ever; and I think my niece she has taken up my views, for I see her many a time looking across and wondering, and I am not clear now what her opinion is.'

'My opinion!' I said, 'Aunt Mary.' I could not help being a little scornful, as one is when one is very young. 'I have no opinion. There is not only a window but there is a room, and I could show you—' I was going to say, 'show you the gentleman who sits and writes in it,' but I stopped, not knowing what they might say, and looked from one to another. 'I could tell you – all the furniture that is in it,' I said. And then I felt something like a flame that went over my face, and that all at once my cheeks were burning. I thought they gave a little glance at each other, but that may have been folly. 'There is a great picture, in a big dim frame,' I said, feeling a little breathless, 'on the wall opposite the window—'

'Is there so?' said Mr Pitmilly, with a little laugh. And he said, 'Now I will tell you what we'll do. You know that there is a conversation party, or whatever they call it, in the big room tonight, and it will be all open and lighted up. And it is a handsome room, and two–three things well worth looking at. I will just step along after we have all got our dinner, and take you over to the pairty, madam – Missy and you—'

'Dear me!' said Aunt Mary. 'I have not gone to a pairty for more years than I would like to say – and never once to the Library Hall.' Then she gave a little shiver, and said quite low, 'I could not go there.'

'Then you will just begin again tonight, madam,' said Mr Pitmilly, taking no notice of this, 'and a proud man will I be leading in Mistress Balcarres that was once the pride of the ball!'

'Ah, once!' said Aunt Mary, with a low little laugh and then a sigh. 'And we'll not say how long ago;' and after that she made a pause, looking always at me: and then she said, 'I accept your offer, and we'll put on our braws; and I hope you will have no occasion to think shame of us. But why not take your dinner here?'

That was how it was settled, and the old gentleman went

away to dress, looking quite pleased. But I came to Aunt Mary as soon as he was gone, and besought her not to make me go. 'I like the long bonnie night and the light that lasts so long. And I cannot bear to dress up and go out, wasting it all in a stupid party. I hate parties, Aunt Mary!' I cried, 'and I would far rather stay here.'

'My honey,' she said, taking both my hands, 'I know it will maybe be a blow to you, – but it's better so.'

'How could it be a blow to me?' I cried; 'but I would far rather not go.'

'You'll just go with me, honey, just this once: it is not often I go out. You will go with me this one night, just this one night, my honey sweet.'

I am sure there were tears in Aunt Mary's eyes, and she kissed me between the words. There was nothing more that I could say; but how I grudged the evening! A mere party, a conversazione (when all the College was away, too, and no-body to make conversation!), instead of my enchanted hour at my window and the soft strange light, and the dim face looking out, which kept me wondering and wondering what was he thinking of, what was he looking for, who was he? all one wonder and mystery and question, through the long, long, slowly fading night!

It occurred to me, however, when I was dressing – though I was so sure that he would prefer his solitude to everything – that he might perhaps, it was just possible, be there. And when I thought of that, I took out my white frock – though Janet had laid out my blue one – and my little pearl necklace which I had thought was too good to wear. They were not very large pearls, but they were real pearls, and very even and lustrous though they were small; and though I did not think much of my appearance then, there must have been some-thing about me – pale as I was but apt to colour in a moment, with my dress so white, and my pearls so white, and my hair all shadowy – perhaps, that was pleasant to look at: for even old Mr Pitmilly had a strange look in his eyes, as if he was not only pleased but sorry too, perhaps thinking me a creature that would have troubles in this life, though I was so young and knew them not. And when Aunt Mary looked at me, there was a little quiver about her mouth. She herself had on her pretty lace and her white hair very nicely done, and looking her best. As for Mr Pitmilly, he had a beautiful fine French cambric frill to his shirt, plaited in the most minute plaits, and with a diamond pin in it which sparkled as much as Lady Carnbee's ring; but this was a fine frank kindly stone, that looked you straight in the face and sparkled, with the light dancing in it as if it were pleased to see you, and to be shining on that old gentleman's honest and faithful breast: for he had been one of Aunt Mary's lovers in their early days, and still thought there was nobody like her in the world.

I had got into quite a happy commotion of mind by the time we set out across the street in the soft light of the evening to the Library Hall. Perhaps, after all, I should see him, and see the room which I was so well acquainted with, and find out why he sat there so constantly and never was seen abroad. I thought I might even hear what he was working at, which would be such a pleasant thing to tell papa when I went home. A friend of mine at St Rule's – oh, far, far more busy than you ever were, papa! – and then my father would laugh as he always did, and say he was but an idler and never busy at all.

The room was all light and bright, flowers wherever flowers could be, and the long lines of the books that went along the walls on each side, lighting up wherever there was a line of gilding or an ornament, with a little response. It dazzled me at first all that light: but I was very eager, though I kept very quiet, looking round to see if perhaps in any corner, in the middle of any group, he would be there. I did not expect to see him among the ladies. He would not be with them, – he was too studious, too silent: but, perhaps among that circle of grey heads at the upper end of the room – perhaps—

No: I am not sure that it was not half a pleasure to me to make quite sure that there was not one whom I could take for him, who was at all like my vague image of him. No: it was absurd to think that he would be here, amid all that sound of voices, under the glare of that light. I felt a little proud to think that he was in his room as usual, doing his work, or thinking so deeply over it, as when he turned round in his chair with his face to the light.

I was thus getting a little composed and quiet in my mind, for now that the expectation of seeing him was over, though it was a disappointment, it was a satisfaction too – when Mr Pitmilly came up to me, holding out his arm. 'Now,' he said, 'I am going to take you to see the curiosities.' I thought to myself that after I had seen them and spoken to everybody I knew, Aunt Mary would let me go home, so I went very willingly, though I did not care for the curiosities. Something, however, struck me strangely as we walked up the room. It was the air, rather fresh and strong, from an open window at the east end of the hall. How should there be a window there? I hardly saw what it meant for the first moment, but it blew in my face as if there was some meaning in it, and I felt very uneasy without seeing why.

Then there was another thing that startled me. On that side of the wall which was to the street there seemed no windows at all. A long line of bookcases filled it from end to end. I could not see what that meant either, but it confused me. I was altogether confused. I felt as if I was in a strange country, not knowing where I was going, not knowing what I might find out next. If there were no windows on the wall to the street, where was my window? My heart, which had been jumping up and calming down again all this time, gave a great leap at this, as if it would have come out of me – but I did not know what it could mean.

Then we stopped before a glass case, and Mr Pitmilly showed me some things in it. I could not pay much attention to them. My head was going round and round. I heard his voice going on, and then myself speaking with a queer sound that was hollow in my ears; but I did not know what I was saying or what he was saying. Then he took me to the very end of the room, the east end, saying something that I caught – that I was pale, that the air would do me good. The air was blowing full on me, lifting the lace of my dress, lifting my hair, almost chilly. The window opened into the pale daylight, into the little lane that ran by the end of the building. Mr Pitmilly went on talking, but I could not make out a word he said. Then I heard my own voice, speaking through it, though I did not seem to be aware that I was speaking. 'Where is my window? – where, then, is my window?' I seemed to be saying, and I turned right round, dragging him with me, still holding his arm. As I did this my eye fell upon something at last which I knew. It was a large picture in a broad frame, hanging against the farther wall.

What did it mean? Oh, what did it mean? I turned round again to the open window at the east end, and to the daylight, the strange light without any shadow, that was all round about this lighted hall, holding it like a bubble that would burst, like something that was not real. The real place was the room I knew, in which that picture was hanging, where the writing-table was, and where he sat with his face to the light. But where was the light and the window through which it came? I think my senses must have left me. I went up to the picture which I knew, and then I walked straight across the room, always dragging Mr Pitmilly, whose face was pale, but who did not struggle but allowed me to lead him, straight across to where the window was – where the window was not; – where there was no sign of it. 'Where is my window? – where is my window?' I said. And all the time I was sure that I was in a dream, and these lights were all some theatrical illusion, and the people talking; and nothing real but the pale, pale, watching, lingering day standing by to wait until that foolish bubble should burst.

'My dear,' said Mr Pitmilly, 'my dear! Mind that you are in public. Mind where you are. You must not make an outcry and frighten your Aunt Mary. Come away with me. Come away, my dear young lady! and you'll take a seat for a minute or two and compose yourself; and I'll get you an ice or a little wine.' He kept patting my hand, which was on his arm, and looking at me very anxiously. 'Bless me! bless me! I never thought it would have this effect,' he said.

But I would not allow him to take me away in that direction. I went to the picture again and looked at it without seeing it: and then I went across the room again, with some kind of wild thought that if I insisted I should find it. 'My window – my window!' I said.

There was one of the professors standing there, and he heard me. 'The window!' said he. 'Ah, you've been taken in with what appears outside. It was put there to be in uniformity with the window on the stair. But it never was a real window. It is just behind that bookcase. Many people are taken in by it,' he said.

His voice seemed to sound from somewhere far away, and as if it would go on for ever; and the hall swam in a dazzle of shining and of noises round me; and the daylight through the open window grew greyer, waiting till it should be over, and the bubble burst.

V

It was Mr Pitmilly who took me home; or rather it was I who took him, pushing him on a little in front of me, holding fast by his arm, not waiting for Aunt Mary or any one. We came out into the daylight again outside, I, without even a cloak or a shawl, with my bare arms, and uncovered head, and the pearls round my neck. There was a rush of the people about, and a baker's boy, that baker's boy, stood right in my way and cried, 'Here's a braw ane!' shouting to the others: the words struck me somehow, as his stone had struck the window, without any reason. But I did not mind the people staring, and hurried across the street, with Mr Pitmilly half a step in advance. The door was open, and Janet standing at it, looking out to see what she could see of the ladies in their grand dresses. She gave a shriek when she saw me hurrying across the street; but I brushed past her, and pushed Mr Pitmilly up the stairs, and took him breathless to the recess, where I threw myself down on the seat, feeling as if I could not have gone another step farther, and waved my hand across to the window. 'There! there!' I cried. Ah! there it was – not that senseless mob – not the theatre and the gas, and the people all in a murmur and clang of talking. Never in all these days had I seen that room so clearly. There was a faint tone of light behind, as if it might have been a reflection from some of those vulgar lights in the hall, and he sat against it, calm, wrapped in his thoughts, with his face turned to the window. Nobody but must have seen him. Janet could have seen him had I called her upstairs. It was like a picture, all the things I knew, and the same attitude, and the atmosphere, full of quietness, not disturbed by any-thing. I pulled Mr Pitmilly's arm before I let him go, – 'You see, you see!' I cried. He gave me the most bewildered look, as if he would have liked to cry. He saw nothing! I was sure of that from his eyes. He was an old man, and there was no vision in him. If I had called up Janet, she would have seen it all. 'My dear!' he said. 'My dear!' waving his hands in a helpless way.

'He has been there all these nights,' I cried, 'and I thought you could tell me who he was and what he was doing; and that he might have taken me in to that room, and showed me, that I might tell papa. Papa would understand, he would like to hear. Oh, can't you tell me what work he is doing, Mr Pitmilly? He never lifts his head as long as the light throws a shadow, and then when it is like this he turns round and thinks, and takes a rest!'

Mr Pitmilly was trembling, whether it was with cold or I know not what. He said, with a shake in his voice, 'My dear young lady – my dear—' and then stopped and looked at me as if he were going to cry. 'It's peetiful, it's peetiful,' he said; and then in another voice, 'I am going across there again to bring your Aunt Mary home; do you understand, my poor little thing, my – I am going to bring her home – you will be better when she is here.' I was glad when he went away, as he could not see anything: and I sat alone in the dark which was not dark, but quite clear light – a light like nothing I ever saw. How clear it was in that room! not glaring like the gas and the voices, but so quiet, everything so visible, as if it were in another world. I heard a little rustle behind me, and there was Janet, standing staring at me with two big eyes wide open. She was only a little older than I was. I called to her, 'Janet, come here, come here, and you will see him, – come here and see him!' impatient that she should be so shy and keep behind. 'Oh, my bonnie young leddy!' she said, and burst out crying. I stamped my foot at her, in my indignation that she would not come, and she fled before me with a rustle and swing of haste, as if she were afraid. None of them, none of them! not even a girl like myself, with the sight in her eyes, would understand. I turned back again, and held out my hands to him sitting there, who was the only one that knew. 'Oh,' I said, 'say something to me! I don't know who you are, or what you are: but you're lonely and so am I; and I only – feel for you. Say something to me!' I neither hoped that he would hear, nor expected any answer. How could he hear, with the street between us, and his window shut, and all the murmuring of the voices and the people standing about? But for one moment it seemed to me that there was only him and me in the whole world.

But I gasped with my breath, that had almost gone from me, when I saw him move in his chair! He had heard me, though I knew not how. He rose up, and I rose too, speechless, incapable of anything but this mechanical movement. He seemed to draw me as if I were a puppet moved by his will. He came forward to the window, and stood looking across at me. I was sure that he looked at me. At last he had seen me: at last he had found out that somebody, though only a girl, was watching him, looking for him, believing in him. I was in such trouble and commotion of mind and trembling, that I could not keep on my feet, but dropped kneeling on the window-seat, supporting myself against the window, feeling as if my heart were being drawn out of me. I cannot describe his face. It was all dim, yet there was a light on it: I think it must have been a smile; and as closely as I looked at him he looked at me. His hair was fair, and there was a little quiver about his lips. Then he put his hands upon the window to open it. It was stiff and hard to move; but at last he forced it open with a sound that echoed all along the street. I saw that the people heard it, and several looked up. As for me, I put my hands together, leaning with my face against the glass, drawn to him as if I could have gone out of myself, my heart out of my bosom, my eyes out of my head. He opened the window with a noise that was heard from the West Port to the Abbey. Could any one doubt that?

And then he leaned forward out of the window, looking out. There was not one in the street but must have seen him. He looked at me first, with a little wave of his hand, as if it were a salutation – yet not exactly that either, for I thought he waved me away; and then he looked up and down in the dim shining of the ending day, first to the east, to the old Abbey towers, and then to the west, along the broad line of the street where so many people were coming and going, but so little noise, all like enchanted folk in an enchanted place. I watched him with such a melting heart, with such a deep satisfaction as words could not say; for nobody could tell me now that he was not there, – nobody could say I was dreaming any more. I watched him as if I could not breathe – my heart in my throat, my eyes upon him. He looked up and down, and then he looked back to me. I was the first, and I was the last, though it was not for long: he did know, he did see, who it was that had recognised him and sympathised with him all the time. I was in a kind of rapture, yet stupor too; my look went with his look, following it as if I were his shadow; and then suddenly he was gone, and I saw him no more.

I dropped back again upon my seat, seeking something to

support me, something to lean upon. He had lifted his hand and waved it once again to me. How he went I cannot tell, nor where he went I cannot tell; but in a moment he was away, and the window standing open, and the room fading into stillness and dimness, yet so clear, with all its space, and the great picture in its gilded frame upon the wall. It gave me no pain to see him go away. My heart was so content, and I was so worn out and satisfied – for what doubt or question could there be about him now? As I was lying back as weak as water, Aunt Mary came in behind me, and flew to me with a little rustle as if she had come on wings, and put her arms round me, and drew my head on to her breast. I had begun to cry a little, with sobs like a child. 'You saw him, you saw him!' I said. To lean upon her, and feel her so soft, so kind, gave me a pleasure I cannot describe, and her arms round me, and her voice saying 'Honey, my honey!' – as if she were nearly crying too. Lying there I came back to myself, quite sweetly, glad of everything. But I wanted some assurance from them that they had seen him too. I waved my hand to the window that was still standing open, and the room that was stealing away into the faint dark. 'This time you saw it all?' I said, getting more eager. 'My honey!' said Aunt Mary, giving me a kiss: and Mr Pitmilly began to walk about the room with short little steps behind, as if he were out of patience. I sat straight up and put away Aunt Mary's arms. 'You cannot be so blind, so blind!' I cried. 'Oh, not tonight, at least not tonight!' But neither the one nor the other made any reply. I shook myself quite free, and raised myself up. And there, in the middle of the street, stood the baker's boy like a statue, staring up at the open window, with his mouth open and his face full of wonder – breathless, as if he could not believe what he saw. I darted forward, calling to him, and beckoned him to come to me. 'Oh, bring him up! bring him, bring him to me!' I cried.

Mr Pitmilly went out directly, and got the boy by the shoulder. He did not want to come. It was strange to see the little old gentleman, with his beautiful frill and his diamond pin, standing out in the street, with his hand upon the boy's shoulder, and the other boys round, all in a little crowd. And presently they came towards the house, the others all following, gaping and wondering. He came in unwilling, almost resisting, looking as if we meant him some harm. 'Come away, my laddie, come and speak to the young lady,' Mr Pitmilly was saying. And Aunt Mary took my hands to keep me back. But I would not be kept back.

'Boy,' I cried, 'you saw it too: you saw it: tell them you saw it! It is that I want, and no more.'

He looked at me as they all did, as if he thought I was mad. 'What's she wantin' wi' me?' he said; and then, 'I did nae harm, even if I did throw a bit stane at it – and it's nae sin to throw a stane.'

'You rascal!' said Mr Pitmilly, giving him a shake; 'have you been throwing stones? You'll kill somebody some of these days with your stones.' The old gentleman was confused and troubled, for he did not understand what I wanted, nor anything that had happened. And then Aunt Mary, holding my hands and drawing me close to her, spoke. 'Laddie,' she said, 'answer the young lady, like a good lad. There's no intention of finding fault with you. Answer her, my man, and then Janet will give ye your supper before you go.'

'Oh speak, speak!' I cried; 'answer them and tell them! you saw that window opened, and the gentleman look out and wave his hand?'

'I saw nae gentleman,' he said, with his head down, 'except this wee gentleman here.'

'Listen, laddie,' said Aunt Mary. 'I saw ye standing in the middle of the street staring. What were ye looking at?'

'It was naething to make a wark about. It was just yon windy yonder in the library that is nae windy. And it was open – as sure's death. You may laugh if you like. Is that a' she's wantin' wi' me?'

'You are telling a pack of lies, laddie,' Mr Pitmilly said.

'I'm tellin' nae lees – it was standin' open just like ony ither windy. It's as sure's death. I couldna believe it mysel'; but it's true.'

'And there it is,' I cried, turning round and pointing it out to them with great triumph in my heart. But the light was all grey, it had faded, it had changed. The window was just as it had always been, a sombre break upon the wall.

I was treated like an invalid all that evening, and taken upstairs to bed, and Aunt Mary sat up in my room the whole night through. Whenever I opened my eyes she was always sitting there close to me, watching. And there never was in all my life so strange a night. When I would talk in my excitement, she kissed me and hushed me like a child. 'Oh, honey,

you are not the only one!' she said. 'Oh whisht, whisht, bairn!
I should never have let you be there!'

'Aunt Mary, Aunt Mary, you have seen him too?'

'Oh whisht, whisht, honey!' Aunt Mary said: her eyes were
shining – there were tears in them. 'Oh whisht, whisht! Put it
out of your mind, and try to sleep. I will not speak another
word,' she cried.

But I had my arms round her, and my mouth at her ear.
'Who is he there? – tell me that and I will ask no more—'

'Oh honey, rest, and try to sleep! It is just – how can I tell
you? – a dream, a dream! Did you not hear what Lady
Carnbee said? – the women of our blood—'

'What? what? Aunt Mary, oh Aunt Mary—'

'I canna tell you,' she cried in her agitation, 'I canna tell
you! How can I tell you, when I know just what you know and
no more? It is a longing all your life after – it is a looking – for
what never comes.'

'He will come,' I cried. 'I shall see him tomorrow – that I
know, I know!'

She kissed me and cried over me, her cheek hot and wet like
mine. 'My honey, try if you can sleep – try if you can sleep:
and we'll wait to see what tomorrow brings.'

'I have no fear,' said I; and then I suppose, though it is strange
to think of, I must have fallen asleep – I was so worn-out, and
young, and not used to lying in my bed awake. From time to
time I opened my eyes, and sometimes jumped up remembering
everything: but Aunt Mary was always there to soothe me, and I
lay down again in her shelter like a bird in its nest.

But I would not let them keep me in bed next day. I was in a
kind of fever, not knowing what I did. The window was quite
opaque, without the least glimmer in it, flat and blank like a
piece of wood. Never from the first day had I seen it so little
like a window. 'It cannot be wondered at,' I said to myself,
'that seeing it like that, and with eyes that are old, not so clear
as mine, they should think what they do.' And then I smiled
to myself to think of the evening and the long light, and
whether he would look out again, or only give me a signal with
his hand. I decided I would like that best: not that he should
take the trouble to come forward and open it again, but just a
turn of his head and a wave of his hand. It would be more
friendly and show more confidence, – not as if I wanted that
kind of demonstration every night.

I did not come down in the afternoon, but kept at my own window upstairs alone, till the tea-party should be over. I could hear them making a great talk; and I was sure they were all in the recess staring at the window, and laughing at the silly lassie. Let them laugh! I felt above all that now. At dinner I was very restless, hurrying to get it over; and I think Aunt Mary was restless too. I doubt whether she read her 'Times' when it came; she opened it up so as to shield her, and watched from a corner. And I settled myself in the recess, with my heart full of expectation. I wanted nothing more than to see him writing at his table, and to turn his head and give me a little wave of his hand, just to show that he knew I was there. I sat from half-past seven o'clock to ten o'clock: and the daylight grew softer and softer, till at last it was as if it was shining through a pearl, and not a shadow to be seen. But the window all the time was as black as night, and there was nothing, nothing there.

Well: but other nights it had been like that; he would not be there every night only to please me. There are other things in a man's life, a great learned man like that. I said to myself I was not disappointed. Why should I be disappointed? There had been other nights when he was not there. Aunt Mary watched me, every movement I made, her eyes shining, often wet, with a pity in them that almost made me cry: but I felt as if I were more sorry for her than for myself. And then I flung myself upon her, and asked her, again and again, what it was, and who it was, imploring her to tell me if she knew? and when she had seen him, and what had happened? and what it meant about the women of our blood? She told me that how it was she could not tell, nor when: it was just at the time it had to be; and that we all saw him in our time – 'that is,' she said, 'the ones that are like you and me.' What was it that made her and me different from the rest? but she only shook her head and would not tell me. 'They say,' she said, and then stopped short. 'Oh, honey, try and forget all about it – if I had but known you were of that kind! They say – that once there was one that was a Scholar, and liked his books more than any lady's love. Honey, do not look at me like that. To think I should have brought all this on you!'

'He was a Scholar?' I cried.

'And one of us, that must have been a light woman, not like you and me – But maybe it was just in innocence; for who can tell? She waved to him and waved to him to come over: and yon ring was the token: but he would not come. But still she sat at her window and waved and waved – till at last her brothers heard of it, that were stirring men; and then – oh, my honey, let us speak of it no more!'

'They killed him!' I cried, carried away. And then I grasped her with my hands, and gave her a shake, and flung away from her. 'You tell me that to throw dust in my eyes – when I saw him only last night: and he as living as I am, and as young!'

'My honey, my honey!' Aunt Mary said.

After that I would not speak to her for a long time; but she kept close to me, never leaving me when she could help it, and always with that pity in her eyes. For the next night it was the same; and the third night. That third night I thought I could not bear it any longer. I would have to do something – if only I knew what to do! If it would ever get dark, quite dark, there might be something to be done. I had wild dreams of stealing out of the house and getting a ladder, and mounting up to try if I could not open that window, in the middle of the night – if perhaps I could get the baker's boy to help me; and then my mind got into a whirl, and it was as if I had done it; and I could almost see the boy put the ladder to the window, and hear him cry out that there was nothing there. Oh, how slow it was, the night! and how light it was, and everything so clear – no darkness to cover you, no shadow, whether on one side of the street or on the other side! I could not sleep, though I was forced to go to bed. And in the deep midnight, when it is dark dark in every other place, I slipped very softly downstairs, though there was one board on the landing-place that creaked – and opened the door and stepped out. There was not a soul to be seen, up or down, from the Abbey to the West Port: and the trees stood like ghosts, and the silence was terrible, and everything as clear as day. You don't know what silence is till you find it in the light like that, not morning but night, no sunrising, no shadow, but everything as clear as the day.

It did not make any difference as the slow minutes went on: one o'clock, two o'clock. How strange it was to hear the clocks striking in that dead light when there was nobody to hear them! But it made no difference. The window was quite blank; even the marking of the panes seemed to have melted away. I stole up again after a long time, through the silent house, in the clear light, cold and trembling, with despair in my heart.

I am sure Aunt Mary must have watched and seen me coming back, for after a while I heard faint sounds in the house; and very early, when there had come a little sunshine into the air, she came to my bedside with a cup of tea in her hand; and she, too, was looking like a ghost. 'Are you warm, honey – are you comfortable?' she said. 'It doesn't matter,' said I. I did not feel as if anything mattered; unless if one could get into the dark somewhere – the soft, deep dark that would cover you over and hide you – but I could not tell from what. The dreadful thing was that there was nothing, nothing to look for, nothing to hide from – only the silence and the light.

That day my mother came and took me home. I had not heard she was coming; she arrived quite unexpectedly, and said she had no time to stay, but must start the same evening so as to be in London next day, papa having settled to go abroad. At first I had a wild thought I would not go. But how can a girl say I will not, when her mother has come for her, and there is no reason, no reason in the world, to resist, and no right! I had to go, whatever I might wish or any one might say. Aunt Mary's dear eyes were wet; she went about the house drying them quietly with her handkerchief, but she always said, 'It is the best thing for you, honey – the best thing for you!' Oh, how I hated to hear it said that it was the best thing, as if anything mattered, one more than another! The old ladies were all there in the afternoon, Lady Carnbee looking at me from under her black lace, and the diamond lurking, sending out darts from under her finger. She patted me on the shoulder, and told me to be a good bairn. 'And never lippen to what you see from the window,' she said. 'The eye is deceitful as well as the heart.' She kept patting me on the shoulder, and I felt again as if that sharp wicked stone stung me. Was that what Aunt Mary meant when she said yon ring was the token? I thought afterwards I saw the mark on my shoulder. You will say why? How can I tell why? If I had known, I should have been contented, and it would not have mattered any more.

I never went back to St Rule's, and for years of my life I never again looked out of a window when any other window was in sight. You ask me did I ever see him again? I cannot tell: the imagination is a great deceiver, as Lady Carnbee said: and if he stayed there so long, only to punish the race that had wronged him, why should I ever have seen him again? for I had received my share. But who can tell what happens in a heart that often, often, and so long as that, comes back to do its errand? If it was he whom I have seen again, the anger is gone from him, and he means good and no longer harm to the house of the woman that loved him. I have seen his face looking at me from a crowd. There was one time when I came home a widow from India, very sad, with my little children: I am certain I saw him there among all the people coming to welcome their friends. There was nobody to welcome me, – for I was not expected: and very sad was I, without a face I knew: when all at once I saw him, and he waved his hand to me. My heart leaped up again: I had forgotten who he was, but only that it was a face I knew, and I landed almost cheerfully, thinking here was some one who would help me. But he had disappeared, as he did from the window, with that one wave of his hand.

And again I was reminded of it all when old Lady Carnbee died – an old, old woman – and it was found in her will that she had left me that diamond ring. I am afraid of it still. It is locked up in an old sandal-wood box in the lumber-room in the little old country-house which belongs to me, but where I never live. If any one would steal it, it would be a relief to my mind. Yet I never knew what Aunt Mary meant when she said, 'Yon ring was the token,' nor what it could have to do with that strange window in the old College Library of St Rule's.

Author's Notes

1. The reader will remember that the ringing of the Cathedral bells happened in fact very soon after the exodus of the citizens; so that the self-reproaches of M. Lecamus had less foundation than he thought.

2. Prima vuol ben: ma non lascia il talento
   Che divina guistizia contra voglia,
   Come fü al peccar, pone al tormento.
                         PURGATORIO, Cant. xxi

Notes

Notes to *A Beleaguered City* and 'The Open Door' by J C. All other stories are annotated by M G, with one or two additions by J C.

A BELEAGUERED CITY

An abridged version of *A Beleaguered City* was published in the *New Quarterly Magazine*, January, 1879. The first book version was published in 1880, with the full title *A Beleaguered City, Being A Narrative of Certain Recent Events in the City of Semur, in the Department of the haute Bourgogne, A Story of the Seen and the Unseen.*

p. 1   Margaret Oliphant visited Semur en Auxois in 1871. The Franco-Prussian War had come to an end in January of that year, which was followed by the Paris Commune and several years of upheaval leading to the declaration of the Third Republic in 1875. *A Beleaguered City* contains a number of references to the unsettled politics of this period.
         rez-de-chaussez: ground floor

p. 2   *soutane*: cassock

p. 3   *vive l'argent*: long live money

p. 5   *dot*: dowry
         gros paysan: fat peasant
         dévote: devout person
         des anges: angels

p. 6   *chef-lieu*: chief town of the department
         en cachette: secretly, on the quiet

p. 7   'Monte Christo' is a reference to Alexandre Dumas' novel *The Count of Monte Cristo*, 1844-5.

p. 8   The 'clerical party'. This is a reference to the opposition to the Third Republic by Catholics as well as monarchists.

p. 9   *plaisant pays de France*: pleasant land of France

p. 10   *adjoint*: deputy

p. 11   The 'officers of the *octroi*' were the equivalent of city guards – the *octroi* was the toll house.

p. 13   *Carmes dechausés*: barefoot Carmelite friars. There were two branches of the Order of Carmelites, of which the barefoot, or discalced, were the more strict.

p. 22   *sommation*: summons
           NOUS AUTRES MORTS: we other dead

p. 26   *porte-cochère*: carriage entrance or main entrance

p. 31   St Jean: the feast of St Jean (St John) is 27 December. Oliphant may have intended a reference here to the fact that St John the Evangelist is reputed to have written the Book of Revelation.

p. 33   The 'invader' is the Prussian army, which had invaded France in 1870.
           cabaret: inn, tavern

p. 37   *vaurien*: worthless person, bounder

p. 39   Sebastapol is a reference to the Crimean War, 1853–6, during which Russian-held Sebastopol was besieged for a year by the allied French and English armies.

p. 41   'An ancient city' is a reference to Jericho, the walls of which, in the description in the Old Testament Book of Joshua, fell when Joshua's army sounded their trumpets.

p. 55   'A poet' is Dante. Oliphant had published her book on Dante in 1877. His influence is clearly present.

p. 57   *porte*: gate

p. 66   *lætatus sum*: I am joyful
           enfant de chœur: choirboy

p. 68   'Unhappy circumstances of France': M. de Bois-Sombre is a monarchist, and therefore not a supporter of the Third Republic.

p. 69   *tendu*: strained

p. 71   *campagne*: place in the country

p. 72   La Corbeille des Raisins: the Basket of Grapes

p. 77   The psalm referred to is Psalm 127:2 – 'He giveth his beloved sleep'.

p. 80   *veuve*: widow
           procès verbal: official report

p. 83   'The holy Pucelle' is the Maid, i.e. Joan of Arc.

p. 84   *garde*: watchman
           canaille: rabble

p. 85   *bon sens*: good sense
           femme de ménage: housekeeper

p. 86   *va-nu-pieds*: people without shoes

p. 87   'The war' is the Franco-Prussian war.

p. 90   *Salut*: Salutation to the Virgin Mary

p. 93   'The cleansing fires' are the fires of Purgatory, a clear reference to Dante.

p. 94   *charrettes*: carts

p. 101   *mousquetaire*: musketeer

p. 104   *jour des morts*: All Souls Day, 2 November, which marks the Catholic belief that the deliverance of souls expiating their sins in Purgatory could be helped through prayer.

THE SECRET CHAMBER

'The Secret Chamber' was first published in *Blackwood's Edinburgh Magazine* in December 1876, and Oliphant later expanded its theme into the unsatisfactory three-decker novel *The Wizard's Son* (1884).

p. 107   Dedication 'To the inquirers in the Norman Tower': reference not traced.

Castle Gowrie would have been instantly identified by the Victorian reading public as Glamis Castle. There was a legend – which persists to this day – that somewhere in the castle there was a secret room in which was kept a horrifically deformed creature whose identity was revealed only to the eldest son of the family.

'The first Stuart rising' was the unsuccessful Jacobite rebellion of 1715.

p. 108   After the Union of the Scottish and English parliaments in 1707, Scottish peers were entitled to elect representatives from among their number to sit in the House of Lords.

p. 111   The quotation is from the song 'High Germany'. See *Cecil Sharp's Collection of English Folk Songs*, edited by Maud Karpeles, 2 vols (London, 1974), no. 131 and no. 132.

p. 112   Daniel Douglas Home (1823–86) was a spiritualist medium whose seances were attended by the Brownings and Edward Bulwer-Lytton, among others. Home claimed to have the powers of levitation and telepathy, as well as the ability to make contact with spirits.

p. 113   According to the Oxford English Dictionary the phrase 'unconscious cerebration', first used in 1853, expresses 'that action of the brain which, though unaccompanied by consciousness, produces results which might have been produced by thought'.

esprit fort: a bold spirit

p. 115   Tokay is a rich sweet Hungarian wine.

p. 121   The quotation is from Coleridge's poem 'Love'.

p. 126   Aurora was goddess of the dawn.

p. 128   The reference is to John 3:20.

p. 135   Andrea Ferrara was a celebrated Italian swordsmith of the late sixteenth century. In his notes to *Waverley* Scott records that 'the name of Andrea de Ferrara is inscribed on all the Scottish broadswords which are accounted of peculiar excellence.' Many of the blades were in fact made in Germany.

EARTHBOUND

First published in *Fraser's Magazine* in January 1880, 'Earthbound' was the first of four short stories by Oliphant dealing with 'earthbound' spirits – the other three being 'The Open Door' (1882), 'The Lady's Walk' (1883) and 'The Library Window' (1896). 'Earthbound' was the first of Oliphant's tales of the supernatural to bear the generic title 'A Story of the Seen and Unseen'. This phrase – an echo of the Nicene Creed – is used of all her later works which tell of life beyond the grave, except 'The Land of Darkness' and 'On the Dark Mountains'.

p. 141   *corps de logis*: main part of the house

p. 145   *espiegle*: mischievous

p. 164   Sir Joshua Reynolds (1723–92) was one of the outstanding portrait-painters of the eighteenth century.

p. 167   The phrase 'To minister to a mind diseased' is an echo of *Macbeth* V.3.40.

         The passage from Dante's *Purgatorio* (Canto XXI, 1.64), given in the original Italian in the Notes on page 403, is rendered in the Dorothy L. Sayers translation:

> True, it wills always, but can nothing win
> So long as hevanely justice keeps desire
> Set towards the pain as once 'twas toward the sin.

THE OPEN DOOR

'The Open Door' was first published in *Blackwood's Edinburgh Magazine* in January 1882.

p. 171   The village of Brentwood is fictional, but the area Oliphant describes is readily identifiable as the countryside around the River Esk, to the east and south of Edinburgh, which she knew very well. The village could be Lasswade, on the North Esk. 'Grimy with paper-making': the Esk was well-known for its paper mills.

         accidenté: uneven

p. 200   Burns: this may be a reference to Robert Burns's 'Address to the Deil', which ends by sympathetically suggesting that even the Devil might mend his ways and be saved.

p. 207   'The tenets of the Church' refers to the Protestant (including the Church of Scotland) rejection of the doctrine of Purgatory.

OLD LADY MARY

'Old Lady Mary', first published in *Blackwood's Edinburgh Magazine* in January 1884, belongs to the group of fictions in which Oliphant wrote of spirits who return to earth in the hope – usually vain – of helping their loved ones in some way.

The others in the group are the short stories 'The Portrait' (1885) and 'A Visitor and his Opinions' (1893); and the superb novel *A Beleaguered City* (1880). In 'Old Lady Mary' the spirit is the central character of the story; in this respect the tale is a transitional one between those supernatural stories which take place on earth and those which tell of the voyages of spirits in the world beyond the grave.

Old Lady Mary had a real-life prototype – Mrs Duncan Stewart, whose London salon in Sloane Square was often filled with the leading social and literary figures of the day. Mrs Stewart died shortly after the publication of 'Old Lady Mary', and when the story was subsequently reprinted (with 'The Open Door') in *Two Stories of the Seen and Unseen* (1885), it bore the dedication: 'To an old lady ever young, Harriet Stewart, now gone where youth and age are no distinction'.

p. 215 Newspapers were originally in the form of broadsheets which the servant of the house would cut to a more manageable size.

p. 217 Six-and-eightpence, being a third of a pound, was a standard unit.

p. 227 The quotation is from 'A Lyke-Wake Dirge'. See Scott, *Minstrelsy of the Scottish Border*, 3 vols (Kelso and Edinburgh, 1802–3), I, 226–34.

p. 243 The reference is to the song 'The Angel's Whisper' by Samuel Lover (1797-1868), an Irish songwriter, novelist and painter.

THE PORTRAIT

'The Portrait' was first published in *Blackwood's Edinburgh Magazine* in January 1885.

p. 282 An echo of Matthew 10, in which Christ sends His disciples out to preach, and promises that words will be given to them in their time of need.

p. 287 Cowper's poem 'On the Receipt of my Mother's Picture out of Norfolk' begins 'O that those lips had language!'

p. 299 The economist Adam Smith (1723–90), author of *The Wealth of Nations* (1776).

THE LAND OF DARKNESS

'The Land of Darkness' is, for intensity and horror, unique among Oliphant's short stories, reminding the modern reader forcefully of such twentieth-century novels as Aldous Huxley's *Brave New World*, George Orwell's *Nineteen Eighty-Four*, and Neil M. Gunn's *The Green Isle of the Great Deep*. First published in *Blackwood's Edinburgh Magazine* in January 1887, it was reprinted in the volume *The Land of Darkness, Along with Some Further Chapters in the Experiences of a Little Pilgrim* (1888). The 'further chapters' were a reprint of *A Little Pilgrim in the Seen and Unseen* (1882) – a novel that had proved enormously popular on both sides of the Atlantic, though modern readers would find its sentimentality cloying; and the short story 'On the Dark Mountains' (1888), in which the 'Little Pilgrim' becomes a guide to those who have struggled out of the Land of Darkness and are making their slow, arduous way to God.

In 'The Land of Darkness' one can clearly see Oliphant's detailed knowledge of Dante: there are elements of his *Purgatorio* in the story, especially in her incorporation of Dante's premise that purgatory is a place of inverted love – pride on earth becoming hatred and contempt for others, envy becoming a wish to deprive others of any succour, love of justice becoming vengeance, and love of pleasure becoming gluttony and lust.

p. 313   In Dante's *Divine Comedy* the monster Geryon carries the poet down to Hell.

p. 315   Ateliers are artists' studios or workshops. [JC]

p. 316   Compare Ecclesiastes 7.6: 'For the crackling of thorns under a pot, so is the laughter of a fool: this also is vanity.'

p. 319   *Misericordia* is Italian for mercy. In Florence, where Oliphant had lived, there was a religious order called Arciconfraternita della Misericordia. [JC]

p. 321   'Good-bye' is a shortened version of 'God be with you'.

p. 334   In Greek mythology Pluto is god of the underworld.

p. 359   An echo of *Hamlet* II.2.303.

p. 361   In Oliphant's slightly later story 'On the Dark Mountains' the saved are described as 'a little whiteness in the great dark'. [JC]

THE LIBRARY WINDOW

First published in *Blackwood's Edinburgh Magazine* in January 1896, 'The Library Window' was the last of Oliphant's tales of the supernatural to deal with a spirit who is 'earthbound', but it stands apart from her other stories in the genre in that it is not religious in subject or tone. In her fiction Oliphant often utilised people and places she knew well, and nowhere is this more clearly demonstrated than in 'The Library Window'. The 'St Rule's' of the story is plainly St Andrews, a town she visited often throughout her life. It was St Rule who, it is believed, brought the relics of St Andrew to what became the town: St Rule's Tower is a well-known St Andrews landmark. By tradition a fair is held in summer in the street outside the old library in St Andrews, as it is in 'St Rule's'. 'The Library Window' has proved to be one of the most popular of Oliphant's short stories and it has been reprinted on numerous occasions.

p. 364   Madge Wildfire is a character of unbalanced mind in Scott's *The Heart of Midlothian*. Oliphant read Scott as a child, and acknowledged his influence. [MG, JC]

p. 365   Oliphant clearly has in mind the row of windows in the old University Library building in South Street, St Andrews.

p. 366   Window duty was a tax levied on windows and to avoid it windows were often blocked up: it was abolished in 1851. [MG, JC]

p. 368   The Earthen Mound (now simply the Mound) in Edinburgh was created out of the spoil from the foundations of the New Town and crossed the drained Nor' Loch to the Old Town. It was completed around 1820. [JC]

p. 372   The heroine of Richardson's novel *Pamela* (1740–1) is 'a support to virtue'.

p. 376   In folklore, Midsummer Eve (St John's Eve) is a time when supernatural beings of all kinds, both good and evil, are especially active. All magic is particularly potent at this time, and the festival is regarded as being especially for lovers.

p. 380   The reference is to Lockhart's famous anecdote about Sir Walter Scott, 'the Great Unknown', in which Scott is seen from a library window, working indefatigably at his desk in his Edinburgh study. See J G Lockhart, *Memoirs of the life of Sir Walter Scott*, Bart., 7 vols (Edinburgh and London, 1837-8), III, 128-9.

p. 384   'Like a dream when one awaketh': Psalm 73.20.

p. 386   'It was between the night and the day, when the fairy folk have power': quotation not traced.
A conversazione was a polite social gathering. [JC]

p. 391   In the Upper Hall of the old St Andrews University Library in South Street, the windows that face the street were blocked off in the early nineteenth century by bookcases running the whole length of the wall.

Glossary

a'
  all
aye
  always
bairn
  a child
ben
  the inner room of a two-roomed cottage; within, inside; hence 'far ben', far forward, on intimate terms
bit
  (used as an adjective) little
bogle
  ghost
braw
  fine
braws
  best clothes
clatter
  gossip
cry upon
  to call for
divert
  a diversion
dogue
  a dog
gane gyte
  gone mad, lost one's sense
greet
  weep
hame
  home
hizzies
  hussies, pert girls
inower
  within
ither
  other
ken
  to know
kent
  known
lane, 'her lane'
  by herself

leddy
  lady
lees
  lies
lippen to
  to trust, to put confidence in
lug
  ear
mind
  to remember
muckle
  large
naething
  nothing
nae
  no
pairty
  party
peetiful
  pitiful
pented
  painted
perfitt
  perfect
siller
  money
sore set
  determined
stirring men
  quick-tempered, fighting men
uncanny
  dangerous, hurtful; open to suspicion of evil
wark, 'make a wark'
  to make a fuss
wee Fifish
  a trace of a Fife accent
whisht
  a call for silence or calm
wi'
  with
windy
  a window
yon
  that